THE WATCH

The Watches of de Gressier

1991 - 2014

Charles Bunker

YOUCAXTON
PUBLICATIONS

ISBN 978-1-914424-26-7
Published by YouCaxton Publications 2021
YCBN: 01

YouCaxton Publications
www.youcaxton.co.uk

Typeset and cover design by Ella Knight Designs

Books in the de Gressier Series

Dedication

I dedicate this book, and the three earlier ones in the de Gressier series, to my wife Suzie, our family and to my very close friends who know who they are.

You are all reflected in these pages somewhere, for a writer is affected by everything and everyone who comes into their life.

Apart from my son James's songs, particularly the song Hero from which my books were conceived, I cannot say where or how I was touched and inspired, for most will have been in my subconscious. Nevertheless, be assured that your influences are in here somewhere, and for that, I say a sincere thank you.

C.S. Bunker
July 2021

de Gressier Saga - Family Tree

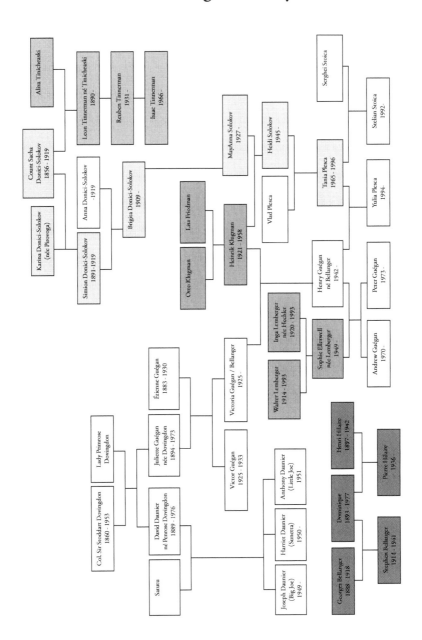

The Watches of de Gressier

This is a story which only the grandchildren can tell, for they are not the secret keepers.

Chapter 1

Kishinev February 1991

"IT'S DOWNHILL ALL the way from here," said the stranger to Henry Guégan as they walked across the tarmac at Vienna airport towards the Tupolev aeroplane from Moldova Air. From the look of the plane and the way the luggage was being loaded into the passenger seats at the back, it seemed to Henry that the prediction was probably right.

Now aged 49, Henry had been finding life tedious. He was prepared to consider almost anything provided it gave him a change to his daily routine. However, as he took his seat on the aeroplane and looked down the cabin, it was apparent that the change he sought, certainly in the short term, was not necessarily going to be for the better.

The daily pressure of working for himself had given Henry a reason to get up in the morning. He used to be excited to start the day. However, following the sale in 1977 of Found Vintners, the wine trading business he had started as a young man, his motivation had slowly disappeared, to the point that it was now hardly noticeable. With a small fortune in his bank account, he no longer felt he served any purpose.

He could have managed projects at Château de Gressier and Château Rabôut, the vineyards and wineries he owned in Bordeaux, and these would have kept him busy. However, these were run on a daily basis by two incredibly good general managers. They respected

Henry's knowledge of wine and viticulture, for there were few with his expertise, but they didn't need him. In fact, they had started to resent his involvement as he dipped whimsically in and out, causing chaos to the smooth running of what they believed to be 'their' businesses. So they politely rejected Henry's involvement which added to his lethargy and general state of depression.

When Sophie, his wife, first fell ill, Henry had made a point of visiting her every three or four weeks in her nursing home in Germany. However, he had started to feel guilty as his trips to see her were now less frequent. For years, he sought to prove to Sophie's parents the responsibility he felt for her by visiting regularly, but his need to demonstrate his caring had abated following their deaths. Although his love for her had not diminished in any way, it had changed.

Sophie remained resolutely beautiful and, through extensive exercise, had maintained the figure which had given her a commanding presence on the modelling catwalk and magazine page. However, it was her mind that had gone. As a result of recreational drugs, she could no longer recognise her children, let alone her husband. Most of the time they were together, Henry and she would either sit or walk the same endless walk that Sophie liked, always holding hands and in silence. During the day, when they weren't walking, Henry might read a novel or poetry out loud to her, and in the evenings, they would watch the DVD he had brought especially for them to see. For all of this, Sophie was no longer capable of reciprocating Henry's love or providing him with the companionship he yearned. Every day he was with her, it upset him and depressed him just that little bit more.

Henry's sons' growing years had been delegated to his mother, Victoria. It meant he was a weekend father, doing the things single parents do. During these times, he never felt good enough. As a father, he found no joy in the simplicity of his children's daily lives. The only time he was truly comfortable with Andrew and Peter was when they were all together at either of his vineyards. Here he would teach them the art of winemaking and share with them his love of its science. Most of all, he enjoyed the freedom of being outdoors with them, whether it be their swims in the river or sleeping out at night under the stars. But now, aged twenty-one and eighteen, his children were no longer that; they were young adults striving to make lives of their own.

It was a mixture of boredom and a long-held curiosity about what had happened to his father, which persuaded Henry to take a short-term consultancy assignment with the Commission of the European Union. They wanted him to examine and report on the ways in which the Commission might help the Moldovan Government privatise its wine industry now communism was at an end, and free-market capitalism was the economic catchword throughout all former USSR satellite countries.

Henry always thought it odd that Bordeaux University had conferred on him the title of Visiting Professor of Viticulture, despite the fact that he had walked out of their degree course before the end of his first year. He thought it even stranger that they had recommended him for such a consultancy assignment, but this was to belie Henry's recognised expertise in the chemistry of wine, and his knowledge of the wines of the world.

It was evening when Henry landed at Kishinev[1] airport. It was dingy, unappealing, and dimly lit with the lowest possible wattage of lightbulbs. He quickly passed through the immigration procedures carried out with an efficiency unknown in other Eastern European airports. Once through the customs hall and onto the public concourse, Henry looked around wantonly. He had been told he would be met.

"This isn't going downhill," said Henry to himself as he looked at the woman walking towards him carrying a placard with his name on it. She was stunningly attractive. If this was a honey trap, he thought, then he had been well and truly trapped.

---

[1] Kishinev is now known by its original name of Chişinău. After Bessarabia was ceded to Russia by the Turks in 1812, Chişinău became known by its Russian name of Kishinyou. After World War II, when Moldova became part of the USSR, the English language spelling of its name changed slightly to Kishinev. In 1991, with the collapsed of the Soviet Union, when Moldova became an independent country, the former Romanian language spelling of its name was formally re-adopted. The spelling of Kishinev has been used throughout this book as this was the recognised spelling of the city's name when Henry first arrived in Moldova.

Henry recognised her face. He'd seen it somewhere before. Then he reflected, wearing a light grey military-style fur cossack beanies cap on top of her golden blonde hair, and with a highly tailored overcoat, the woman could have come straight from Hollywood central casting for a female KGB spy.

Henry smiled enthusiastically as he went up to her, only for that smile to disappear as a man, she obviously knew well, stopped at her side. The man was tall, very fit, well-groomed, and handsome.

"Henry Guégan?" asked the man in a strong Russian accent as he offered Henry his gloved hand.

"Yes," said Henry, returning the handshake.

"My name is Eduard Borisovich, but everyone calls me Edik. I'm from the President's Office, and he has asked me to welcome you formally. This is my wife, Evelina Kirillovich. She will be looking after you while you are here." His voice, although very formal, was friendly.

Evelina and Henry shook hands. As they did so, he looked into her grey-green eyes. He was immediately reminded of his wife. Not because they looked alike. They didn't. What they shared was the same natural beauty that comes from a well-proportioned and symmetric face with large eyes and a mouth that cannot help but smile. He thought her face could have sold millions of beauty products too.

It was a Moldovan government car that took them from the airport to the Steffaco Hotel in central Kishinev. Edik sat in the front passenger's seat but, throughout the journey, he turned around to talk animatedly to Henry, who sat in the back with Evelina by his side.

As Edik spoke proudly of his country's history, Henry could not help but keep looking down at Evelina's long slender legs as they revealed themselves through the opening of her sensibly long winter coat.

Henry checked in to the hotel quickly. He found his room easily, only to discover it had just a single bed in it. He returned to the reception desk to ask for the double room with single occupancy which he had ordered.

"You are on your own, are you not?" said the receptionist.

"Yes," said Henry.

"Then you have a single room," said the receptionist as though the matter was not for debate, and debate was certainly not going to make her change her mind.

Is this what the man meant when he said it was all downhill, Henry wondered, for it was evident that the receptionist had failed to grasp the rudiments of a free market economy. Had his bathroom basin been provided with a plug, he wondered as he returned to his room. Was he going to need the one he had been advised to bring with him?

Henry, Edik and Evelina ate that night in what was supposed to be the best restaurant in Kishinev. The recommended delicacy was the carp caught freshly in the local Dniester River, but it had a muddy taste to it which Henry found unappetising.

"What's your interest in Moldovan wine?" asked Edik after they had placed their order.

"I'm here on behalf of the EU commission," replied Henry. "They're keen to help Moldova develop a free-market economy. One of the areas they've chosen to support is your wine industry. It's why the EU office in Paris is involved. It's why I'm here."

"Why would a Frenchman want to help a potential competitor?" asked Edik.

"I'm only one-quarter French," said Henry defensively. "One-quarter English and one-half German," he added, appreciating it was a good question which he deliberately chose to ignore in his answer.

"Moldova is the home of the Romanov vineyards," said Edik proudly. "The best in the world. Uniquely, our fields are untainted by chemicals. Do you know we produce more wine than France and Italy put together?" he continued boastfully.

"I do," said Henry appreciatively. "For a long time, I've wanted to come, but sadly it's been impossible."

"Why has the EU chosen you?" asked Edik in a less than friendly manner.

"I'm a wine scientist," continued Henry defensively. "I had a business importing wines from all around the world into England and France until I sold it. Also, I own a couple of small vineyards in France. The EU commission must assume I have some value to bring otherwise they wouldn't be paying for me to be here."

"Mr Guégan?" asked Evelina formally.

Please call me Henry," he interrupted.

Evelina started again. "Henry, where were you when the Berlin Wall came down? You know, when the cold war truly ended."

"I was in Bamberg, West Germany," he replied, at the same time thinking it was a strange question. "I watched it on television with my wife. I followed every moment of it. I wanted to drive to Berlin to be there, to take my own piece of the wall, but I didn't. I regret that now. Why do you ask?"

"It's probably the defining moment in my life, in our lives, said Evelina correcting herself. We were on the streets that day. You've no idea how it felt."

"I do, in part, I think I do," said Henry. "All my life travel restrictions to Russia, Ukraine and East Germany stopped me from finding my father, but now, it's probably all far too late."

Henry began to feel uncomfortable as Evelina studied him with an intensity he was not used to. It made him talk more. "I'm told my father was a pilot during the war. He was flying on the Eastern Front, but his plane never returned. I believe the reason is held somewhere in Ukraine."

"Which side of the Great War were you on Mr Guégan? It seems you have reason to be on both sides," asked Evelina.

Another strange question thought Henry. "I didn't know my father was German until I was about twenty, so I was only on one side; the side of the English, French and of course the Russians," he replied. "We were allies then, weren't we? Why do you ask?"

"Because Romania was on both sides then, just as you have a reason to be. It's why this country has always been treated with suspicion by Russia. The statistics say that three-quarters of our population is Moldovan, but this ignores our long history. Half our population has Romanian heritage. It is in Europe they see this country's future. The rest are descended from Russians, Ukrainians and Turks," said Evelina as though she were presenting an argument in a dissertation.

Edik saw the expression of confusion on Henry's face, so he sought to end the discussion. "That was our parents' war, as was the cold

6

war which followed," said Edik, revealing the age difference between Henry and them.

"I was a war baby," said Henry. "I had a food rationing card and everything, but the cold war, that was definitely my era. I can't tell you how scared we were on occasions, especially during the Cuban missile crisis."

"Cuban missile crisis?" asked Edik and Evelina together. It was part of the USSR's history which they professed to know nothing about. Henry told, in detail, the story of the stand-off between Kennedy and Khrushchev, which brought the world to the brink of nuclear war. They listened with interest as Henry reported how it was only a flashlight, caught in the hatch of a Russian submarine's conning tower, which stopped a nuclear war. However, it was when Henry criticised the hypocrisy of the United States for thinking it perfectly alright to put US missiles on Turkey's soil pointing towards Russia, while not accepting that it was alright for Russian to have missiles on Cuba pointing to the USA, that Henry passed Evelina's test of character. He had her seal of approval. However, Edik was still withholding his judgement.

At the end of the meal Henry decided he liked Edik and Evelina. Their English was so good it was easy to converse. There was a lovely warm, supportive relationship between the two of them. Most importantly, they carried all the enthusiasm that the Moldovan people, free from Communism and Russia, were going to need if their country was to succeed as an independent state.

Chapter 2

Kishinev February 1991

THE FOLLOWING MORNING Evelina picked up Henry promptly at nine o'clock from his hotel. She was to accompany him on the extensive itinerary prepared for him by the Ministry of Agriculture. They travelled in her small, battered Lada car with its broken windscreen.

"We never drive in puddles," said Evelina as she manoeuvred the car from one side of the road to another to keep on the tarmac she could see in front of her. "You never know if it's hiding a missing drain cover. If it's gone, it can badly damage a wheel."

"Missing a drain cover," repeated Henry.

"Yes, people steal them, melt them down and sell the metal as scrap."

"Really," said Henry, truly astonished that people could behave in such a way. "Why would they do that?"

"They need the money," she answered matter of factly.

"You mean they put their needs before everyone else!" he commented aghast. "Did this happen in communist times, too?"

Evelina didn't answer.

Their first visit was to a wine bottling plant. Henry had seen many of these around the world, but nothing had prepared him for what he was about to experience.

"Christ, what was that?" shouted Henry as he ducked to the ground in response to a massive explosion. Evelina ducked too, but the plant manager, who was showing them around, did not move.

"That's a bottle exploding," he replied as though there was nothing wrong. "We hot fill and sometimes that happens."

"Where do you get your bottles from," asked Henry through Evelina, who acted as his translator throughout.

"We import most from Romania, but we also get some from here too."

"How many explode like that?"

"About two, may be three in every hundred bottles on the line, but we get many more breakages during transport."

Henry scrutinized the whole process from the moment the bottles, labels, corks, and wine arrived to the moment the filled bottles were packed in cardboard boxes ready for delivery. It was when Henry saw the way the bottles were inspected before they were filled that, for the first time, he appreciated the extent of the problem. The empty bottles were placed manually on a single line conveyor. These then passed in front of three forty-watt light bulbs as they were looked at cursorily by three ladies who were sitting on the other side. It was, Henry concluded, no inspection at all. No western retailer was going to allow Moldovan wine on their shelves until things had materially changed.

The tour of the plant, the science and testing laboratories and the administration departments, which took all morning, had been well planned. Henry and Evelina joined the plant manager and some of his senior colleagues for lunch in the refectory. The meal comprised sarma, which were battered and then fried stuffed cabbage rolls, sauerkraunt and mamaliga, a cornmeal mush garnished with sour cream. It was also the time set aside in the itinerary for a formal wine tasting with eight different bottles of wine laid out to be tried.

"I don't drink," said Henry shaking his head and putting out his hand when they came to fill his glass from the first bottle of wine.

The table went silent; a wine expert who doesn't drink wine. They'd never heard of such a thing.

Evelina translated for him, but it needed no translation.

"Have you never drunk? How do you do your job?" she asked perplexed.

"I'm sorry, but I never have. I don't like the way it makes me feel. I'd love to taste the wine, but I'd need a bowl to spit it out into and some water.

As they worked through the wines, Henry found one which was excellent and would sit alongside the best in the world, many that were passably good table wines, and some which were truly dreadful. This led to a discussion on pricing, for the excellent wine wasn't premium priced as it would have been in Western Europe. The reason soon became apparent. This wine had been reserved for the communist party bosses, and although their main customer remained the government, no one had thought to change the price upwards to reflect its quality.

When they were leaving, and just as Henry was skipping through puddles of snowy slush, once again soaking his feet, he saw a man sawing rough-cut planks of oak. "What's happening here?" he asked.

"Our oak barrels are so old that they have stopped yielding the oak flavours associated with our brandy, and we can't get new ones," said the plant manager. He then added brightly, "so we put freshly cut oak blocks in each of the old barrels to give the same flavour."

"Ingenious," said Henry as he climbed into Evelina's car, albeit he was a little shocked.

That evening Henry sat at the hotel bar in a room which was the epitome of austere. He was watching the football on the silent television sipping a coke when he was joined by Edik and Evelina at precisely 7.30 pm, just as they said they would. Edik looked incredibly smart in his white tailored shirt, designer tie and sharply cut mohair suit. Evelina had, once again, transformed herself. Throughout the day she had appeared dull and dowdy in heavy winter work clothes and practical boots. Now she was looking slim and trim. She was wearing long beige tight-fitting trousers which fell to the floor covering the high heel boots she was wearing. These made her appear incredibly tall and her legs very long. She was wearing an expensive, heavily embroidered cardigan which accentuated her bust. For whatever reason, these two were dressed to impress.

"What happened today?" asked Edik as soon as they sat down at a table away from the bar. There were no niceties.

Henry summarised what he had seen.

"And your thoughts?" demanded Edik.

"Too early to say," replied Henry. "It's been interesting. I can say that I see potential."

Edik drilled on. "Evelina said you thought our prices needed changing."

"Yes," said Henry, "possibly for some wines, not all. A much bigger study needs to be done."

Getting fed up at answering a series of similar questions, Henry thought it was time the tables were turned. Although Edik had spoken a lot, neither of them had revealed anything about themselves.

"What are your backgrounds?" he asked.

"My degree is in international relations with politics, after which I did another degree in computer studies," said Edik.

"I did international relations with law," said Evelina.

"At the same University?" asked Henry.

"Yes," said Edik, who was clearly trying to re-take control of the conversation.

"When were you married?"

"We're not," said Evelina.

"But you said ..."

"We always say that when we first meet a diplomat," said Edik. "It is far too complicated to explain."

"We live together," interjected Evelina, speaking in such a way as to make it clear that this was her decision.

"I'm not a diplomat," said Henry adding, "but in London, you'll find living together is now almost the norm."

"Yes perhaps," acknowledged Edik dismissively.

"Your job in the President's office; what do you do exactly?" asked Henry, directing his question firmly at Edik.

"I advise on policy."

"What does that mean?" persisted Henry.

"I'm working on land privatisation. We have huge collective farms created by Stalin, which the State still owns. They're not very efficient. But, it is fundamental to our future and akin to what you're doing," said Edik confidently.

"And you Evelina?" asked Henry.

"I used to work in a bank. I had a good job, but since independence, there's been a policy to sack all Russians in jobs like mine. I've applied to work with the United Nations, but until then ... well, this time, I'm lucky. Edik got me this job working for the Ministry of Agriculture to help you."

Immediately Evelina had finished speaking Edik stood up. "We need to go," he said. "Evelina will pick you up in the morning, same time, nine o'clock."

They were gone as quickly as they had come.

Chapter 3

Moldova February 1991

LONDON HAS THE Tower of London. Paris has the Eiffel Tower, and New York has the Statue of Liberty. Moldova has Cricova. It is a winery, about sixteen kilometres north of Kishinev, made famous by its wine cellars which boast 120 km of underground roadways going down to a depth of about 300m below ground. It is a perfect location for storing its 1.25 million bottles of wine, some dating back to 1902.

Henry, like every visitor, was taken to see the remnants of Herman Goering's private collection of wine taken from his cellars in Berlin in 1945 and brought to Cricova by the Red Army for safe keeping.

As Henry was driven through the caves, some of which were wide enough to allow lorries to pass with ease, he was undoubtedly envious. He'd gone to huge trouble to build a large wine cellar in the chalk hills near Folkestone, England which was just a fraction of the size of this 500 year old work of human ingenuity.

After driving around the cellars for 45 minutes, Henry was taken to the European Hall in the winery where he was proudly shown a large collection of silver, gold and grand prix awards for their Cricova wines, but none, he noticed, were from competitions outside the USSR.

Once again, surprise was expressed when it came to the wine-tasting and Henry admitted he didn't drink. This time forewarned, Evelina dealt with the issue with much less fuss. Water, bowl and napkin quickly found their way to the table. All the Cricova wines they served were passably good, but when Henry came to taste their sparkling dark red wine, called *Kodrinskoie*, he found his tee-total days were almost over. It was a wine exactly to his taste.

It was when Henry saw, and was asked to comment on, their new design of labels for Cricova's latest vintage that he found himself in difficulties. They had abandoned their old design, similar to the great French wine labels of history, and replaced them with something modern and contemporary making them look more like the cheap plonk sold in the aisles of supermarkets around the world. To use his grandmother's expression, they had taken the lace off the ladies' underwear, and in the process, had destroyed its image and thus its perceived value.

It was away from the display cases, and the selling formalities of the winery, and with the men who earned no more than $5 a day, that Henry learnt the most. They were uncomfortable at first for, in his London suit, he looked like the kind of man they instinctively wouldn't trust. As Evelina translated, and they used chemical symbols to find a common technical language, Henry found the soulmates he always discovered at the heart of any well-run vineyard or winery. There was no issue which these men had not considered nor any problem to which they had not found a solution. It was Henry's obvious appreciation of their ingenuity which created the thaw, and then the laughter as translations went wrong, as they inevitably do. There was something else which struck him. Unlike those who worked at his vineyard, these men were not interested in what any other vineyard did; but like them, they were interested in what made their wine better. For that, you needed to understand the land. It is what the French call 'La Terroire' and, like Henry, the men who worked the vineyards of Moldova understood this perfectly.

Over the next few days Evelina took Henry to visit Purcari, Brănești and Milestii Mici wineries, the latter of which has the largest cellars in the world. At every vineyard he would walk the fields, examine the vines and look at the soil. You could learn so much from the way the soil is cared for and the way the vines are pruned. The trellis posts were old, and the wires had stretched under the weight of grapes in previous years. They had not been replaced as they should have been. It was indicative of the whole of the country's wine industry. It was as a result of these solitary walks that Henry concluded that the Moldovan wine had enormous potential, capable of competing with the best of the Western wines. It just needed modernising which meant investment, a lot of investment.

After each trip Henry would be dropped off at his hotel and then, at exactly 7.30 pm Edik and Evelina would appear, both dressed in their evening refinery. Evelina always wore something different, but equally fetching. Both looked as though they were going to an important reception. Edik would grill Henry for half an hour on the day, picking up on any comments which Evelina had made to him earlier. Then, as before, they would quickly disappear. Henry didn't realise it, but their appointment was always with the President of Moldova. He was taking a special interest in the privatisation of the Moldovan wine industry and, in particular, what Henry Guégan, from the Commission of the European Union, had to say.

Early on Saturday morning Evelina took Henry to Kishinev airport. "You will come back?" she asked.

"I think so," said Henry as he checked in several cases of wine to take back to France for analysis.

"I hope you do," she said. "I think Moldova needs what you can do".

She walked with him to the security desk where they shook hands formally and he thanked her for all her help. Taken completely unawares Evelina responded by kissing him tenderly on the cheek. "Let's see each other again," she said.

At Charles de Gaulle airport it was the best Henry could do not to swear out loud. Half the bottles of wine he had tried to bring back to France had broken in one red, soggy, glass infested, cardboard mess.

Chapter 4

Kishinev June 1991

BY THE TIME Henry returned home, written and submitted his report to the EU Commission, inspected the de Gressier and Rabôut vineyards, had his mother and children to stay for the Easter holiday, and taken his two boys to see Sophie in Bamberg, and dealt with all his personal administration matters, it wasn't until early June before he was able to return to Moldova.

The EU commission had read his fact-finding report and, as a second piece of work, commissioned him to carry out a full feasibility study. His plan was a simple one. The bottle making factory, the bottling plants and the major wineries, together with their vineyards, should each be privatised - not as one lot but in a series of tenders, where each tender benefited with a predetermined amount of EU grant aid. Henry was certain that, properly packaged, the large international drinks companies and many of Europe's largest private equity firms would come to the party. Having sold his own business, Henry was confident he knew exactly what was required.

Early summer was firmly in the air when Henry arrived at Kishinev airport. This time he had paid to be collected at the aeroplane steps as a VIP passenger but, once through immigration, customs and on the concourse, he was disappointed to find there was no one to meet him. He had hoped Evelina would be there. Henry took a taxi to his hotel and checked in. Once again, despite his instructions being clear, and an argument with the receptionist, he was allocated a single room with a single bed.

At the Ministry of Agriculture, Henry was provided with a large room, and courtesy of the European Commission, a large team of eager men and women from the local associate offices of Arthur Andersen[2] had been gathered. Together their task was to prepare detailed business plans, financial forecasts and sales brochures for each of the business units which Henry thought should comprise the first set of tenders. There were two consultants to each project and, at first, the data started to flow in from the bottle making factory, two wine bottling plants and eight wineries and what was thought to be their vineyards. What should have been a simple issue was made more complicated as some of the documents were in Russian and others in Moldovan. This reflected the Government's decision to change the official language to Moldovan so as to emphasise the country's new found independence from Russia.

It was on the fourth day of Henry being ensconced in his work at the Ministry of Agriculture, that Edik and Evelina arrived at his hotel unannounced. They greeted each other formally and they took their usual table in the bar. They were smart but the sharp suit and designer wear were not in evidence.

"Tomorrow morning you have a meeting with Kurepin Maximovich," said Edik. "He's the chief of one of the largest collective farms in Moldova. He's at the sanatorium, but he has agreed to see you," said Edik enthusiastically.

"We can't go and see someone at the sanatorium," protested Henry, assuming it was a hospital. Later he was to learn that the sanatorium was a state-sponsored health farm available to those of enough seniority so they could take one or two weeks holiday each year. It was the Communist version of a company paid spa break.

Edik ignored Henry's protests. "Also," said Edik proudly, "Evelina has been permanently seconded from the Ministry of Agriculture to help you. I gather there is a lot to translate, and her banking knowledge will be useful too."

For the first time Henry began to feel nervous about Edik. Did he never ask? Did he always tell? he wondered.

---

[2] In 1991, Arthur Andersen was one of the 'big five' international accounting firms providing auditing, tax and consulting services to governments and large corporations worldwide. Its implication in a series of very large fraudulent accounting and auditing scandals, combined with the findings of criminal complicity, destroyed the firm in 2002.

Evelina picked Henry up from his hotel in her car to take him to see Maximovich. They had gone less than a mile when she was stopped by a policeman. She handed over her driving licence and Henry handed over his passport. There then proceeded to be a heated argument which was ended when Evelina handed over ten lei.

"Bloody police," she said. It was the first time Henry had heard her swear in English. "They wanted 50 lei just because you are a foreigner."

"What had you done wrong?" Henry asked.

"Nothing. They don't get paid, so they stop drivers on a random excuse. It's how they earn their money. Everyone gives them ten lei so they can just get on with their lives, otherwise its hours of form filling and sometimes worse as they cart you off to the police station."

"So how did you get him to accept only ten lei?"

"I showed him President Stanescu's business card. I said you were President Stanescu's personal guest and told him to phone his number and check." She thought for a little while and smiled to herself. "I think you have an expression ... my Ace just trumped his King!"

Henry was surprised at the large deputation which had come to the sanatorium to be at the meeting with Kurepin Maximovich. He was a man in his sixties for whom his seniority in the communist party had represented his life's work. This was evidenced by the fact that he thought it perfectly acceptable to come to the meeting in his dressing gown. However, like many others of his age, he had no grasp of the economic revolution taking place in his country.

Also, at the meeting was the Minister of Agriculture and his deputy whom Henry had not previously met. There were several general managers from the wineries who Henry had met the last time he was in the country and, of course, Edik and Evelina.

Once they were gathered, Edik took control of the meeting. Without warning Henry was asked, almost ordered, to outline his plans. He was beginning to dislike this man for his brashness.

Henry spoke cautiously outlining his earlier proposals to the EU Commission and the Moldovan government, allowing time for Evelina to translate. He praised the potential quality of Moldovan wine. He spoke admiringly of the Moldovan workforce and told of the need for a very large investment. For the first time he shared his plans to preserve cash flow during the transitional period, when all the existing plant and machinery would be upgraded. They would do this by continuing to serve their existing customers in the countries of the former USSR. Once the upgrade was done then the wines produced in the new bottles could go to the higher-priced Western European and American markets.

Henry was only asked one question: "When will the markets in Europe and America start buying? "

"When you have new bottles which don't break, new quality-controlled filling lines and proper inspection systems!" he answered forcefully.

Despite Evelina translating all the way through Henry's speech, she gave him no report at all about what the others were saying. The knowledge flow was just one way – from Henry to them. One thing was apparent, whatever Edik had said after Henry had finished speaking had caused an enormous row. One other thing was obvious, it was Edik against the rest.

In the car journey, on the way back to the Ministry of Agriculture, Henry asked Evelina about the conversation after he had spoken. "It was nothing," she said. "To make what you suggest happens, there has to be land reform legislation in parliament. It's what they were arguing about."

Henry was not at all certain he had been told the truth.

Chapter 5

Moldova, its wineries and cellars. June 1991

HENRY LEFT THE Ministry of Agriculture during the middle of the afternoon. He could not bear the smog of cigarette smoke he was being asked to work in any longer. He had tried to ban smoking but, in the new found democracy of Moldova, there had been a team vote on his proposed ban and he had lost. Further, he was becoming exceptionally frustrated. He was used to things happening promptly, but it seemed to him as though everything was getting bogged down. The flow of information he needed was proving to be slow and piecemeal. He couldn't create the urgency he thought the task required, and he found this desperately upsetting. There appeared to be a culture of deliberately not doing something today if it could be left until tomorrow.

As he walked back to his hotel, Henry stopped to visit the National Museum of Moldova; a large, most impressive building. Immediately, he noticed a huge display on his left as he walked in. He paid and headed towards the re-creation of part of the battle of the Jassy-Kishinev Offensive in World War II. Henry walked around a large scene depicting the Russian army taking control of the River Prut. Several times he thought about his father, before he wandered aimlessly around the rest of the museum. His mind was never far from the scene of the river fighting as he felt a nagging wonderment which he couldn't articulate. It was a place he was to revisit many times when the trials and tribulations of the Ministry of Agriculture became too much.

Henry also visited the only department store in Kishinev, on the Boulevard Ştefan cel Mare, for some therapeutic shopping. He soon realised there was nothing he wanted to buy, and this depressed him even more, so he walked back to his hotel arriving early evening and headed to the bar. The barman was wearing his usual white coat and was slowly polishing a solitary glass. He probably polished it all day long, thought Henry, so as to look busy, for there were few customers. Henry ordered a Coke and looked around the room.

"What is it with the women over there?" Henry asked quietly, leaning in to speak to the barman as there was no television or background music to muffle what he wanted to say. "They seem to be always here," he observed. "All the time, there are two or three out of the same four."

"One hundred forty dollar," said the barman. "One hour."

Henry pulled a face, for it was now obvious what he was being told. He cursed himself for his naivety.

"Except Turkish, he added "Turkish one hundred ninety, also Arab."

Henry looked puzzled but said nothing.

"Turkish make girls work hard. Don't like. English, French not good payers. German's good, Italians very good, and Americans ..." the barman wobbled his hands in the air. "Russian's pay more to show off," he said. "They make it clear who customer."

Henry squirmed. He really didn't need an international run down on the sexual proclivities of the male, and so he looked away towards the three women. They were quietly chattering away nursing one drink which, as part of the skills of their trade, they made last an exceptionally long time. They were all in their twenties. The one in the middle looked up and smiled at Henry. Seeing her smile the other two looked in his direction. A woman with a bobbed hairstyle beckoned him over. Henry shook his head to decline her invitation. It was not his scene.

The barman saw his refusal. "One hundred forty-dollar, girl get one hundred dollar, hotel get twenty dollar, me ten dollar and door man ten dollar," said the barman in an effort to explain that, by refusing her invitation, Henry had just cost him ten dollars.

"Turn on the television, please," said Henry as he moved away to the table and chair he always sat at. He aimlessly watched the football match between two teams in which he had no interest and slowly sipped his glass of coke. He would phone home he decided. It was on that positive note he downed his coke and headed to his bedroom.

Over the next three hours Henry stayed in his bedroom working on the faxes he had received from his vineyards and swapping impatiently between the two novels he had brought to read. Slowly he became gripped in a form of claustrophobia to the point where he started to pace the room. He still hadn't been able to persuade the hotel to give him a double room. In such a small space he felt trapped. His television had no English and no films. He had to get out and go somewhere else.

He left the bedroom and walked down the hotel corridor. Why was he in this bloody country he asked himself as he noticed for the umpteenth time that the carpet had no underlay. It was hard against the wooden floor. This was the only four-star hotel in Moldova and the lessons of European soft furnishings were still to come.

Henry turned right into the hotel bar and was immediately struck by the noise. Only one of the prostitutes was sitting at the table, abandoned by her colleagues, who were undoubtedly earning their fee. She smiled hopefully. Henry smiled back and shook his head in decline. He found there was something uncomfortable about being propositioned for the money in his wallet.

Henry ordered a coke from the barman and returned to sit in his regular chair at his regular table. He took his pen out of his pocket and, on the pad of paper he had bought with him, he started to write a letter to Sophie. Although his wife would be able to read it, he knew she would forget each word the moment she had seen it, and so his letters would be read to her by her nurses. He knew that she did not remember him, but Henry also knew of the joy in her face every time one of his letters was read as, in that millisecond, she had a memory.

Henry hadn't taken much notice of the group of eight or nine women sitting around two tables pulled together, who were talking animatedly; except that, as their noise grew, he couldn't help but be distracted by them.

"Excuse me," said one of the women interrupting Henry's concentration. "Would you mind telling me your nationality?"

"Why? Haven't you just worked it out by asking in English," he replied. His less than friendly mood was reflected in the tone of his voice.

"We've been having a wager, a bet, on whether you're English, French or Italian," continued the woman.

"Not American?" he asked.

"Oh, definitely not American," said the woman confidently. "We've all decided you're not fat enough to be an American."

"What's the wager worth?"

"We have a sweepstake but it's of no benefit because the winner has to spend their winnings on buying the next round of drinks."

"What nationality do you think I am?" asked Henry directly to the woman who interrupted him.

"Your shoes are definitely English, but your clothes are Italian. So, I'm not sure. In the end I said you were French."

Everyone was now listening intensely to the conversation for there was prize money at stake.

"I think it is best if I buy the next round," said Henry, as he signalled to the Barman to join them. "The answer's too complicated to get a winner," he added.

"But we need to know," said the woman who started the conversation.

"As long as I can buy you all a drink," said Henry.

It was quickly agreed.

"I am one quarter English, one quarter French and half German," he explained for the second time in Moldova. "None of me is Italian."

"Come and join us," they said almost in unison. "It would be nice to practice our French, German and English," continued the woman who spoke to him first.

"Perhaps not German," said Henry as, although his wife was German, it was not his strongest language.

Henry folded away the letter he had been writing and placed it in his inside jacket pocket. They all shuffled their chairs around to create a space so he could join them.

"What do you all do?" Henry asked.

"We're all teachers," replied the woman on his left. "Except we haven't been paid for four months," she added bitterly.

"Five months," corrected another voice.

"Five months," repeated the woman on his left, "so we all have other jobs."

"And you still teach every day?" asked Henry amazed.

"Yes," said the woman on his left.

"What's your other job?"

"My mother, she's a teacher too. We're now florists. We provide flowers to all the new embassies and consulates that have started here. It's a good business."

"Then why don't you stop being a teacher and concentrate on that," asked Henry, thinking it was the obvious thing to do.

"Because teaching is an important job. In our society it has status," she answered seriously.

"What do you do?" asked the woman on his left, looking Henry straight in the eye.

Henry explained to everyone around what he was doing in Moldova. They were all impressed, although the woman who asked the question was adamant that it was all going to be stolen, "by the gangsters who now run our government," she said loudly.

There was a general discussion about the need to emigrate as each was certain that their country had no future. The United States, England, Canada, France and Germany were the chosen countries of the majority, and Henry was quizzed intensely on each of these, and in particular, whether France or England was the better country to go to. There was good fun and laughter all around.

Slowly everyone disappeared, leaving the woman on Henry's left engaged in a detailed conversation with him about the Battle of the River Prut. It was a strange conversation because Henry had only idly mentioned that he had been to the museum. However, this woman had researched the battle carefully because she had taken a party from her school to see it and wanted to be prepared.

"The museum display has a number of inaccuracies" she said. "They're small but they're mistakes all the same. I know because my grandmother and great-grandmother fought in the battle. They were nurses then. My great-grandmother's now 82 and she remembers it clearly. "She says the scene's wrong because it's been created by the Russians, and excludes us Moldovans. History is always written by the winners because they're the winners," she added sardonically.

"Do you know what else she said? She said that, when the Germans first invaded the Moldovan and Ukrainian people welcomed them with open arms. They saw it as an opportunity to rid themselves of the Russians, who we've hated ever since they'd starved thirty million of us in 1932. Do you know the Holodomor killed over ten percent of the population?

Henry nodded animatedly.

"And then the Germans, as they invaded, set about exterminating about another three million of us. Not just Jews and not in battle. It was a simple extermination of peoples they saw as an underclass. Everyone knows about the Jewish holocaust, but there was a Moldovan and Ukrainian one too. Can you imagine how different history would have been if they hadn't done that?"

As the woman spoke, Henry studied her for the first time. She had a slightly oblong face, with a high forehead and a sleek, well-proportioned nose. She had large deep brown eyes and full, well proportion lips. All this was surrounded and enhanced by thick bouncy auburn hair. Unquestionably, she was attractive.

"I am in room 225," said Henry suddenly after a long pause in the conversation. Would you like to join me there?" he asked. He had never said anything like that before.

The woman looked at him and smiled. Without a word being said he had his answer.

"Give me two minutes," said Henry, as he stood up to go to the bar to sign his bill.

He returned to the woman. "Two two five," repeated Henry. "I need a couple more minutes," he said and was gone.

Neither knew the other's name.

Chapter 6

Kishinev. June 1991

AS HENRY STARTED tidying up his bedroom, putting things in his briefcase, and folding up his clothes, the woman he had been speaking to was wondering whether she should follow the man who had invited her to his room. She knew exactly what it would mean. She looked at the two prostitutes who had regrouped to wait for their next trick. If they could, she thought, so could she. Perhaps she might charge him two hundred, three hundred, no five hundred dollars.

The woman got up and walked purposefully towards Henry's room. She knew exactly why she was going there, and it was not for money.

All too soon for Henry, the woman with the auburn hair was tapping gently on his door. He opened it stood back and let her in. She was carrying a large cheap handbag and a red raincoat which she put on the ground.

"Let's have a shower first," said Henry, as soon as she was in the room.

"A bed for one?" said the woman surprised.

"Every time I try and book a double bed, but clearly a man travelling alone in post-communist Moldova is permitted just a single room with a single bed," said Henry apologetically. "I've asked them to move me into a double room but ...."

"A shower?" she queried, picking up on Henry's first suggestion.

Yes, said Henry as he moved to the bathroom and push the door ajar. He held it open for her. She went in.

"Would you like something to drink?" asked Henry as he came out of the bathroom.

"Yes please, orange juice, no ice."

As soon as Henry heard the sound of running water he stripped off, walked quickly into the bathroom, closed the door and stepped into the shower with her. Nothing was said between them. Taking some soap in his hands, Henry started to wash her ample breasts which lay on her tiny ribcage. Her areola were large and dark. Henry moved his hands still bathed in soap and started to massage her nipples. As he did, so they became more erect in his hands.

It was obvious that the woman was trying not to get her hair wet. Henry got out of the shower, to retrieve the shower cap from the box near the wash basin. The woman made a point of studying Henry's firm buttocks, his tight leg muscles and groin. His body, with its broad chest and slim hips, had the chisel looks she found attractive.

Henry returned and placed the shower cap on her head. She pulled down the loose ends so that there were no gaps. She looked upwards and allowed the hot water to pour directly onto her face and into her mouth.

Once again, with the soap in his hands, Henry worked it around the small of her back. He was amazed at how thin she was between tummy and backbone as it exaggerated the curve of her firm buttocks. Bending down and using both hands, he soaped her tummy allowing the lather to float into her pubic hair before he started washing around her buttocks and the top of her legs. Henry stood up and soaped under her breasts once again, down past her tummy button and then between her legs where he allowed his fingers to play gently. Involuntarily, she bent her knees and slowly gyrated her hips in response.

The woman took the soap from Henry's hands. She did not try and wash any other part of him, just the shaft of his swollen penis and his balls beneath.

"Please," said the woman, now aroused by Henry's touch, "Let's go to bed."

Each wrapped in a large towel, they made their way back to the bedroom. The woman threw off her shower cap, reached into her bag, took out a hair brush and rapidly brushed her hair. She shook her head vigorously, so her locks fell naturally. Very quickly she dried herself and, discarding her towel at the last moment, she climbed into bed.

"Condom?" she said just as Henry was thinking the same thing.

"No, ... you?" he replied.

"No," she said.

"It was all going too fast. Both were thinking that this was the moment they could pull out, stop it all, when the woman said: "the women in the bar..."

"Good idea," said Henry.

He dialled reception, was put through to the barman and Henry made his request.

"Fifty dollars?" said Henry, repeating the words of the barman. "That sounds too much."

"Tell him ten," said the woman, who was listening to his conversation.

They struck a deal at thirty dollars and with that the barman was with them in seconds. Henry gave him forty dollars. "Ten dollars, that's for you," he said alluding to their earlier conversation before he rapidly closed the door. It was a serious mistake. Firstly, the barman had already made his margin when the price of thirty dollars was struck, but far worse, the woman in his bed was now categorised with the women who had sat at the other table - a cash machine that was never going to be allowed to escape.

There is an immediate intimacy about two people sharing a single bed with one side pushed up against the wall, and so it was natural that Henry and the woman squeezed up close. Each took the other in to their arms and, for the first time, they kissed tentatively. They broke away naturally, looked into each other's eyes, smiled and kissed again.

As they kissed, the woman deliberately moved herself under him for a coupling in which she took frantic control, working her hips, grabbing the bed head and yelping short, muffled screams. It was only when she screwed up her face, and her body seized underneath him that Henry felt he had her permission to release himself.

As they lay side-by-side, both short of breath, the woman started to cry.

"I'm sorry," said Henry concerned.

"I not. I cry because I happy," said the woman with a smile designed to remove the worried look on Henry's face.

Henry reached for the orange juice he had poured earlier and they each took a sip.

"You're the only man other than my husband," she said.

"You're married?" asked Henry looking at her hand. There was no wedding ring.

"I'm getting divorced. He cheated on me, another woman, when I was pregnant," she said.

"You have a child?" asked Henry nervously.

"No, lost before born," she said, not knowing the word for miscarriage.

"I am sorry, really sorry," said Henry sympathetically. "I'm the only man other than your husband?" he repeated, just to make sure he understood what she had said.

"For sure," replied the woman using an expression which seemed strange coming from her lips.

They talked, made love twice more in unions which were exciting, happy and natural so it was 3 am when they got out of bed and the woman started to get dressed.

"My name's Tania Plesca," she said just as she was ready to leave. It was the first time she had told him her name.

"I'm Henry, Henry Guégan," he replied.

They shook hands as though they had just been formally introduced. Not another word was said between them as she left, and Henry closed the door behind her.

Chapter 7

Kishinev June 1991

HENRY STROLLED THROUGH Park Katedrainy towards the Presidential Palace. He was early and in no hurry. The sky was clear blue, and the trees were just beginning to turn from the bright green of spring into the deep green of summer.

Henry stopped walking to tarry a while on a park bench. He should have been thinking about his forthcoming meeting, but his mind was on Tania Plesca and the night before. He had read about 'revenge shags' promoted in the more avant-garde women's magazines. It was one of their new strategies in their mission to empower women. He had dismissed it as all nonsense, until now. Had that just happened to him, he wondered. Henry couldn't work out exactly how he felt, not least because, the moment they touched, he felt some instant connectivity, and he knew it was the same for her.

As Henry sat there, he started to hear the faint sound of choral singing. His thoughts changed as he concentrated on listening to one of the most beautifully clear pitched sounds he had ever heard. It was carried with clarity in the cool stillness of the early morning. Henry got up, picked up his case and walked towards the sound. Into Henry's view came a large imposing building in white and cream. He changed direction and walked towards its square and circular towers caped with domes, from which the singing was radiating. The Catedrala Naşterea Domnului[3] stood strong and magnificently within its park surrounds.

---

[3] The Cathedral of Christ's Nativity

Henry entered the cathedral walked past the small shop selling candles and icons. He remembered the words Jesus is said to have spoken, "my house shall be called a house of prayer, but you are making it a robbers' den." It was those words "robbers' den" which summarised Henry's views on organised religion, but at that moment, he was prepared to forgive any religion that could make music as beautiful as this.

Henry knew he would be entering an orthodox Christian cathedral, but his surprise was to see it so full so early in the morning. It was quite different to a church, or even a cathedral, in France or England where, at such a time, the congregation would be no more than a handful.

Henry listened to the voices of the male priests as they sang the canticles with the highest of pitch, which only a choirboy would attempt in England. It was truly a beautiful sound. Absorbed by the music, he stood disconnected and observed the congregation. It was either standing still, making the sign of the cross over their hearts and then bowing as they joined the priests in their prayers, or were moving from icon to icon in private worship. There were no obvious or immediate pews to sit in.

Henry retraced his steps and selected and paid for three candles, one each for his sons and one for his wife. Slowly he wandered around the church, looking at the congregation and the candles which were alight in front of the different icons. He chose to stand quietly at the side of a large candle holder in front of an icon of Mary holding Jesus as a small child. There were some four or five candles already alight, each throwing off a different size flame. With Sophie and his children in his thoughts, Henry decided that this was where he wanted to place his lighted candles. He pointed the wick of each of his unlit candles into the flames of one already alight, and, when it too was alight, he buried its base deep into the sandbox so that it stood upright. When Henry had lit all three candles, he stood back and watched the flames flicker in a warm orange-yellow glow. He thought of his family. He was so proud of his two sons. Once again, he felt the ever so familiar sense of despair at the fact that their mother could not know them. There was never-ending loneliness in him not being able to share his pride with her.

Beyond the glow, there was a woman looking at him intently. Immediately their eyes touched, they both look down, embarrassed. Henry raised his eyes again and looked back at the woman who was now staring firmly at the ground. A bright yellow, blue and green silk scarf was wrapped over her hair and around her face, accentuating its prettiness. She raised her eyes again to look at him. Immediately they recognised each other. They had been bed companions the night before. Henry smiled in recognition, but Tania looked right through him. She was in a state of shock.

Henry gently nodded and smiled again. Tania looked at him once more for only a brief second, but in doing so, she gave him the smallest hint of a smile. Henry smiled back, a wider smile this time as, at that moment, he had become completely smitten.

Chapter 8

Kishinev June 1991

EVELINA AND HENRY met on the steps of the Presidential Palace as planned. He was a fraction late as he had taken time to write a note to Tania and thrust it into her hand. It asked her to have dinner with him that evening.

Where's Edik?" asked Henry as the two of them entered the building.

"He's gone to Belarus on behalf of the President," replied Evelina.

They went through security and waited to be met as Henry tried, unobserved, to study Evelina. Once again, she had proven to be a chameleon in what she chose to wear. In the Ministry of Agriculture, her dress sense was dowdy and certainly cheap. Now she was in a smart, very expensive navy trouser suit, with the jacket length coming down to sit halfway down her buttocks. It was cut around the bust and deep into her waist to show off her figure. Again, Evelina had created the illusion of much longer legs by wearing high heels with the trouser hems coming to the ground. She had a light blue silk scarf thrown gently over the shoulder to add some colour.

"You look nice," said Henry. "Very London lawyerly," he added.

Evelina was thrilled with the comment. She had met the President many times socially where she saw her role as supporting Edik by dressing glamorously. As soon as she heard she was attending this business meeting with Henry and the President, she had decided that the look Henry had commented on was the one she wanted to obtain.

Outside the door to the President's office, Evelina paced nervously while Henry stood still. He was calm and collected. Whilst he was emotionally attached to this project, if it ended with nothing happening, then it wouldn't affect his life one iota.

As they entered the President's room, the power play was immediately obvious. President Mircea Stanescu did not get up. He stayed seated behind his huge desk and looked admiringly at Evelina. He turned to her and, with a big encouraging smile, said in Russian: "You look nice."

Stanescu then turned to look at Henry. "You think everything in this country is for sale," were his opening words. "You buy our women, and now you try to buy our wine and our land. Is that why you've come here too?" Without a pause, he continued in one breathless stream. "Do you know, most of the money that comes into this country comes from the women who have left?" It was all said in perfect English but with a strong Russian accent. "The diaspora, those who go abroad, they're the betrayers." There was bitterness in his voice. "They should be here helping to build our country. We educated them well, and instead they've run abroad for money, and where do they end up, in the hands of the sex traffickers and cities like London." Stanescu paused to read Henry's business card. "Your London, your Paris, Mr Guégan," he said accusingly. "We tell 'em, but it makes no difference; still they go."

At first Henry was shocked, but then he remembered the briefing papers helpfully provided by the EU Commission in Paris. Stanescu was a former Chairman of the Presidium of the Supreme Soviet. This helped explain what had just happened. Stanescu had played his opening move just as in a game of chess. A move that was designed to throw the other side off-guard.

"If that's what you think Mr President," said Henry speaking deliberately softly, "then you have been misinformed. I don't want to buy anything. I only bring something. I don't take it away. I bring the opportunity for an investment in your wine industry that's all." Evelina started to translate what Henry had said, but the President's translator quickly took over.

"I imagine you know the outline plan for the investment and grant money from the EU?" asked Henry.

"Yes of course," said Stanescu in English, before turning to his translator and speaking in Russian.

"How much are you investing?" asked the translator.

"I don't know yet. We haven't finished our work but overall, I guess it will be around €85 million over a five-year period," replied Henry.

"How many hectares are you buying for this?" asked the translator, on behalf of Stanescu.

"That work still has to be done. However, it will be whatever it has to be to provide the volume of grapes needed. The project won't need more and can't work on less," said Henry. He knew Stanescu would understand the point without debate. He was a trained agronomist and a former director of the Main Agricultural Science Directorate of the Ministry of Agriculture.

"The €85 million, will that be spent here, or will it just bring in the machinery bought from France, Germany or Italy?" asked Stanescu through his translator.

"I don't know," said Henry. "We haven't done the analysis, but I would expect the investment to create good quality jobs in Moldova."

"With modernisation we lose jobs'" said the translator, this time speaking on his own account.

"What percentage do we end up with after all this is done?" asked Stanescu in English.

"I don't know. It all depends on the size of the EU grants and what people bid."

"All the money is going to the company, nothing to the government? asked the President through his translator.

"Yes, that's right," said Henry.

"No," said Stanescu speaking himself. "The money must be paid to the government."

"I can make that clear in the tender documents, but the percentage the government owns after the deal will fall.

"No," repeated Stanescu. "We must have money and 51%."

"As I've already told your Minister of Agriculture," continued Henry, "this is a matter for the accountants and the economists; yours, the EU's and those who invest. They will pay whatever they think is fair. If there are a lot of bidders, the price will rise. If not, then ..."

"I won't have less than 50%," said Stanescu.

"I can't tell you what the percentage will be," said Henry. "The market will decide when people put in their bids. You can then decide whether you accept or not."

"I won't have less than 50%," repeated Stanescu.

"That's entirely your privilege," said Henry as he gently shook his head. "You can decide what to do once the bids are in. But I suggest you decide once the market has spoken, not before."

"For Cricova, I want $25 million cash plus 51% to the Government," said Stanescu, "or you're wasting my time."

"That values Cricova in its present state at $50 million," said Henry. "I can't see it's worth that."

"It's the deal. If you want it then we can talk more. If not goodbye."

"What do you want from the President?" asked the translator after Stanescu had spoken to him at length.

"Obviously, the whole plan requires land reform, but I am told you are working on that. However, given the President's concern about percentages, I think we should have an economist from the President's Office seconded to us."

"You have that already," said the translator, not waiting for Stanescu to speak. "You have Miss Kirillovich. She's a financier. She understands these things."

Henry looked straight at Evelina with a flash of anger in his eyes. She went deep red with embarrassment. Her true position was now known. All along she had been a mole, reporting straight into the President's office.

"The only other thing I need is the total integrity of your government," said Henry pointedly. This time he looked directly at Evelina as he spoke, before turning to look at Stanescu. "I need a promise that all the tenders will be treated fairly," said Henry.

"That's not right," said Evelina quickly, commenting on the translator's translation of what was said, but it was too late.

"Don't tell me about bribes," shouted Stanescu. "Look at your arms industry, look at your Prime Minister's son. What was his name?"

"Are you talking about Mark Thatcher?" volunteered Henry confused.

"He was involved in one of the UK's biggest arms contracts with Saudi Arabia, and the bribes went everywhere. How dare you come here preaching about bribes with hands as dirty as that?" yelled Stanescu, clearly upset.

"Fuck the British government," said Stanescu. "Fuck all Englishmen. They're so pathetic that they have to fuck with their socks on." He laughed at his own joke. "They wash their hands after they've pissed because they piss on their hands. No Russian is so stupid as to piss on his own hands, on someone else's yes, but not on his own," and he laughed again.

"I am French Monsieur," said Henry exaggerating his French accent. "This project is the European Union's; with the Paris office of the EU to be precise and there are certain rules which must be followed."

"You don't understand this job," said Stanescu in a conciliatory tone. "This job is dangerous. Russia can crush us at any time. It is down now but it will rise. Yeltsin is a fool. He's always too drunk to know his own problems. Who will succeed him?" Whoever comes after Yeltsin will be a strong man, ruthless," he predicted. "It's the Russian way." The translator was struggling to keep up. "Where do I go?" he said in English. "Where do my family go when Russia comes back? To the Gulag? I do this job for my country, but my country must make sure I'm safe. Do you understand?" he asked.

It was the first time Henry had heard a politician explain why he had to act corruptly. It was not an argument he was prepared to accept, and certainly not from President Stanescu, a man who he had already started to dislike.

Chapter 9

Kishinev June 1991

HENRY AND EVELINA left the Presidential Palace without a word being said between them. He was cross with her, but more importantly, he was cross with himself. He had been honey-trapped and, to make it worse, without the benefit of any sex. But then Evelina didn't need to sleep with him. He had given her access to everything. But why not, he thought as he walked. There were no secrets. There should be no secrets.

Henry didn't go to the Ministry of Agriculture or back to his hotel. Instead, he returned to the museum, paid the entrance fee, and dragged a wooden chair so he could sit by the display of the Battle of the River Prut. The room was cold, damp and empty. He was to discover it was always like that. It was where he could think in peace; something he found impossible to do in the noise of the Ministry of Agriculture or the confines of his hotel room.

What was happening? he asked himself. He knew the game he was playing. It was all spelt out in advance. But what about the others, what were they all doing? Stanescu's motives were clear. He was going to take as much out of this deal personally as he possibly could. The same was true of the Minister of Agriculture and his deputy, but they were unsure they had the political power to get a cut of the spoils. The Chief of the Collective would happily accept the few scraps Stanescu threw him, provided it was enough to live out his days in comfort. As he thought about everyone and what they had done, it suddenly dawned on him, both Edik and Evelina were ex-KGB and now in the pay of Stanescu. They were there to do his spying, his bidding, and his dirty work. Henry was sure of it. Apart from the people from Arthur Andersen, the only one he was sure of was Tania. Her motive had been simple, revenge on her ex-husband.

After an hour of sitting, standing and pacing in the museum, Henry returned to his large, shared office within the Ministry of Agriculture.

"We need to go for a walk," said Henry to Evelina as soon as he got back.

It was obvious from the way she looked up at him that she had been dreading this moment.

"We need that walk, now!" he said, making it clear from his tone that he expected her to move immediately.

They walked side-by-side at a sharp pace, and in silence, along the Boulevard Ştefan cel Mare until Henry turned into the park. Once amongst the trees, Henry slowed down. One hundred metres inside, he stopped, turned, looked at Evelina straight in the eye and asked: "When did you join the KGB?"

Evelina looked at him hard. Her brain went into overdrive as her training kicked in. She thought about denying it, but she knew he wouldn't believe her.

"I was recruited from school just before I went to university," she answered. "They sponsored me."

"When did you leave?"

"I don't think you can ever leave," she said, "but they stop paying me when the wall came down. I suppose I left when all those I reported to disappeared into other jobs too."

"And Edik?" asked Henry.

"You need to ask him," she said. "I'm sorry but I can't talk for him."

They walked some more, and talked as they went, until they came to a small café with outside tables. It was open but had no customers. They sat down at one of the tables, and a man carrying a tablecloth laid it and passed out a couple of menus.

"I think you should have a glass of wine too," said Henry, as he ordered coffees for the two of them, and a large glass of Kodrinskoie for Evelina. "I know I don't drink wine, but this is my favourite of everything I've tried in Moldova so far. I don't need an excuse to order it when I see it on the menu."

Evelina smiled, and they started to chatter some more.

"Tell me about you and Edik?" asked Henry, after her wine glass was nearly empty.

"He's very ambitious," she said, almost apologetically.

It was the way Evelina spoke which made Henry ask his next question. "Do you love him?" he asked, surprised at his audacity.

Evelina looked at the tablecloth for a long time as she contemplated her answer. No one had asked her that question before. Edik and her had got to that stage in their relationship where she had even stopped asking it of herself.

"I thought I did, maybe once, but now, I'm not sure ... no, I don't think so," she said. There was sadness in her voice as she recognised that something, which she once thought perfect, had gone wrong.

Henry reached across and comfortingly touched Evelina's arm.

"I am not sure I even like him anymore. Now he has money he's changed," she said, as her face reflected the bitterness which she had felt for a long time but had kept hidden.

"Where does he get his money from, Stanescu?" Henry asked.

"Some for sure, but I don't think a lot, but he uses his place in the President's office to ..." Evelina stopped talking. They both knew she had possibly said too much.

Henry ordered two more coffees and another glass of wine.

"Why don't you leave him?" he asked.

"It's true what I said about being dismissed from the bank. The KGB put me there. I had an excellent position, but then it was gone. I needed a job. I needed money. Edik gets me jobs, he gets me money."

Henry nodded sympathetically.

"Do you know I was one year ahead of my age group at school, even then I was always top of the year in everything ... except sport? I didn't like sport, just tennis."

"It means you can do anything you want," said Henry encouragingly. "Come on, let's go back, but we'll need to be honest with our colleagues as to what it is you do. From now on, we'll tell everyone that you're the new liaison officer with the President's office. We can say it was the outcome of today's meeting."

Evelina said nothing in reply. She just nodded.

Henry paid the bill.

"In fact," he said, as he joined her at the gate to walk out of the restaurant area, "I'll get you put on contract with Arthur Andersen as a consultant. You can be paid by them and be included as part of the EU's project costs, that way you are no longer dependent upon Edik for your job."

"You want me to change sides?" asked Evelina, hiding the fact that she was really thinking Henry wanted her to change beds. From Edik's bed to his. Could it be any worse, she wondered.

"Good God no!" said Henry. "I want you to stay on the same side. The side which does the best for everyone in Moldova."

Chapter 10

Kishinev June 1991

TANIA AND HENRY met in the reception hall of Henry's hotel. He was thrilled to see her, as he wasn't sure she would come. They went to dinner in an unappetising restaurant where, amongst very few other customers, they talked, and they talked. When the restaurant closed, they went to a newly opened nightclub in a basement and there, away from the music, they talked some more. It was past midnight when they left the club. Both instinctively knew they would be returning to Henry's hotel.

"Have you been shopping?" asked Henry pointedly as they climbed the stairs to his floor.

"Yes," she said with a smile on her face.

They showered together, made love all night and again in the morning. They left together. Henry to the airport. Tania to go home. They exchanged telephone numbers, and Henry promised to get back in touch with her when he returned to Kishinev in late July.

When they parted, each felt a slight twinge of loss, for they weren't sure that they would see the other again, and neither liked the idea of that.

Chapter 11

Kishinev June 1991

HENRY CHECKED HIS case in at the Air Moldovan desk, collected his boarding card and passed through security. He put his briefcase on the conveyer belt for it to go through the scanning machine, and his keys, pens, and odd coins were placed in a plastic container and were quickly scanned too. He was waved through the security body scanner without any problems and, as he turned to collect his case, he found it had been selected for a routine search.

"Your case?" questioned the security man, pointing to Henry's briefcase.

"Yes," said Henry.

"Open," said the security man.

The man rummaged through Henry's case and picked up a round, cylindrical object with a plastic top.

"What is this?" said the man.

Before Henry had any chance to answer, the security man blew his whistle and was pointing towards him. Within seconds Henry had two men at his side grabbing him viciously. One pointed a rifle at his kidney, the other a pistol at his neck. Henry froze in fear. These men were now shouting at him, all at once in a language he didn't understand.

The man with the pistol took Henry firmly by the arm, twisting his thumb and hand, which forced him to lean forward. Forcefully, he was led away while the man with the rifle followed, now pointing it firmly at his back.

"Call British Council," Henry shouted to the crowd. "Call the British Embassy," he shouted again before he was pushed into a corridor and then into a room. The man with the rifle stayed outside, taking up a guarding position while the man with the pistol shouted to Henry in Russian, demanding he sit on a large black leather settee placed against the wall in the middle of the room.

Henry studied his surroundings. Straight ahead of him was a huge oak partner desk with long pedestals. It abutted the opposite wall. It had two chairs on either end of the desk so that its occupants would sit opposite each other.

An attractive woman in early middle age came in. She was very elegantly dressed in plain clothes. "Empty pockets," she instructed and then, very carefully, she laid everything out from both his pockets and his case on top of the partner's desk in front of him.

"This, what?" asked the woman in plain clothes as she pointed to the pepper spray Henry had in his brief case and which he had long forgotten about.

No sooner had the plain-clothed woman asked her questions than another younger woman came in, this time dressed in a neat uniform, tailored, far distant from the standard issue. Epaulettes indicated her senior rank. She picked up the pepper spray and pointed to a board that covered the whole of the end wall from top to bottom and from side to side. It was loaded with different types of weapons. Henry looked and studied it carefully. At the top left, there was an AK47 and then, spread from left to right, row upon row, there was every kind of weapon, from guns, knives, knuckle-dusters, and chains. At the bottom, far right, the final item was a canister of spray like the one which was in his bag and now being shown to him.

Oh fuck, thought Henry as he identified his pepper spray with the canister.

"Crime," said the woman in uniform in English. Then, reading from a hand-written sheet, she said, again in English, "possession of illegal weapon and attempted skyjacking, crime!"

"What?" said Henry shocked. "I bought that in a petrol station in the United States. It's journeyed through JFK, Heathrow, and Vienna airports before it arrived here," he protested.

"Clothes off," demanded the woman in plain clothes.

"Undress?" asked Henry.

"Yes."

Slowly Henry undressed until he was, without his under pants and socks, standing there completely naked.

The woman in the uniform indicated, with a twist of her fingers, that he had to turn around, which Henry did, coming back to face her. She looked at him, up and down, and when she came back to look into his eyes, she smiled.

"Sit," said the woman in the uniform and pointed to a leather settee before the two women left, leaving him on his own.

Henry sat down. Although it was June, he found the black leather settee cold against his naked skin. He could feel his heart beating through his chest in fright as he contemplated the mess he was now in. He thought of his family and wondered who was going to take care of them while he got himself out of this not insignificant difficulty

A few minutes later, a gaggle of women and girls arrived, seven or eight of them. Henry was not sure of their number, but they were of different ages and sizes, and all dressed differently. Some were in uniform, some were cleaners, and others were office staff. Henry moved his hands in front of him to give him some modesty.

A middle-aged woman in a white coat moved forward as the leader of the group. She beckoned him to stand up, which he did. Two of them then pushed him against a wall while another girl marked his height and a third measured, pronouncing 1.97. There was then a lot of whispering as each girl gave a number and another wrote it down.

Surely, but very deliberately, the woman in the white coat put on a latex surgical glove. Henry froze. Oh my God, he thought, as he feared a rectal examination. Isn't it obvious to these idiots I'm just a businessman and not a hijacker."

A small, very round woman wearing one yellow washing-up glove pushed herself forward and grabbed Henry's private parts quite forcefully. His hands immediately moved down to protect him, but they were forcefully taken away and pushed against his side and the wall.

"No, whoa, no, hang on" said Henry, protesting in a polite, nonaggressive manner. The yellow glove was now around his penis, being vigorously pumped up and down by the small woman who was laughing and showing her black teeth. She was being as rough as hell as she worked at him ridiculously hard. With each stroke down, bashing his testicles, causing an ache and nauseating pain in Henry stomach.

After what seemed like a lifetime of manhandling, his manhood lay limp and his face grimaced in pain. This time the white-coated woman came forward and took over masturbating him with a surgical glove. She was softer to the touch, gently stroked his testicles and rubbed the inside of his legs. Soon his penis started to grow and now, taking the shaft between her fingers, she worked vigorously until his penis was strong and erect. Soon a ruler was produced. One edge was dug deep into his pubic bone until it hurt, and the measurement was announced.

This measurement was hotly disputed by another woman who fought forward, this time with no gloves. She attacked his genitals with both hands, trying to force a bigger erection. Out came the ruler again, which was stabbed into him, trying to get a bigger reading. Now each wanted their turn and Henry put his head back against the wall and closed his eyes. His mind was only capable of thinking about the discomfort and pain below. After what seemed like an age, the woman in the white coat took control, and Henry opened his eyes to watch the other women leave as she stayed behind.

"Not good," she said, looking at his penis. "But not bad either, seen better, but not good measure," she added, shaking her head

"I haven't had any complaints so far," said Henry in his defence, immediately regretting he had said anything.

"Woman too polite to complain," she responded dismissively before instructing him to: "Get dressed." With that, the woman in the white coat was gone. Henry winced as he was now in quite a lot of pain in his stomach. He proceeded to get dressed, and just as he was putting on his jacket, a large man came into the room. He was wearing an enormous military cap, and on his jacket, he had oversized epaulettes.

"Sit," he instructed.

Henry duly sat down on the settee.

"Crime," said the man in the large cap and epaulettes. "Attempted skyjacking," he said. This time there was no mention of the possession of a weapon. Henry said nothing.

"I gather our women have been having fun with you," he said, laughing. "But not so bad as Moldovan jail," he continued. "Very bad, very bad," he added, shaking his head forlornly from side to side

The man in the large cap and epaulettes studied Henry's possessions. He counted the money. A mixture of pounds, dollars, and Euros, along with some Moldovan money.

"It's a shame you didn't buy an export license for this," he said, waving the pepper spray in the air.

"An export licence?" said Henry in bewilderment.

"Yes, an export licence."

"How much is an export licence?" questioned Henry.

The man with the epaulettes said nothing. Instead, he started to do some calculations.

Instantly, Henry knew what had been happening. The gang of women had been sent to soften him up, to frighten him as to his prospects in a Moldovan jail.

After a long period, during which the man with the epaulettes did his sums several times, a figure was quoted. Henry nodded in agreement, not really understanding what was happening. The man with the epaulettes then produced a book, a stamp and wrote out a hand receipt, which he handed to Henry. He also handed him just one of his ten-pound notes and the few coins that were left.

Henry packed his case and put his items back in his pocket. As he was packing, the man with the epaulettes ceremoniously handed him the pepper spray, which Henry put back in his case. They then walked out to the gate together. Henry was certain that, by now, he would have missed his plane, but it was still there waiting.

"The women here think height goes with the size of dick," said the man in the cap, "ridiculous," he commented.

What had he just said? Was this real! Henry wondered.

"In England they think it goes with shoe-size," replied Henry.

"Shoe size?" enquired the man with the cap.

"The bigger the shoes, the bigger the dick," said Henry.

The man with the epaulettes and Henry both looked down at his feet. To Henry's relief the man was wearing a huge pair of brightly shone boots.

"I will have to tell them," he said with a huge smile on his face as he turned to leave.

Henry looked around and found a waste-paper bin in which he threw the pepper spray. The thought of a similar experience, as he passed through Otopeni airport, was too much to contemplate.

As Henry walked through the check-in towards his aeroplane, one of the women ground crew held his passport and ticket for an unusually long time. She stared at him and smiled a most delightful smile. He looked into her sweet face. Had she been one of the women in the room? He had no idea. What he did know was that he had just been shaken down for nearly five hundred dollars. That would buy an awful lot in Moldova, but better than prison, he thought. The experience was not something he was going to shout about, nor forget.

Chapter 12

Kishinev and the Woodman's Dacha September 1991

HENRY RETURNED TO Kishinev at the end of September. Nothing was going to get in the way of his long summer holiday with his children and seeing his wife. His recent experience with Moldovan airport security made him a little anxious, but with diplomatic credentials provided by the European Union and remembering he had direct access to the President's office for any future problems, he felt far more confident about going back.

On his return, he found little progress had been made on any of the individual privatisation projects. It appeared everyone working on it saw it as a gravy train with the objective of keeping it running as long as possible. The situation was made far worse by the bureaucracy placed on the project by the European Union. One-third of the total employment costs were now being spent in gathering and providing them with monitoring information on what was going on. Henry knew that, shortly after he had got back to Paris, he was going to have to go to Brussels as the European Union had created a project which was spinning wildly but was achieving little forward momentum.

The bottling plants, wineries and vineyards had provided as little information as they could and then as slowly as possible. They were frightened by having to live from hand to mouth in this new capitalist world, but they were even more frightened by the prospects of what lay ahead.

Politically, land reform legislation was going nowhere, bogged down in debates between too many internal and vested factions.

Evelina was still living with Edik. She accompanied Henry to each of the units being privatised to see what was holding things up. With her accompanying the local manager in the consumption of many a bottle of wine, and with Henry drinking orange juice and black tea, they managed to re-galvanise the unit managers' initial enthusiasm for their privatisation project. In short, they had numerous well-founded fears about capitalism which, without experience, they did not know how to solve.

Each of those involved in a unit's management could see that having the lowest price would give them a competitive advantage, but they also assumed that their competitors would lower their prices too. If they all did this, then they were in a zero-sum game, with future losses and certain bankruptcy guaranteed. They marvelled at how free-market capitalism had ever become so successful, for it was, they thought, a mad system.

It was when Henry spoke of different marketing strategies, peppered with loads of examples from his experience, did they regained confidence in the privatisation plan, only to lose it time and time again when another business issue, which they had not previously experienced, came to the fore.

The evenings and night-times were reserved for Tania. At last, the hotel acceded to his request for a double room and with a double bed. They would have their evening meal delivered as room service and then work, with her marking her children's books and him reading until late. They would go to bed together just as though they were a married couple, sometimes making love and sometimes not. They both enjoyed the quiet presence of the other Not once was Henry invited to Tania's apartment, but likewise, not once had he realised it.

From the very first days of being a wine wholesaler, Henry had a golden rule that, wherever he was in the world, he would leave for home on Friday evening, or occasionally, Saturday morning, so he could have at least one day of the weekend with his family. However, with his children getting older and more established, the rule had started to lapse.

On this trip, he intended to go home on a Friday, but at the last minute, he changed his plans and extended his visit so he could spend his last Saturday in Moldova meeting members of Tania's family at their rural Dacha.

At the Dacha, Henry discovered that Tania came from a long dynasty of proudly Moldovan women. He was first introduced to Tania's mother Heidi Solokov and then her father Vlad Plesca. It was immediately obvious that they were devoted to each other and their only daughter. Away from their work they did almost everything together. Tania's mother was warm and welcoming. Her father scowled at Henry. The fact that Henry was taking his daughter to bed without the benefit of a wedding ring was enough to upset him, but once Tania had shared Henry circumstances, married with a wife and children, he ended up thoroughly disapproving. Tania could tell her mother how this man made her feel, and she understood, but not her father.

This is my grandmother, Mayanna Solokov but we all call her Anna, and this is my great-grandmother Brigita Solokov," said Tania excitedly as she introduced them. "You know the Battle of the River Prut?"

Henry nodded.

"Brigita fought as a partisan just before the battle, and both Brigita and Anna were nurses during it." She spoke proudly. "Do you know they set up a field hospital just here in our Dacha and down to the river," she said, waving her arms around to indicate the size.

Henry stood on the veranda of the Woodman's Dacha and looked out over the fields, down to the river and beyond. He could smell a mix of crops and soil in the air so reminiscent of the smell at Château de Gressier at this time of year. He loved places like this and had an immediate affinity with all those who loved their terroir. Tania's family, like his, were at one with the earth beneath their feet, and it made him feel as though he were at home.

Chapter 13

Kishinev December 1991

HENRY RETURNED TO Kishinev in December to see Tania and give her a Christmas present, but he also wanted to see President Mircea Stanescu. The EU grant money to develop the privatisation plans for his country's wine industry was nearly all gone. A new application had to be made early in the New Year if the project was to go forward, and this needed Stanescu's commitment. Thankfully, Stanescu realised how important the wine project was to his country's internal politics. He needed to keep the EU's money flowing into Moldova. His whole political future was based on getting as close to Europe and its money as possible, and Henry was a tiny cog in the wheel of making that happen.

This time Henry was received most cordially by Stanescu, who was accompanied by his Minister of Agriculture. Edik appeared in a suit well beyond his pay grade, and Evelina wore not the clothes she would wear to go to the Ministry of Agriculture but, once again, another brand-new trouser suit in the style chosen by Europe's leading businesswomen.

The meeting was unusually cordial and ended with a series of promises which, being political promises, were not promises at all.

As Henry left the Presidential Palace, he felt quite depressed. It was nearly a year since he had first arrived in the country, and since then, he had only been able to achieve a fraction of what he had expected. It was as though Brussels and Kishinev had their own kind of bureaucratic treacle, not found in Paris or London, which made it impossibly hard to wade through.

Henry's only pleasure was when Tania joined him at his hotel after work. For her, this wasn't just spending time with a man she really liked and who treated her well. It was also the convenience of his hotel, which gave her a holiday from the grind of daily living.

The day after Henry's meeting with Stanescu, it was Tania who left the bedroom first. It was early in the morning, and she had to get to school for the autumn term was close to its end. At the front door of the hotel, Tania was stopped by the doorman, complete with earpiece and walkie-talkie.

"Mr Frolov Ilyich, the hotel owner wants to see you," said the doorman, taking Tania roughly by the arm and squeezing it tightly. "I have her," he reported to his walkie-talkie.

"OK, bring her in," came the reply.

Ilyich's room was through a panelled door off the main reception hall. It was no better furnished than the rest of the hotel and was typical of communist Eastern Europe. The room reflected austerity, poor quality and bad workmanship in every direction.

"You haven't paid me," said Ilyich as soon as Tania had been placed in the chair on the other side of his cigarette burned desk. "Why not?" he asked. It was said in a way which was designed to frighten and intimidate.

Although Ilyich was the named director and shown as the owner of the hotel shares, he was just the secret nominee for Mircea Stanescu and his son, Constin. However, the income he got from the prostitutes working from the hotel bar didn't go through the books. He deemed it his money to keep.

"What have I got to pay for?" asked Tania confused. Instantly she became worried that Henry might not have been paying his hotel bills.

"Working here for twenty-one nights," said Ilyich. He looked at the doorman. "Twenty-one nights?" he said again to check the number.

"Yes, twenty-one nights" confirmed the doorman.

"That's $840 you owe us. It's $420 for me, $210 for the Barman and $210 for the doorman," said Ilyich. "Those are the rules of this hotel, and you should know them."

"I haven't been working here," protested Tania shaking her head vigorously.

"You've been fucking the Frenchman," said Ilyich. "In my book that's working."

"But he's not been paying me. What do you think I am?" There was now anger in Tania's voice.

"More fool you," said Ilyich. "A pretty girl like you can charge a lot, but that's not my concern. You fuck in my hotel; you pay my fee. It's the rule.

"How much do you want?" said Tania, not having fully grasped what she was being charged

"$840," said Ilyich.

"It's ridiculous. I'm a teacher. I don't have that kind of money," she replied emphatically.

"Ask your Frenchman for it,"

"I can't do that," objected Tania.

"Look girl, protest as much as you like. You've been fucking here, he's been paying you, and I want my money. I don't care where it comes from," said Ilyich shaking his head.

"He hasn't been paying me," said Tania firmly, placing strong emphasis on the word hasn't.

Ilyich got up from his desk and stood in front of Tania. He leant down so that his face was just inches from hers.

"This is a good one to fuck," said Ilyich looking up at his body guard, who had just entered the room. "A pretty face and big tits," he added, before taking Tania's wrist and then, taking the little finger of that hand, he placed his thumb on her nail and squeezed it hard into itself.

Tania twisted her hand and body and yelled out in pain," as she tried to escape.

"I will have my money!" said Ilyich. "Tell her, show her what happens when I don't get my money," he said, turning to his bodyguard.

The bodyguard reached into his pocket and took out a wooden handle about 6 inches long. Wrapped around it were six or eight strands of thin plastic-coated electric wire, each about a meter long, pinned and bound into the handle to create a lethal whip. Very quickly the bodyguard shook the strands of wire, so they were dangling free. He handed it to Ilyich who immediately thrashed the strands of wire over the back of a leather seat placed at the edge of his desk, cutting the leather. Then, in a sudden frenzy, once, twice, three, four times, he frantically whipped its leather seat cutting it to shreds.

"See that," said Ilyich, said pointing to the strands of cut leather. "That will be you if I don't get my money." He was breathing hard out of the physical effort he'd put into whipping the chair.

Tania shivered and bit her lip. She was certain that this man was quite mad.

"Then what happens?" said Ilyich turning to his bodyguard.

"You give her to me boss."

"Why's that?" asked Ilyich.

"A bit of fun boss."

"Do you want to have some fun with her now?" The implication of that question was obvious to everyone.

"No boss not now, we've got a meeting, remember?" said the bodyguard shaking his head, "perhaps later."

"And after the fun, then what happens?"

"I'll sell 'er. She'll get good money in Albania. Two hundred, three hundred dollars, maybe more. They'll probably get a thousand for her."

Every syllable from the bodyguard's lips was designed to frighten Tania into getting Ilyich his money. That was their only interest, and it had the right effect. She was well and truly frightened!

Chapter 14

Kishinev December 1991

UNKNOWN TO HENRY, Tania was facing her ordeal in Ilyich's office just as he was walking through the hotel lobby to go to the Ministry of Agriculture. Even if he had been there when she left, it is unlikely that it would have made any difference. As soon as she got to the door and the doorman had let Tania go, she ran and ran. She was in an almost uncontrollable state when she arrived at school but, ten minutes later, she did what every teacher in the world has to do when they walk into their classroom, she left her problems outside the door, and that's where they stayed for the next two hours.

At the first play break, Tania used the school telephone to phone Henry on his mobile phone. Everyone in the office heard as she told what had happened. She described the events so dramatically that, on several occasions, she burst uncontrollably in to tears.

Henry and Evelina were outside Tania's school within forty-five minutes of her ending their telephone call. It meant they were there waiting long before Tania dismissed her class for the day and could leave. Seeing Henry, Tania ran into his arms and sobbed whilst shaking uncontrollably. They both ignored the cold rain which was falling heavily upon them.

In Evelina's car, with Henry sitting in the rear, Tania re-told her story.

"Phone Edik," said Evelina as soon as she heard. "You have to phone Edik," she repeated. "He'll be able to sort it out."

Henry handed Evelina his mobile phone, and she dialled his office from memory. He wasn't there. Evelina left a message that he had to telephone her urgently and cut the call. They were each contemplating in silence what to do when Edik phoned back. Evelina snatched the phone from Henry as soon as she heard his voice. There was a frantic conversation between them in Russian which Henry didn't understand.

"He's agreed to meet us at a small coffee shop on Strada Doina," said Evelina handing back his phone. It was one of the large living-quarter areas of Kishinev with its badly built blocks of 1960 style apartments. It was an area of Kishinev Henry had never been to before.

Edik was already in the cafe wearing jeans and an expensive black leather jacket, the uniform of the Kishinev's mafia, when Evelina, Tania and Henry arrived.

The four of them settled at a table, and Evelina told Edik exactly what had happened in graphic detail. Tania listened and said nothing, for Evelina had, in one hearing, grasped every aspect of what had happened.

"I will sort it," said Edik, his voice unruffled.

"How?" said Henry.

"I will sort it," he repeated. "I will talk to the hotel owner."

"Do you know him?"

"Yes."

"How?"

"Doesn't matter."

"I'm sorry Mr KGB man," said Henry, "But I don't trust you or them. So tomorrow you and I are going to the bank. I am going to get the money which you'll take to them. You'll give them their fucking $840. You'll pay my bill, which I'll give you the money for too, and you'll get Tania and my things, then..." Henry paused to gather his thoughts. "Then," he repeated, you'll get your mate, the President, to phone the owner of that shit hotel and tell them to leave Tania and me alone. He's then to phone me to tell us that he's done it."

"Stanescu will never do that," said Edik.

"Yes, he bloody well will," said Henry, "because I can assure you, I will spend the rest of my life making sure that the European Union never gives this country a single lei whilst Stanescu's in charge. And believe me, when I say, that promise has a lot of money and influence behind it!"

"I'll sort it," said Edik, now concerned about Henry's demand for Stanescu's involvement. Did he know, had he worked out who was the real owner of the Steffaco Hotel, Edik wondered.

"I leave Saturday morning. Make sure he's made his call to me by the time I am gone," said Henry.

"I'll sort it," said Edik again. "I promise I'll sort it."

"Did I tell you my grandmother was great friends of the Kennedys?" said Henry. "You'll have heard of them, remember, President of the United States?" There was deep sarcasm in Henry's voice. "They're my direct access to the White House when I need it."

"Of course, I've heard of Kennedy. What do you think I am, an idiot," replied Edik crossly. "When we first met, you lectured us on the Cuban missile crisis as though we were fools. Of course we studied it. We analysed every move to make sure the next time it's not us who has to give in!" There was real bite in Edik's voice. He spoke as a warrior that had lost one battle and was not going to lose another.

"Do you know why we lost, why we gave in?" he continued.

Henry didn't answer. He was studying Edik's body language looking for signals, clues as to what was really going on.

"Humanity! We gave in for humanity!" continued Edik. "The Americans thought we had ten thousand men deployed on Cuba; we had forty-three thousand. On the island, we had bombers and medium-range missiles capable of striking the US mainland. They knew nothing about these. But do you know what caused Krushhchev to give in? We had over fifty short-range nuclear missiles down there too which they knew nothing about. Each missile had the same power as was dropped on Hiroshima. They wouldn't have reached Florida, but they would have destroyed, wiped out any American invasion force. The thing is, each of our battlefield commanders is authorised to use such weapons if they are attacked. Khrushchev was scared stiff that the Americans might just be stupid enough to try and invade, and then ... the end! And do you know what? They were that stupid. In complete fucking ignorance, the American military not only prepared invasion plans but went out of their way to encourage Kennedy to attack! So say thank you, Mr European man, because if it wasn't for us, you wouldn't be sitting here right now."

The animosity between the two men was now as strong as the intense dislike Russia and the USA had for each other at the worst of times. Once again, the Cold War was being re-fought, but this time in a coffee shop in a small suburb of a city and in a country most people had never heard of.

"Yeh, well get this, Mr KGB man. Unless I hear from your President, I'll use every sodding contact I have in the US to make sure that the State Department doesn't give a cent to Moldova whilst Stanescu's in charge."

"Don't threaten us," said Edik, in a tone so menacing that if he'd had a weapon on him, he would have produced it.

"I am not the one threatening or being threatened," said Henry calmly. "It's Tania here ... it reflects badly on your country. I can say good things or bad things about Moldova when I get home and report, that's my choice."

"If you get home!" said Edik menacingly.

"Edik, shut up!" said Evelina, digging him hard in the ribs.

"Your country needs friends," continued Henry. "Stanescu needs friends. I'm his friend. He needs to understand that, and this friend needs a favour. Are we clear? Do you understand?"

Edik didn't reply. It enabled Henry to decide he'd said enough. He got up from the table. "Come," he said taking Tania's hand. "We'll leave Edik and Evelina to pay the bill and work their power games."

Evelina smiled encouragingly at Henry. She had taken a perverse joy in seeing someone take on Edik and, at the least, meet his match. It was a rare event. For his part, Edik scowled his goodbye.

It was dark and still raining when they got outside. Tania spotted a taxi and hailed it. Sitting sopping wet in the back of the cab Tania gave the instructions.

"We'll go to my apartment," she said, taking Henry's hand. They made their journey in silence. She knew that bad luck had put her in a terrible position, but perhaps good luck had found her the right man to deal with it.

"Hell Edik, how can they have been so stupid?" said Evelina as soon as Henry and Tania had gone.

"I know," said Edik.

"The one man in the whole of Moldova we don't want to upset, and they've done just that!" said Evelina.

"I know, I know," repeated Edik as he reached into his pocket to take out a mobile phone.

"When did you get that?" said Evelina shocked. Mobile phones, although not new, were still expensive to buy and only owned by the elite.

Edik didn't answer. Instead he dialled. It wasn't President Mircea Stanescu he called. It was Costin Stanescu, the President's son, the real owner of Steffaco Hotel.

Three hours later, Frolov Ilyich, Costin Stanescu, Edik and Evelina were together in the same room in which Tania had been frightened witless. Immediately, Evelina spotted the leather torn by Ilyich's whip. She deliberately ran her hand over it to signal she knew how it had been made. In the meantime, Costin and Evelina had shared a secret smile which only past lovers can share.

Evelina had once been tempted to trade Edik for Costin. While they'd had a few dinners together followed by sessions of rough, unsatisfying sex, she had abandoned her ambitions when she realised how selfish and narcissistic he was.

Evelina watched as the three men argued. Costin was furious that Ilyich had been syphoning money from the prostitutes which he thought should belong to him. Ilyich disagreed. What made Costin even crosser was the demand to involve his father. It was not something he was going to do. There was an impasse as the men went around and around their alternatives, including killing the two of them. "Then say good-bye to your father's political career," was Evelina's response to that remark, shaking her head as she spoke. It was her only comment throughout their debate.

It was ninety minutes into their conversation, made more incomprehensible by the amount of vodka drunk, that Evelina, completely exasperated, took control. "This is what happens," she said. "Get Guégan and his woman's things out their room right now and give them to me. Tomorrow Edik will go to the bank with Guégan and get the money which will be paid to the hotel, just as he wants."

"It will be paid to me," said Costin.

"For Christ sake shut up!" said Evelina sharply. "It will be paid to the hotel, because the hotel will give Edik a receipt which he can give to Mr Guégan, okay! I don't give a shit what the hotel does with the money, sort it out between you! Then, Costin you're going to phone Mr Guégan. You're going to tell him who you are, the President's son, and that you own the hotel. You're going to apologise and assure him that nothing will happen to Tania Plesca."

"Then he's bound to ask for his money back," protested Costin.

"You really are pathetic, aren't you?" said Evelina, disgust pouring through every syllable.

"Evelina!" shouted Edik, "You can't say that."

"We're worrying about Moldova and its wine industry. We're worrying about his father's political career, and all he's worrying about is eight hundred dollars. So yes, I can say that!" shouted Evelina. "But in any case, he won't ask for the money back."

"How do you know?" asked Edik.

"I do, okay. I've worked with him long enough now to know."

Edik flashed a look at her. Was she sleeping with Henry, he wondered.

In any case, I'll talk to him too. I'll tell him about this meeting. He trusts me," she said.

"Does he know you're ex KGB?" asked Edik.

"Yes, of course he does. He worked it out ages ago. Why do you think he called you Mr KGB man?"

Edik was now certain of it. She was sleeping with him! She would only have told him that as pillow talk.

"Edik, let's go," said Evelina continuing to be in control. "There's no more to be said."

"I'm not coming," he replied crossly. "Go on your own," he instructed. There was a woman in the bar upstairs who was going to be paid $140 and provide him with a joint to smoke. It was going to be far more fun than being with an angry girlfriend complaining about the friends he keeps.

Chapter 15

Kishinev December 1991

WITH TORCH IN hand, Tania led Henry through the puddles of mud in the yard, up some concrete steps to a steel door. They went through the door into an unlit concrete stairwell. With the light of the torch, they climbed two flights of stairs until they came to a landing with a lift entrance and three more steel front doors, one of which was the entrance to Tania's apartment. Several keys and two doors later they were inside. Tania turned on the lights, locked the two doors behind her and closed the curtain. It was warm and cosy. A bolt hole of safety, away from the nastiness of the elements bashing away at the windows, and those threatening to do them harm.

"This was my great grandmother's apartment," said Tania proudly, as soon as she had taken off her coat. "The other one over there," she pointed to the way they came in, "on the same floor is my grandmother's. This is the absolute best area of the city and these are the best apartments. We have them because my great-grandmother was a partisan hero. With her husband, they were big in the Communist Party."

"She doesn't live here anymore?" asked Henry.

"No, she lives with my grandmother at the Dacha. She can't climb the stairs. My grandmother's apartment, the one next door, is let to the American Embassy. The money gives them a good pension," continued Tania as she rubbed her thick hair with a towel to dry it.

"This is my grandmother's bedroom," said Tania leading him into the second room. "My mother and grandmother were born on that bed," said Tania. "It was retrieved from the rubble at the end of the war. It has a new mattress, but everything else is the same," she said proudly. "It is good to have heritage."

Henry looked at the single bed against the wall, for it looked none too comfortable for one, let alone two.

"We sleep next door, in the room we've just been" said Tania, answering the question in Henry's mind, while only adding to his confusion as there was no bed next door.

Tania cut some bread and sliced some cheese which she served with tea. They said little as neither knew what to say. It was late evening when Evelina phoned Henry. She told him exactly what had happened after they had left. Not a single detail was left out.

"I will take you to the nearest Moldindconbank when you get in to work tomorrow. We'll meet Edik there," she said.

The call was played hands-free on Henry's mobile phone, so both Tania and he could listen and say goodbye at the end of the conversation.

"She's very pretty," said Tania.

"Yes," acknowledged Henry. "She's ex KGB."

"Have you...?"

"No," said Henry firmly, knowing the question before it was asked.

"If she's KGB, then she'll be very bright."

"She is," acknowledged Henry.

"If she wasn't KGB, then perhaps I could have liked her," said Tania.

"I think you could like her irrespective of that," said Henry.

"D'ya know what? I don't think she was given the choice. When you are that clever and good looking, they come hunting for you and tell you that you have a duty to be one of them," said Tania as she cleared the table and closed it up. It gave her room to unpack the double bed which was folded away in a wooden cabinet behind double doors. To make her bed was a task she did freshly every night.

It was when Tania came from the bathroom wearing cream pyjamas that Henry had to take a double look. Sophie had worn the same style and now, with her hair dyed blonde, the resemblance between the two of them was too striking for comfort.

"Are you coming to bed?" she asked.

"Yes," said Henry, although he knew it was far too early for him to sleep.

Tania turned on her torch and turned off the lights. Then as part of her bedtime routine she went to the curtains, drew them wide, and opened a window.

"Why have you done that?" asked Henry, as he proceeded to undress.

"I always do it."

"Why?

"I don't know my mother always did. I think it so that we would be woken by the morning light. Why do you ask?"

"It's just that KGB women do that. It's so they can be photographed from outside with the men they're compromising,"

"You think I'm KGB too?" scoffed Tania jokingly. "I think you read too many of the wrong books."

As Henry got into bed Tania turned away so that he could cuddle up into her; her buttocks into his hips, her breasts cupped into his hand. The soft feeling of Tania's cream pyjama jacket, the thickness of her blonde hair and her perfume were all too reminiscent of his wife when they were first married. It all felt so good and yet so wrong.

Tania turned her head around towards him. "I do love you," she said. "I hope you know that, I really do love you."

Henry had only told one woman that he loved her. It was his wife, Sophie, but she had changed. Yes, he still loved her, but not in the way he once did. How could he? As he thought about Sophie, he realised that he now had the same feelings for Tania that he once had for his wife. "I do love you too," he said as he squeezed her tightly so as to reinforce those four little words.

As the night passed, Henry lay awake listening to Tania's breath as he watched the electric power cables outside shorting in the rain, throwing out huge blue arcs which illuminated the whole room in a yellow hue. Yes, he was sure he loved her, but their future together. He didn't know. It was all far too complex. He would just take one day at a time. It was all he could do.

On the top of the wooden cabinet of the bed in which Henry and Tania were lying, there was an old, polished and much-loved wooden box. It had laid in that place since Brigita Solokov, Tania's great grandmother and Anna Solokov, Tania's grandmother, had made this apartment their home just after the end of the war. If, as he lay there, Henry had known the contents of that box then Tania and his life would have taken an entirely different turn.

Chapter 16

Château de Gressier June 1992

TANIA'S PROBLEMS WITH Steffaco Hotel, Frolov Ilyich and Costin Stanescu were sorted exactly as Evelina had ordained. It allowed Henry to leave Tania safely in Kishinev and return to Château de Gressier for Christmas to be with his mother and his two boys.

Henry telephoned Evelina at least twice a week from wherever he was. He was determined to keep track of the Moldovan wine privatisation programme. It had become a personal mission and it was progressing too slowly. All the business plans had been written, prospectuses drafted, and tender documents prepared. All they were waiting for was the surveyors to produce detailed maps of the vineyards which were going to be sold with each winery. There were some strange complexities as some wineries had more vineyards than they needed, and others had less. Complex land swapping negotiations were having to take place.

Once a week, typically on a Thursday, just after he had spoken to Evelina, and because he knew she would be home, Henry would phone Tania. Not only did he want to make sure no harm had come to her, but he liked to hear her voice. This week, his call to Tania was more important than most because he was going to Kishinev on Monday for a series of progress meetings. He wanted to confirm that she was happy for him to stay with her. If he was honest with himself, Henry had become so disenchanted with the whole wine project, he might well have given it up long ago if it hadn't been for the prospects of him sharing her bed.

They chatted quite naturally, talking about the arrangements for his visit until Tania asked: "Do you know what day it is?"

"No," said Henry cautiously, for people only ask that question if it's something special.

"It's the anniversary of the day we met," said Tania.

"Oh," said Henry, "I forgot. Hey, that was a great day, wasn't it?" he continued enthusiastically.

Tania started to cry. "I am so sorry ..." she said, and then she stopped speaking.

Instinctively Henry knew what she was going to say next; she was pregnant!

"I'm sorry, I forgot?" he said.

Again, Tania tried to speak, but the words wouldn't come out.

"What's the matter?" he asked.

"I pregnant," said Tania. "I sorry, I pregnant."

Henry was silent. He didn't know what to say.

"Am I going to be a father?" he asked.

"No, I sorry, no," said Tania, who didn't hear Henry's sigh of relief, tainted with painful disappointment.

"I need help," she said.

"Who's the father?" asked Henry, ignoring her plea for help.

"He's a young journalist, writer, reporter."

"Are you living together?" asked Henry.

"No," said Tania. "He lives with his mother."

"Are you going to ...?" Henry was going to ask whether they were going to get married.

"No, it's not like that. .... Will you say good-bye to me?" she asked.

There was a long pause as both tried to control their emotions.

"I cannot abort," said Tania. "I abort once."

"When?" asked Henry sharply, wondering whether it'd been a child of his.

"Before married," Tania replied.

Why is she speaking in pidgin English? Henry wondered. This was so unlike her.

"Then miscarriage," she said, having learnt the word after the last time she needed to use it, but couldn't.

"Are you divorced now?" he asked, remembering it was her husband's baby that she'd miscarried.

"No, but I need to," she replied.

"Look," said Henry." My brain can't cope. I need to think. I'll phone you back."

"When?" she asked.

"Not long."

"Promise?" she asked.

"Yes," he replied.

"Henry ... please. I need help." Those were the final words in their conversation.

Henry put down the phone rapidly. He had to stop talking. He rose from the wooden chair and threw his pen onto the large leather edge blotting pad on the desk on which he had been scribbling. It was the same desk used by the most senior male member of the Guégan family since it had been placed in the Gallery by Henry's great-great-grandfather shortly after he'd had it made.

The Gallery had been the workplace of the masters of Château de Gressier ever since it had been built, joining together the two houses of the Cellars and the Cottage. It was the defining work that made the Château stand proudly as one building under one continuous roof.

Henry started to pace the Gallery from one side to the other. He would stop at the large window at the front of the house and look out across the lawn, past his vineyards to the north and into the trees beyond. He would then go to the corresponding rear window and look over his lands to the south. There he could see row upon row of vines flowing down to the river, then into the fields of vines beyond and up into the blue summer evening sky.

He should stop now, Henry thought. He should not go back, he told himself. Twice he had been shaken down for money, a lot of money. The whole place was as crooked, corrupt and dangerous as anywhere in the world. For Christ sake, they even steal the drain covers allowing people to fall into the sewers! He couldn't hail a taxi off the streets for fear of being taken to the edge of the city, beaten up and robbed. It would be foolish, truly foolish, to go back. No, he decided. It was time to end this adventure and say goodbye to her.

As he paced, Henry tossed a corn-dolly table mat into the air which he caught, time after time. It had been made as a table stand for a glass or wine bottle by one of the men whom he'd spent time talking to at the Milestii Mici winery. The man had plaited the wheat stems as they talked, creating the most wonderfully patterned designed mat. It was so skilfully done that Henry admired it when he was given it, and he admired it again as he caught it for the last time. It epitomised the real people of Moldova; the people who worked in the bottling plants and the wineries and on the land. They were a wonderfully generous people. They were good and true, loyal and committed. They were the salt of the earth, just as the people who worked at his de Gressier and Rabôut vineyards and wineries.

Henry then thought about the wonderful land of Moldova. It was a rich land with rolling hills and rivers and trees. He felt the same attachment to the land there as he did here in Bordeaux. It was a bond that he knew he couldn't break. They all deserved so much better.

He remembered Tania's family at the dacha, her loving mum and dad. The bravery of her grandmother and great-grandmother. It was truly a happy day, in such a calm and glorious place. It was where true peace could be found.

Finally, Henry thought about Tania. Did he love her? he asked himself. He knew that, for some inexplicable reason, he needed her in his life. He knew he had a deep and true love for her. He knew there was an emotional bond between them, and he could not be the one to break it. He knew he couldn't leave her, but he also knew he should never see her again. He had to go back. He knew it was wrong. He knew it was stupid, but he had to go back; he had to!

And then Henry thought about her baby. Does it matter it's not mine? he asked himself. Had she let him down by sleeping with another man? he wondered, and then, when he realised he had not seen her for six months, he had his answer. What had he offered her? Nothing? What had he promised her? Nothing? What could he offer? What could he promise? His answer was in the singular: security. There was nothing else, but was this enough for her to want him. He pondered his answer to this last question long and hard. She had asked him to come, hadn't she? She'd almost pleaded for him to come, hadn't she?

It was fifteen minutes after he had put the phone down that Henry called Tania back. For Tania, it seemed like a lifetime. It was as though she had been charged with a crime and had been waiting anxiously for the jury to announce its verdict. She felt sick in the stomach at the thought that Henry might be gone from her life forever.

"I'll see you next week," said Henry, as his opening words.

Tania winced, and her body froze tight on the news. She didn't know what to say.

"But I think I'll need to sleep in your grandmother's room. Somehow, I don't think it's right ..." He didn't finish his sentence.

"Yes of course," said Tania. "Thank you."

As Henry climbed the stairs to go to the bed he once shared with Sophie, he realised that, in all the time he had been thinking about his relationship with Tania, he had not thought about Sophie once, and immediately he was overcome by an emotional conflict which caused him to have a very restless night.

Chapter 17

Kishinev June 1992

IT WAS LATE in the evening when Tania met Henry at the airport. She had been taken out there by a teacher friend as Tania had never learnt to drive. The moment Tania saw him, she beamed the widest of smiles before she collapsed into his arms and held him tightly. Seeing him again lifted a great weight off her shoulders. Immediately Henry felt the firmness of Tania's tummy and the child she was carrying.

They went straight to Tania's apartment where, in Tania's great-grandmother's bedroom, he unpacked sufficiently to wash and change before they went to eat in a nearby restaurant. Things were beginning to improve in Kishinev, for the menu was much better with a much wider selection.

Tania spent a long time talking about Serghei Stoica, the father of her baby. Henry wasn't sure he wanted to hear as, quite frankly, it made him feel jealous, but it was obvious that Tania needed to explain.

"We met at a friend's wedding," she said. "He's nice, a bit too shy and thoughtful for me. We ended up on the dance floor because ... well, there was no one else for us to dance with, and then, you know, things happened. And then they happened again, and again and here I am with a baby."

"Are you going to get married?" asked Henry.

"No," she said firmly. "He has nothing to offer me. He doesn't have a good job. Maybe one day but today he has no money and lives at home with his mother. I like him, and I am sure he will be a good father, but not enough to marry him. I've been married once, and I'm not doing that again, she said emphatically. Well, not in a hurry."

"What do your parents say?"

"My father's pleased the baby's not yours ... because you're married," said Tania, thinking her answer needed an explanation. "My mother's really excited and wants to have the baby living with her, but so do Serghei's parents. My grandmother and great-grandmother are pleased. They both had a child, and they were never married, so they think it's in keeping with the best of the family's tradition."

"I thought we were in an exclusive relationship," said Henry trying to express as gently as he could his disappointment.

"Please Henry, that's not fair," said Tania with pain in her voice. "You're not here most of the time. You do not look after me. You cannot look after me. I have no promise, no commitment from you. You're nice to me, but without ... well, it's just not fair to say that you thought me all yours."

Henry swallowed hard. Tania was right in what she had said. It made him feel quite guilty. In fact, it was the other way around. It was her who had given him so much, and not just her body. She had given him support, encouragement, advice during everything he had done in Moldova, even the confidence to go on, and he realised he had given her nothing in return.

That night, after Tania was in her bed, Henry left the bathroom with a torch in his hand to make his way to her great-grandmother's bed. He stopped where Tania was lying. He knelt at the side of her bed and, in the torch light, he looked fondly in to her eyes. Henry kissed her as softy and gently on the lips as he could. It was the sweetest kiss they had ever shared.

"I'm here because I love you," he said, touching his finger to her lips so she needed to make no reply. As he rose and went to his own bed, Tania sighed the deepest of sighs of regret.

The next day was Henry's first day in the office. The situation was worse than he'd been led to believe. Little progress had been made with the privatisation project since he was last here. Everyone had gone from the project room other than Evelina. The project director and partner from the accountancy firm had turned up specifically for the meeting, but no one else was there. There was nothing more anyone could do. Henry was told the project was stuck politically, and no one knew why or could find out why.

The fact was that the investment experts, who had come from London, had put into the tender documents a series of contractual protections which they said the investment community would require if they were to have less than 50.1% of the shares in each company being privatised. Except it was not what Stanescu wanted. What he wanted was their money without the investors having any future say in how the businesses they were being asked to invest in were run. He was being naively unrealistic.

"Time and time again, we've told the Minister of Agriculture that, if the Moldovan government were to give up their insistence on having over 50%, then these minority interest protection terms could go," said Evelina. "It's become something of a deal-breaker where pride and macho behaviour is defeating logic."

After a frustrating morning, Evelina and Henry had lunch at the little cafe in the park where Henry had first asked Evelina if she was a member of the KGB.

"Tania's pregnant," said Henry after they had ordered.

"Oh," said Evelina. "May I ask, are you the ..."

"No," said Henry rapidly before Evelina could finish asking her question.

"But you are staying with her?"

"Yes, separate beds."

"Who's the father?" asked Evelina. "Do you know him?"

"I don't, no. I don't really understand it."

"You sound as though you're disappointed?" said Evelina.

"I am, I think. Not for her, I think she'll be a good mother and happy. I'm sad about it, but I can't explain why."

"Edik's left me," said Evelina with a shrug of her shoulders. "He's moved to a new place. I am told it's smart and awfully expensive."

"Oh, I am sorry," said Henry, "But you know you weren't right together. You deserve much better than him," he added, in what he hoped she would find as words of comfort.

"He left me on the day you went back to Paris. He accused me of sleeping with you. He said we were having an affair."

"I wish," said Henry clumsily and in a tone that had no escape to its meaning.

"If it is difficult with Tania you can come and stay with me," said Evelina, and there was no mistaking her meaning either.

They looked at each other as though each was daring the other to take the first step.

"What does Edik say about the impasse we have with the Government? Do you know?" asked Henry, deliberately ignoring her invitation.

"No, he's not interested anymore. He now organises for barges to go up to a refinery in Russia which he loads up with gasoline. He pays a price of ten cents on the dollar in cash to the refinery manager. He then ships it to a Romanian refinery that pays him sixty cents on the dollar."

"Is he using special barges?" asked Henry. "Otherwise, they'll explode."

"No, they're fairly ordinary. They come all the way through Europe by river and no one seems to stop them. I've told him, one spark, and it would take out a whole town."

"Christ, that sounds hugely dangerous," said Henry shocked.

"It is, but he doesn't make the journey. He organises it, pays everyone. He's a good businessman," said Tania.

"Maybe," replied Henry. "But he's not a very good KGB agent."

"Why?"

"A good agent would've known not to wear the most expensive suit in the room. It draws attention to you."

"Ah, yes," admitted Evelina. "It's amazing how quickly we forget the little things they taught us. But Edik's a multi-millionaire now," she added, as she sought to justify his behaviour.

"Edik's a criminal," said Henry.

Evelina didn't reply. She had not thought of it that way, but as soon as Henry had said the word, she knew he was right.

They wandered slowly back to the Ministry of Agriculture walking closely side by side as though they were a couple. Neither felt that there was much they could do other than arrange a meeting with Stanescu.

"I feel sorry for the wineries," said Evelina. "They wait and wait for this money and in the meantime their plant is dying under their feet. Some wineries will not produce any wine this year if they don't get some of the new equipment they need."

"Is it as bad as that?" asked Henry.

"Probably worse," said Evelina. "All we're talking about is five thousand, maybe ten thousand dollars which needs to be invested in each plant. Without it, some will have no income from this year's harvest at all."

"What about the bottling factory?" asked Henry.

"They're buying better quality bottles, so the explosions have stopped, but the motors have gone, so the production line keeps breaking down. Of course, they still haven't done anything about putting in proper quality control procedures to make sure the bottles are clean before they are filled."

"Surely the banks here will lend to these businesses?" asked Henry.

"Yes, they'll lend in dollars and at a thirty-five per cent interest rate. No one takes their terms. They can't afford to!"

"This project; we've always been looking at the big picture, haven't we?" said Henry. "But the big picture's getting us nowhere. We need to re-examine the whole thing at the grass roots level. Hey, tomorrow we'll start and revisit them all again. Let's see if we can solve some of the immediate problems."

Henry increased his walking pace in response to his new enthusiasm. Who was he here for? He knew exactly. It was the man who made his corn-dolly mat and all those like him. And who else was like him? Tania was.

Chapter 18

Kishinev June 1992

SYSTEMATICALLY HENRY AND Evelina visited all the wineries in the privatisation programme. Cricova and Mileștii Mici wineries were not at all welcoming. As far as they were concerned, Henry's reputation was busted. They had worked so hard and enthusiastically to meet his demands and he had delivered nothing. They were no further forward than when they first met. There was another reason its senior management chose to avoid him. They were in the middle of an intimidation war from two of Kishinev's rival mafia groups for control of their wineries, and, quite frankly, they preferred to do nothing. It was, they believed, their best chance of keeping alive.

It was at every other winery that Henry and Evelina found more fertile ground. Over the next few days, Henry found he had accidentally entered a new business; to purchase whatever equipment the winery most urgently needed and then rent it to them under an ordinary finance lease. However, there was one big difference. It was that the interest and capital repayments would not be made in money but wine. Once a year, at the end of the harvest, Henry would take delivery of an agreed number of barrels of wine from their first pressing to be stored at Cricova cellars. It was why every evening he had a phone call with his general managers at his de Gressier and Rabôut estates. He was getting them to source the equipment and machinery that was needed from around Europe.

It was late afternoon, as they were returning from a winery, that Henry spotted, through the trees and in the valley below, a church surrounded by a monastery. It was placed within a village with nursery farmlands all around. It appeared wonderfully charming and idyllic.

"Look, look," shouted Henry excitedly. "Let's go and have a look."

Evelina turned the car around and retraced their steps. They turned into a small, badly made road and drove through some trees. The church, the monastery, and the village sat below, bathed in the late afternoon sun. They proceeded to drive down the track, which meandered viciously from one side to another, allowing them to go down a very steep escarpment.

"We shouldn't go any further," said Evelina, suddenly stopping.

"Why not?" asked Henry.

"They'll think we're here to steal their children," she said, as though it were a normal thing to worry about.

"What!"

"They will," said Evelina seriously. "A strange man and woman; we'll likely be attacked."

"What," repeated Henry, not really understanding.

"Our children get stolen for their body parts," she continued, matter of factly.

"You're joking?" said Henry, looking completely shocked.

"No, Henry, I'm not!" said Evelina angrily. "We have many children disappearing, and it's what people believe. It's what I believe!"

Henry looked through the windscreen of the car to the most beautiful view below. How could it be that people lived in such a majestic place, with such peace at its heart, and yet must live with such a fear?

"The situation is much worse in the villages than the city," continued Evelina. "In the cities, people see. They also have power. But here, people must work hard; they don't see when their children are taken, and they have no power, so no one takes any notice of them when their children have gone."

"Don't you worry about this?" asked Henry.

"Yes," said Evelina, "but what can I do?"

What can I do? It was an expression Henry had heard time and time again when in Moldova. It was the communist excuse for doing nothing. It usually made him very cross when he heard it, but this time he had real sympathy with the expression, as he had no idea what he would do if a child of his was stolen from here. Yes, prevention was the best thing, and if that meant keeping out strangers, then good for them.

Henry got out of the car and sat on its bonnet. Evelina came and sat next to him. They said nothing. They both closed their eyes and enjoyed the warmth of the sun, and breathed deeply.

"What are you going to do when this project ends?" asked Henry. "I think it is likely to end any moment now unless the politics change."

"Arthur Andersen has given me a permanent contract in their management consultancy team," she said. "It's conditional upon me passing the accountancy exams which I'm now studying."

Henry said nothing, he just nodded.

"I'd like to find a way to do an MBA either at Harvard or the London Business School," she added.

Although Evelina didn't know it, she had just answered the question Henry did not ask. He decided that she would not be interested in working with him in his nascent business. It would be too small for her he concluded.

"I'll never be rich," said Evelina, "but I'll have a good job and a good income. Also, I will be able to leave here and work anywhere. It's sad but Moldova has no future," she added.

"How can you say that?" said Henry. "Look," he said, waving his arms over the view beyond. "It's such a beautiful place. Why would you want to leave?" he asked.

"We have no natural resources, so we have to import all our energy. It means we are dependent on Russia, Ukraine, Romania. Our only major industry is agriculture, and that doesn't earn us enough to pay for the energy we need. Unless we find some way to be energy independent, we will always be a poor country, permanently in debt and at the mercy of these other countries." As one would have expected from a well-trained KGB officer, Evelina's assessment was as thorough and as compact as anyone was going to give.

"Our people are well educated, but our women and the brightest men go abroad, so our potential for economic growth leaves with them," continued Evelina. "It's why we have no future!"

The last statement was made so strongly that Henry had no further response. Instead, he hung his head as a sense of sadness overwhelmed him.

Evelina felt the sudden loss of energy from Henry's body as his optimism deflated on hearing her analysis. She tucked her arm through his and pulled him towards her. It was a squeeze of comfort designed to say, don't worry about Moldova, don't worry about me, but strangely, as she drew Henry into her, she noticed the strength in his muscles, and that surprised her. She had assumed he lacked any real physical strength. She had not taken account of the fact that, from the age of seven, Henry had constantly lifted wine barrels and cases. It was this which gave him a core strength throughout his body. She squeezed him again. This time to make sure she was not mistaken. She liked physically strong men. She needed her men to be strong. It was what attracted her to Edik. Suddenly, it was Evelina who, reassured by his strength, was taking comfort from Henry's presence. They looked at each other and smiled. It was a moment to kiss, but each held back as though they were in suspended animation, neither knowing whether to move forwards or backwards.

"Come on," said Henry, taking her hand. "Let's go!"

Evelina couldn't concentrate on her driving as she took Henry home. Her thoughts were only on the man sitting next to her. Why was he sleeping with Tania and not her?" she wondered. She answered her own question when she realised that, at first, she didn't fancy him; but in any case, at that stage she had Edik. But now Edik was no longer in her life, and she knew Henry so much better. Perhaps it was time to take him from Tania. After all, Tania was pregnant, and her child wasn't Henry's? Could she, should she take him as her own? It was the question Evelina still had not answered when, for the first time, they kissed each other on the cheek when they said goodbye in the drive outside Tania's apartment block.

Chapter 19

Kishinev June 1992

ALL THOSE PRESENT remember how the debates started. It was the evening before Henry was due to fly home.

Henry, Tania, and a group of her friends had agreed to meet at a nightclub on Strada Mitropolit Varlaam. They arrived to find it closed. As with many things in Moldova, Henry was convinced it was only a matter of paying enough money, and they would be allowed in.

"We're only a small group," he insisted, as he sent one of their group back inside the club to negotiate an entrance fee. The answer was an emphatic no.

In the car park outside the nightclub, his group was huddled, wondering what to do next, when suddenly a siren alarm rang out through the air. Henry was standing aimlessly at the front door of the nightclub when he saw another group of men walking purposely, almost running towards him. Henry, having no sense as to what was going on, politely opened the door to let them rush through. Suddenly he was grabbed by two of the young men in his group and forcibly bundled into one of his group's cars, which was moving at speed as it reversed out of its parking slot.

Henry had no idea what was happening but from the nervous chatter of those bundled in the same car and the frantic way it was being driven, he knew that something was seriously wrong.

"What's happening? Where are we going?" Where's Tania?" Henry shouted, for she was not with them, and he was worried about her safety.

As they arrived at Tania's apartment, Henry was relieved to see her outside. "What the hell's happened," asked Henry.

"It was a mafia-on-mafia raid," said Tania, her heightened adrenaline making her short of breath.

Although Tania was the host, it was others around who served the coffees and poured the wine. She took her place close to Henry on the sofa. After much hubbub, the room went strangely quiet as each disappeared into their own thoughts, internalising the fact that each had been on the edge of an extremely dangerous situation.

"You know, you can't let it go on like this," said Henry, addressing the whole room very quietly.

As often happens, it is sometimes the quietest voice which makes the loudest noise.

"You have to sort it out for your children and your children's children," Henry continued.

The room remained noticeably quiet and still. Each person understood that Henry had not just made a statement, but had laid down a challenge.

"And please don't say, 'what can I do?' That's an expression for doing nothing. That's a saying from the Communist era. Today, such a saying can only be uttered by the lazy and the cowards." He stopped, allowing his words to hang gently in their ears.

Most present spoke good English and they knew exactly what he had said. However, Tania decided she should translate. The words lazy and cowards were repeated by her in Russian, again quietly, but in a different tone. They were not said challengingly, as Henry had said them, but repeated in a contemplative questioning way.

"It's corruption," said a young woman, seated on the floor, leaning slightly forward, with her arms wrapped around her knees, her long hair hanging down, covering her face. The room murmured in agreement.

"You all know, until you've solved the corruption problem, you're not going to move forward as a country," said Henry. "You all know it, so you have to do something about it."

"So how do we do that?" asked a woman sitting on the floor, missing off the words which she sarcastically wanted to add: 'Mr Bigshot.'

"To solve the corruption problem, you have to have political control. To have political control, you need to develop a political philosophy and then a political party to further that philosophy so its policies can be implemented." Henry paused. "I am not telling you something you don't already know, but I can tell you that, as a country, you're stalled. I see you debate amongst yourselves, knowing exactly how to put the issues right, but you are so busy worrying about your needs of today that you don't deal with the issues which could make your lives better tomorrow."

"But you have not told us how to solve corruption?" said the woman on the floor challenging Henry for not having answered the question.

"It's easy," said Henry, almost condescendingly. "You make the penalties big enough for everyone who pays or receives a bribe."

"We have those laws, but no one enforces them because they are all so corrupt," said the same woman in a resigned and sarcastic voice.

"Of course," said Henry. "But those laws aren't enforced because the police and the judges aren't paid properly. They're not paid properly because you don't collect your taxes. You don't collect your taxes because the tax people aren't paid properly. Any new government in this country should, on the first day in power, do a number of things."

Henry paused, wondering whether they wanted him to speak, for he was about twice the age of everyone else in the room.

"Go on," he was urged by several voices.

"Firstly, a new government should announce an amnesty for all corruption below an agreed figure, say, $25,000. Choose the sum, I'm not bothered, but the idea is to keep the big fish in the criminal net and let the small fish out. Everyone here's paid a traffic cop a few lei, and we don't want ordinary people caught for past petty bribes like that. You want to catch all past big bribes and all bribes, whatever their size going forward, including the ten lie paid to the traffic cop, because that nonsense needs to stop. For example, there are university professors here who've made a fortune by selling degrees to their students. Some will have made well over $20,000 each year by taking brides. They should remain liable to prosecution, but each of their students, who will have paid much less than that to get their degree, should not. By having a de minimis, the student doesn't get prosecuted, just the crooked lecturers. In fact, it's the student who will provide the evidence to catch the big fish."

"But no student wants to admit they bought their degree," said a voice.

"Why not, everyone knows that a degree issued after 1989 is worthless because it is likely to have been brought," added Tania.

"I didn't buy my degree," protested a mellow female voice.

"That's because you'd been sleeping with him all term," came a female response. It caused everyone to laugh, because this woman's affair with her professor had been widely broadcast by the woman herself.

"Secondly, make the penalties for bribery and corruption much bigger. Life imprisonment should be the norm for serious offences, like bribing a judge. I don't think you realise that these people are killing your country. It's like murder, except they're not killing just one person, their killing the hopes of a complete nation."

There was a murmur of approval at the analogy.

"Third, you announce an amnesty for all unpaid past taxes; no interest, no penalties, just pay the tax, possibly at a special low tax rate. In every country this has happened it has been hugely successful. It you want an example, look at Ireland. Finally, you increase the salaries for all tax officers, policemen, judges, customs officers. You must pay these people properly. They must be able to go to work every day, not having to worry about money. After the amnesty period, then the tax penalties should be huge and include long terms of imprisonment."

Henry stopped speaking. Whilst talking, he had been leaning forward into those gathered to take control. Now he leant back intending to relinquish the floor to other contributors, but he didn't "Finally," he said: "You have to stop, no, you must stop politicians appointing your top lawyers – judges, prosecutors, policemen. Until you've done that, then the whole system will remain rotten to the core and there is no hope!" There was sadness in Henry's voice as he realised the magnitude of the challenge he was giving to this group of young men and women.

There was a prolonged silence after his diatribe. Then slowly, conversations started amongst the group in gossipy whispery Russian or Moldovan. Although, he did not know what was being said, there seemed to be a consensus that Henry had made a statement of the 'bleeding obvious', and they were cross that it took an outsider to say it.

After a while, Henry got up. "I think it's time I left you younger ones," he said as he headed to his bedroom. Twenty minutes later, and very quietly and without saying anything, Tania left to join him, not saying goodbye to any of her guests. In their clothes, they fell asleep on Tania's great-grandmother's bed.

Serghei Stoica, who had arrived at Tania's flat much later than the others, tidied up after all her other guests had gone. He then left hurt, really hurt as, when he popped his head around the door to say good night to Tania, he saw the natural intimacy between her and Henry as they lay side by side, fully clothed and asleep. It was when he saw Henry's hand resting gently on Tania's belly, knowing it was his baby she was carrying, that he felt truly humiliated. He was totally crushed by his inability to provide. It was, he incorrectly told himself, the only reason she would choose Henry over him.

Tania accompanied Henry to the airport the next day. They said an uncomfortable goodbye in the car park. She watched him go, and with each of his steps, she felt a little lonelier. Sitting in the taxi, she could not bring herself to give instructions to the driver to leave. A sense of despair overwhelmed her thoughts as she knew that he could never be hers. She sat and thought of their lovemaking and those very precious moments, although they now seemed long ago. These thoughts gave her some comfort for, it reaffirmed in her mind that Henry genuinely loved her.

"He really believes in me," she said to herself under her breath. "Come back soon, please, please come back soon," she pleaded silently.

Chapter 20

London July 1992

HENRY LOOKED AROUND the panelled meeting room with its portraits of famous faces of years gone by, none of which he could name. He wondered where to put his briefcase as the furniture was clearly antique and expensive. The room was reminiscent of a time, one hundred years before, when Britain had an Empire on which the sun never set.

Henry chose a chair in the middle of the table with the window behind him and the door set diagonally opposite so he could see who came in. As he sat down he placed his case on the carpet. He started to play with the sharpened pencil laid neatly across the paper placed on top of a blotting-pad. Henry had no idea why he had been summoned to London and the UK Government's Cabinet Office for this meeting, but summoned he had.

Two men rushed in. "The Cabinet Secretary sends his apologies. He's been called away to see the PM, and he's asked me to take this meeting. I'm Paul Cryer," said the first man through the door. "I'm an assistant permanent secretary in the Cabinet Office. This is ...." Henry didn't catch the second man's name as the words were jumbled, one into the other. There was a third man, much younger, who was not introduced. Other than Cryer, Henry started the meeting with no idea as to who the other two men in front of him were or what they did.

"Tea, coffee?" asked the second man assertively.

"Coffee," answered Henry taken aback by the force of character which he found unusual in a British civil servant.

"Biscuits?" enquired the second man offering a plate of plain rich tea biscuits.

"Tell me, what's been going on in Moldova?" asked Cryer.

"What's been going on in Moldova," repeated Henry, stressing the words 'going on' so as to give him time to think. "In what context?" he enquired.

"In the context of the privatisation of their wine industry which the EU commission is paying you handsomely to project manage," said the second man, with the same assertive manner.

"The EU Commission in Paris is paying me, not London," said Henry in a tone which, whilst not designed to rebuke, was made to let them know he wasn't going to be intimidated. "It's been going reasonably well, so far, thank you," he added with a sarcastic emphasis on the words 'thank you'.

"It's not what we hear," said the second man.

"What do you hear?" asked Henry. "I'd be very surprised if you are hearing anything about this from the French office of the EU."

"Let me brief you," said Cryer. "Early last week, the Prime Minister had the chairman of British American Tobacco, BAT, in at Number 10. He complained bitterly that Reemtsma, the German cigarette manufacturer, had bribed the Moldovan President and his government to sell them the Moldovan tobacco industry, even though BAT says their offer was worth far more. The Prime Minister has asked the Cabinet Office to make some enquiries. We know you've spent quite a lot of time there over the last eighteen months and suspect you have an interesting insight which we would like you to share with us."

"From what I see of Moldova, it's highly probable," said Henry with a Gallic shrug of his shoulders.

"What do you see of Moldova?" asked the second man.

"It's in the hands of organised crime, just as Italy or Greece were after the Second World War. In fact, in many parts of those countries, they are still in its grip. When one order collapses, this time communism, and until another order rises to take its place, then organised crime thrives in the chaos. Look at Italy; it's the children of those who were born after the war who have started to tackle the issue of organised crime. The second and third generations rarely accept the gangsterism of the first. Even now, corruption remains deep in the culture of Italian society." He paused as he thought about what he had said. "Eventually, every rutting stag gets deposed," he added.

"Is that what's happening in Moldova?" asked the second man.

"It's the poorest country in Europe, poorer than Romania or Bulgaria, or even Albania. It's a place where a boyfriend will sell his girlfriend into a sex trafficking ring for $25. It's a country where any Westerner gets in to a taxi at his peril as he is likely to get taken to the edge of the city and robbed. If you cross the river into Transnistria and walk through the market in Tiraspol you can buy a gun and any amount of ammunition without any questions, just as if you were at a US gun fair. But you know all this!" said Henry, who decided to stop talking as he was now getting cross. Not with the men asking the questions, as they were reasonable ones, but for the nastiness of the situation Moldova found itself in.

"What of the wine privatisation plans?" asked Cryer.

"What do you know of their wine industry?" asked Henry.

"Assume nothing," said Cryer.

Henry quickly recapped. He told them that Moldova was the home of the Romanov's vineyards, that the country produced as much wine as France and Italy combined and had the potential to be one of the finest wine-growing regions in the world. He also told them of exploding bottles, missing manhole covers, and stolen children.

"The problems in the Moldovan wine industry are huge," said Henry, "but they are not insurmountable. It needs investment, a lot of investment. It also needs its managers to be trained, not in making wine, they know how to do that. They need to understand, to learn, how a western economy works. At the moment, they don't seem to appreciate how consumerism sits at its heart and how sophisticated the consumer can be." Henry paused for a moment. "Adam Smith had a metaphor for the unseen forces that move the free market economy. He called it 'the invisible hand.' They've lived all their lives in a command-and-control economy. It takes a lot to believe in a system driven by an invisible hand."

Cryer smiled and nodded his approval of the explanation.

"Would you be so kind as to write all this up for me"? asked the second man.

"If the EU Commission in Paris say you can have a copy of my reports, then I will be happy to send them to you," said Henry. "They're quite comprehensive. Of course, you'll need to get them translated because they're in French."

"I gather you've been in touch with Clydesdale International, Drinsbergs, Cain Partners, Abbey Partners and quite a few others about them bidding in the privatisation programme you've been organising," said the second man.

Henry was surprised they had this amount of information as his talks with this group of private equity firms and investment funds had been highly confidential, under binding non-disclosure agreements.

"Given your apparent knowledge, I don't think you need my reports, do you?" said Henry tartly.

"The Prime Minister is pretty damn cross about the tobacco bribery thing," said Cryer. "He won't spend any political capital trying to stop the European Commission putting its grant aid money into Moldova. He wants that to happen. His government wants Moldova to be close to Europe, even a member of the EU one day."

"Good, I'm pleased," said Henry. "It's a country which needs help," he added, before using Evelina's example of the imbalance between the cost of its energy needs and the value of its agricultural outputs to explain why.

"However, the Prime Minister wants President Stanescu to know that the wine privatisation programme is dead if the auction for its tobacco industry isn't conducted fairly, openly and above board."

"Oh, and how will that happen?" asked Henry sharply.

"I think a phone call from this office to those who you've been speaking to about bidding will be enough to make sure the tender process fails, don't you?" said Cryer.

"And you want me to tell Stanescu this?"

Neither man answered. Instead, the second man got up to indicate the meeting was over. The message had been given. The third man, who'd said nothing but had written copious notes throughout, shuffled his papers together. The second man walked around the table shook Henry warmly by the hand before saying: "Mr Cryer will see you out." With that, he was gone.

"Who was that?" asked Henry, as soon as the second man had left the room. "I'm afraid I didn't catch his name when he was first introduced."

"Oh, I don't think you need that," said Cryer. "I would be surprised if you and he were to speak on this matter again. Here's my card, please send whatever you feel appropriate to me."

"Let me get this straight, said Henry. "You want me to go to Stanescu and tell him that the UK Prime Minister says that he will make sure that the EU sponsored wine privatisation programme will fail if Stanescu doesn't accept BAT's bid." Henry knew this was not the message, but he deliberately sought to be provocative to see what the reaction would be.

"That is not what the Prime Minister wants, and it is not what you have been asked to do," said Cryer sharply. "Her Majesty's government is only interested in seeing a fair auction for the Moldovan tobacco industry. Given its other privatisation plans, the Prime Minister thinks it would be helpful if the Moldovan government were to know that anything other than an open, fair and properly conducted auction is likely to bring an unfavourable reaction from Her Majesty's government. If might be something you could share when you are next there."

"Yeh, I think that's what I said," said Henry, with a big grin on his face, letting Cryer know that his earlier remarks had been a tease.

"I think you should know that the threat to stop their wine privatisation programme is not a big one," said Henry. I think it's already stalled for internal political reasons; too much infighting with too many trying to get their snout in the trough. Certainly, it was like that when I left a few weeks ago."

Outside on Whitehall, Henry paused, wondering what to do next. It was then that he remembered he was a member of the Reform Club on Pall Mall. It was his Grandfather's Club and his mother had arranged for Henry's membership as part of his 40th Birthday celebrations. He rarely entered its hallowed portals but today the

Reform Club, with all its history, was just the place to contemplate what had happened.

Henry sat down with the lunchtime edition of the Evening Standard in a leather chair in the morning room. His eyes moved over the pages, not really taking in their contents, as he thought about what he should do next. The most perplexing thing about the whole conversation was how much the British government seemed to know about what was going on. It was as though they were spying on him.

After some while, Henry wandered into the dining room and sat at the club table for lunch where, amongst convivial strangers, he joined a discussion on why the conservatives, in the European parliament elections, had just had the worst election results ever, and who was going to replace the late John Smith as leader of the Labour Party.

It was on a whim that Henry headed to Heathrow to catch the first available plane to Paris. At the airport he phoned and agreed a meeting, early the next day, with the Chef de Représentation of the EU's Paris Office.

Over a most convivial meeting in which all those present assumed Henry was one hundred per cent French, with no idea about his English upbringing, they discussed his mysterious meeting in the Cabinet office the previous day.

After much debate, they concluded there was no harm in Henry providing a note to the UK government, but the rest they found most perplexing. Was the British Government really going to help the French wine industry by stopping the privatisation of the Moldovan wine industry just because a German cigarette manufacturer had offered a bribe?

In the eyes of those Frenchmen around the table, it was not plausible. It made no sense. There had to be a deeper reason. Henry tried to explain that, because of the British culture, it was probably exactly as he had described. There were others in the room who decided it was the continuation of one thousand years of British foreign policy of keeping the nations of Europe apart so that they alone could remain strong. Their problem was that, on this occasion, they couldn't work out exactly how the British reaction fitted into their belief of the British strategy.

After hours of strategising, it was agreed that the Chef de Représentation would contact the EU Commissioner for International Cooperation and Development, who would strongly suggest to the President of Moldova that he invited Henry to an early meeting with him.

It meant that three days later, Henry was back in Kishinev.

Chapter 21

Kishinev July 1992

EVELINA WOULDN'T ADMIT it to herself, let alone anyone else, mainly because it happened in her subconscious, but she had become attracted to Henry.

Arthur Andersen had done a large study amongst all its European offices of their clients. Both their London and Paris offices had identified Henry as a 'Person of Influence'. He was a client who should receive extra care and attention, the Kishinev office was told. There was no explanation why.

Using the services of the librarians in both the London and Paris offices, Evelina soon had a file of press cuttings on Henry Guégan. There she found two things which amazed her. Firstly, he wasn't just wealthy, but very wealthy. Secondly, and what intrigued her most, was the fact that he was married to a woman who appeared in almost every list of the world's top 10 most beautiful women. Why was he sleeping with a Moldovan teacher when he could have anyone? Evelina wondered.

Perhaps, what upset Evelina most was the fact that he had not even tried to seduce her. They'd had their moments, when that frisson between them might have gone one way or the other, and yet it always ended with them moving apart; each just a little too scared. Evelina's upset manifested itself by her becoming almost obsessional about finding pictures of Sophie so that she could copy her fashion style, not realising that she had been naturally doing it.

Henry arrived early in the morning at Kishinev airport for his meeting with President Stanescu. He had stayed overnight in Vienna. Evelina met Henry wearing a short floral summer dress. It had the desired effect, as it put Henry into the same honey trap mentality he had when they first met.

They drove immediately to Arthur Andersen's offices in Evelina's newly acquired second hand Volkswagen Polo which, even she admitted, had probably been stolen somewhere in Western Europe.

As soon as they were in the car, Evelina asked the question that she had been bursting to ask despite knowing the answer. "Is your wife Sophie Elleswell?" she asked, knowing the answer perfectly well.

"Yes," said Henry.

"She's very beautiful."

"Yes, she is," acknowledged Henry.

"Several times she's been named as one of the world's most beautiful women."

"Yes," said Henry, "but she'd argue against that."

"But she doesn't model anymore?"

"No, no more."

"Why, did you stop her?"

"No."

"Not even after she became a mother?"

"No."

"I'm surprised. It must be horrible knowing that other men are constantly trying to steal her from you?"

Henry puckered his lips, for it seemed a strange remark.

"It doesn't work like that," he said. "When you love someone, and you know they love you, then you know that, whatever happens, you're meant to be together. So, while you both find other members of the opposite sex attractive, they're never as attractive as the person you love. In any case, as Sophie will tell you, most ordinary men are frightened by beautiful women; like you and her. She says its only narcissistic alpha males who have the confidence to approach an attractive woman. What they want is a trophy wife, and that's the last thing Sophie would be. She is .... was far too intelligent for that."

"Are you a narcissistic alpha male?" asked Evelina seriously.

"Probably until I met Sophie, and then I realised I love someone more than I loved me."

93

"Oh, that's so sweet," commented Evelina, as she smiled and frowned at the same time.

"Edik proves the thesis," said Henry. "He's a narcissistic alpha male who had you as his 'trophy' girlfriend until you realised you were cleverer than that."

Evelina sat at the traffic lights in silence, thinking deeply about Henry's last remark. She didn't spot the lights turning from red to green and only came out of her trance at the beep of the horn from the car behind.

"Why's Sophie no longer modelling?" asked Evelina.

Henry sighed.

"It all started when we bought some counterfeit wine," he said.

Henry told their story to the point of taking Evelina into his confidence. He very rarely told anyone that Sophie was living in a nursing home suffering from drug-induced permanent memory loss, but he told Evelina.

"The strange thing about all of this," he said, as the car pulled up outside Arthur Andersen's offices and Evelina switched off the engine. "Neither of us drank alcohol. It was probably that and the fact that neither of us was looking for anyone, which got us together."

"It's strange how love comes along when you're not looking for it," said Evelina pointedly.

Chapter 22

Kishinev July 1992

THE MORNING MEETING with the partner and directors of Arthur Andersen working on the privatisation programme was of little help in preparing Henry for his afternoon meeting with the President of Moldova. For the first time, he went into the meeting with Stanescu feeling nervous and he knew why. All his life he had acted as principal, now he was acting as agent with a clear diplomatic message to deliver.

"Good morning Mr Guégan," said Stanescu in English and welcomingly, as Henry entered his office. This time he walked around his desk to greet them.

"Good morning Miss Kirillovich," said Stanescu in Moldovan. "I see Mr Guégan continues to benefit from the services of one of our women," he continued. It was the smirk on his face which made it clear he thought Henry and Evelina were sleeping together.

"We just work together," said Evelina sharply in Russian.

"That's not what Edik Borisovich says," said Stanescu.

"Edik's wrong, in any case Mr Guégan's my father's age," she said testily.

"Miss Kirillovich," said Stanescu looking straight into her eyes. "I hear what I hear. I observe what I observe."

Stanescu turned to Henry and again he spoke English: "The EU commission tells me I should see you," he said. "I'm intrigued."

"The EU commission's office in Paris thought you might like to hear what the British Government told me after I had been summoned to see them," said Henry.

"A Frenchman summoned to see the British government," said Stanescu feigning surprise. "Such is the animosity between the UK and France; I didn't think such things could happen."

"I have many business interests in the UK; not least it's where my children live."

Stanescu frowned as, tactfully and with great accuracy and without embellishment, Henry repeated the message he had got from the civil servants in the Cabinet Office.

"It seems to me that the British government is telling me to choose between Britain and Germany," said Stanescu. "Am I not right?"

"No, that's not right," said Henry. "It is telling you ...., no, that's not right either," he added, correcting himself. "It's asking you to have an open auction for the privatisation of your country's tobacco industry, just as we have spent months preparing for your more complex wine industry."

Stanescu either didn't hear or chose not to take any notice of Henry's clarification.

"If I have to choose," said Stanescu, then I will choose Germany. Now it has been re-unified, it will soon be the strongest country in Europe if it is not already. One day Russia will be strong again with a strong man in charge. When that happens, Moldova will need a strong Germany on its side. In this game, France and Britain bring me nothing."

"Perhaps we could reflect on history for a moment?" asked Henry.

"Indeed," said Stanescu through his translator. "About one-third of my population wants us to be part of Romania again. They think that, as part of Romania, they will get early admission into the European Union, be able to work there, and it will be our defence against Russia. Another part of our population, some of whom are in Transnistria, want us to be part of Russia. They've already tried to break away and caused a war. The strangest thing about Transnistria is that it sits between us and that part of Ukraine which, because of the Holodomor, is particularly anti-Russia. The rest of Moldova wants us to be independent. That's how history has left my country Mr Guégan."

"History also records that twice in the last hundred years Germany has invaded Russia. It's gone through Romania and Ukraine as part of those wars," said Henry. It has been the aggressor; Britain and France have been your allies. Do you not think it strange that you choose an alliance with your former enemy rather than with your historic allies?"

"Britain and Russia were allies only to defeat Hitler. What do they say, my enemy's enemy is my friend? Before and after, you and Russia have always been enemies," said Stanescu.

"Only because Russia became a totalitarian state, and totalitarianism is probably the one thing that is a complete anathema to the British culture; always has been, for nearly a thousand years," responded Henry.

The conversation stalled as Evelina and Stanescu's translators argued about what Henry had really said.

"I really don't understand it," said Henry. Why choose to have Germany as your ally when it was responsible for forcing on the Russian people communism and totalitarianism, all of which gave rise to the Great Terror and mass starvation? These events killed tens of millions of people."

"What do you mean?" said Stanescu inquisitively. "Germany didn't force communism on anyone."

"The Russian people didn't want the Bolsheviks," said Henry sharply. "They didn't even want communism. What they wanted were soviets – democratic councils, and in 1917 that's what the provisional government was giving them."

"How can you say that?" snapped Stanescu.

"Because it's true; the Bolsheviks came to power because the German government financed their coup d'état. It must be one of the most cynical foreign policy actions of the 20th-century. It was designed and implemented by Germany to take Russia out of the First World War, which is what it did. Once the Bolsheviks were in power it meant that Germany could move its soldiers from fighting Russia on the Eastern Front to fighting France and Britain on the Western Front."

"Our history says something very different," said Stanescu speaking in English.

"So did ours," said Henry, "but now our historians have access to Russia's records, it is all having to be revised. They can now see what happened from both sides. What we know now is that a middle man, I can't remember his name, something like Helphand, organised it all. I remember his name as being one of the most hypocritical names in history. He arranged for Lenin and thirty or so of his Bolshevik cronies, who were hiding in Switzerland, to travel through Germany in blacked out carriages to Finland and then into Russia. It only happened because it was in Germany's best interest to let it happen." Henry paused.

"Parvus Helphand, yes that was his name, 'help' and 'hand', also arranged for millions of Deutschmarks of gold to go to the Bolsheviks on the condition that, when they seized power, they would stop the war with Germany. This money was used to pay the soldiers recruited into the Bolsheviks' new Red Army from Russia's imperial army, who'd stopped paying them. I don't wish to upset the Russian people, but they didn't have a revolution in 1917. They suffered from a coup d'état by a bunch of ideological thugs who held power for over thirty-five years; until Stalin, Beria and their like were dead."

"Leon Trotsky, in his book on the History of the Russian Revolution, says that Germany was not involved in the way you say," rebuked Evelina strongly. "He specifically says so!" Her voice was sharp and defensive.

"Of course it does," said Henry. "History is always written by the winners," he said remembering Tania's words. "Trotsky had to keep to the script that theirs was a victory for the proletariat. He couldn't tell the truth. How could he? It would undermine everything he did."

How do you know this?" asked Stanescu's translator, who had become fascinated by the conversation.

"Since I started coming here, I have read a lot of your history."

"History that's been written by the West," said the Translator.

"No, not all. Some of it's been written by Russians and then translated in to English, some in to French."

The translator snorted his disapproval.

"Our history and your history of the Russian Revolution is fundamentally the same. I assure you we are taught almost the same thing in our schools. What I am saying is not mainstream thinking. However, it is a fact that Helpland worked with the Austrian and German intelligence agencies to finance the Bolsheviks. It cannot be disputed."

The room fell silent as Henry's analysis was absorbed. Had Germany really paid for the Russian Revolution so it could win the First World War?

Stanescu got up from his desk. "Let's go and sit over there," he said in English, pointing to some softer chairs. Then, speaking in Moldovan to his translator, he asked: "Could you organise more coffee, please."

"Germany is the biggest contributor to the EU budget," said Stanescu, immediately they were settled in armchairs arranged around a table. Stanescu had insisted that Henry sat by the side of him and Evelina sat directly opposite. "It means that they are the most influential voice when it comes to aiding countries like ours," he added confidently.

"Yes, and France and the UK are the next largest net contributors, they swap between being second and third. The amount they contribute together is more than Germany's and their two votes would defeat Germany's one."

"But France always sides with Germany, doesn't it," said Stanescu.

Suddenly, Henry realised he was having fun, particularly enjoying the art of diplomatic debate, which is when your opponent makes a good point, not to acknowledge it.

"If you're worried about Russia, you don't look at the EU, you look at NATO," said Henry continuing his argument. "That's where your defence will come from. Germany doesn't pay for its own defences. It can hardly put a tank battalion together. It's the UK and the US which has paid for the defence of Germany; something which the Germans conveniently and far too easily forget."

The conversation stopped while pots of coffee and tea were placed on the table, allowing them to sit there until Evelina, impatient for any of the men to assume it was their role to hand out the cups, took the initiative. Her infuriation was increased as every man pointedly enjoyed the sight of her cleavage as she leaned over to serve them.

"There's one other thing you should think of in your Germany v Britain debate," said Henry. The fact that Germany is dependent upon Russia for its energy, its gas and oil. Britain has the oil and gas from the North Sea. If Germany ever had to choose between either shutting down its industries because it couldn't get gas from Russia, or supporting Moldova in its fight against Russia, then please believe me when I say, Moldova would be easily and quickly sacrificed. Germany will not come to your aid. It's not what the German people do."

"You speak very disparagingly of the Germans," said Stanescu.

"You're right; if I heard anyone else say these things, I would be very cross and immediately rush to Germany's defence. The thing is though, I'm half German. My father's German. I think it gives me the right to speak freely."

"Thank you," said Stanescu, almost spluttering with surprise. "It's probably the most interesting geopolitical conversation I've had with a non-politician or non-diplomat for a long time. We should have dinner to discuss this more," he added. "Your viewpoint is, how shall I put it, unusual!"

"Mr President," said Henry taking an American tone, "You have a very challenging job. I think it's an almost impossible job. Keep your independence, don't align yourself to one geopolitical group too soon. Yes, you need money but don't exclude one side, and don't try and play one side against the other. Try and be friends with both sides, Europe and Russia. How to do this? Take small amounts of money from both sides. Not all from one side. This way, you don't have to sell your country's soul."

"I'm glad you said that," said Stanescu, "because the wine privatisation project is not going to happen. The businesses are better organised now, so that's been a benefit, but I'm not going to be the man who sells the family silver to foreigners. Our wine industry is our country's soul, as you would call it, and I cannot be the one who sells it."

"I understand," said Henry sympathetically. "I really do."

"We need EU aid money to revitalise our wine industry, but it needs to be done under our ownership and no one else's. As regards the tobacco industry, your government, or perhaps I should say the UK's government, is wrong. We've not chosen any party, as the time is not right for us to choose. It is true, both British American Tobacco and Reemtsma sought exclusive negotiating rights and were prepared to pay quite a handsome non-refundable deposit to get those rights, but no deal has been done or will be done in the near future. So, if you would be so kind, I would like you to take a message back to the UK Government. It's a short one. I am sure you will put it more gracefully than this but tell them please, they need to butt out of our affairs! No, no, no," he said as he changed his mind. "It is simpler than that. Tell them to fuck off!"

"I don't think that message needs changing. It's elegantly succinct," said Henry with a wide smile on his face.

Chapter 23

Kishinev July 1992

THE AIR, STIFLING hot and thick with diesel and petrol fumes, struck Henry and Evelina hard as they came out of the cool of the Presidential Palace building.

"Christ, I hate it," said Evelina as she stormed down the steps. Henry had no idea what she was talking about. "Every time I'm with that man he spends most of his time trying to look up my skirt or ogling my tits!" she said angrily.

Henry said nothing. He wasn't sure he'd not been doing the same thing.

"What do you want to do now?" asked Evelina sharply.

"I don't know," said Henry. "Tania is not expecting me until after she's home at about 6 o'clock. Why, what have you got to do?"

"Nothing, I am signed out to look after you until you fly back tomorrow afternoon."

Henry raised his eyebrows teasingly as she said the words 'look after you.'

"No don't!" rebuked Evelina, irritated by the innuendo, so they walked in silence to her car.

"We could get out of the city and go to a dacha I know," she suggested. "It's near the river and in some trees. It will be much cooler, and the air will be much better than this. It's close to where our national football team have their training ground,".

"Sounds good to me," said Henry as they continued to walk to the car.

"The seats burned as they climbed in and so they wound the windows down to let the hot air out. As the air conditioning kicked in, they wound the windows back up again.

"It looks as though you and Stanescu have just become the best of friends," said Evelina contemptuously, as she drove out of the car park.

"I thought it went reasonably well," said Henry.

"Are you not disappointed at his decision not to privatise the wine industry, given how hard we've all worked?"

"In some respects, yes."

"Do you know why Russia has produced so many world champions at chess when compared to the rest of the world?" asked Evelina appearing to change the subject.

"No," said Henry shaking his head, too hot to think of anything witty to say.

"It's because you see everything in two dimensions; yes or no, in or out, noughts or ones, whereas Russia trains us to see everything in three or four dimensions. You don't understand us. It's why Churchill described Russia as 'a riddle wrapped in a mystery inside an enigma.'

"You know that expression," asked Henry.

"Yes of course, we're very proud of it."

"He also said that the only thing that could be guaranteed about Russia was that it would always act in its best interest."

"True, but only partially," said Evelina. It will always act in the best interests of those in charge, and those in charge don't care about the ordinary people."

"I don't get the point you're making," said Henry, as he could tell from Evelina's tone she was seeking to communicate something more significant than her words suggested.

"You've given him exactly what he wants. The Moldovan wine industry neatly parcelled up, thanks to you and the considerable fees paid by the European Union. He can now dish them out to his cronies. You watch, they will all end up in their hands and he'll end up with a huge amount of money in his Cyprus bank account."

"And tobacco?" asked Henry.

"I don't know enough about it. I guess now the wine industry's been done, we should go and get a consultancy job from the EU to privatise that," said Evelina sneeringly.

They drove on for half an hour, rarely talking. Evelina stopped to buy some bread, cheese, fruit and drinks. When she was back in the car, she asked: "Would you like to buy a vineyard?"

"How can I?" said Henry. "I didn't think people could do that."

"The vineyards and wineries you've been dealing with are the big ones, but there are several vineyards which have been privately owned by communes throughout the whole of the communist era. I think I know where one might be for sale."

"What's it like?" asked Henry.

I don't know. It's close to one of the villages in the Orhei District. It's about 50 miles north of here, close to the Brănești winery which you visited.

"Has it got a river?"

"I don't know but the River Raut runs right through that area before it goes into the Dniester."

"How much land is there?"

"I am told it's a small commune outside of a village with four owners, each owning somewhere around thirty to forty hectares.

"That makes it big, possibly too big," said Henry. "How much do they want for it?"

"My guess is a thousand dollars a hectare."

"That's a big chunk of change."

"No, it's not," rebutted Evelina. "I've been looking at international land prices. That makes it dirt cheap."

"And it's dirt cheap because of the political and legal risks," countered Henry. As I say, it's a big chunk of change to risk."

"Being a foreigner, if you were to buy it, you would need a partner who lives in this country as you can't own more than fifty per cent.

"Could you be my partner?" asked Henry, forgetting that her ambition had ruled her out for a job offer once before.

"I would like to, but no. Arthur Andersen wouldn't let me. The obvious person is Tania," said Evelina as she drove into a complex with dachas hidden behind big wire fences and steel gates.

Evelina stopped at one gate, unlocked the padlock with a key she had on her car keyring and swung it open. She drove in and then shut and padlocked the gate behind her.

"Whose is this?" asked Henry.

"It's my aunt's, my father's sister."

"Is she not here?"

"No, in the summer, she goes to Cyprus where she works in a small shop she owns there. She makes good money from all the Russian tourists."

As Evelina hunted around, found the house key, opened up and got everything ready, Henry did nothing except wander around the swimming pool. He picked up a pool net and started to scoop out the leaves floating on the top of the water as Evelina switched on the filtration system.

Evelina produced two sun loungers which she placed side by side, and some towels, which she laid out on top. Then, within seconds, she stripped completely naked and, with a shout to Henry to "come on in," she dived, a long sleek dive, allowing her stretched body to skim across the top of the water.

"Come in, come on in," she shouted when she reached the shallow end. There she stood up and stroked her wet hair behind her head, in the process thrusting her bust forward, as the hairs on her pubic bone were caressed by the waves.

Clumsily Henry undressed, feeling very conscientious that Evelina was watching him. She studied, with approval, his muscular legs and admired their length in proportion to his height. She noted how, even naked, he stood with a commanding presence. She wondered why Edik was never that confident when he had his clothes off.

As Henry stood at the side of the pool and contemplated the shock from the cold water, Evelina swam up to him and soaked him in a series of well-aimed splashes.

"One, two, three," he yelled as he ran and jumped with his arms around his knees to come down heavily in the water in a dive-bomb designed to swamp her and everything around.

As Henry came up for air, Evelina jumped on his head to duck him down. As he went under the water, his feet touched the floor of the swimming pool. He grabbed her legs, and then wrapping his arms around her knees, he lifted her up high and threw her into the air until she came crashing down deep into the water with an enormous splash.

Evelina was standing when she came up for air, so Henry squatted down and, with his arms wrapped around her legs, he picked her up once again. This time he allowed her to slowly slide down his body until his arms were squeezed tightly around her buttocks and her tummy button was almost level with his lips. He felt her pubic bone press into his chest. Slowly, he lowered Evelina further until her breasts came to level with his eyes. He moved his hands under her buttocks to lower her further, at which point she lifted her legs and wrapped them around him. Both knew that, at that moment, she was open to him. They looked into each other's eyes. Like that, he could have carried her anywhere and made her his. Instead, he held on to her a little longer, savouring the moment, until he allowed her to slide down to a point where she unwrapped her legs, and her feet touched the swimming pool floor. They looked intensely at each other, their lips almost touching. For fraction of a second, they shared a hesitancy which meant that they did not kiss. They both knew they were playing a strange and potentially dangerous game. Undoubtedly, each wanted the other, but was it for the conquest? Neither was sure that, having won, whether they would want to keep their prize.

It was Evelina who broke away. With three strokes, she was at the edge of the pool. She pushed herself up with her arms and with an athletic lift of her leg, she stepped out and ran around its edge. Henry watched her run with long graceful strides. She stooped, picked up a ball, threw it into the pool and returned to his side by doing the same running bomb. They laughed and smiled as they thumped, bumped and skimmed the ball at each other.

Evelina was the first to leave the pool; this time by the steps. Again, Henry watched carefully as she walked around the edge. He was enjoying everything about the way she moved and looked. It was as though he was in his own Hollywood movie. At the sun lounger, Evelina didn't dry herself, instead she lay face down on the towel she had placed earlier on the canvas. The sun would dry the water globules on her skin.

Evelina watched as Henry laboured out of the pool. She had felt the strength of his arms but now she looked admiringly at his tight buttocks and leg muscles. He took the towel from the spare lounger and rapidly rubbed the water from his face and the hair on his body whilst unashamedly Evelina studied his manhood, shrivelled by the cold water. He wrapped the towel around his waist, to give himself some modesty before he lay face down on the lounger next to her.

Henry and Evelina looked at each other fondly. She reached across to him and they held hands before they both closed their eyes to rest them from the burning sun.

"Can I have a finder's fee if you buy the vineyards?" asked Evelina suddenly and after a long period of silence. "Of course, only if you buy them," she added for clarity. She was proving what Henry had already established. In Moldova, those aged under thirty-five were having no difficulty adjusting to capitalism.

For you or for Arthur Andersen?" he asked

"For me, it's my idea," she answered.

"I suppose so," said Henry. "How much?"

"Ten percent," said Evelina quickly.

"In France and England, the finder's fee is usually between two and three percent."

"This is not France," said Evelina, with a look to show that she did not appreciate the need to negotiate.

"That's true," said Henry. I'll do a deal with you at five percent.

Evelina propped herself up on one arm, reached across and shook Henry's hand before she turned over to lay completely naked on her back. As she moved, Henry once again admired the elegance and beauty of her perfectly formed body. He thought she was the most perfect painting, really beautiful live art. A picture he wanted all to himself and for no one else to see.

"Shall we go tomorrow?" Evelina asked. "If we go early enough, we can have a good look around and I'll get you back to the airport in time to catch your plane home."

"Sounds good to me," said Henry, as he watched Evelina rise and with just three strides dive into the pool again, this time taking a long deep underwater dive.

Chapter 24

Kishinev July 1992

TANIA LOOKED TIRED when she opened the door to let Henry into her apartment. The windows were open but there was little breeze, and the humidity was stifling. It drove a feeling of lethargy which was hard to fight. It was perhaps one of the reasons why Tania was not as effusive in her welcoming of Henry as she usually was, just offering him a peck on the cheek. This was in sharp contrast with joie de vivre shown by Evelina as they said their goodbyes just moments before.

The second reason was sitting on the settee in her living-cum-bedroom. Henry was surprised and embarrassed to find Serghei Stoica sitting there. Although, he might have been more uncomfortable had he known that Serghei had seen him laying peacefully with Tania, his hand rested on her belly, pregnant with Serghei's child.

Tania introduced the two men. Serghei stayed seated as the two men reluctantly shook hands. Both men shared an expression telling it was not a meeting either wanted to have, ever!

"Is it alright that I stay here?" Henry asked. "I can easily book into a hotel."

"No, no you must stay," said Tania. "I've made everything ready for you."

"Are you sure?"

A frantic nod of Tania's head told him that he had to stay.

"Am I next door?" asked Henry picking up his suitcase and pointing to her great-grandmother's bedroom.

"Yes," said Tania, who then immediately asked, "would you like something to eat?"

"Would you like to go out to eat?" Henry responded.

"No thank you. I am too tired. I'll prepare something. I have some cold meats, cheese and salad in the fridge."

In Tania's great-grandmother's bedroom Henry changed his shirt and combed his hair. He returned to sit on a hard chair at the dining table.

"The wine privatisation project is over," said Henry to both Tania and Serghei, after he'd consumed half a glass of apple juice. "Stanescu effectively killed it off today," he added.

"You're not surprised, are you?" asked Serghei in perfect English.

"Why?" asked Henry.

"He's a crook. He was never going to allow an outsider to get hold of a national prize like Cricova or Mileştii Mici. He'll want them for himself and the others for one of his mates. All that's happened is that he hasn't worked out how he's going to get hold of it, that's all."

"Everyone says that about every politician in this country. It's the first and only cry everyone makes after the refrain 'what can I do'." said Henry crossly. "There is a permanent presumption of guilt over every politician. Where's the evidence? Show me the evidence because I haven't seen it," said Henry challengingly hard. He had taken an instant dislike to Serghei without any real reason to do so, other than it was Serghei who had got Tania pregnant and not him.

"You won't find it around Mircea Stanescu. He is too clever," said Serghei. "You know his son, Costin. You've had your dealings with him. You know how rotten he is. He's the beneficiary. Between Mircea and he, they extort everything. Costin is deep in the Mafia, almost untouchable, because his father controls the police and the judges and, if he doesn't control them with money, he either has them killed or arrested on false corruption charges," said Serghei.

"You know the nightclub on Strada Mitropolit Varlaam, the one you were standing at when the Mafia raided?" asked Tania.

"Yes," acknowledged Henry. "It's not something easily forgotten."

"Well seven men were shot, three killed. It's said that it was Costin Stanescu's gang who made the attack to take control of the club," continued Serghei.

"You're a writer, a journalist," said Henry, "why aren't you writing about these things?"

"It's too dangerous," he replied, with the protest in his tone which was much louder than the volume of his voice.

Henry said nothing. He wasn't sure he would be brave enough to tackle them either.

Tania served a simple meal for the three of them as Serghei told story after story of political corruption. She said little, leaving the table after they had eaten to fall asleep on the settee. The two men chatted as cordially as any two men, who both knew they were in love with the same woman, could possibly manage.

It was late, and Tania was still asleep when Serghei left to go home to his mother's flat. Henry cleared the things from the dining table, folded it up and went into the kitchen to wash up. Back in the living-cum-bedroom he moved Tania's treasure box, holding all that was precious to her, from the top of the cupboard containing her bed which he unfolded and made ready for her to sleep in.

Taking Tania gently by the hand he woke her and, as she stood restfully still, he helped her step out of her dress, leaving her in just her bra, panties and short white socks.

"I need a drink," she said.

"Okay I'll get you one."

As Henry returned from the kitchen with a glass of apple juice, Tania came out of the bathroom completely naked, her eyes still half closed. Her tummy was swollen, her breasts were full, and her hips and thighs had taken on a lot of extra weight, but none of those things mattered to him. Her face was as pretty as ever. It radiated with a healthy glow.

Tania drank the cold juice and laid her head on the pillow. Henry lifted her legs on to the bed and covered her in a thin sheet, protecting her body from the draft which was beginning to move around the room. He sat on the settee and watched her sleep. He had no right to be here he thought. Perhaps her life, and her baby's life, were best served by them being with Serghei for, as she had already said, what had he to offer? He could only offer her two things; maybe financial security, but above that ... he cared, he really cared.

Chapter 25

Kishinev July 1992

THE NEXT MORNING was cool. A thunderstorm had passed over during the night and freshened the air. Tania was up early sitting drinking coffee at the kitchen table when Henry joined her.

"I am sorry about last night," she said. "I was very tired."

"It was fine," said Henry. Serghei and I chatted for a little while. He's a nice man."

Tania nodded. "He's very clever," she said. "He wants to be a professor of journalism and communication at Moldova State University. "

"Yes, you said. He and I talked about it last night. He said it was why his English was so good."

"Would you like a coffee?" asked Tania, as she got up from the table anticipating his reply.

"Yes please," said Henry, then asked: "What would you say if I said I was thinking of buying a vineyard out at Orhei?"

"Why would you want to do that?" asked Tania, her tone revealing her surprise at the question.

"To prove that private capital can make Moldovan wine great again, one of the best in the world. To prove to Stanescu that he is wrong to reject the privatisation of his wine industry."

"Orhei is a good wine district," said Tania, "but I didn't know that there were any private vineyards there that could be bought. I thought they were all owned by the government."

"The thing is, to buy it, I need a Moldova national to be my partner; to own at least 50% of the shares. Would you do that with me? he asked.

"I don't have any money to do that kind of thing," said Tania, thinking Henry was crazy.

"You don't need money. I've got all that. You've just got to own half the shares."

Tania thought hard for a long time. "Do I own them, or do I just hold them for you?" she asked.

It was a good question causing Henry to think hard too. "You'll own them. They'll be yours to do what you like with. If you want to sell them you just have to offer them to me, or the person I say first."

"Yes, why not?" said Tania. "If you want."

"You'll need to help me look after it, not manage it, just make sure that everything is all right."

"I know nothing about making wine," protested Tania.

"I know all we need to know," said Henry.

"Would you want me to go there?" she asked.

"Yes, of course."

"It's just, it's a long way and I don't drive. I don't have a car."

"You can learn," said Henry frustrated that such a small matter should be put in the way of the big picture.

"Yes, but it's expensive," protested Tania, without Henry taking any notice.

"I am going out to Orhei this morning to take a look," said Henry. "Evelina is going to take me."

"Oh," said Tania with obvious disappointment. "Will you be back here before you leave to go home?"

"No, I'll go straight to the airport. I really only flew in to see Stanescu and this cropped up,"

"When will you be back?

"I don't know. It will depend on what happens later today. Perhaps late September, just after Peter's gone back to university."

"After my baby's born," said Tania.

"Yes," acknowledged Henry, and from that moment there was an embarrassed strain between the two of them which lasted until Henry saw Evelina's car pull up in the square outside.

They kissed goodbye, not as though they were lovers but close friends. Henry left wishing Tania good luck with her birth. He didn't know what else he could say.

Chapter 26

Faterini Village July 1992

EVELINA FOUND FATERINI village quite easily. Finding the abandoned hamlet, which was at the heart of the vineyards being sold, was much harder. Three times Evelina stopped to ask directions. Eventually, after asking themselves many times whether they were travelling in the right direction, they found the hamlet they were looking for. It was to the side of the village, down a rutted track which ran for about a mile along the edge of a large wood. As they drove the length of the track, they both admitted that the panoramic views on the opposite side to the woods were quite spectacular.

The Hamlet was on the top of a small hill, about 700 metres from the river, which curved around the land at the bottom of the hill. At its heart were a set of badly run-down buildings surrounding a large courtyard with an impressive well in the middle. To the right of them, with their backs to the woods, were two large oblong barns with clay tiles on their roofs. They looked as though they had stood there for two hundred years and would stand there for just as long again. To the south of the yard, and before you got to the slopes of the vineyards, there were four separate, but identical two-storey houses set in a crescent, with views fanning out over the vineyards below. The damp and decay in each building was palpable, with broken windows, doors and gaps in the roof. Foliage sprouted from all parts of the building.

The news that a foreigner, accompanied by a woman from the city, had come to see the hamlet spread quickly amongst the inhabitants of Faterini village. It was why, when Henry and Evelina had been there just minutes, two men arrived in an old Russian Military Zil lorry, which only kept working through the ingenuity of its owners.

The two men were exactly the same as all the men that Henry had met at every winery he had visited. They were very poorly dressed, with leathery skin, unshaven beards, raggedly cut hair and bad teeth with gaps in their mouths from unanesthetised extractions. As they approached, Henry felt a sense of aggression. Evelina sensed the same thing. In response, she untucked her shirt tails from her trousers which she then tied into a bow under her bust, exaggerating it's size, whilst revealing the flatness of her white stomach and the curve of her hips into her waist. Henry thought it most odd, as it was as deliberate as it was provocatively non-threatening.

Evelina spoke rapidly. Henry had no idea what was being said. It was obvious from the way she stroked her hair, puckered her lips and posed, that she was flirting with them to get her way. Was that what she been doing with him yesterday, Henry wondered.

It was agreed that one man would go and get the keys while the other, a man called Efrim Cazac would show Henry and Evelina around the land. As they walked between the two central houses towards the vineyards, Henry and Evelina were stopped in their tracks by the view, as was every other person who ever saw it. From the north-east through two hundred and seventy degrees to the north-west there was a truly magnificent panorama which captured Henry's heart as obviously as it had captured the man's who was standing next to him.

"Tell him this is the best view in the whole of Moldova," said Efrim Cazac. "No," he said suddenly correcting himself. "Tell him it's the best view in the whole of the world!"

Evelina translated and Henry could only agree. He searched hard into the horizon to look for, what he thought blighted every view, but were not there. There was not an electricity pylon to be seen!

"How come this is all yours?" asked Henry through Evelina.

"When the communists came, and collective farms were started, we were allowed to keep 20 hectares." Then the man started pointing. "One brother this house this land," he said to Evelina. Then he pointed to another house and in a different direction, "Another brother this house this land," he said eventually doing it six times in all.

"There are six lots of land but only four houses, why?" asked Evelina.

"The two barns, they were houses once," replied Efrim Cazac with a disapproving shrug of his shoulders.

"So, six brothers are selling this land?" said Henry to make sure he understood.

"It's the relatives of six brothers," said Evelina.

"Please asked them why they are selling?"

There was a long explanation. "They say Russia no longer wants to buy Moldovan wine. The winery only takes grapes from the collectives, so their grapes are no longer wanted," said Evelina, succinctly translating a long conversation. "All the family now lives in the village and they all work in the chicken factory so there is no one to look after the land."

Henry walked between the vines. He could see that they were already full of grapes, but no one was caring for them. The soil was no longer piled up against the roots, so the rain wouldn't be captured in the gullies set between the rows. It wouldn't stand in pools ready to sink deep into the chalk bed below. There would be no reservoir of water for the vines to draw upon in the heat of the summer. It would mean a poor harvest. Unless something happened soon, thought Henry, the rainwater would start to leach the soil away; a catastrophe as it can never be replaced. Everywhere the trellis wires had sagged. In many places they had snapped, leaving the vines to grow wild. It was like every vineyard he'd visited in Moldova, but worse. It was in desperate need of care and maintenance and that meant investment.

The three of them walked the boundary of the land for a little while until they heard the noise of the diesel lorry returning. Independently, and without saying anything, they all turned to walk back up the hill to the hamlet.

The doors were opened to each of the houses which could only be described as ruins. They were all the same. There were no concrete or wooden ground floor, just the caked earth. There was no electricity, running water or toilet. There was just one room downstairs with a staircase which led to two rooms upstairs. It would be easier to knock them down and start again, thought Henry.

Just as he was beginning to think that it needed too much work, Henry was taken into the second barn off the court yard. As the door opened, he saw in front of him a large, beautifully made copper still. Once again emotion forced on him an immediate change of mind.

"You make brandy?" asked Henry through Evelina.

"Yes," said Cazac. "We did."

"And the wood for the brandy?" asked Henry.

"Like the wine, from the forest," said Cazac with an expression which indicated it had been a stupid question.

"Who makes them?" asked Henry.

"They're made in the village," said Evelina when she heard the reply, "and the man who makes them still lives there."

"Please tell them I am very interested in buying these vineyards," said Henry. "Please tell them I need a surveyor and architect to examine and report. If they say it's okay, then I'd like to buy."

Evelina translated. "They want to know how much."

"I don't know," said Henry. "It depends on what the architects and surveyors say."

"Thousand dollars hectare," said the man who drove the lorry and had bought the keys. It was the only English either Cazac or he had spoken.

"Maybe, maybe not," said Henry. "It depends on the reports."

"Can I suggest you say one thousand dollars; that way you can get your architects and surveyors onto the land, otherwise they might not let them come. You can always negotiate it down later," said Evelina.

"Okay," said Henry, "but make sure they know that, at that price, it includes the four houses and the two barns, and they are not to sell it to anyone else.

Henry wandered around by himself for another twenty minutes, pacing out measurements whilst Evelina talked earnestly to the two men. Unknown to Henry she was negotiating, and had agreed, a finder's fee for herself with them too; seven and a half percent.

As Evelina drove out through the village with Henry at her side, he said: "I'm going to name it after Sophie. I promised her a long time ago that I would name a wine after her and I never did. Well in addition to wine, I'm going to make the best brandy in the world here, and I'm going to name it after her!

Chapter 27

Faterini Village October 1992

HENRY'S FIRST TELEPHONE call on his return to Château de Gressier, back in July, had been to Tania. He was going to buy a vineyard in Faterini near Orsie, he told her excitedly. She was to come onto the de Gressier payroll immediately and most importantly she was to buy a car. The fact that Tania was heavily pregnant and about to have a new baby didn't come into his calculations. For Tania, the news of a proper salary at last, rather than worrying about living from hand to mouth on her teacher's salary, eclipsed anything else which Henry had said.

Henry then spent the rest of the summer obsessing about his vineyard purchase and its refurbishment. He sent out his general managers, Pierre Hilaire from Château de Gressier and Thomas Cannen from Château Rabôut to study the vineyard and its hamlet. They both came back with a long list of issues which, in summary, concluded he was mad to contemplate it, and completely bonkers if he went ahead and actually bought it.

The first and biggest issue he had identified himself, and that was how the hamlet had to live off the grid because it was a long way from mains power and drinking water in the village. Both were essential for the business he was going to run there. The second issue identified by his general managers was the lack of cellars for long-term local wine storage. It was, as they both strongly pointed out, the one feature common to de Gressier and Rabôut which made their business model a success. Recognising it as a good point, Henry's answer was a simple one. He would knock down the four dilapidated houses, dig a huge cellar and then put four new bigger houses, in the existing style, back on top. If there was one thing he knew how to do, it was to build waterproof cellars.

Henry hired Moldovan and French architects and Moldovan and English surveyors. Each brought further expertise into the mix of advisers and so the problems to be solved became more extensive. However, just as happened with each of Henry's earlier building projects, there was not an issue which was going to defeat him. Once again, he saw each problem not as an obstacle but as a maths formula or crossword to be solve. Nothing was going to get in the way of his main ambition, creating great wines and an award-winning cognac at Sophie Estate.

With Henry's eldest son, Andrew, now beginning to establish himself in his own career and with Peter, his youngest son, in his last year at University, Henry went back to Kishinev in the last week of September with a complete project plan in his pocket. Most importantly, he had a purpose which had eluded him since he had sold his wine import and distribution business nearly eighteen years before.

Tania met Henry at Kishinev airport. She had proudly driven there in her newly acquired Opel Corsa. They each found there was something truly magical, almost spiritual, about seeing the other again. As they embraced it seemed that they had never been apart. Tania's figure was once again slim and trim, making it almost impossible to believe that her son, Stelian, had been born just a few weeks before, in mid-August.

Tania took Henry straight to her apartment to show off her son of whom she was justifiably bursting with pride. It was immediately apparent to Henry, as soon as he saw mother and child together, that there was an overpowering bond of love between them. It made him think of when his children were born, when his wife Sophie had suffered with 'baby blues' so badly that she had been diagnosed with psychotic depression. It saddened him to think of those times. He could now see the mother's love which his sons had been denied for weeks on end. Henry's sadness was not long lived because he could see Tania glowing with true happiness and this made her incredibly attractive.

Tania and Henry had already agreed that, now she had Stelian to look after, it would be impossible for him to stay with her in her apartment. Instead, and because he was totally committed to buying the vineyard near Faterini Village, he agreed to take a one-year lease on Tania's grandmother's flat opposite her own. It was the one which had previously been modernised so it could be let to a diplomat from the US embassy. Henry therefore had his own apartment, and it was from its dining table that he started to implement his plans to build the best vineyard and winery in the whole of Moldova in earnest.

Evelina had taken Tania out to see the vineyard almost immediately after Henry had made Tania a formal job offer. At first, both women were uncomfortable with the thought of meeting, each feeling possessive about Henry. It was as though they considered they had some exclusive right to him which the other was not to enjoy. Whilst their half-day together didn't end with Tania and Evelina being the best of friends, any animosity which had been there at the start was nearly all gone at the end.

Henry's meeting with the owners the Faterini vineyard to negotiate its purchase was difficult to arrange as there were twenty-one sellers, each with a slightly different agenda. After much toing and froing, Evelina was to arrange a meeting on Saturday 1st October in Faterini Village Hall at 12 noon. Tania's mother baby sat so she could go to the meeting with Henry and Evelina.

The sellers had already gathered in the village hall by the time Henry, Evelina and Tania arrived. Immediately Evelina took charge so that within minutes, Henry was standing before his audience who were seated in front of him in theatre style.

After Evelina's introduction, Henry stood completely still. He allowed the room to go silent before he started to speak. He had dressed carefully for the occasion, wanting to look like an old-fashioned London solicitor. He made sure that none of the trappings of ostentatious wealth were on show - no expensive watch, or bracelet or pen as he guessed rightly that these things would only upset his audience. He had to look as far away from a mafia spiv as he possibly could.

With Evelina translating, Henry slowly and deliberately told of his family's background in the wine business, his experiences of vineyards around the world and of his failed efforts to privatise the Moldovan wine industry. He spoke enthusiastically about his ambition for 'Sophie Estate', as he called it. He then reported, in detail, the huge impediments which had to be overcome if a great vineyard and winery was to be created on the site of the hamlet. He closed by setting out the huge investment he would have to make.

"Nevertheless," said Henry, "I am prepared to pay your asking price of $1,000 per hectare subject to certain conditions being agreed. I'll set out the conditions in a moment," he continued, "but before I do that, I want to make sure that there is agreement between us on this price?"

A middle-aged man, who was much better dressed than all the others, stood up. It was obvious to Henry, Tania and Evelina, from the man's demeanour, that he had been chosen to speak on behalf of all those who were sellers.

"I don't know where the price of $1,000 per hectare has come from," said the man, "but the advertised price was $1,500 and no one in this room is prepared to sell it at less than that price," before adding, "as had been agreed." He then promptly sat down.

As Evelina translated their new demand, Henry looked at her with a mix of shock and disappointment. Instantly Evelina was on her feet arguing animatedly, as Tania whispered into Henry's ear an explanation of what was happening.

It took Henry a nanosecond to understand. He folded up his papers and put them in his briefcase. His eyes moved slowly around the room making sure he looked directly into the eyes of everyone there. "Come on, let's go," said Henry firmly but quietly to Evelina and Tania so he wouldn't be overheard.

"This has been a bit of a waste of time, hasn't it" said Tania. There was sadness in her voice.

"I've been conned twice before in this country, and it's not going to happen again!" replied Henry.

Tania and Henry left and walked quickly to Tania's car. As far as Henry was concerned the negotiations were over before they had begun. Neither said anything as they climbed inside and stared at the hall door waiting for Evelina to appear. Either Evelina didn't hear, or chose not to, as she was in full fight when Tania and Henry left. With her finder's fee at stake, she was not going to give up that easily.

Henry and Tania sat in the car for nearly fifteen minutes. Tania was surprised at how sanguine Henry was at the whole thing. She knew that, in similar circumstances, she would be seething. It was true; Henry was cross but mainly with himself. He'd put a huge amount of effort, and spent a large sum of money, creating a project plan and they knew it. They were now seeking to leverage that knowledge for their personal gain. Well, he said to himself, it was not going to happen.

"Tania, please understand," said Henry. "This is not about me winning .... Well yes, it is, but it is more important than that. We're going to be here for generations to come. It's about fair dealing. If we start out like this, then everything from now on becomes a negotiation. There'll be two sides fighting; one winning, one losing and it's not a good way to do business. It really isn't. There's far more to good capitalism than a fight over today's price. It's far more subtle, more nuanced than that."

Tania squeezed Henry on the arm to show she understood and the two sat in silence until eventually, Tania suggested that she should go back and get Evelina from the meeting. Henry agreed.

When Tania returned to the room, she found Evelina still battling strongly. The price had apparently come down to $1,100 per hectare, and Evelina was being urged to go to Henry to present him with their lower number. She was valiantly resisting.

On seeing Tania, Evelina stopped talking and the two women huddled together to have an intense whispered conversation. Immediately Tania had been briefed, she returned to the car and told Henry of the revise price.

"I am sorry, but the answer is no," he said emphatically.

Tania went back to the room and this time it was her turn to address the audience which had grown bigger as family members had joined to see what was going on.

"I just asked Mr Guégan whether he would increase his offer to $1,100 per hectare. He has told me that he will not."

There was no immediate reaction to the news, so Tania moved forward and started to walk between her audience, as though she was walking between the desks of the children in her class.

"I think it might be helpful if I were to explain some of the background. I think you will then understand why Mr Guégan won't increase the amount you asked him to pay," she said. Immediately, but without going into too much detail, she told them of his experience at the airport, him standing outside a night club witnessing a mafia-on-mafia shooting, then at the Steffaco Hotel and finally the way he felt he had been let down by the Moldovan government with its wine privatisation programme.

"He's sitting outside in the car convinced that no one in Moldova can be trusted," Tania said. "He tells me that it was two of you who set the price at his first meeting. Now you tell him that you want 50% more. I don't think you understand. You are dealing with a Frenchman, who was brought up in England. In these countries, your behaviour today is called gazumping. It is not common because it is socially disapproved of. Mr Guégan's cultural experiences are different to ours. He is not being difficult. It is just our way is not the way he is used to doing business."

Tania moved away from being in the centre of her audience to stand in front of them again. It was as though she were now standing in front of the parents of her class telling them exactly the kind of behaviour she expected from their children this term.

"I can assure you," said Tania, "Mr Guégan will leave if you do not accept the price of $1,000 per hectare. In fact, I'm not sure, even if you were to agree such an amount now, he would still go ahead. You see, he was about to invest three hundred thousand, maybe four hundred thousand dollars in rebuilding that vineyard, and to do that he needs to be able to trust the people around him. And let us remember, a lot of that money will be spent here."

"But we can only sell our land once," protested a young voice from the back.

"And there is only one buyer," responded Evelina rapidly. "Please, I'm a consultant with one of the world's leading consultancy firms. I worked with Mr Guégan on the wine privatisation programme that Ms Plesca told you about. There are ten, twenty, possibly more vineyards that people will try to buy before they come to try and buy yours. Yes, there might be one other person out there who might be interested in buying your land, but no one knows who or where they are. It might take five years, ten, twenty to find them. Do you want to wait that long and perhaps not get as much?"

Tania moved forward again. The deal price is a thousand dollars or nothing. You need to decide, and rapidly. If you do agree to go back to the original price then Miss Kirillovich and I will do our best to persuade him to go ahead at that price, but neither of us can promise anything."

Efrim Cazac, the man who first met with Henry, and who everyone else in the room knew was responsible for the attempted price hike, was sitting in the corner in the front row. He'd put on his best suit, was wearing a tie and had shaven for the event, as he did at every one of the village council meetings. As he stood up, it was immediately clear, from the way that everyone looked at him, that he was the most senior member of their village and the man who was going to decide the price. He had said nothing until that moment. "Please tell Mr Guégan that the price is agreed. Perhaps he would be so kind as to come back so we can discuss his other terms," said Cazac. There was a murmur of approval around the whole room.

Tania went to get Henry, who came back into the room to a round of applause.

Immediately Henry was in front of them, once again, he deliberately stood still, allowing the room to fall silent, but this time he looked at the floor as though he were in prayer.

"I'm very sorry if there was a cultural misunderstanding," he said, as Evelina translated for him. "It is just that in Paris or London or New York, whenever I'm in a shop and select a chocolate bar to buy which has a price of two dollars on it, I do not expect to be asked to pay three dollars when I get to the till." It was a simple analogy that had a resonance amongst his audience.

Henry went ahead and listed his preconditions. He needed licences and permits to build a cellar to store the wine and cognac the estate was going to produce. He needed a licence to double the size of each of the four houses so that he and his General Manager could each have somewhere to live and international wine buyers could have a place to stay. He needed permission to connect to the mains water and mains electricity in the village, and a licence to extract water from the river. Finally, he wanted a memorandum of understanding between the village and the vineyard. "I don't think there is anything unreasonable here," said Henry, winding up his list of issues.

Efrim Cazac stood up. "Thank you," he said, "that is clear. I don't think they will provide any difficulties. Miss Kirillovich and Mrs Plesca both spoke of you creating jobs. I think everyone would like to know about that."

"Thank you," said Henry. "Yes, I'm looking to employ two highly experienced viticulturists and an experienced distiller almost immediately. Then there will be part-time and seasonal jobs for between another eight and twelve people."

"How much will you pay?" asked Cazac.

Henry smiled. As part of his business planning process, he had enquired extensively on local wage rates. He knew exactly what he was going to do. He was going to pay twenty per cent more than the local chicken factory. "For the viticulturists and the distiller, I will be offering $3.50 per hour, for everyone else I will pay $2.60 per hour," he said.

There was a general murmur of excited approval; particularly from the women folk who were finding it hard to manage the welfare of their families on the wages they, and their husbands, were being paid.

"I have one special employment condition," said Henry. "Everyone who works at Sophie Estate will have to learn to speak English. I do this, not because I have no respect for the Moldovan language, far from it." Henry paused as Evelina had difficulty translating the double negative. "However," he went on, "I intend to make this vineyard, this winery, into one of the most famous in the world. Those people who come here will expect us all to speak English. It is the international language. I expect all of us to be able to do so too. So, every day for one hour a day I will pay everyone who works on Sophie Estate to learn English from a teacher I will employ. However old you are you can learn, but if you don't want to learn then please, don't apply for a job with us."

Chapter 28

Kishinev October 1992

HENRY SAT QUIETLY in the back of Tania's car, next to Stelian's empty baby seat, while Tania and Evelina sat in the front for the journey from Faterini Village to Tania's flat. Henry was deep in thought as the women chattered in Moldovan congratulating each other on the way they turned the meeting around in Henry's favour. Neither knew how much the other needed the deal to go through. As new found companions with a common vested interest, it was quite natural for Tania to invite Evelina in when, late in the afternoon, they arrived outside her flat.

As Tania struggled to unlock the outer steel door to her apartment, she was surprised to find Serghei there, helping her by unlocking the inner door. He had bought their son, now sleeping restlessly in his cot, back from her parents. Tania was feeling heavy breasted and knew that her son needed to be fed, so it only took a few minutes before Tania was seated calmly with Stelian latched contentedly to her breast.

At Tania's behest, Serghei made tea for all those present as he listened to Evelina tell him what had happened in the village hall. The excitement of their discussion in the car of what had happened was now missing from this retelling.

"We'll need to take great care about the Notary Public we use," said Evelina as the conversation began to slow down.

"Why is that?" asked Serghei, highly tuned to the words 'Notary Public'.

"My father's flat was stolen from him using a corrupt Notary. These men are supposed to certify the truth, but they certify lies and, because they are so powerful, it's hard to fight back," said Evelina.

"It's not just hard, it's impossible," said Serghei. "The courts will take the document signed by the Notary Public as the definitive document. They simply won't believe you when you tell them that you didn't sell it and, more importantly, when you say you didn't get the money, even though you can prove the apartment was yours."

"Yes, I know," said Evelina. "The people who illegally sold my father's property are fraudsters. They wouldn't have been able to have committed their fraud if the notary had done his job properly, or more likely, wasn't involved in the fraud in the first place. I'm sure he's done it many times to many people."

"You're right. You're not alone on this, you know that, don't you?" said Serghei. "It's now taking place on an industrial scale. It is something I've been investigating, and so far I've found over twenty, possibly twenty-five people who have been cheated out of their homes."

Tania and Evelina looked at Serghei anxiously, for they were concerned as to what Henry's reaction might be. They'd bought this transaction too far to lose it now because Henry might change his mind on the basis that Moldovan lawyers could not be trusted.

"What was the name of the Notary in your case?" asked Serghei.

"Notary Tigran Tarvel," said Evelina with disgust.

"Yes, that's one of them," said Serghei animatedly.

"The whole thing is a heathen, backed dated practice," said Henry, in a matter-of-fact way. As an international businessman, he knew the negative grip these people had on doing business. "God knows why it is still going on. Do you know it goes back to Roman times and then spread throughout the Holy Roman Empire? It was appropriate when most people couldn't read or write, and they needed somebody independent to read out and explain to them the contract they were signing, but why this should still be happening as we come to the 21st-century is beyond me."

Tania and Evelina said nothing. They could sense Henry's frustration at finding so little worked properly in Moldova.

Henry stood up moved and over to Tania and kissed her gently on the cheek. He did the same to Evelina and nodded to Serghei. "It's been a good day," he said as he got to the door to go to his own flat. "We'll just have to have two notaries for our deal," said Henry, "one for our side and one for them." He then paused before continuing. "I make one comment; if you Moldovans can't trust your notary publics then who, in this darned country, can you trust?

While Tania fed, winded and changed Stelian, and laid him down to sleep, Serghei and Evelina swapped notes on the corrupt notaries.

"You are going to have to do something about it," said Tania when she re-joined them. "The courts are useless and, until it is stopped, families are going to continue to have their homes stolen. The only thing which is going to stop it is publicity. We need to publicly shame those notaries who are cheating so that no one uses them again. You're the journalist," said Tania pointing to Serghei. "I am sure if you put your mind to it you could make it a headline story and kill their filthy business."

Chapter 29

The Woodman's Dacha October 1992

STILL GLORYING IN the success of their meeting in Faterini village hall, Tania invited Henry to join her and Stelian for her family's weekly Sunday gathering at the Woodman's Dacha.

It was a beautiful warm autumn day when Tania, Stelian and Henry arrived at Brigita and Anna's home. The clouds were high and billowed slowly across the sky. The crops had all been gathered in from the fields. It meant that the view from the Woodman's Dacha down to the river looked bare and tired, ready for its winter's sleep.

Their harvest had been carefully dried with Brigita and Anna working to protect every morsel of food as though their lives depended on it as, in the past, it had done just that.

Unusually, Vlad Plesca, Tania's father was not there. He had been offered a day's fishing. Despite owning a stretch of river bank, they had been refused a permit to catch fish. It meant the opportunity to catch six fish from a government controlled lake was one which Tania's family was not going to allow him to turn down. It was therefore natural that Henry should be conscripted as a porter to help carry some of the sacks of grain, maize and flour to their hidden store in the woods at the back of the Woodman's Dacha. It was just as Brigita and Anna had done every year since the harvest of 1945. It was a habit engraved on their minds for Brigita remembered the Holodomor of 1933, and they both remembered the starvation of 1946. It was this hidden store which had kept Brigita, Anna and Heidi alive in the last of those famines.

"My grandfather, Count Donici-Solokov, built it in 1914," said Brigita using his full title and name proudly. It was built so we could hideaway when the Germans came," she explained, "but thankfully they didn't come, and we didn't need it." Tania translated.

"So, they stopped using it," said Anna bitterly. "It meant my whole family died in the Great Hunger. My mother and I were the only ones who survived," said Tania continuing to translate for her grandmother.

"The Great Hunger ... in 1933?" asked Henry, conscious that the Holodomor was being discussed for the third time.

"Yes," said Tania shaking her head in sorrow. "It's one of the most important events in our history. It's why Moldovans loathe the Russians," she continued. "A hate made worse because they did the same again in 1946. It's why we don't understand the people in Transnistria. They're supposed to be Moldovan, but they're mostly Russians who still have a big statue of Stalin in the centre of Tiraspol."

As Anna, Heidi, Tania and Henry marched into the woods carrying heavy sacks of food, Henry had a history lesson.

"We lived here for four or five days in June 1944," said Anna when they arrived at the appointed family den. When the Russians counter-attacked and recaptured Kishinev, it was too dangerous to be anywhere other than hidden away, so we left the field hospital, which had been established at the Woodman's Dacha, and came here."

Henry was glad to put down his load. He stretched to relieve his stiffness as he looked around the clearing. It had one large shed to the edge and then five or six smaller huts, built on stilts about a metre above the ground and spanning out into the undergrowth in different directions and distances from the main shed. The original thinking had been that someone might find one or two but not all of their hidden stores.

"My mother and I stayed here until we ran out of water," said Anna. There was regret in her voice. "When my mother went to get it, she found so many casualties back at the Woodman's Dacha we left immediately and returned home to help."

As Anna moved away to unlock the shed and the huts, which had all been refurbished with new waterproof roofs, she said: "Do you know, I think those few days I spent here were some of the happiest in my life. Don't you think that strange?"

Henry said nothing. Instead, he listened and observed carefully. One additional question, one extra remark and he might have learnt why Anna was so happy to be here then. She had spent those days with a man with whom she was desperately in love. He was Heinrik Klugman, a shot down German pilot. It was a magical, thrilling, exciting time for her. A memory made most precious because he was the first and last man she'd ever made love with.

With Tania at his side, Henry sat down on the same huge log that Anna and his father had sat on years before, for age had not wearied it. Tania and Henry both looked up into the sky as the sun shone through the canopy of the trees where the leaves were now turning a golden yellow-brown. They closed their eyes. They felt the warmth of the sunbeams on their faces. It was such a magical moment that both Tania and Henry could have sworn that they had been touched by the love of God.

Overwhelmed by their feelings and a little confused, they opened their eyes and looked at each other. Stunned into silence, they found that, under each other's gaze, they felt a powerful, heart-aching sensation of love. This time it was accompanied by a sense of fear and inadequacy as they knew they would never be able to express to the person opposite them how much they were loved. Words and actions would never be enough.

It was a shout from Heidi, Tania's Mother, telling them to come along because they had to return to the Woodman's Dacha to collect the next load, which shocked Tania and Henry out of their *'stupor amour.'*

"We should create one of these in the woods at the back of our barns at Faterini," said Henry to Tania in a whisper. "We'll make it a home for fairies, pixies, elms, gnomes and goblins," he continued to Tania's utter dismay, for she had never heard any of those words before.

Tania and Henry returned to their apartments in Kishinev early in the evening, separating on arrival to go about their own chores. It was late, and Stelian was asleep, when Tania tiptoed nervously across the landing and rang the doorbell to Henry's apartment. He looked through the spy hole and he saw her standing there in cream silk pyjamas. He, on the other hand, was looking far from attractive as he opened the door in his tea shirt and underpants.

"I think we should have a shower," said Tania seriously.

"I'm about to ......," Henry started to say, and then he saw Tania's face, her wide smile and instantly he translated the code in her message.

That night with Henry in Tania's bed she took from him as vigorously as she had done when they made love together for the very first time.

"Please no more," said Tania exhausted as, in the early hours of the morning, Henry found his libido renewed.

"What happened to my little sex machine?" teased Henry, disappointedly.

"She fell in love ... and that's an exhausting experience," said Tania, as she rose from their bed to give her son an early-morning feed.

Chapter 30

Kishinev December 1992

IT WAS THE third Thursday in the month; 17th December to be precise. It was a day Henry would hate for the rest of his life because he could trace everything that happened back to this point. It was the singularity in his own black hole before it exploded, leaving his life and those of many others spinning out of control.

This day should have been no different to all the other Thursdays before or the many others which were to follow. From early evening a group of Tania's friends would come for coffee, some would bring wine, most would bring food. There was never any music. Right from the very first gathering, immediately after the nightclub shooting six months before, these had been sombre, constrained affairs, but more so now that Stelian was sleeping in the bedroom next door.

Serghei and Evelina were now regular attendees, as was Henry when he was in the country, which was now far more frequent. There was just one condition for membership to the group; you had to be able to speak good English, for that was the language spoken throughout. Some thought that this was the reason for their 'club' but it was not that. You had to be able to speak English so you could have an appreciation of what was going on in the wider world and therefore bring this knowledge into the room.

There was never any structure to their debates. No one proposed a subject, and the arguments could be free and wide-ranging, covering many issues as happens in an ordinary conversation. What distinguished it from any other discussion group was how people waited courteously to make their point. This was because those who had proved too dominant were quietly left off the list of invitees when the group reformed after each of the school holidays.

Apart from her role as host, Tania had two other functions during the evening. Firstly, she was the mediator if an argument arose. Her second and most important role was to keep pressing to find the alternative point of view. She was a natural adversary to group thought.

The debate on this Thursday night was started because there were news reports, which many had seen, of desperately poor Moldavians selling one of their kidneys for a pittance so they could buy medical treatment for a member of their family. It was a very distressing story.

"Did you see the news this evening?" said someone referring to the news report.

"Yes," said another. "There should be a law against it." The words tripped easily off their lips.

"In the days of the Communist Party, you didn't have to sell your kidney to buy medicines, but now we have capitalism; everything has to be for sale."

"You forget, in the last few years of communism, we didn't have any medicines, and no one was around then who you could sell your kidney to!" came a reply.

"Who owns my kidney?" asked Evelina. "If it's mine, do I not have a right to sell it?" she continued, a little confused.

"There was an English philosopher called John Locke who lived back in the seventeenth century," said Serghie. "He said: *Every man has a property in his own person and nobody else has a right to it, but himself.* In addition, the UN Declaration on Human Rights gives everyone the right to own property by themselves and requires that no one shall be arbitrarily deprived of it," continued Serghei using his photographic memory. So I'd say yes, your kidney is yours to do whatever you like with, although the law doesn't make it specifically clear that's the case."

"If I own my organs in my lifetime, do my next of kin own them after I've died, or do they belong to the state?" asked Evelina.

There was silence as everyone thought about the question, but no one spoke because they didn't know the answer.

"I can only tell you what happens in the UK," said Henry before starting a long soliloquy on the moral conflicts which arose from Evelina's question. It was the only contribution Henry made all evening to the debate, which ranged widely. It included a significant objection on the grounds that transplants were a mutilation of the body, which were specifically prohibited by Christian and Islamic teaching. Given the long history of secularism in Moldova, the introduction of this religious element surprised Henry, but then he remembered Tania and their second meeting in the cathedral.

If there was one thing that frustrated Henry about these evenings, it was that there was never any conclusion. A subject had been aired, everyone knew what they thought, but there was no attempt to find a consensus.

After everyone was gone, Henry and Tania would wash and tidy up as though they were any married couple and discuss what people had said. They would move Stelian's cot into the living room with them and go to bed together as a matter of routine. It was the next day after the transplant debate, which Henry would remember so very well.

He woke up early to find Tania not by his side. He waited a little while, thinking she was looking after Stelian, or in the bathroom, but he heard no movement, so he got up and went to look for her. Tania was sitting at the kitchen table and writing furiously in an exercise book.

"What are you doing?" asked Henry.

"I'm just writing up my thoughts after last night," said Tania with embarrassment before closing her exercise book.

"What were your thoughts?" asked Henry.

"It's a big subject," replied Tania. "I suppose I think people should be free to deal with their body as they choose. The important thing is that the seller is not exploited so I'm beginning to think that there should be a law which says that the person who sells their kidney should get not less than half of the total costs of the operation."

"Good Lord," said Henry, "That's clever, really novel," he continued as he filled the kettle with water.

"Do you always do that after you've had people around to one of your discussion groups? he asked.

"Nearly always, yes. It helps me decide what I think. The trouble is one week I find myself thinking one thing and then, maybe a month later, when the subject comes up again in a different context, I find myself thinking something different."

"Such as?" asked Henry.

"The big things, like the death penalty, I'm certain on. It's on the nuances of economics or foreign policy where I find my opinion can waiver."

"For example?" asked Henry.

"Transnistria ... look at the war we've had with them," replied Tania quickly. "A few weeks ago, we discussed the Croat-Bosniak War which is going on and we agreed that the people there should have the right to self-determine their own government, and yet I still think Transnistria should belong to Moldova. It's as though they're part of us."

"Even though they're the other side of the Dniester River, so there's a big geographical divide, and most of them speak and identify themselves with Russia and not with you?" asked Henry.

"I know. It's daft and certainly not worth the lives of the seven people who died in the independence war we had earlier this year."

Tania heard Stelian stir so she went to deal with him as Henry made himself a cup of coffee. He casually picked up Tania's exercise book. The writing was perfectly neat and tidy. It was written in the copybook handwriting of a teacher. Even the crossings out were done with a ruler. What surprised Henry, even more, was that most of it was written in English, just the occasional words in Russian or Moldovan.

As he sipped his coffee, Henry started to read what Tania had written. He was immediately drawn into her writing. It was obvious he was reading the work of a polemicist of considerable note. But it was the emotion of the moment which he would always remember, for the mind of the woman he loved was spread across the page. His profound admiration of her was tempered with real envy because he wished he could write with such clarity.

Unknown to Tania, when Henry went home to spend Christmas with his mother and sons and to see his wife, he took photocopies of her handwritten notebook. At Château de Gressier, he arranged to have her work typed up and then, over the next few months, using scissors and glue and a red pen, he set about editing her work, bringing subject matters together. Where there were conflicts of opinion, he would carefully present both of her arguments and come down with a policy that he thought she would favour. However, nature being what it is, Henry couldn't stop Tania's work from being flavoured with what he thought she should think.

Chapter 31

Kishinev Spring 1993

HENRY AND TANIA signed the contract to purchase the vineyards at the side of Faterini village the day before Henry returned to England and his mother's for Christmas.

For months they'd been negotiating to get a contract agreed and the permissions Henry had insisted on. It was only when he made it clear he was leaving on 20th December and would not be back until after Easter did everything started to come together. The Moldovans didn't believe him at first. Why create such an arbitrary deadline, they wondered. It was only when everyone began to recognise that Henry had the stubbornness of the English, the intransigence of the French, and a double dose of the arrogance of both nationalities that they realised he meant it, and the deal got done. Too many people were owed too much in fees to let things drift on for another few months.

Henry spent two weeks in late January with Harriet Russell (née Sunetta Daunier), a long-standing girlfriend at her vineyard in South Africa, then Easter in England as usual with his mother and his two sons. On the Easter Monday, Henry, accompanied by Andrew and Peter, flew to spend two days with Sophie in Bamberg. They had been there just four weeks earlier for the joint funeral for Sophie's parents. Walter and Inga Lemberg had died within two weeks of each other. They weren't particularly elderly, aged 79 and 73 respectively, but in later years their health had failed them to such an extent that every day became a struggle, only fighting onwards because of their need to look after Sophie, whose condition had not changed.

Henry always found his visits to see Sophie painful for, whilst she still looked as lovely as ever and was ageing with grace and beauty, he could not help but get depressed by her mental state. However, on this occasion, sitting with Sophie by his side, he listened with great joy as their two sons chattered together about their lives. In these conversations, he could see that his two boys had a friendship which was loving, admiring and disapproving in equal measure. He knew that they would be there for each other long after he had left this life.

Henry returned to Moldova just before the Orthodox Church celebrated Easter. It was always later than the Church of Rome. It had been too cold to get on the land to do any serious work before then. Between New Year and Easter, Henry's architects had prepared a detailed, day by day, item by item, project plan as Henry was determined that all building projects should be completed before the winter came.

Henry arrived at the vineyard on the day that the excavators, diggers and bulldozers came on site. He was pleased to see that, during the winter, the four old cottages had been demolished whilst keeping the roof tiles, the wooden beams, lintels and doors so these could be incorporated as original features in the four larger replica houses which were going to be built.

Immediately the diggers and bulldozers started to clear the top soil to make the foundations for the road, and the excavator started digging the cellars, Henry knew they were never going to make their timetable. All the equipment brought on-site was 1950 - 1960 ex Russian military equipment. It was strong but prone to regular breakdown and needed to be repaired. It was to start a feature which was to run throughout the project. Henry began to buy and import new and good quality second-hand equipment from Western Europe to get his job done; even down to buying electrical generators and small powered hand tools such as saws, drills, and planes. His intention was to recoup his losses by selling the equipment when he stopped needing them.

While it was easy to buy earth moving equipment in Germany or Italy the job of getting it across so many borders and into Moldova was extremely challenging. It wasn't just about having the right paperwork. It involved the payment of cash bribes at each border crossing point. Nevertheless, it was the right move because, three weeks after Henry made the decision to buy his own equipment, he had the additional plant on-site, and very quickly, they caught up with the planned timetable.

Henry watched as long trenches were dug along the drive, many pipes of different widths, and in different colours, for the different services, were laid. The chalk, which was excavated to make the new cellars, was compacted into the ground to make the sub-base for a proper road which would take the heaviest of lorries. It was a fact that, of all the building work he had ever done, Henry loved building cellars, roads and driveways the most.

The only snag to getting the drive built was that there wasn't enough chalk to finish the job. Very rashly, Henry gave instructions that a hole for a swimming pool should be dug. Something he intended to do later because, as he had discovered in France, it could be an important part of a vineyard's irrigation system.

While the architects supervised the building of the cellar and the four homes, Henry's immediate focus was on the regeneration of the vineyards. He started by taking out half of the vines in the fields on the western and eastern sides of the vineyard, returning them to meadows. The villagers thought he was completely mad, but they didn't appreciate the economics. Tending vines costs money, and to have more grapes produced than the planned production capacity of his winery would simply be a waste of money.

An enthusiastic work force came in the morning, in the evenings and all day on any day when they were not working in the chicken factory. All those that worked enjoyed the extra pay they got from replacing the trellis systems holding the vines, or hoeing around them to recreate the gullies, and laying straw to protect the soil from leaching away when it rained. In fact, such was the volume of the extra labour that the transformation of the vineyard to something which, in later years Henry would be proud of, was very quickly done.

Henry started and ended the day in the fields, but during it he spent most of his time in the big barns at the back of the hamlet. He cleared them out, one at a time, so they were just a shell, four bare walls and a pitched roof. He organised concrete foundations to be poured under the wooden walls and the huge supporting wooden posts. He then laid a concrete floor. Once this was done, he called in the local fire brigade to fire their water jets inside the building to clear away 200 years of accumulated dirt. In the process, a few roof tiles were broken but these were quickly replaced. The buildings were then heavily insulated, plastic-coated plasterboard was fitted over the top, and finally, they were wired for electricity and plumbed for running water and a sewage system; to be ready when these were brought on site. Finally, laying ceramic tiles on the floor, Henry made his two barns as clean and hygienic for food preparation as the very best wineries anywhere in the world.

Henry ended every day exhausted but delighted. So much progress had been made that, in June, he placed an order for twenty new wine barrels. It was the first new order the village cooper had received in over ten years. He purchased two new narrow-wheelbase tractors with trailers to go between the vines and ordered the carpenter in the village to repair the existing grape collection boxes and make twenty new ones.

When Henry returned to France at the end of July, he had spent twice the amount he had intended but was way ahead of schedule. He was also certain he would recoup some of that cost when he came to sell the digging equipment when he no longer needed it.

Once again, Henry secretly took with him photocopies of Tania's exercise books and the essays she had written in the early mornings. Back at Château de Gressier, Henry had these typed up too, and in the cool of the evening, while sitting at his desk in the Gallery, he worked on editing them. He then integrated them comfortably into the first set of her work, making it a new revised whole. It gave Henry comfort to read her words, for in his head, he could hear Tania speak them, and as he did so, it brought her closer to him.

Chapter 32

Vienna September 1993

FOR SOME TIME, Henry felt he was a supernumerary at his own vineyards and wineries. At Château de Gressier Pierre Hilaire had everything under control. Likewise, at Château Raboût, where Thomas Cannen had run the estate long before Henry had bought it. It meant that, in the middle of September, Henry was content to return to Moldova, going via Bamberg to see Sophie. He wanted to supervise the harvest at Sophie Estate but, before that, he had promised Tania a few days holiday in Vienna; just the two of them.

Henry had never been to Vienna before, and it would be the first time that Tania had visited a country outside of the Eastern bloc. The city had been at the centre of the Austria-Hungry Empire and was steeped in the history of the Habsburg Monarchy, but at the end of their second day of their holiday, Henry had seen none of it. He had accompanied Tania on endless tours of the shops, comparison shopping; looking, choosing, differentiating and then often going back to buy the items she'd first seen. Henry began to feel resentful as it all seemed an excessive waste of time. No man would shop in this way, he thought. Not only was he being made to shop for hours on end, but the environment was always hot and noisy, with piped music played far too loudly, filling the vacuous minds of the shoppers. It was far from Henry's idea of fun. It seemed to him that he was acting as an endless cash machine. By the time they returned to the hotel in the late afternoon of the second day, Henry was fuming and Tania, feeling his reaction, was livid. By the time they got to the hotel room they both exploded with rage.

"Never," he said, "never ask me to come shopping again, as I won't."

"I'm not your wife, so it's what you have to do," said Tania matter-of-factly. "Without your ring, how else is our relationship judged?" she snapped back.

"Judged, by whom?" asked Henry, really surprised by the remark. "I hope it's not judged at all!"

"It's judged by others; my friends judge it. It's the way they judge the value you place on me."

"What have your friends got to do with us?" He paused, "and why are they making a value judgement about us?" he questioned angrily.

"They use it to judge the way you treat me. What I bring back shows them what I am worth to you. I'm an unmarried Moldovan girl, and these things are important when it comes to others judging us. They ask, is she getting the best for herself, or should she be with someone else?"

"You make it sound as though our relationship is a commercial bargain. It's as though this shopping is the price you're charging me for being here. Is it?"

"Look at you, you treat me as a sex machine," she retorted.

"Sex machine! Sex machine? I don't do anything of the sort – that was our little joke," he protested angrily. The accusation hurt him, for Henry had been careful to make sure their relationship was fully consensual.

"Do you think your salary is me paying you to sleep with me? Is that what you're thinking? Well, I am not. I am not doing anything of the sort. I am simply looking after you because ...." Henry couldn't find the words to explain how he felt.

"Well you can stop," said Tania angrily. "I didn't need you before and I don't need you now." There was real resentment in her tone. With that Tania got up and walked to the bathroom. She didn't want to be in the same room as him.

"Hang on," shouted Henry after her. "Are you saying the last two years has simply been a financial bargain to you? Well, let me tell you, it's not been that for me!"

Henry waited for a reply, but Tania said nothing. Upset by their row Henry moved to lie on the bed and he stared at the ceiling. He couldn't understand what was happening. How could she feel any resentment towards him?

In his tension, Henry noticed his mouth was dry, so he got up and selected a carton of orange juice from the fridge, turned on the television and tuned it to an English news channel. He went to sit in an armchair. His anger was still manifest when Tania returned to the bedroom and started to unpack her day's shopping, trying on everything she had bought. She started a monologue commenting on her purchases. "Perhaps too big, too small, perhaps she should have had a smaller size or bigger size. Should she change it tomorrow?"

Henry tried to show a disinterest as she wriggled into and out of jeans and tried on tops, but the graceful way she moved her exquisite body and waived her hair was too much to resist. He had to concede that she was one hell of an attractive woman.

Henry picked up one of the books Tania had bought to read. As he turned the pages, he could see where she had underlined passages and made notes in the margin, how he hated that. It destroyed a perfectly good book for others to read. Henry picked up the book he had bought on the Habsburgs and became absorbed in their story. Quietly he took the book back to the bed where he lay down to read, until his eyes closed, and he was asleep.

Tania sat in the chair close to where Henry was sleeping. She leant forward and examined his face. His deep breathing gave her a calmness which she had not felt earlier. It was time to leave him, she concluded. Henry was never going to make her his wife. She was always going to have to share him, and that was just not good enough. She deserved better. Serghei would marry her tomorrow and with that marriage came certainty. Oh how, she loved Henry, she thought. He had been a good man to her, but now she needed more. She knew that, for her son's sake, she had to stop being the mistress and plaything of a rich European. It was time to become the wife of her son's father.

Henry woke to see Tania gazing at him. Her eyes were full of water, and he could see the salt stains where the tears had fallen down her cheeks. She smiled, and in that one look Henry knew immediately what she had been thinking. Silently, he reached for her hand to come to him. Slowly, almost reluctantly, she joined him on the bed. They kissed and said sorry to each other. Not once had they argued about their relationship before and, knowing that this would be the last time they would share a bed, each was overgenerous in their lovemaking.

With those words of sex machine still ringing in his head, Henry gently turned Tania onto her stomach and secretly unfurled the condom he had been wearing. He kissed her gently on the back of her neck, and then, with her buttocks pressing firmly into his thighs, he entered her for the first time in the nakedness of his skin. He allowed his seeds to travel in search of creating a new life. He so wanted a part of him to be with her always; whatever happened, wherever she went.

In the evening, they dined in perfect harmony, walked the city and chattered just as old friends do, and when they went to bed that night, they lay side by side holding hands until they drifted off to sleep.

In the early morning, whilst Tania was sleeping on her side, Henry slowly and very gently wriggled up to lay close into her buttocks where, once again unsheathed, he slipped gently inside her. Within a few seconds, his mind was overtaken on sustaining, for as long as possible, a pulsating joy of release. As he lay in the afterglow, Henry wondered whether Tania would now be pregnant. At that very moment, he did not know what he thought of the idea. Whatever happened, he was satisfied that he had now branded her as his.

Chapter 33

Faterini Village Autumn 1993

ON THEIR RETURN from Vienna, Tania deliberately didn't ask Henry to 'join her for a shower.' Instead, she made it clear that, after they had eaten together in her apartment, she expected him to return to his. From now on she would keep their relationship professional. It was precisely how she approached the next day and their drive to Faterini Village.

At the entrance to his new estate were two new impressive walls built either side in a mix of local bricks and limestone blocks, just as Henry had ordered. However, in the middle of each wall was not the name Sophie Estate as Henry had expected. Instead, carved in wood, six feet long and two feet high, were the words 'St Sophia Estate.'

"I didn't dare tell them," said Tania apologetically when she stopped the car at the entrance so Henry could have a good look. "They're a present to you from the villagers," she added, wincing. "They've been carved by the local carpenter. They are all enormously proud of them, as they are to work here."

"Faith, Hope and Love," said Henry reading the words carved underneath the St Sophia Estate name.

"Yes, in both English and Moldovan. They're the names of St Sophia's three daughters," she explained.

"They're lovely," said Henry wistfully, knowing he had been defeated over the name, but he didn't mind as it had a nice ring to it. St. Sophia Estate sounded so much better in marketing terms, he told himself.

He had only been away seven weeks, but Henry was delighted to see the progress which had been made. The roof of his newly dug cellar had been completely covered over with either the four houses or with garden soil. The only thing which could be seen of the cellars were the deliberately narrow ramps of its entrance and exit, just wide enough for a forklift truck carrying a standard pallet or wine barrel.

The four houses were up; the roofs were on with the old tiles carefully blended in with the new. The old wooden beams and lintels had been reused above the windows and door apertures. Once the doors and windows were fitted, the buildings would be watertight. It was all ahead of schedule thanks to the extra skilled labour which was available in the village.

There was just one big snag. The electricity and clean drinking water, which was supposed to have been connected at the end of June, were still nowhere in sight.

Now it was nearing harvest time, each day at noon, Henry collected exactly three hundred berries from the top and bottom of the grape clusters, both sun exposed and sun shaded, on different sides of the rows and at different heights. The idea was to get as representative a sample of the whole vineyard as he could. He weighed them, and using a small hand press, the juice was extracted. It was passed through a fine muslin sieve, and the sugar and acid concentrations were measured. He did this day after day as he also very carefully watched the weather forecasts. When he was certain that sugar and pH levels were right, Henry ordered the harvest to begin.

It was at this point Efrim Cazac, the man whom Henry had met on his first day and had hired as his senior viticulturist, refused to obey Henry's order. It was too soon, he complained. "These are my fields, my vines, my grapes, my wine, not those of a Frenchman," he told his compatriots. "Whatever he does he cannot take the land with him. Look at the amount of money he has spent. When he goes he will leave it all behind. Do as I say and not the Frenchman," Cazac ordered his fellow workers.

Tania came out to St Sophia Estate immediately Henry had told her of the problems he'd had the day before. Within seconds she understood what was happening. She instantly recognised the destructive nature of the dissent Henry was facing. For too long, she had watched as the power of the ignorant had crushed reason and common-sense. It was steeped in the traditions of the Soviets. Like dry rot, unless it was tackled and cut out, she knew it would spread and destroy everything.

Within minutes of her arrival, Tania had ordered Cazac to go to the caravan, which Henry had brought on site as a temporary office. "Wait for me there," she instructed forcefully. She then called everyone she could find, including the junior viticulturist and the distiller together. She told them, in no uncertain terms, that she owned half the vineyard, she was Moldovan and was going nowhere. If they wanted jobs, and to be paid, then they had to support her and the Frenchman. If they didn't, they should leave now.

Tania then instructed the junior viticulturist and the distiller to come with her to the caravan. There, in front of Henry but without him knowing what was happening, she sacked Efrim Cazac. She did not do it on the grounds of him challenging Henry because that could be debated. Further, for her to fight his battles would make him appear weak. She fired him for failing to attend any of the English classes, contrary to the terms of his employment and for which he had been paid. She then ordered the two men who had come with her "to escort Mr Cazac off the premises and make sure he never returns."

"Why did you do that?" asked Henry as soon as he was told what had happened.

"The man's too old to understand the changes which are going on, she said. "He is fighting for a past which we can't return to."

"But you didn't ask me first," said Henry showing hurt.

"No, but it had to be dealt with swiftly," she answered. "But in any case, isn't that why I have fifty per cent of this business, so I can make these decisions for you?"

"But ...," protested Henry, conscious as to how their relationship had changed since they had got back from Vienna.

Before Henry could continue, Tania interjected. "Seriously, Henry," she said, "that man's an ignorant bully. He had to be taken out permanently, otherwise everything would have gone wrong forever."

That night at about 1am in the morning, a pile of wooden crates was stacked up underneath and around one of Henry's brand-new tractors and set on fire. The culprit was not identified but everyone knew who it was; the coincidence was too great.

In the morning, Henry and Tania called everyone who was on the Estate into the newly refurbished barn, including all the building contractors. Henry spoke. Tania translated.

"Yesterday Mr Efrim Cazac was dismissed for not attending any of the English classes which he was both contracted and paid to attend. To claim and be paid for something you are supposed to have done, but have not, is theft. It is stealing. It is gross misconduct, and that is why Mr Cazac was sacked. If anyone doesn't understand that, then they need to say so now!"

No one looked at Henry or Tania as she translated. They all looked at the floor.

"As you all now know, last night one of my tractors was deliberately set on fire," said Henry. "Be in no doubt, it was not an accident," he continued. "That tractor cost me over forty thousand dollars. I would like to accuse Mr Cazac of arson, but I cannot because I have no evidence. However, I have been in business too long to believe in coincidences!

Henry paused for breath and to clear his mind as to what he was going to say next.

"With two tractors working in the fields we would have been able to bring in the harvest in much shorter time. With only one, it is now going to take much longer. However, the value of the wine I get from the harvest will only be the same amount. Out of this money I cannot pay twice. I cannot pay for a new tractor and for you to work longer hours. I am sorry, but because of the fire I have to cut everyone's wage by ten lei an hour." Henry stopped talking again to allow everyone time to understand what he was saying.

"I will understand if you no longer want to work for me," he said, "but this problem is not of my making." Henry placed heavy emphasis on the word not. "Anyone who no longer wishes to work here needs to tell me straight away because I have to harvest now," he continued. "And if it is not you who's working in my fields, then I'll have to get people from elsewhere."

No one moved. They had each worked out how much extra money they were going to earn from the harvest, and to have none of it was not a proposition they wanted to contemplate.

Seeing no response, Tania decided to phrase the question the other way. "Who wants to stay here and work?" she asked.

Everyone held up their hands.

"There is one other issue which I think is connected," said Henry on the basis of a hunch. "The agreement with the village and with the district council is that St Sophia Estate is to be connected to the mains electricity and the water. I have agreed to pay for these connections, but they are not happening. I now think the burning of my tractor and the lack of these connections are all part of a long-term plan to see me gone off this land so you can have it back!"

There was a howl of protests.

"You may protest," said Henry "but I've received reports of such discussions being held amongst you," he lied.

Henry looked at every man and woman standing there directly in the eye. In turn, they all looked accusingly at Tania.

"Do not think that I didn't consider this possibility before I bought this land. Of course I did," he said. "Before I invested a single dollar, I decided that, if I was forced off the land by foul dealings or sabotage, then I would burn everything before I left; every house, every barn, every vine, every tree, every tractor, everything. Everywhere will become bare and desolate. I will leave a permanent scar on the landscape, which will last one thousand years. There will be nothing here for anyone to have, and certainly nothing which will give you an income! I promise you, if I am forced to go then, before I do, I will destroy it!"

Henry stood still for a moment. Someone put up their hand to ask a question. "There are no questions necessary," said Henry. "I have made a statement and that is all that I have to say except this."

Henry stepped down from the crate on which he had been speaking and moved closer to his staff to create a more intimate feeling. He worked hard to control his anger by softening his voice.

"You all see me as the owner, the boss," he said, "but I am more than just that". He spoke slowly, allowing Tania time to translate. "We

... you and me ... we are the custodians of this land for our lifetime. It was here before us and will be here after us. Neither you nor I can take it away. It's not like a car or a watch or a bicycle. It can't be moved. It has to stay here. Yes, I am the senior custodian, but only because it's my money. It means I get to make the decisions. Yes, it is unfair I get to make those decisions because undoubtedly they affect you, your lives and those of your family, but I say this - each of you are custodians too. If you think of this as our project - a project which is for the common good, then we will all have worthy and fulfilling lives amongst these vines, not just for our generation but for generations to come."

With that Henry turned on his heels and walked past the newly built houses, down through the vineyard to the river's edge. When he had both started and finished speaking, he was calm and purposeful. Now he was upset and furious. It was better he was by himself. It was Tania who answered the questions from a shaken group of individuals.

That evening there was another fire. This time it was Cazac's shed in Faterini village, and there was no question as to who set it on fire. Hearing what had happened, the village council had an early meeting without Mr Efrim Cazac being there. Its decisions were simple. Cazac had been voted off the village council. He no longer represented them. The burning of his shed was in reprisal for Cazac setting Henry's tractor on fire and, unless he paid $5,000 from the sale of his land to the council so they could pay this in compensation to Henry, then they would torch his whole house too. It was local justice Moldovan style. Naturally, Cazac chose to pay up, which he did the very next day. However, the loss of his money was nothing like the loss of Cazac's reputation for every day, until he died, he was shunned by everyone in the village, except the priest, who could not help but notice that Efrim Cazac no longer went to confession.

The next afternoon the new elected council chairman came to see Henry. He was one of the few from the village who did not work on St. Sophia Estate. He offered Henry his apologies for the damage done to his tractor and gave him Moldavian Lei worth exactly $5,000 in compensation, explaining that, whilst it was not enough, it was all the village could afford.

Henry accepted the money gracefully and mentioned the problems he'd had in getting connections to mains water and electricity. It would be sorted in two weeks, he was told. The newly elected council chairman proved to be as good as his word.

The next day, in recognition of the goodwill from the village, Tania announced that, because of the compensation payment Henry had received, the wage rates were going back up to the same level as before the fire. Peace was duly restored.

The harvest was a good one, but like Henry's Bordeaux wines of that year, the St. Sophia Estate's red and white wines turned out to be a disappointment. They were quite austere and lacked charm.

The brandy they produced was smooth and with a high alcohol content. Henry was not a brandy connoisseur, so he didn't know the exact taste he was seeking but likewise, to him, it seemed poor. However, the distiller was pleased, so Henry filled and laid down a modest five barrels of St Sophia Brandy in Moldovan oak casks. He would wait patiently to see whether, over the years, the tannin in the wood would do its work and improve the taste.

Henry left St. Sophia Estate and Moldova in early December to return to France. He was pleased with his years' work. There was only one problem and it was a big one. The mains water pressure was just enough to deliver water at ground level and that was assuming the chicken factory wasn't using a lot of water that day. But the pressure was not strong enough to get water from the ground floor level to a kitchen sink tap, let alone to the upstairs bathrooms.

The village council were sympathetic to Henry's plight but cleverly pointed out that their agreement only required them to make sure he was connected to the water grid and they had met their obligation to him. When Henry suggested pumping water from the mains to the hamlet, he was referred to an old rule book which showed this to be illegal. When Henry discussed his plight with his architect in Paris and Surveyor in London, he found similar rules existed in these countries too.

As Henry caught the aeroplane out of Kishinev in early December, he was very conscious that he had spent the best part of $400,000 to create a winery on a spot which had one of the best views in the world, but would be economically useless, and a complete waste of money, if there was no water.

Henry took the opportunity to fly to South Africa to spend time with Harriet Russell at New Found Estate just outside Paarl, before going to Bamberg to be with Sophie, and then back to England to spend Christmas with his mother, Andrew and Peter.

Henry shipped several bottles of St. Sophia's 1995 harvest to Château de Gressier. He wanted to analyse its chemistry properly as he used to do. Much later, Henry decided that the wines were not good enough to be sold under the St. Sophia's brand name. They would be emptied into the river.

For the third time, Henry took with him secret photocopies of Tania's exercise books which contained the essays she had written since June. He had peeked at her writing whilst copying them and thought it was sharper and more concise. He was looking forward to incorporating her new work into what she had already written.

Chapter 34

Kishinev January 1994

FOR SEVERAL DAYS Tania wondered how she was going to raise the subject with Serghei, but one evening, when they were on their own and Stelian was asleep in his bed, Tania turned down the television, which had been dominating the room. She sat beside him and, without saying a word, she showed him the positive results of a pregnancy testing kit.

"Are you sure, Serghei?" asked, recognising the white stick and knowing exactly what it meant.

"I've been feeling so sick in the morning, and my breasts are feeling heavier. So yes, I'm sure."

Serghei leaned forward, kissed her gently on the forehead, enfolded her arm in his, squeezed her hand and smiled. "When's the baby due?" he asked.

"I don't know," she said. "I haven't been to the doctors yet."

"But we can work it out from the date of your last period," he said enthusiastically.

"I don't remember when my last period was," she replied.

"Yes you do. You always pencil it in your diary," said Serghei. "I wonder whether it's a girl. We said we would like a girl. We should get married to celebrate," he added excitedly.

In all innocence, Tania fetched her diary, and together they counted back the weeks.

There was a sudden freeze in the atmosphere as they both realised Serghei could not be the father. Neither said anything as they counted back for a second time.

"It's not mine, is it?" said Serghei, both matter of factly and in a quiet voice. "It can't be. I wasn't here then. I was in Moscow all that time.

Tania said nothing, for she couldn't believe that the baby could be Henry's, for they never took risks. She wouldn't let him.

"You said," Serghei paused. "We agreed." He paused again. "You were going to end it with him."

"I did, I did," said Tania. There was desperation in her whispered voice. I have not been with him since Vienna. I promise you. I ended it then."

"He still paying you. I've seen your bank statements."

"I know, but that's only because I work for him, but this baby can't be his. I never let him have me that way. You are the only one who ...." Tania stopped mid-sentence. "I've always saved myself like that for you."

Serghei got up from the settee and started to pace the room. He said nothing as he marched the four paces from one wall to another and turned around. There was quiet purposeful agitation in his movements.

"Serghei, I must have the dates wrong," Tania suggested desperately. "There must be some dates I've missed out from my diary," but as she said this, she knew it was not true.

Serghei said nothing. He went into the bedroom and bathroom, where he gathered a few things which he placed into a holdall. He picked up his heavy winter coat which he threw over his shoulders, and without saying a word, he walked out of the door.

Tania got up to follow him but changed her mind. Instead, she moved to a chair and sat at the empty table where, just a few minutes before, they had enjoyed the chicken borscht she'd cooked, in the unspoken expectation that they were going to be together forever.

The muscles in Tania's face were so tight with fear that she couldn't cry. Inside, her heart was breaking in pain, for she genuinely loved both men and yet in choosing one, she had managed to lose them both. She cuddled her tummy and the baby she could not yet feel and promised that it would be the most loved and cherished person in the world.

Chapter 35

Kishinev Spring 1994

HENRY SPENT JANUARY and February at Château de Gressier bored and lonely. He phoned Tania almost every night. He knew nothing was going to progress at St. Sophia Estate until he returned at the end of March, but he just wanted to hear her voice and chatter.

As Henry discovered after selling his business, life without a purpose was meaningless, and he hated it. His solution was to work at his desk in the Gallery day after day, night after night, editing Tania's latest work into his earlier scripts of her writings. He found it much harder this time because she had covered several subjects three or four times with subtle differences, and he didn't want to lose the fine nuances of debate that she had brought to her latest work.

Once Henry had completed his work on the script, he gave a copy to his mother and Harriet to read and comment on. He also sent a copy to a professional editor to go through word by word, line by line. By the end of February, he had taken all their comments and incorporated them into what he thought was a final version. However, Henry lost his nerve as to its accuracy, so he sent it for one last edit with somebody entirely new. With those editor's changes made, Henry read through the script one last time, made a few further amendments and then ordered it to be printed, six copies to be leather-bound, and thirty copies in hardback. The leather copies he had embossed in gold with the words 'A Manifesto for a Modern Land, A Collection of Essays' by Anastasi (Tania) Alekseevna Plesca, edited by Henry Guégan.

Tania met Henry at Kishinev airport. Her news was obvious. She was pregnant, and there was a huge beam on her face to show her delight. There was never the question in Henry's mind that he wasn't the father. He grabbed Tania tightly and swung her around, thrilled by the news.

Tania felt instant relief at seeing Henry's joy. Her fears that he would say it was not his had kept her awake night after night with a feeling of sickness in her stomach, but with Henry's instant acceptance, the false smile she had presented when she first saw him was replaced with a genuine smile and sobs of relief.

"Why didn't you say?" he asked.

"I wanted you to be here to tell you," she said.

"When?" he asked.

"July," she replied.

"Where's Stelian?" asked Henry, referring to Tania's son, as they walked to her car.

"Serghei is looking after him," she said.

"What does Serghei say about you being pregnant?" Henry asked.

"He's not happy," she admitted. "I don't know why. I think it's made him realise that he and I could never be together."

"Do you think it's a boy or a girl?" asked Henry as Tania drove out of the airport car park.

"I don't know. I really don't mind."

"What do you think?" he asked.

"I don't know. If I had to guess, I'd say a girl. What do you think Andrew and Peter will say when they learn you are going to be a father again?" asked Tania.

"Erm," said Henry, not knowing the answer to that question.

Once Henry had unpacked, he left his apartment and crossed the hall to join Tania. He took a leather-bound copy of 'A Manifesto for a Modern Land' in his hand to give her as a gift. Suddenly, he felt incredibly nervous about giving her a book of her work. He had prepared it in secret. He was now worried that she might see it as an invasion of her privacy.

"I have a present for you," he said cautiously. "I've had your essays made into a book."

Tania looked at him puzzled, then at the leather-bound book and then at the pages inside. It was when she started to read the printed page that she recognised her words. She turned the pages rapidly. Page after page, she found paragraphs she could remember writing. "Why?" asked Tania, totally confused.

"I thought it was exceptionally good writing. Not to be hidden in an old exercise book or lost," he said apologetically. "I hope you don't mind?"

"It's lovely, thank you," she said, rather bewildered.

"May I ask, why did you write in English?" asked Henry.

"It was the phrases people used. The way they spoke. All I did was write down what I heard."

"You did more than that. When you were writing, which language did you think in?

"Both," she replied as the doorbell rang.

It was Serghei who had been looking after Stelian while Tania collected Henry. Stelian was now nineteen months old and most definitely a toddler, as he proved soon after Tania had cuddled her son and put him down on the settee.

"You now know?" said Serghei bitterly, as he pointed to Tania.

"Yes," said Henry. "It's lovely news. It really is. I'm thrilled."

"Will you get married?" Serghei asked pointedly.

"I'm already married," said Henry defensively.

"You could get a divorce," commented Serghei harshly as though he were her father, her protector.

Tania listened anxiously, but Henry didn't respond. Instead, he gave Serghei two leather-bound copies of Tania's book. "I've brought this for you and a copy for Stelian," he said. "It's of Tania's writing," he added.

Serghei took the book, moved to the chair he always sat in. He browsed at first, flicking the pages, doing the same as Tania had done, reading and recognising in the paragraphs what had been said in their group meetings. Serghei then turned to the front and started to read in earnest; so focused was his concentration that he heard nothing else of what was going on around him.

Chapter 36

St. Sophia Estate Spring 1994

TANIA HAD KEPT Henry briefed on what had been happening at St. Sophia Estate, but nothing she said prepared him for the chaos he found. It looked as though all the work of the previous year had been undone as there were holes and piles of earth and chalk stacked up everywhere some appearing to reach the height of the bedroom windows.

The solution to the water pressure problem had proven to be complex and expensive. It involved the well in the middle of the large courtyard between the new houses and the old barns, being dismantled to a depth of over fifteen metres until they were deep in the chalk. It was then relined with huge concrete collars and rebuilt. Henry insisted that it needed to be put back exactly as it was but with one difference. There would be a clear thick laminated glass plate on top to stop anyone from falling in. Next to the well, an underground water tank was constructed. It was sealed to make it water, dust and animal proof. Henry would swear it was big enough to float a battleship. The idea was that the mains water would feed into the huge tank from where it would be pumped around the rest of the hamlet. The drinking water in the well would automatically be pumped into the underground tank if there was not enough water coming from the mains. It was as neat, foolproof and gold-plated a solution as the architects could devise.

The worst part of the whole operation was dealing with the soakaways and septic tanks albeit the latter had not yet been used. These all needed to be moved a long way from the houses and further down the hill so that there was no risk of contaminating the water in the well.

Henry could find three saving graces out of the mess he was in. The first was modest. He hadn't sold his excavating and earth moving equipment, so it was already on-site to deal with this huge groundworks project. The second was that the chalk provided the foundations for the new roadways he wanted built along the fields' edges and running down to the river. Thirdly, in the courtyard, under a couple of inches of accumulated mud, there was a mosaic of cobblestones laid in a circular pattern around the well. The architect, knowing Henry's passion for preserving as much of the history as was feasible, made sure that all the brick blocks were lifted, cleaned and prepared, ready for relaying once all the groundworks had been done.

Just as Henry was beginning to think that his water issue and sewage problems had been solved, he realised the mains electricity supply coming into Faterini Village was completely unreliable. It was such a common feature of Moldovan life that no one seemed to notice when it went on or off. Henry found that it was all part of the government's policy of reducing the amount of gas it imported. During the day, and particularly in the summer months, they would switch off the electricity supply to domestic areas allowing the factories to keep working. Faterini Village was in a residential area and was therefore constantly having its power turned off, particularly when it was sweltering hot and Henry was desperate for the air-conditioning units he'd installed in the houses and the barns to work.

Henry knew that the solution would involve self-generation, certainly by diesel oil and possibly by solar and wind but, until the water issues were solved, it was not something he was prepared to commit to. What he did do, while the groundworks people were on-site and before the cobblestones were re-laid, he reconfigured the electrical supply system feeding all the premises around the Hamlet to a central distribution point. It meant that one day, standby generators could be installed, which would automatically switch on if there was a power cut.

The good news was that all the houses had been completed with identical kitchens and bathrooms. Once furnished and water was available, they could be occupied. Tania had moved their office out of the caravan and into the first house, where one room was used by the accountant, who Tania had recruited on Henry's behalf. Just as had happened when he first started in business, more money was going out than coming in. Back then, it had been thanks to a commercially astute accountant that had stopped Henry from going bankrupt.

It wasn't just controlling the expenditure at St. Sophia that Henry was worried about. He had also spent another winter buying equipment to lease to other Moldovan wineries on the same basis as previous years, taking capital and interest payments in the form of future bottles of wine.

Getting hold of Henry's payment in barrels of wine for the 1993 harvests had been something that Henry had always meant to do, but now, with an accountant on board, he had someone who could enforce payment. But instead of going to Cricova, the wine went straight into storage at his newly constructed cellars on the St. Sophia's Estate.

It was a fact that, as soon as he saw them, Henry detested the St. Sophia Estate cellars. The cellars at Château de Gressier and Château Rabôut were made from brick, with roofs of curved arches. They carried with them the smell of hundreds of years of damp, oak barrels and the aroma of wine which had leached into the atmosphere. Each had a romance which suited the wine which was being held there. The cellars at St. Sophia Estate were rigid, cold and heartless with a horrible smell of concrete dust. He thought them reminiscent of a Gulag prison block and hated them. He thought everyone else would feel the same

Just as Henry had done with the huge sellers he had built in Folkestone, he sealed the walls, floor and ceiling to stop the dust swirling around and getting into people's lungs. He bought in two large dehumidifiers to get the excess damp out of the concrete, down to an ideal 65%. Below this level, the alcohol in the barrels would be diluted which would affect the taste he wanted to achieve. It was then, in a pique of total craziness, and knowing that they would hardly ever be seen, that Henry commissioned a local artist to paint a series of large murals of people working both in the vineyards and in winemaking on the concrete walls. Once the paintings were dry, he had piles of fresh sawdust scattered around the floor. Finally, he insisted that seven strategically placed large church candles should be alight all the time, so as to create a warmer atmosphere and to get the air gently moving.

In fact, many times, in the spring and summer of 1994, Henry felt like giving up on the whole St. Sophia's Estate redevelopment project. There was just one thing that kept him going. His eldest son Andrew was going to inherit Château de Gressier and his second son, Peter, was going to inherit Château Rabôut. He was now determined that his baby by Tania was going to inherit St. Sophia Estate, and it was going to be just as good as the other two.

Chapter 37

Kishinev June 1994

ON 16TH JUNE 1994, everyone gathered in Tania's flat, just as the discussion group had done on every Thursday evening during term time since the shooting at the nightclub. However, tonight's agenda was different. There would be no discussion. The message had gone around the group that they were going to watch a programme on national television, written and researched by Serghei and Evelina, filmed and edited by Serghei, with Evelina as the presenter. It was a true joint venture between the two of them and had been carried out in total secrecy. Only when the film had been completed had they approached and sold it to Moldova's national television channel, a process undoubtedly aided by Evelina's sex appeal.

No one knew what the programme was about, but the excitement in Tania's apartment was such that Stelian could not get to sleep, so he sat on Serghei's lap, not knowing that his father was about to become a national hero.

"Congratulations Daddy," said Evelina to Henry as she sat down next to him.

"I know, it's lovely, isn't it?" he replied with a big grin, as Tania came and sat on the other side of him.

Then, for the next fifty minutes, everyone watched in almost complete silence, the only sound being Tania and Evelina whispering to Henry to let him know what was going on until the advertising breaks came when everyone erupted with questions. The breaks were carefully edited to leave the watcher in frightened suspense, petrified for Evelina's safety.

Evelina and Serghei had produced a television programme exposing the story of homes being fraudulently stolen with the aid of corrupt Notary Publics. It included Notary Tigran Tarvel, who had been involved in the theft of Evelina's father's home. It was tough, brave and ruthless investigative journalism of the highest order. It contained the most wonderful scenes of entrapment by secret filming. When the credits rolled, there was a genuine and heartfelt round of applause and cheers of congratulations from everyone in the room.

"It will be in tomorrow's newspapers," said Evelina. "We sold the story to them as well, so it will get a double exposé. They'll get hit twice," she added with real vengeance in her voice.

"Aren't you now in real danger?" came a voice from one of their number.

"Yes," said Serghei.

"Tarvel's the notary that Costin Stanescu uses on all his transactions," explained Evelina.

"The President's son?" asked a voice, seeking to clarify.

"Yes," replied Serghei, continuing the double act between them. "We decided it was too dangerous to report that relationship. Also, neither of the National Networks would have shown it. We thought it best just to stop these two men by putting them out of business and hopefully in jail."

There was a murmur of approval for they were right. Such was the grip of the President on the two national broadcasters that nothing was going to be shown which criticised Stanescu or his son.

"We think a lot of families who were defrauded will petition the courts to have every document notarised by these two publicly re-examined. That will be the time to release the relationship between Costin and Tarvel.

"We need to go," said Evelina, no more than ten minutes after the programme had ended. "Serghei's driving me to Bucharest. I am catching a plane from there to spend a few weeks in Cyprus. I think I'll be safer there. At least until all this dies down," she explained.

While Evelina and Serghei were receiving their congratulations and saying goodbye, Henry went to his apartment and gathered up a pile of the books he'd had printed. He couldn't think of a better time to hand them out.

"Some aeroplane reading for you," said Henry as he handed Evelina the last leather-bound copy of A Manifesto for a Modern Land.

"I am really very proud of you," said Henry. "Call me as soon as you're back. No, call me as soon as you've got to Cyprus."

While Henry and Evelina were having a friendly conversation in the hall, in the kitchen, behind closed doors, Tania was in an animated discussion with Serghei.

"Why didn't you tell me?" she protested, angry that she had learnt, at the same time as everyone else, what he had been doing for the last few months.

"Isn't it obvious," he replied, looking at her swollen tummy. "You chose him …."

"I didn't choose," snapped Tania before Serghie had completed his sentence. "It just happened. Like with you, it just happened."

"Well a lot has just happened, hasn't it," Serghie retorted.

"Are you and Evelina …?"

"No," answered Serghei. "We've managed to keep our relationship professional," he added, emphasising the words managed and professional to have a dig.

"What about your son?" Tania scolded. "What you've done is dangerous!"

"Don't you understand, I did it for him. Night after night, we've discussed what's wrong, well, this time I could do something about it, … and I did," he added as he opened the kitchen door and left.

That night, with Serghei living back at his mother's and Henry alone in his apartment, Tania picked Stelian up from his cot, where he was sleeping, and carried him into her bed. With Serghei being so physically and emotionally distant, she needed to have their son by her side.

Those few weeks when Serghei had lived with her, just before she found she was pregnant again, had been an especially happy time. They had been a proper family, she thought, and now it was gone.

She remembered the time when she fell pregnant with Serghei's baby. She was sure she didn't love him then, but since he had been such a good father and so loving and kind towards her that an emotional bond had been created between them. It was not the kind of lustful all-consuming love that she first shared with Henry. Her relationship with Serghei was much deeper than that. It was like that of a fellow kinsman on a life's journey; a journey to be shared. There was no sharing of Henry's life. You had to be in it on his terms or not at all. The two men were quite different.

A cloud of total despair descended over Tania as she realised that she couldn't choose between the two men who were the fathers to her children. Gentle, thoughtful, loving, kind, young and poor, versus exciting, determined, powerful, rich and old. It was the old story, she thought, having to choose between the good man and the bad. But she knew she couldn't choose. She wanted them, no she needed them, both.

Chapter 38

England and France July 1994

WITH TANIA'S BABY due in July, Henry had been planning on not going to England or France in the summer. It would have been only the third time he had not been at the Château de Gressier's harvest since he was five years old. However, his plans changed rapidly when he got a text message from his son Andrew to say that his mother was in hospital, very poorly and he needed to come home.

Henry dropped everything. He caught the last plane from Kishinev into Berlin where he had a few hours stop over before catching the first flight into London in the morning. He was on his way to the local hospital in Welwyn Garden City when Andrew texted him to tell him his mother had been transferred to the Royal Free Hospital in London.

Victoria had been fit and healthy all her life but, said her friends later, for a few weeks before her death, she had started to complain about headaches. She struggled through each day, not wanting to let anyone down. She got up, as usual, to go to the hospice, where she worked three days a week as a volunteer fundraiser. The moment Victoria had parked her car in the hospital car park, she had collapsed unconscious inside. It was the car park ticket inspector who discovered her, and within minutes she was admitted as an emergency into the hospital, which was only hundreds of yards away.

X-rays showed that Victoria had a complex brain tumour. It was why she was transferred to the Royal Free Hospital. That night, Victoria had an emergency operation to remove the tumour. It went on into the early hours of the morning.

Andrew and Peter were sitting by Victoria's side when Henry arrived. She had come out of theatre, but a rapid fall in blood pressure suggested she was suffering from a post-operative haemorrhage. They were preparing to take her back into theatre for a second time.

It was late afternoon by the time Victoria was back in the intensive care unit connected to a series of life support machines and monitoring devices. In the early evening, with Henry, Andrew and Peter by her side, Victoria died. She was just seventy-one. Her heart had just stopped pumping, and the three of them just knew that she would not want to be resuscitated. Victoria had never regained consciousness.

Henry watched as his mother's soul left her body. With one hand covering his face and eyes, he gave himself permission to cry. He suddenly felt a heart-breaking loneliness and a tremendous sense of guilt. All her life, she had done so much for him, and he had done so little for her.

Henry was devastated by his mother's death, and for a long time, he found the whole grieving process hard to deal with. He would describe it as an internal fight between his logical brain and emotional brain with, far too often, the latter winning. It left him in a state of exhausted lethargy, finding it impossible to think about anything else but his mother, her death, and his eventual demise.

Andrew and Peter were far more stoical, although Peter, being the artist, was the more emotional of the two of them. To all intents and purposes, following Sophie's illness, Victoria had been their surrogate mother. It was she who had bought them up, looked after them and given them a quality of life that was enviable. But it was in their sibling relationship that each of Henry's boys found the support they needed in their grandmother's death.

That night, the three of them went back to Victoria's home in Hertford. It was the one place all three of them called home, for it still had the beds they slept in when they were growing up and when they visited. Without Victoria being there, the house felt empty. It no longer seemed a home.

Immediately they walked through the front door, it was obvious that something had been wrong. Very unusually for Victoria, the house was unkempt. It had never been like that before. If anyone of them had seen it, they would instinctively have known that she had not been managing and was unwell.

Each of them felt uncomfortable seeing the house in that state and so, without anyone saying anything to anyone else, the three men started to tidy up, doing the washing-up, hoovering and putting everything in its place.

With pizza ordered for supper, they started turning the pages on Victoria's photograph album and watching old cine films and videos of their growing up.

For the first time, Henry told his sons about Victoria and his German pilot father. They listened attentively as he told them about her twin brother Victor, and how they were both given gold and diamond pocket watches by their grandfather when they were born. They already knew that had Victor drowned in the river at Château de Gressier when he was young because it had been impressed on them many times how dangerous the river was. They were told how Victoria had given Victor's watch to Henry's father as a token of her love and in the expectation that he would return with it after the war ended. He never did. Henry stressed the significance of Victor's watch to the family and how it might lead to his father being discovered. Just as Henry's mother and grandmother had avoided discussions on their family, so had Henry. He had never spoken to his boys in this way before.

This was a time when Henry could have told his sons he was going to be a father again; they were going to have a half-brother or half-sister, but he didn't. He couldn't do it. Somehow it didn't seem right to share what he thought was good news at the same time as they were grieving over bad. The moment was lost and the subject of Andrew and Peter having a half-sibling was never raised with them.

There was never any discussion, because it had been her lifelong wish; Victoria was going to be buried in the same plot in the churchyard at Latoire Village as her twin brother. Ever since Victor's death at the age of eight, Victoria had never been truly at peace. With the threadbare remnants of Victor's pillowcase nestling close to her face, where it had lain every night since his death, brother and sister would, once again, lie side by side for the rest of eternity.

Tania and Henry's baby was born on the day of Victoria's funeral. Henry had promised Tania faithfully he would be there, but he was not. Instead, he heard of his daughter's birth via a text message as he was walking in a crowd back to Château de Gressier after the funeral service. He wanted to scream and shout in delight, but instead, both worried and embarrassed, he said nothing.

Standing outside the maternity room, as Henry's daughter was born, was Heidi, Tania's mother, and Serghei, who had rushed Tania to hospital. It was not lost on Henry that it was Serghei who sent him the text telling of the birth of his daughter.

That night, after the guests had left, Henry took his sons into the library in the Cellars side of Château de Gressier. For the first time, they discussed the importance of the diaries that had been written by the women of Château de Gressier and most recently by him. Some parts had been written by people he never knew. Some were by his grandmother, Juliette, other parts written by Sophie and Victoria. He told them the golden rules of diary writing as laid down by his grandmother. Only tell the truth as you perceive it to be. Never lie, and if you find you are wrong, the correction is recorded on the date of the discovery. You never go back and amend. The two boys only took a cursory interest in the content of the diaries, but both would remember the rules.

Henry brought down his mother's gold pocket watch engraved with the word 'Victoria' from his desk in the Gallery where it was safely kept. "We're looking for this one's twin," he said to them earnestly. "It's engraved Victor and it's out there somewhere. We'll find it one day, and when we do, we'll find my father."

"I have to go," he told them a little while later as a taxi pulled up on the gravel outside. "I have a crisis in Moldova."

"Now?" protested his sons in unison.

"Yeh, I'm taking a taxi to Charles de Gaulle airport so I can catch a plane from there first thing in the morning."

They kissed and hugged each other fondly goodbye, and Henry promised to phone.

"Papa's mad privatisation programme," said Andrew to Peter, neither knowing the double life their father had created for himself there.

As Henry travelled, he thought of names for his daughter. He thought of calling her after his mother, but somehow, it didn't seem appropriate given the sadness in her life. No, he was certain that she should be named after his grandmother Juliette. She'd had a fair share of unhappiness too, but Henry had always seen her as positive, optimistic, and indefatigable.

Without even seeing his daughter, Juliette Plesca Guégan had been named.

Chapter 39

Kishinev July 1994

"OH MY GOD, she's beautiful," said Henry, on seeing his daughter for the very first time.

"I'm sorry I wasn't here," he said to Tania. "I really am."

"I understand," she said smiling. The joy of having a daughter outweighed anything which Henry might or might not have done, and it certainly outweighed the discomfort she was feeling throughout her body. Importantly, she really did understand.

"How did it go?" Tania asked

"More importantly, how did it go for you?" said Henry.

"Much quicker this time, only three hours, and the funeral?"

"That was okay, sad, but okay," said Henry. "At least she's with her brother now, so she'll be happy."

Henry looked down at his little daughter, who was nestled in her mother's arms, and studied her squidgy, wrinkly face, which was relaxed and expressionless as she slept.

"I'd like to suggest a name for her," he said. "It is my grandmother's name, Juliette."

"Juliette, Juliette," said Tania, savouring the word. She pulled her daughter up closer and studied her face. Tears swelled into her eyes as a flood of emotions surged wildly through both her mind and her body.

"Hello, Yulia," she said. "Privet Pape," and then added, "say hello to daddy."

"Hello Yulia," said Henry willingly accepting Tania's shortened version.

"I'd like you to wear this," said Henry handing Tania a small jewellery box. It contained a ring with a large central diamond, with smaller diamonds clustered all around. It was the prettiest and most expensive ring that Henry could buy from the jewellery shop in the transit lounge at Vienna airport.

"It's beautiful," said Tania, that's really beautiful. It was unquestionably the most stunning of rings.

Henry reached across and kissed Tania very gently on the lips. He took the ring out of its box and moved it towards her right hand. She didn't offer her wedding finger as he expected. Instead, she offered the same finger on the other hand. Confused, he gently slipped it on.

Tania held her hand up to the light and moved it about as she studied the diamonds and their sparkle. "I'll only wear it on special occasions," she said. "It's too good to wear all the time." In her mind, she was thinking about Serghei. She knew it would hurt him if he saw her wear it, and she couldn't, wouldn't hurt him.

Chapter 40

Kishinev July to December 1994

THE TIME BETWEEN Yulia being born in July and Henry leaving to spend Christmas at Château de Gressier went quickly.

Tania was focused entirely on her two children.

All the building work at St. Sophia Estate had been completed, and everything was working well. All the digging and excavating equipment had been sold to the man who did all the groundworks for just a fraction less than Henry had paid for them.

The quality of the 1994 harvest had been better than the year before, albeit Henry lost a lot of grapes in a series of violent thunderstorms. Pierre Hilaire and Thomas Cannen came from Bordeaux to do an audit of St Sophia's winemaking processes. They spotted some areas where oxidisation might have got into the process and damaged the wine. They also suggested ways of increasing the phenolic compounds by adjusting the maceration times and temperature.

Henry had cautiously ordered only 100 oak barrels, far fewer than he should have done given the quantity of juice which the land had produced. Once full these were stored in the cellar at St. Sophia. Everything was ready so that next year, in the second barn, Henry could install a micro-bottling plant. Just as he did at his two wine estates in France, Henry wanted to bottle and case the St. Sophia Estate's red and white wines so that he controlled the whole process from the field to the customer.

As soon as the harvest was in, Henry ordered miles of hedgerows to be planted to give a clear boundary to his land and to create smaller fields. He did this to protect his parched sunburnt soil from being blown away in the summer winds. The villagers thought him mad, but automated hedge cutters had not yet made their way onto the market in Moldova. In the distant fields on either side of the estate, where he had dug up the vines, Henry planted five rows of peach and apricot fruit trees in a straight line running from the top of the hill down to the river. Again, these were planted to help protect the soil from wind erosion, but also on the whim that, one day, he might make peach and apricot based liqueurs using the copper still he had acquired with the hamlet.

As Christmas came on the horizon, Henry was confident that, in St. Sophia Estate, he had created the most modern, up-to-date winery in Moldova. Everything was set fair for the years ahead. One day, Yulia would inherit a vineyard and winery she would be proud of.

Chapter 41

Kishinev Winter 1994 - 1995

"HAVE YOU SEEN this?" demanded the fourth or fifth arrival as she excitedly waved a book in the air. The woman had come to Tania's apartment for the last discussion group meeting before Christmas. As everyone said their hello's, they paid little attention to what was agitating her. It was seconds later, when Evelina and Sergei, who arrived together, started to angrily wave the same book, that Tania and Henry took any notice.

The book they were waving was the Moldovan translation of 'A Manifesto for a Modern Land'. Without Tania's knowledge or consent, it was now being sold throughout the country under the title: 'A Manifesto for Moldova. The book was not advertised, but people heard of it by word of mouth and were going into bookshops and ordering a copy. For weeks it had been an open secret amongst those who considered themselves part of the intellectual class, but the day before, Moldova's leading weekly cultural publication, Literatura şi Arta, had published a favourable review of Tania's work, which was how Evelina, Serghei and others had heard about it.

"A blueprint for government" and "pragmatic politics" was some of the ways Literatura şi Arta described the book. The only criticism they made was: "Far too often Ms Plesca debates a subject and decides the answer is found in moderation. It means her solutions are not always as clear as they otherwise might be." However, it was her essays on dealing with corruption that won Tania their praise. "The one area where Ms Plesca does not advocate moderation is on the matter of corruption," they wrote. "If this government were serious about tackling corruption then it would do exactly as Ms Plesca advocates."

It was very soon afterwards that Tania, as an author with a book in the Moldovan list of top ten non-fiction sales, found herself something of a media celebrity. She was surprised to find invitation after invitation to join discussion panels on the radio and television. Her beauty, grace and poise radiated through the television screen, and her soft voice had a calming resonance which took the wind out of the sails of any aggressive opponent. She didn't preach nor did she argue. Instead, she spoke for a balanced, compassionate and common-sense approach to every problem.

It was as a result of one of these invitations that Tania joined a radio discussion on euthanasia. During the debate, she vacillated between the sanctity of life and the freedom of the individual to choose. Eventually, Tania admitted she didn't know which side of the argument she favoured because it depended on the circumstances where common sense would dictate the most sensible approach.

"It's very strange for a potential presidential candidate not to know what they think on any subject," said the lady interviewer, tartly.

Tania was thrown. "I'm not," she said, "a potential presidential candidate."

"But you wrote a book called A Manifesto for Moldova. Are you saying that you wrote this without political ambition?"

"Yes," said Tania. "I wrote a series of essays after debating the issues with my friends so I could work out what I thought. To me, they're an essay of middle-ground common sense, nothing more. A friend made them into a book as a present for me and a few others who were involved in those debates."

"Then, why are they called A Manifesto for Moldova?"

"They were originally called A Manifesto for a Modern Land; that's what my friend called them. It is what he thought they were," she said. "It's the publisher who changed the name. Please understand, I did not authorise the publication of this book. The copyright has been stolen from me, and the publisher is making a lot of money from my hard work. At the moment, I am getting nothing from the sale of this book, but I intend to rectify that. It will be interesting to see what the Moldovan Court does. It will be a real test of their impartiality," she said, laying down the gauntlet.

Tania's most impressive interview was the one conducted by Evelina, with Serghei behind the camera and doing the editing. It would also be one of her longest.

"It will help your book sales," said Evelina, forgetting that Tania was getting nothing for her books. When this unfortunate fact was pointed out, and ever being a saleswoman, Evelina argued that Tania should do the interview with her to help her court case. Above all, she knew one of the TV channels would pay Serghei and her handsomely for the interview. It was not a fee Evelina was prepared to miss. Further, the idea of Tania being a future presidential candidate was starting to germinate as a possibility in Serghei's mind.

The filming was done in Tania's flat; in her great-grandmother's bedroom to be precise. It was deliberately made to look like every other family home in Moldova, with children's toys lying around; presidential looking, it was definitely not.

"Tell me about your family's history," said Evelina, as her opening question after making an introductory segment.

"We can trace our family history back over 400 years," said Tania. "The family's name was then Donici-Solokov. We've always lived in Moldova, but members have married into the family from Russia, Romania, even England. The family once owned large farms on either side of the Dniester River, a famous glassworks, and the first steam-powered mill in Moldova. The land was confiscated by the Communist Party and aggregated into collective farms, and the businesses were lost in the Revolution." Tania took care not to mention any words of sadness or regret.

"I think you told me that your family lost everything in the Great War," said Evelina as her prompt into the next part of their agreed interview.

"Yes, that's right," said Tania. "Like a lot of other families. The only possession my grandmother and great grandmother had at the end of the war was the bed in this room. They would sleep in it together. It's the bed my mother was born on. It was pulled out from Kishinev's rubble. It's why it is here. It was the start of making this the family home."

"Wasn't one of your relatives a partisan?" asked Evelina, gracefully moving into the next chosen segment.

"Yes," said Tania. "My great-grandmother, Brigita Solokov, lived here in this apartment. She was part of the resistance and was made a Hero of the Soviet Union. She was a markswoman who fought against the Germans when they occupied Kishinev. She also worked disrupting their supply lines. One of the things she did was to act as a decoy to kidnap their soldiers so they could be killed out of sight. If a soldier disappeared, then it could be that they'd deserted. If a body were found, then the Germans would take reprisals against the local population, killing twenty, maybe fifty people. But each kidnapped soldier weakened their army and without cost to ours. The campaign of harassment meant that the German's soldiers had to do everything in two's; one to do the job and the other to stand guard. She also set up and ran a field hospital during the Battle of the River Prut. It was where my grandmother served as a nurse before joining the Russian army and travelling with them as far as Belgrade."

"Do you consider yourself Moldovan, Russian or Romanian?" asked Evelina. "Where do your national loyalties lay?"

"We are a country of mixed heritage," said Tania. "Like many Moldovan families, my heritage is mixed. I think it is best to identify with the people around you. Russia is a long way away. Moldova is here. I speak both Russian and Moldavan. I like to respect both cultures, both heritages."

"But you're avoiding the question. Do you consider yourself a Moldavan allied to Russia or a Moldovan allied to Romania and the wider Europe?" challenged Evelina.

"I consider myself Moldovan," said Tania firmly. "I believe Moldova should be a free and independent country, tied to no-one, friends with all. We should not favour one side or the other on historical or cultural grounds. We should not choose between Russia and the European Union but seek to work with both," said Tania. Henry's script, used at his meeting with Stanescu, had gone straight into Tania's writing, and now it was being repeated, almost word for word, in this television interview.

Time and time again, Evelina challenged Tania to choose. Surely, it's better to choose the democratic rules-based system of Europe rather than the oligarchy system operated by Russia? What happens when these come into conflict? Isn't membership of the European Union the best way to protect our country against the old empirical ambitions of Russia? Tania answered every question thoroughly, and in accordance with her essays. It was preparation work rarely done by any politician, let alone a nascent one.

Serghei was thrilled. In those few questions, Tania's potential as an international stateswoman was there for all to see.

"In your book 'A Manifesto for a Modern Land', you write a large amount about corruption and how to solve it. It's a strong theme throughout the book. Why's that?" asked Evelina.

"Corruption kills. It kills the people who have been wrongly jailed. It kills the people who happen to be in a building when it collapses on them because corruption bought the permissions the owners of the building needed to break our safety laws. It kills when people can't escape a building on fire because the builders paid for a fire certificate certifying that the building was fire compliant when no fire escape had ever been built," said Tania, referring to a couple of specific and well publicised cases. "In short, corruption kills. It kills people and it kills hope, and when enough hope has been lost and individuals killed then it ends up killing the nation itself. You cannot be proud of being a member of a corrupt society. It destroys the soul of the nation and makes each one of us who pays ten lei to a traffic cop a lesser person as a result."

"You admit to bribing traffic cops?" asked Evelina.

"I admit nothing of the sort but show me a driver in Kishinev who says he hasn't paid a bribe to a traffic policeman and I will show you a liar .... or an incredibly lucky man," replied Tania, realising she had just dodged an interviewer's bullet.

Over the remaining ten minutes of the interview, Tania spoke lucidly about corruption and the string of policies which had to be introduced if it was to be eradicated. "One piece of anti-corruption law is mere tokenism," she argued. "To defeat corruption there has to be a whole legislative programme which would bring about a complete culture change, from top to bottom."

By the time Serghei had finished editing Tania's interview and it had been broadcast, she was, in everyone else's eyes, a potential Presidential candidate. The only trouble was that she didn't see it herself. In her eyes she was a mother first; that's what she was, and that's what she wanted to be.

Chapter 42

Kishinev Spring 1995

HAD ANYONE TOLD Tania the extent to which her life was going to be changed by the publication of 'A Manifesto for Moldova', she would not have believed them.

Following the broadcast of her interview by Evelina, Tania was invited to write a weekly column for Literatura şi Arta, for which she was paid handsomely. She also appeared regularly on radio and television. The moderate way Tania expressed herself made her an acceptable guest to producers and directors, who feared that anyone more controversial would put at risk their jobs as the television and radio channels were still government-controlled.

Tania's out of court settlement with the publisher of 'A Manifesto for Moldova' for royalties meant that, for the first time, she felt financially secure. As part of the settlement, Tania agreed she would produce one more book along the same theme for which the title, 'A Route Map for Moldova' was created before she had written a single word. It should, her publishers suggested, be a synthesis of everything she had covered in her weekly magazine articles and more. They would pay a small advance on royalties once it was written, but they wanted the manuscript by the first of September so it could be in the shops for Christmas.

During February and March, Henry had spent a large amount of time out of Moldova, returning for just the odd days. Tania and he telephoned each other every day. There can be no doubt that Henry was completely taken aback at Tania's success. He enjoyed the excitement it gave her, whilst his frustration grew with the fact that she had far less time to give to him.

By Easter 1995, the weekly discussion group meetings had all but petered out. Tania and Serghei were almost always too busy, and Henry's absence meant that the external view, which some thought essential to their debates, was missing.

With Henry's return just before Easter, the discussion group reformed, and the conversations were restarted but not as before. Once again, as in their earlier discussion groups, Tania did not lead or make any comment. She would probe with questions just as she had always done, but now there was a reluctance or hesitation in the responses she received, as they all knew some comment they might make could end up in some philosophical or political writing of hers.

Even though everyone there knew Tania before she had become famous as a political commentator, she was now treated slightly differently. She was no longer one of them. She had become their spokesperson, their voice.

It was the continuing deterioration of the country which caused their debates to become fiercer, more irritated, and less reflective than in the past. As a result of the urgency to find solutions to a desperately upsetting economic situation, the conversations came to be held less and less in English, alternating between Russian and Moldovan. Perhaps it was because he continued to annoy by prefacing each of his remarks with such words as "that's easy" or "that's a problem" that Henry's views were sought less often.

Serghei had changed as well. His new job of working for the United Nations inside Moldova had boosted his confidence enormously. It gave him an insight into the bureaucracy of its government. He had also gained from the extensive philosophical and political reading he had undertaken in the last couple of years, with the result that he could now talk with a new powerful and impressive insight.

As she had always done, Tania would get up early in the morning to write her conclusions of the debate the night before. Sometimes she left Henry's side to do this, but more often he had returned to his apartment long before she climbed into bed.

Often Tania would discuss the topics of the previous evening with Serghei and Henry after she had done her writing. She would re-rehearse the arguments as a prelude to revising and editing her morning's work. This happened most often when Tania found an argument she liked which conflicted with something she had written in the past. Most of her writings ended up in her weekly magazine article. Whereas before, she had written for her own fun and enlightenment and in English, she now wrote in Moldovan. She also spent time honing her views and making her writing more precise, because she knew her words would be widely scrutinised. Henry's services as an editor were no longer required.

Of endless fascination, and the most common conversation amongst Tania's women friends, when Tania was not in earshot, was the relationship between her, Serghei and Henry. "She's not shagging them both, is she? She's not sleeping with them at the same time, is she?" was a common refrain, sometimes said in envy and other times in disgust. The commonly held view was that: "She was fucking Henry for money and using Serghei for sex."

It was obvious that the two men in Tania's life wanted her. It was also obvious that both men refused to compete. Instead, they behaved towards each other with restrained politeness, perhaps not wanting their jealousy to drive Tania permanently into the arms of the other. Their friends noted how, of the three of them, not one of them led, yet they each led in turn; not one of them was subservient or lesser and yet each was prepared to acknowledge the other on level terms.

Other less generous observers of their ménage à trois, cruelly thought that Tania's new celebrity status gave Henry and Serghei a voice-piece for their own ambitions, but this was to ignore Tania's intelligence and strength of character.

Some would see it as one of those rare occasions where there was a meeting of minds on the simple basics of life, like good manners and generosity of spirit. The fact was that everything about Tania's relationship with the two fathers of her children was too complex for the parties themselves to comprehend. Accordingly, any question to Tania on her relationship with Henry or Serghei gave rise to a very sharp and negative response, for it was something which Tania herself could not rationalise, let alone explain. The simple fact was that each father had a driving need to be with their child and if that required a huge amount of tolerance and self-sacrifice, then so be it.

However one chose to describe the relationship between Tania, Serghie and Henry, it was all to change on the evening of the group's last meeting in June, just before the start of the school holidays.

"Dan and Daminika are not coming," said Osip Pasternack. He was physically shaking with anger. Osip was an ophthalmologist and long-time participant in their discussion meetings.

"What, the Susser's?" asked Serghei, referring to Dan and Daminika's married family name.

"Yes, they've left. They've gone back to America ... for good! Worse, Nicholas Radu is in hospital. He's been very badly hurt. He's most likely blind in one eye," continued Osip. He was out of breath from anxiety. He slumped into a chair from the exhaustion which had suddenly overcome him.

"What's happened?" asked Serghie, obviously concerned.

Mostly only coffee was served at their meetings, but Tania, seeing Osip's distress, without asking, poured him a small glass of brandy before making cursory offers to the others that were there.

"Who are Dan and Daminika?" asked Henry, unfamiliar with the names, once a translation had been done for him.

"You know them," replied Tania. "They own six or seven small pizza restaurants in Kishinev. Dan's parents are Jewish. They're the ones who fled Moldova just before the Germans invaded. They met on the boat from Odessa when emigrating to the United States."

"Oh yes, I remember him," said Henry. "He was a good chap, a chemistry teacher."

"Yes, and he taught English for a little while," interrupted Serghei, having half-listened to Henry and Tania's conversation.

"Daminika's the very pretty Belarusian girl you fancy," continued Tania in a whisper. "Dan came here out of interest when the wall came down and stayed to marry her."

"They'll be regretting that now," chipped in Serghei.

"Earlier this week, Dan had a visit from Costin Stanescu and Frolov Ilyich," said Osip, now ready to explain.

"What, the President's son and the owner of the Steffaco Hotel?" said one of those listening.

"Ilyich likes you to think that it's his hotel, but the real owner's Costin," said Evelina who had now joined the conversation.

"Ilyich is mad, dangerously mad," added Tania. She shook her head as she remembered their meeting in the Steffaco Hotel.

"They came with a Notary called Nesto Ivanov," continued Osip.

"We know him," said Serghei excitedly. "He was one of those notaries who we thought was crooked, but we didn't name him, did we, Evelina. We didn't think we had enough proof," he added.

"Well, you've got your proof now because Dan was ambushed by all three of them earlier this week," said Osip. "They turned up at his biggest restaurant and, in front of all the customers, staff, everyone, told him that he had to sell them seventy per cent in each of his restaurants for a total price of $5,000. Apparently, Costin Stanescu and Frolov Ilyich had visited him two or three times before and each time demanded to buy his pizza chain. He told them they could buy it for $500,000 but not for less. Apparently, the last meeting got incredibly angry. Dan ended up shouting in Moldovan: *"No money, no shares, No money, no shares,"* so everyone in the restaurant heard. That really pissed off Ilyich, who danced around the tables screaming in anger forcing everyone to leave. Well, last night, their smallest restaurant in Codru was firebombed."

"It's where they live," said Serghei with panic in his voice.

"They managed to get out," said Osip.

"And their young son?" asked Tania in equal panic.

"Yes, he's out too, but there are two others dead who lived in the top apartment. The fire brigade managed to get them out, but ..." Osip paused. "They were dead, killed by the fumes," he added mournfully.

The whole room went completely still as those present absorbed the incredulity of the news, which they all knew, in post-communist Moldova, was not that incredulous.

"Are you sure Costin and Ilyich are behind this, and it's not some awful accident," asked Evelina, worried that her old boyfriend, Edik Borisovich wasn't also involved.

"Yes, because this morning Dan and Daminika went to see Nicholas Radu. If you remember, he's the manager of their biggest restaurant. Except they couldn't find him," continued Osip. "He's in hospital, severely injured. At the same time as Dan and Daminika's apartment was being fire-bombed, Ilyich was with Nicholas telling him that they were now in charge. When Nicholas insisted on phoning Dan to check that it was true, they beat him to a pulp. One of them whipped his face with electric wire in such a frenzy that they've cut it to shreds. They've probably sliced one of his eyes in two."

"That's Ilyich, that's Ilyich," shouted Tania as her toes curled and her feet ached as she remembered how the leather settee had been torn to shreds from Ilyich's frenzied whipping. "That's him, isn't it Evelina?" said Tania looking for support.

"Nicholas has been hit so hard that his ribs are broken. He's also being operated on this morning to remove his spleen. They are going to wait a few days before they decide whether to remove his eyeball or not."

Although it was warm, a chilled quiet descended upon the whole room as those listening absorbed the news.

"Two other managers arrived just as Ilyich, and they think his bodyguard, were leaving. It was them that took Nicholas to hospital," said Osip. "Apparently, there was going to be a meeting that evening, after the restaurant had shut, amongst the managers to discuss what they were going to do about Costin's threat. They think the attack on Nicholas was recorded on CCTV and they've got the tape."

"Where are Dan and Daminika now?" asked Evelina.

"All five of them, Dan, Daminika, their son and the two managers, are all together. They're in a car travelling as fast as they can to get across the border into Romania. I spoke to them an hour ago. Dan's changed his mobile phone number and everyone else has thrown their sim cards away."

"Are they not coming back?" asked a voice.

"Would you?" responded Osip, before adding, "Just before they left Dan and Daminika emptied their bank accounts. They've given me enough to pay all the staff their wages. They've also told me to tell all the managers to break the pizza ovens, so they are of no use, and then they are to take and sell everything from the kitchens and restaurants and share the proceeds with the staff too. I'm not sure

I want to be involved," Osip continued dejectedly, "but I suppose I must."

"I'll help," said Evelina.

Osip smiled weakly at her as he acknowledged her generous offer.

"He's done this before" said one of the group.

"Who?" asked Osip, naively.

"Costin, he took over an Italian and Japanese motorcycle dealership last year in exactly the same way, and before that, he took over a taxi and courier business, Rapid Taxis. That one is now his."

"How does he get away with this?" asked Henry amazed at the unfolding story. "I thought Moldova's extortion days were over."

"He's the son of the President, and the police don't dare to investigate now the President controls the SIS," said Serghei "

"The SIS?" asked Henry.

"The SIS are the new Intelligence Service, but they act more like a secret police force," explained Evelina to Henry. "The police won't investigate any case in which Costin's name is mentioned. It's not worth the risk. Any policeman who tried to do anything would immediately find they faced a jumped-up corruption charge courtesy of the SIS, so why would they?"

"It's pure racketeering," said Henry, getting annoyed with the ease at which everyone accepted what had happened.

"In any case, $1,000, maybe $2,000, shared amongst a few policemen, and a file is quickly mislaid, and the matter never comes to court."

"Fucking Hell," said Henry, introducing a swear word into their very many meetings for the first time. "Unless you lot sort this out, then Moldova's fucked, and you are all fucked with it. When I first came here and complained about something not working, you would say: what can I do. Well, I tell you, this time, you can do bloody something."

Not everyone in the room fully understood what Henry was saying, but from the passion of his speech, it was clear that he was now pretty angry.

"*Is life so dear, or peace so sweet as to be purchased at the price of chains and slavery?*" said Osip, quietly bringing the meeting back to its earlier calm. "*I know not what course others may take, but as for me, give me liberty or give me death,*" Osip continued, with his voice rising with passion towards the end.

"Who said that?" asked Henry recognising the quote.

"It was said by Patrick Henry in a speech urging all Americans to take up arms against the British during the American War of Independence," said Serghei, once again proving his range of knowledge.

Henry nodded, for once again, he was impressed. Here was a group of men and women quoting from heart something from his history that he had only vaguely been aware of.

Henry lost the thread of their discussions as they all started to speak at once, interplaying between Moldovan and Russian, automatically choosing the best language for what each wanted to say at that moment.

There was no meaningful discussion that evening as too many people needed to express their anger. Much later, when everyone was gone, Serghei, Evelina, and Henry had an informal debrief on what had happened. Tania was not there. She was looking after the children who had been disturbed in the rare noise of the evening.

"In a war, there are many battles," said Serghei philosophically. "We will have to deal with Ilyich in our own way, and we will do so, and you are right about Stanescu and his son, but there's a political fight to be had for which we are not ready."

"You are ready," said Henry in a firm voice. "Tania, in her books and articles, has already articulated the policies needed for the renewal of this nation. You know everyone in this room and way beyond is prepared to support them."

Serghei shook his head once more, rejecting Henry's argument.

"You also have your leaders," continued Henry, "but you don't see it because you are too close. You look around for others to lead, but they are here in front of you. It's Tania and the two of you. She has the intelligence, but more importantly, a known public face and the presentation skills. You two are highly knowledgeable with the ability to organise, promote and publicise. All three of you have the intellect and the ability. You just have to decide if you want to do it."

"Do what exactly?" asked Serghei.

"Get Tania elected as President and establish a new political party to take control of the Parliament; to form the Freedom Party ..."

"The Freedom Party," repeated Evelina. "Why the Freedom Party?"

"It seems an obvious name because ... you are not free at the moment, are you?" added Henry. "Not one of you."

"You should talk to Tania about it," said Serghei.

"We should talk to Tania about it," responded Henry quickly.

"In any case, you don't understand our constitution, answered Serghei. It's not that easy."

"I'm sure you are right, but isn't it worth some thought?" he asked.

Chapter 43

Kishinev May 1995

MAY 9TH, 1995, is a day of abiding memories for Henry. Secretly, he was delighted to have received a formal invitation to Moldova's fiftieth-anniversary commemoration of the Great Victory and then to a formal luncheon given by the Ministry of Agriculture afterwards. He felt it showed that he had 'arrived' in Moldova with someone thinking him important enough to be invited.

As Henry took his place on the grandstand built on the Great National Assembly Square, he started to feel uncomfortable observing a military parade that celebrated the end of World War II, not least because his father had fought on the other side.

The march past of soldiers and military equipment was not, in his mind, impressive. It could easily have been forgotten. It was the march past of the veterans which caught Henry's attention. Thousands of elderly men and women, wearing their best clothes and resplendent in their campaign medals, had travelled with their families many miles to Kishinev to honour their comrades in arms, and pay their respects to those who had paid the highest price. It was when Henry saw the large number of people marching with amputated arms or swinging along on a pair of crutches having lost one leg or being pushed in a wheelchair because they had lost both, that the true cost of Russia's war, came home to him.

Henry had watched armistice day parades in England and France, but they were nothing like this for the scale of hurt and pain which was still before your eyes. Henry knew the numbers. Russia had 24 million civilian and military deaths. France and England had one million between them. The Great Victory Parade reflected that ratio in the injured too, 24 times as many.

After the parade, Henry made his way past the Triumphal Arch built one hundred and fifty years earlier by the governors of Bessarabia to commemorate Russia's victory over the Ottoman Empire. It was here that the veterans and their families were gathering to lay their single red carnations. There was something incredibly touching as young boys and girls, also dressed in their best clothes with many of the girls with fresh flowers sewn into their hair, gathered proudly around their grandfathers and grandmothers with a tangible show of appreciation for what they had been through

As Henry studied these men and women with their families, he was, once again, unable to ignore how many were without limbs. He felt truly humbled. We really don't know, do we, thought Henry. Yes, it was bad in the Blitz, awful in the North African Campaign and up through Italy, dreadful in the Atlantic winter convoys and appalling on the beaches of D-Day, but nothing compared to the total inhumane war fought between Russia and Germany on the eastern front, which even 50 years later, was manifest before his eyes

Feeling rather low and reflective, and with a lot of difficulties, Henry found his way to the large, impressive room where lunch was being served and then to his place at the long banqueting table. Henry was beginning to wonder what the hell he was doing there, for he knew no one around him. He had accepted the invitation on the assumption that Evelina would be there to look after him. He was shocked to find she was not going. The Great Victory Day is a national holiday in Moldova. It is a sacrosanct day in the calendar when families get together, and it was with their families that Tania and Evelina were spending the day.

"How dare he? How dare he?" said the man opposite in perfect French, as Henry was wondering how everyone was going to clamber into the bench seats on either side of the table.

Henry turned around and looked over his shoulder. There were at least another hundred other people in the room, and he could not believe the man was addressing him.

"How dare he? How dare he?" repeated the man who was on the other side of the table and by, his fierce look, made it clear he was speaking to him.

Who? asked Henry, not sure who or what the middle-aged man in a Russian air force uniform was talking about. Henry was later to discover that the man, whose name he never learned, had been in the Soviet Air Forces. He was now the Russian Federation's military attaché to Moldova. He spoke perfect French because, for two years, he had studied International Relations at the Sorbonne.

"Your President," explained the attaché.

"Do what? What did he do?"

"Criticised Russia for keeping control of our western states. How dare he?"

"Which one? The last one François Mitterrand or the new one Jacques Chirac?" asked Henry still confused, for the use of the french language had automatically made him think of France. The weekend before had seen the final of the French presidential elections in France, and after 14 years, President Mitterrand was leaving office.

"Neither, President Clinton, Bill Clinton. Doesn't he realise we've been invaded three times in our modern history? We needed those countries, the border countries - Poland, Czechoslovakia, Hungary, Yugoslavia, Bulgaria, Ukraine, even Moldova, to keep us safe."

"I don't know about Clinton, but I certainly know, and so does everyone taught in our schools," said Henry. "Three times in modern history, we've been Russia's ally when it's been invaded. The first time was against Napoleon when he invaded you in 1812. We'd been fighting him since 1793. The second time was in 1914 when Germany declared war on Russia. As a result, Germany decided to invade France because of some ridiculous treaty. The last time was the Great War, which we're commemorating today."

"But you only came into the Great War after we had started to win it," said the attaché fervently.

"What do you mean?" asked Henry crossly. He knew the dates. He had spent long enough in their national museum to know Moldova's war history as well as any school pupil.

"You only came into the war after we had started to win it," repeated the attaché determined to press home his point. "Germany invaded us in June 1941. You didn't enter the war until December of that year."

"That's wrong. France and England declared war on Germany in September 1939. In June 1940, the Germans invaded, and France was defeated. Britain, my country, stood alone." It was time to be very British, decided Henry. "It wasn't until 21 months later before you got involved, and only then because Hitler invaded you. In fact, if my memory is correct, at the time Britain stood alone against the Nazis, Russia was in the middle of a 10-year nonaggression pact with Germany, which it used to invade Poland. It was just two weeks after Britain had declared war on Germany for going into Poland."

As a gavel hit the top table, a series of bangs acted as the signal for everyone to stop talking and take their place. There was a loud noise as benches were scrapped on the ground as everyone fought to clamber over and sit down.

"That's not what our history books teach us," said the attaché assuredly after both men had sat down.

England and France declared war on Germany on September 3rd 1939. I think you are mistaking me for an American. It was they who declared war on Germany after you."

"Are you not American?"

"No," said Henry. "I'm English."

The attaché looked puzzled before continuing, "That's a shame, perhaps even worse."

"Why do you say that?" asked Henry, somewhat taken aback given the event.

"Do you remember John Kennedy's inaugural speech?"

"Yes, I know some of it."

"Well, at one part, he says: *'remember that, in the past, those who foolishly sought power by riding its back often ended up inside.'* Of course, he was referring to countries seeking to get close to Russia and the USSR, but he could equally have been referring to England and France, but they never realised it. England and France have been, ... What do you call it ...? America's ..."

"Whore?" proffered Henry, having thought he had detected the attaché's general sentiment.

"You could say that, but I was thinking of something more polite. I think the expression is a lap dog. They whistle, and both countries come running."

"Well, riding the tiger, as you call it, has worked for us in the past, hasn't it. For example, the American's only got serious about the development of the nuclear bomb after Churchill had pushed, prodded and bullied them."

"And how many did that kill - Hiroshima and Nagasaki – what 200,000 people?" asked the attaché, before adding, "and note, it's the only country that has used the bomb in anger."

"It ended the war with Japan, probably saved 15 million lives which would have been lost if a conventional war had been fought all the way to Tokyo."

"It didn't matter to us. We weren't coming."

"Not coming?"

"No, not after Yalta[4], why would we. We'd got all we wanted. Of course, we said we would, but we were going to be slow, very slow. Just as the US were slow in getting into the fight in France. You saw all those men with their broken limbs today during the march past. They were as a direct result of the US failing to do its duty as quickly as it promised."

Henry leaned back to allow the food to be served. It allowed a natural pause in the conversation, the hostility of which was causing Henry to feel uncomfortable.

"You think the US is your ally, don't you?" asked the attaché.

Henry nodded cautiously.

"Have you heard the expression military-industrial-political complex?"

Henry shook his head

---

[4] The Yalta Conference was a meeting of three major World War II allies in February 1945. Its agenda was to shape the postwar peace and to give self-determination to the liberated peoples of Europe. A task which it lamentably failed to do for the Easter European countries of the former USSR.

"It was a phrase coined by President Eisenhower in his farewell address. He warned of the incestuous relationship between the American military as the buyer of weapons, American industry who makes money by supplying the weapons and the American politicians who pay for them. The trouble with this is that the industry needs the military to use its weapons so it can sell them some more, so what better than to start and maintain a little war somewhere, like Vietnam.

"I'd hardly call that a little war," commented Henry.

"Do you know of the Pentagon Papers?"

"No," said Henry

"During the Vietnam War, the US Government decided to make a critical study of the war, right from the very start in 1955 to see what lessons they could learn. The report was supposed to remain secret, except it was leaked. Do you know what it concluded?"

Henry shook his head.

"It said that the decision making was flawed. It showed that throughout the whole war, the politicians lied to the American people. They knew the war could not be won. Most importantly, the study weighted the reason that the war was being fought. Do you know what the highest weighting was?"

"No," said Henry, knowing he was about to be told

"Seventy per cent."

"Do you know the reason?"

Henry shook his head.

"The Pentagon concluded the biggest reason, seventy per cents worth, that the war continued to be fought was to avoid America being humiliated. Can you believe that – sending young men to fight in a war they knew could not be won to stop America from being humiliated!"

"A bit like Russia's war in Afghanistan," retorted Henry before asking, "What was the name again of the report?" as he was now taking serious note.

"I can't remember what the report was formerly called, but they're known as the Pentagon Papers. It was huge in the press, all over the world."

Once again, their conversation was stopped, this time by wine being poured.

In the US, its big business which buys the politician. In fact, it's the same in France and Britain too. These countries are not democracies as you'd all like to think. They're plutocracies. They're countries controlled by the wealthy, the seriously wealthy."

Well, a plutocracy is certainly better than a totalitarian dictatorship," responded Henry quickly.

"You think so? The Vietnam War was a war the plutocrats wanted to fight to make money out of. If they'd wanted to stop communism in Vietnam, and Cambodia, they'd have done it with money and investment in its economy. It could have outbought China and us together ten times over, and yet it didn't. The industrial complex wanted the war. The military wanted somewhere to play with their new toys, and it was the job of the politicians to oblige. As is widely acknowledged, the military-industrial-political complex makes America the most dangerous country on earth. It's why Russia has to be strong. Very strong."

With those words, the attaché stopped talking to Henry and started talking to the person to the left and right of him. He was not to say another word to Henry for the rest of the time he sat opposite. It was as though he had been planted there to give Henry the messages he had just received.

No one around Henry could speak any of the languages he could communicate in, and so he sat there in silence, gesticulating when necessary to be understood, while enjoying some dishes and decidedly disliking others. As soon as he thought it reasonable to leave, Henry started to head to the door.

"You're leaving?" asked the attaché as Henry was close to the exit.

Henry nodded.

"I thought I might share one final thought, Mr Guégan, if that is alright."

That's strange, thought Henry as he nodded again. He now knows my name.

"Russia is weak now. We are led by a drunk.[5] He will soon be gone and will be replaced by a strong man. It is always the case with Russia."

It was the third or fourth time Henry had heard that prediction since he had been in Moldova

"America and Europe, they've both humiliated us. We'll never forget that," said the attaché

"How?"

"By agreeing that our former allies can join Nato – Poland, the Czechs, Hungary. You've coerced them to change sides, and in the process, you've brought your weapons right to our front door. It's aggressive. It is not the way friendly nations should behave."

"They'd have only asked to join if they hadn't felt threaten by Russia, would they?"

"It's a mistake. Europe doesn't realise how strategically weak it is. It's too dependant upon Russia's energy. We cut the gas pipeline, and Europe's finished. It will destroy itself in a civil war."

That's interesting, thought Henry. It was precisely the point he had made earlier to Mircea Stanescu. "But you need dollars to keep your economy afloat, don't you?" responded Henry.

"Yes, for now, but you are not thinking strategically. Do you know the most successful capitalist country on earth? And don't say the States."

Henry shook his head.

"China. It has got 1.3 billion people. Russia's got 150 million."

"And the life expectancy of Russia is falling," interrupted Henry.

"China needs Russia's oil and its other raw materials. Think of the surface area under a twisted elastic band and then untwist it. It becomes much bigger."

Henry copied the attaché as he put his thumbs and forefingers together and then moved them to touch on both hands. He looked down at the two circles he'd made. He then moved his thumbs and fingers apart and saw how much bigger the hole had become. Henry looked up at the attaché and silently acknowledged the point he was making.

---

[5] President Boris Yeltsin

"That's what we are going to do. We're going to untwist the rubber band with China. When that's happened in ten or twenty year's time, Europe's going to need friends, and unless it rapidly rethinks, Russia's not going to be one of them. Believe me when I say this Mr Guégan, the seduction of Moldova by EU's money will not be in France or Britain's long term best interest. It is as certain as the sun will rise tomorrow."

Chapter 44

Kishinev May 1995

HENRY WAS PLEASED to get outside of the hall and into the fresh air. He'd sat bored during the speeches as he had not understood a word. Even worse, the event had turned into a vodka drinking competition that had no appealed to him at all.

Outside he deliberately stretched his hand. Everyone he said good-bye to had applied the usual vice-like grip adopted by every Russian when shaking hands with a Westerner. The message with every handshake was clear – we're Russian, we're strong, respect us! He didn't detect any looks of surprise when he squeezed back, perhaps a little harder. Another benefit from years of working in the wine industry.

Henry walked casually to the Caterdrala Nasterea Domnului. As he expected, it was full of veterans with their families saying prayers. Inside he purchased three candles as he always did when in a church. Sometimes, he thought the candles represented the past, present and future. Another time he would think of them being lit for the previous, present and future generations, but once again, he lit them for Andrew, Peter and Yulia. Or were they for Tania, Yulia and Stelian? He could not make up his mind.

As Henry watched the flames, he wondered about his father. He had told Tania that his father was German, but he had never mentioned that he was a pilot, personally decorated for valour by Hitler for fighting in the war whose victory everyone around him was commemorating. Should he tell her, he wondered.

Often, he'd thought about driving to Kropyvnytskyi in Ukraine. His father's last known whereabouts. He knew it was only 200 miles away, but he had not gone before because he did not know what he would do when he got there. Who would he speak to? What would he say? If today's sights had confirmed one thing, Germany's war in Eastern Europe had caused a lot of harm to the people of the region. In the end, Henry decided it would be best if nothing more was said or done about his father. But it was a decision he would revisit time and time again.

As Henry left the Cathedral he wondered what he might do next. It would be a long time before Tania would be home. She had gone with Stelian and Yulia to be with her family at the Woodman's Dacha, as they always did on public holidays. Henry had been invited to join them, but because Tania was so pleased and impressed that he'd received a formal invitation to the Victory Parade, she was certain he should go there instead of being with her.

Henry wandered aimlessly. He walked past the National Museum, which he had visited many times, and then past Moldova State University before crossing in to Valea Morilor Park. He would join the many people strolling around its enormous lake.

As he walked, looking at the glistening water, he thought about his conversation with the Attaché. Had France and Britain really been so silly to have been America's allies? Had they been riding the tiger Kennedy spoke of? Had they ended up inside? After many a step, Henry decided France and Britain had not been swallowed up, as the Attaché claim. He knew France had re-occupied Vietnam immediately after the war but had pulled out after nine years following its defeat by the pro-independence communist forces and, despite much urging by the US, Britain had decided not to get involved. The charge that France and Britain had been the US's lapdog was, in Henry's mind, unproven.

But the Pentagon Papers, the military-industrial-political complex, and possibility of a Sino-Russian trade pact, now those were matters for concern. He would talk to Tania, Evelina and Serghei about them.

Chapter 45

Kishinev May 1995

THE THING THAT shocked Tania and Evelina when Henry told them about his conversation with the attaché was how naive he had been. Had it not occurred to him strange that, of all the people in the room, the Russian attaché had been positioned to sit next to him?

"I'm of no use to anyone like that," said Henry as he defended the charge that he was being tested on his loyalties. "In any case, he thought I was America."

"I agree. Not today, not tomorrow, but remember their files run deep. Believe me, one day, you will find yourself being approached again," said Evelina, confirming what Tania had already said.

Two days after the Victory Parade, Henry was up very early in the morning. He'd had two successive sleepless nights. In his dressing gown, he let himself into Tania's flat where she was, as he had expected, writing at her small kitchen table.

"Tania, how does Moldova defend itself against a country like Russia?" asked Henry without any of the usual morning pleasantries.

"Or Germany or Turkey, because they've all invaded over the last four hundred years," she replied, as she got up to make him a cup of coffee

"Seriously, how do you defend yourselves?" he asked again. "With you, and Yulia and Stelian here, and with the St. Sophia Estate, I need to know."

"We don't. To defend Moldova would be an utter waste of time, money and lives," she answered swiftly. "To choose sides would be folly. We would soon become the battleground for a proxy war."

Henry looked shocked

"For a thousand years, perhaps longer, armies have marched through Moldova from east to west and west to east, and we've never been able to stop them. Our defence is not in armies. I spoke to Great-Grandma Brigita about this. She was here when the Germans invaded in 1941. It was their planes that did the damage. Then the Russians blew everything up as they retreated to stop the Germans using them. She says, and I'm sure she is right, we don't need aeroplanes as we should not be attacking anyone. Her view is that we only need missiles to shoot down anything which might attack us from above. I think I agree with her."

"You've not written any of this, have you? Why's that."

"I'm a woman. Because of that, the army won't like me. I don't say anything because I don't want to antagonise them."

"What would you write if you had to?"

"I'd make the army a professionally trained and equipped civil defence force ready to deal with anything. It would have missiles, transport helicopters but no aeroplanes. That would be it."

"Utrinque Paratus," interrupted Henry.

Tania looked at him, confused.

"Utrinque Paratus. It means 'Ready for Anything.' It's the motto of the Parachute Regiment."

"How many times have you told me the first duty of government is the defence of its people?" asked Tania, ignoring Henry's flaunt of knowledge.

"Lots," acknowledged Henry.

"Well it's not just wars we need to be prepared for. There are floods, there's fire, there's famine. We have to be prepared for everything, and we're not. You know the Woodman's Dacha?"

Henry nodded.

"It's been my families shelter for over one hundred years. When something goes wrong, we always go there. It has meant there are still Solokov's in Moldova. But not everyone's been so lucky. We survived because we prepared. It is the same for Moldova. We have to be prepared for every eventuality, every possible natural and man-made disaster, and that means shelter, clothing, food and medicines and, of course, civil control. If I am ever asked, that's the job I'd want the army to do. Would I order a Moldovan soldier to fight to keep Transnistria part of Moldova? No, never, what a waste of life! For what?"

"And what do I do about Mr Attaché man?" asked Henry.

"You have to report your conversation to the UK Government in London and to the EU Commission in Paris."

"But he's bound to find out, isn't he?" asked Henry perplexed.

"You need to spend more time playing three-dimensional chess," scoffed Evelina, without a shred of sympathy, when he'd asked her the same question and she had given the same reply as Tania.

Chapter 46

Kishinev Summer 1995

IT WAS A lovely sunny evening. Like very many other families, Henry and Tania had taken Stelian and Yulia to the park. They stopped to allow Stelian to play on the swings. Yulia was getting used to the feel of grass beneath her bare feet. She was using her father, who was lying down, as a climbing frame to pull herself up before toddling a few steps and falling over.

"Serghei tells me that you want me to run for President," said Tania, interrupting Henry's daydream.

"Yes," he replied without adding any explanation.

"And how do you propose I do that," she asked.

"Slowly, quietly and assuredly," he replied.

"And money, where do we get the money."

"I will help, but we'll get it from everyone. Small amounts, ten and twenty lei, but if we can get many people to actively support you, campaign for you, then we will need less money. We find those people who are cash poor and time rich. They're the ones who will be able to help the most in the campaign.

"Serghei thinks that most of the students would come and campaign with us, because we would be new and idealistic."

"I'm sure that's right," said Henry encouragingly.

What are our policies? asked Tania vaguely as she picked at the grass, while keeping a beady eye on her son who was running about furiously.

"Manifesto for Moldova, surely, and your new book when it comes out," said Henry, confused that she should even think to ask the question.

"But these don't have much in the way of economic or monetary policies, do they?"

"That can be easily fixed." Henry paused before adding: "In fact, you've already indirectly written about them. Don't you remember the discussions on a mixed economy, a balanced budget, borrowing only for capital expenditure and the country taking in taxes between thirty-seven and forty-two per cent of GDP."

Tania nodded before continuing: "Serghei thinks we should try and get some members of parliament elected too. He thinks the presidency will not be enough to change things."

"He's probably right, but that means establishing a party machinery to select candidates and everything. That's a huge task," protested Henry.

"I know I can do the job, said Tania confidently, particularly if Serghei is there to help me and protect my back. It's just I have Stelian and Yulia to think of."

"You would be doing this for them and every other Stelian and Yulia in the country," said Henry sympathetically. They won't understand now, but one day they will, and then they will be proud, ever so proud."

"I'm worried about the Kremlin," Tania continued. "They would hate it if someone from the proletariat was to take power. It would mean they've lost their influence, and they are not going to let that happen, are they?"

"The Kremlin's in total disarray. It's probably the best time to do it. In any case, at first, we would do everything very slowly, without a fuss. By the time they find the Freedom Party exists it will be so strong they won't be able to do anything about it."

Tania and Henry got up and walked on to buy Stelian and Yulia ice creams.

"We could go to England or France, couldn't we? asked Tania."

"And take Stelian away from his Father?" replied Henry, "and leave your mother, father and grandmother behind?"

"I suppose not," she said, smiling at him. "Just an idea".

"There is one thing," said Henry, who then paused.

"And?"

"It's just that we will need to clear out the stable yard first."

"Meaning?"

"If you are going to do this, then you're going to come under intense scrutiny, and any indiscretions in your past will come out."

"Like what"

"Your first husband, abortions, miscarriages etc., even what happened to us at Steffaco Hotel. It's bound to come out, and you would need to put it out there first, in your own way," said Henry adding, "Evelina would do a brilliant job at that."

"If we have to do that, then I'm not doing it," said Tania firmly. "They can have so much of me but not all!" Her voice was resolute.

"Who?" asked Henry confused.

"The electorate, they can have so much of me but not all. My private life has to remain private," said Tania.

"There's no such thing as a private life for a politician. What the media can't get, then they'll invent. For example, your ex-husband will have pages and pages of rubbish devoted to him and what he thinks of you. He'll be paid something for past photographs but most of it will be made up. The angle will depend on the political persuasion of the paper, but most of it will be nasty, horrible!"

Look, I can't explain you and Serghei to myself, so how do you think I'll explain it to someone else," said Tania. It was the first time she had ever acknowledged to Henry the complex relationship they all found themselves in.

"I'm not doing it, announced Tania, after no thought at all. "I'm just not doing it!"

Chapter 47

Kishinev November 1995

TANIA AND HENRY sat in the back of the taxi. It was old, dirty, very noisy and with the usual cracks in the windscreen. They reached out to hold hands. It was dark and raining. They were returning from a birthday gathering for one of Tania's friends.

"What were you talking about," asked Henry. "It was a very serious discussion at your end of the table."

"It was nothing," she replied. "How was your end?"

"Very boring, lots of excited young men working out how to make their fortune from the Internet," said Henry before adding, "there was a lot of money changing hands at your end of the table. The discussion was very intense for it to be nothing."

"It's a problem we have to deal with," said Tania turning to look at him in the eyes.

A problem? repeated Henry.

"Yes, but this time the problem doesn't create an opportunity, as you always argue."

"Every problem creates an opportunity," said Henry cockily. "It's just the way you think about these things."

"No, Henry, it's not!" replied Tania very firmly, "and definitely not this time."

Henry said nothing. Sensing the rebuke he had been given, he turned and studied the raindrops as they moved on the steamed-up door window, the outside lights making them twinkle in the darkness.

"You know Mitina Denisovna?" said Tania.

"No."

"Yes, you do. She's the ballerina," said Tania, continuing in her rebuking tone. "She sat next to me at the end of the table."

Immediately he heard the description he remembered, for Mitina was a woman you could not but help notice. She was slight, very pretty with poise and a beauty which made him want to stare, but to do so would appear rude, so he only took fleeting glances.

"Er yes, I remember," he said cautiously.

There was a pause as Tania wondered whether she should go on. She knew she would be breaking Mitina's confidence, but she needed to tell someone, talk to them about what had happened, to get their approval.

"She was raped. Mitina was raped. I can't see how that can be said to create an opportunity," said Tania, spitting out the words.

Henry stopped looking out of the window and turned towards Tania.

"She was raped by her boyfriend's best friend when he called at her apartment," explained Tania.

"Boyfriend's best friend? repeated Henry, with a hint of incredulity.

"I don't want to talk about it," she said, but after a little while later, Tania continued.

"Adam, her boyfriend, asked Gogu Stancu to pick Mitina up to take her to a party they were going to as he was at work and was running late. Gogu arrived early and Mitina wasn't ready. She'd just got out of the shower, but nevertheless, she invited him in to be polite. She has two rooms, so it shouldn't have been a problem, but then ... well, it happened."

Henry said nothing. He didn't know what to say as he could detect the upset in Tania's voice.

"She escaped from Gogu, ran downstairs to the flat two floors below just dressed in a bath towel. You men are such bloody animals," she said angrily, vile, vile animals. All he did was to get dressed and go to the party. He acted as though nothing had happened."

Henry felt uncomfortable as it was as though Tania was accusing him of the attack.

"The woman downstairs took Minita back to her flat, helped get her dressed and called the police," continued Tania in a contemptuous sneer. "Gogu was arrested for rape but was quickly let out, and nothing has happened since. It was six months ago, and nothing has happened," she said, repeating herself. "His family is rich. They have political and mafia connections. They have paid off the police to do nothing about it, so Gogu now walks around with a big cock in his hands. None of us is safe," she said. "None of us is safe," she repeated, emphasising the words safe, "whilst he thinks he's got away with it."

The quizzical look on Henry's face was enough to encourage Tania to continue talking. "In Moldova," she said, "when the police don't act, it is the job of the husband, or boyfriend or father to get justice. Adam's a coward. He said she encouraged Gogu by opening the door when undressed, but this is ridiculous. Her bruises show this is untrue. He wants to stay Gogu's best friend as his family have money. Money rules everything in Moldova."

Tania then let out a very deep sigh.

"Mitina's father is too old and frail to take on Gogu. Also, he doesn't have money. So, we're doing it," she said defiantly. "We're paying to have him shot in both knees and have both his hands broken as well. He'll damn well learn then, won't he," she said, defiantly.

"You're paying?"

"Yes, I've put two hundred and fifty dollars in to the pool," replied Tania matter-of-factly. "It's going to cost twelve hundred dollars, a bit more than normal 'cause two people are needed to break his hands.

"Why are you breaking his hands?" asked Henry innocently.

"For Christ sakes Henry, use your imagination. He can't hold his dick for weeks, months if his hands are broken, can he? In any case, it's nothing less than the little shit deserves."

"Why not just shoot him in the balls?" asked Henry.

"That might happen too, but you have to be careful. There are two big arteries at the top of his legs, and if he were to be hit there, he would die. We can't commit murder," said Tania, clinically repeating one of the reasons someone had given for shooting Gogu in the knees. "He has to be punished, and this is a good punishment. It will do well, as all the newspapers will know that it's a punishment shooting for rape. It will be a good thing as it will be a lesson for other ... attackers."

"And you've helped pay for this?" asked Henry, making sure he understood.

"Yes," replied Tania. "I paid the most as they knew I could afford it."

"This is crazy," said Henry turning to look at Tania. "There has to be a better way than this. "The opportunity that comes is the opportunity to stop corruption," said Henry without any empathy, only seeking to prove his point.

For Christ sake shut up, just shut up!" snapped Tania furiously. "You just don't get it, you just don't get it, do you!" she continued, her anger growing. "The fact is his dirty filthy semen is inside her forever, and it can't be got out. The fear she had waiting to learn whether she was pregnant or caught a disease. The fact that she knows she's not strong enough to defend herself and this could happen again. The fact that every man knows she's been raped, and who'd want to marry her now?"

The taxi pulled up outside their apartment block. Henry gave Tania the money to pay the fare as he always did. They then negotiated the puddles to the door of their stairwell. There they waited as Tania found her torch. All the light bulbs in the stairway, which Henry had bought and fitted, had long since disappeared.

"Not tonight," said Tania exasperated, as they stood on the landing outside their front doors.

"I'm sorry, you're right," said Henry, both chastened and embarrassed by his own insensitivity. "There's no opportunity which comes out of rape," he admitted as they parted to their own apartments for the night.

Both Tania and Henry had a bad night's sleep. Tania was burdened by the decision she had made the evening before. Henry worried about the reality of living in Moldova, where the things that a citizen should be able to rely on were dangerously absent.

At 5.00 am Henry tapped on Tania's front door and let himself in. He knew she would be up, sitting at her kitchen table with unsweetened black coffee and her notebook open, writing away. Tania invited him into the kitchen, made him a coffee, and they sat down. Tania's notebook was not open. It was on the table with her pen resting across the top.

"Have you finished writing for today?" Henry asked after his first sip of coffee.

"No, I've been thinking about yesterday. I want to write about it, but I don't know how, or even if I should," she replied.

"One of the US Presidents, I can't remember which one, once said that 'everyone is the president of their own life.' I think he said it because he was fed up with so many people blaming him for the many things which went wrong, which he didn't have the power to fix," said Henry.

Tania looked at Henry, making a mental note of the saying, for she was sure she would be able to use it in one of her articles.

"You and your friends have to decide whether you want to do something to effect change or just complain," said Henry patiently. "I don't mean by shooting some rapist in the balls. You have to do that, but it doesn't change your society for the better. It just perpetuates the pain. Believe me, corruption in this country could be defeated. It could be ended. You all know that. You just have to put your minds to it."

"We can't, Henry, the task is too big, too complicated."

"It isn't, I assure you. One day a black woman called Rosa Parks refused to move from an area in a bus reserved for whites. Out of that one moment of defiance, a whole civil rights movement started in America. One woman, one protest and the course of American history was changed for ever."

Tania picked up her pen, opened her notebook and wrote down the name - Rosa Parks.

"Of course, it will be dangerous, of course it will be hard," said Henry, "but you and your friends need to want it enough for themselves, their children ... our children and our ... their children's children."

Henry stood up and perched his bottom on the window sill. Tania could tell from his demeanour that he wanted to make a pronouncement.

"Everything is changed through politics," he said. "Force doesn't bring permanent change. It's always temporary. Young men, who use guns to try and bring change, end up as common criminals. They grow old, and old men grow weak. Good political argument, matched by political will, brings change. Complacency will achieve nothing, except keeping you all permanently subservient."

Tania jotted in her notebook as Henry shared his thoughts.

"What you guys need, above all else, is to end the corruption. In turn, that will bring down the Mafia and organised crime which runs on the back of it. The questions of being part of Europe or Russia, whether you have a capitalist, communist or socialist economy, they're all secondary. We've discussed it many times, the first duty of government is the security of its people. The people aren't secure when the police and judges can be bribed. Corruption is endemically dangerous. But you know this. You've written about it so often."

Tania looked up at Henry and sighed. She knew he was right, and it made her feel sick in the stomach to know that it was so.

"As, Serghei and I have both said. What you guys need is the Freedom Party, and for that you have to choose someone who will not be afraid to lead it," said Henry before he turned to the sound of pattering feet as Stelian joined them.

Chapter 48

Kishinev November 1995

THEY MET IN a small, unimpressive restaurant at the university end of Strada Pushkin where there was a booth that would sit eight people. Tania had issued the invitations, more in the form of an instruction. Those invited had three things in common. They were her friends, and they had attended most of the discussion group meetings in her apartment. But, most importantly, each had spoken to her privately about her standing in the next election to become President of Moldova.

As each guest arrived at the booth, they were presented with a copy of Tania's new book, 'A Partnership for Moldova', which was being rushed into the shops in the hope of catching the Christmas sales. They also noticed how Tania welcomed each of them solemnly, which was unusual for a group of Moldovans dining out. It was clear she had something on her mind.

When they were all gathered, and drinks had been served, Tania banged the table with the handle end of a fork.

"I want to talk to you about Project Freedom," said Tania in English as she handed out photocopies of a handwritten agenda. It was deliberately written in English not just so Henry could participate, but to make sure no casual observer could know what they were talking about.

"Each of you has approached me over the last few months about putting myself forward to try and become the President of Moldova. I really don't know why," she said. "Some of you have spoken to me about it many times. I've always said no, but things have happened which have made me think about changing my mind."

Tania didn't say what had been the catalyst to bring about her change of heart. Undoubtedly her discussions with Henry about Mitina's rape was the driving influence. Every time she held Yulia in her arms she would think of Mitina and fear for her daughter's safety. It was this single thing which compelled her to do something. It was why they were now meeting.

"The thing is, I don't know how to do this," said Tania. "For example, where do we get the money, where do we get the support? There's no political party I would want to join, and I doubt they would want me."

There was complete silence around the table as everyone stared at the agenda in front of them. It was true, each of them had said, not just to Tania but amongst themselves, that she should try and become President, but they did not know how to answer her question, for each had no idea how it could be made to happen.

"Thank God for that," said Evelina breaking the silence. "I've been waiting a long time for you to say that."

Once Evelina had spoken, there was a Mexican wave of approval around the table.

"Are you sure?" asked Henry touching Tania gently on the arm. Not only was he surprised, but the truth was that he was deeply upset. They had walked together to the restaurant, and she had said nothing about her intentions until that moment.

"No," said Tania. "I'm not sure, but I need to see if it's feasible. That's why we're here. I need to see if it can be made to happen."

"It's feasible," said Henry, ever the optimist. "We have to make it so. Remember," he continued, quoting from his school poem:

"Life's battles don't always go
To the stronger or faster man.
But sooner or later the one who wins
Is the one who Thinks he can!"[6]

"Where do we get the money from?" she asked. We'll have nothing like the money of the other candidates. Corruption will get them all their money, and money buys elections."

---

[6] From the poem 'Thinking' written by Walter D. Wintle

"You're right," said Serghei, "but elections are 90% about emotion. The emotion of trust. You vote for the person you trust the most. Everyone trusts you, and that's worth millions of dollars in anyone's campaign. You against Stanescu, and it's no contest."

"Except he's paying people to stuff the election boxes with false ballot papers," said Evelina, in a statement of acknowledged truth.

"You start by finding members and getting them to pay a membership subscription. Not a lot, maybe ten, twenty, fifty lei. We build slowly from the ground up," Serghei continued enthusiastically.

When's the next election?" asked Henry.

"December next year."

"So we've got 12 months to get organised," said Henry to a murmur of agreement around the table.

"If we could get one thousand members, then that would give us ten, maybe twenty thousand Lei," said Osip Pasternack encouragingly.

"It's nothing like enough, but if we did things, like they do in other countries, and get the members to hold fundraising events, then we might double or treble that amount," added Serghei. "Look what happens in America. Once people know who they think is going to win, then the money pours in. People want to donate in the hope that it will buy them some kind of preferment later on."

"I'm not doing that!" said Tania firmly. "No one is buying me!"

"It's not always like that," countered Serghei. "Some just want to have their photograph taken to hang on the wall. It makes them look a bigshot with their friends."

"I could help with some initial funding," said Henry. "I could provide say $50,000 to get you started and then $20,000 a month for the next ten months, but that would be it - a quarter of a million dollars. I couldn't afford any more."

"Really," said Tania shocked.

"I suppose so. I've been one of those telling you to do this." There was caution and concern in his voice, for he wasn't sure it was an offer he should be making. He knew it would lead to a change, and he was fearful of what that change might be.

"You can't," said Serghei. "It's illegal for a political party to take money from somebody outside of the country, from a non-national."

"Is that the law?" asked Evelina.

"I don't know," replied Serghei honestly. "Even if it is not, it's a law that should be there, and so it's one we will obey in its absence."

"Tania owns fifty per cent of the Moldovan company, which owns the St. Sophia vineyard and winery. I will lend the money to that, and it can then gift it to Tania's campaign. I don't see how anyone can complain about Tania gifting money from her company to herself."

"We shouldn't start out as a political party," said Osip. "Otherwise, we will have to register with the government, and you can guarantee that will cause a whole host of problems and masses of interference. Remember, at some stage we'll be taking on Costin Stanescu. You don't think he's going to let his father lose without some very rough play, do you?"

The mention of Costin Stanescu sobered up everyone around the table. They each realised what a dangerous task Tania was taking on.

"We should start as a members' voluntary association first, becoming a political party at the last moment," said Osip, bringing the conversation back to his original point.

"Good thinking," said Serghei, who then asked: "What are we called?"

"We'll be the Freedom Party," said Tania firmly, looking lovingly at Serghei as she spoke, wrongly thinking that the name originated with him. "It's on the top of the agenda. It's what we're doing; we're making this country free from corruption. So, we'll start as the Freedom Association."

There was no dissent. It seemed reasonable that the candidate should name her own political party.

"If I could be paid, I would be happy to give up my job and work full-time on the campaign, getting everything set up and running," said Evelina coyly at the same time as emitting a rare moment of shyness.

"Would you?" said Tania excitedly. "Would you really?"

"Yes, so long as Serghei comes and works on the campaign too."

Serghei's heart sank when he heard Evelina's condition. He'd only just got himself established at the United Nations, and their employment conditions forbad him from working or volunteering for a political party. Serghei looked imploringly at Tania. He did not want to let her down. "Do you think I could be paid too?" he asked tentatively.

Tania looked at Henry who nodded furiously. "This is only going to happen if there's a core team working full time and they need to be paid. They need money to live like everyone else," he said, adding what he thought was a statement of the obvious.

From that moment, the Freedom Association had Evelina as its first General Secretary and Serghei as its first Campaign and Membership Director. Within a few seconds Osip Pasternack was volunteered as its first unpaid Treasurer and Finance Director.

"We'll need an office and computers," said Evelina and, very slowly, those around the table started to address the issues of forming a political party working through them one by one.

As the evening progressed and the conversation diverged into smaller groups, Tania thought it was time to bring the discussion towards her biggest concern. She banged the table once again, this time with a glass.

"It seems as though we might have a plan," said Tania, bringing their small gathering back to order. "However, we have one issue we still have to discuss. Henry calls it, 'cleaning out the stable yard.'" Tania paused before continuing. "Everyone here knows my domestic arrangements are, er ... unusual."

"You can say that again," chipped in Evelina.

"I expect to be quizzed on my past life. I have no difficulty with that," said Tania, but it's my children, our children," she added, looking pointedly at Serghei and Henry in turn.

Over the next few minutes, Tania laid out her terms. Her children were never to be mentioned by name in the campaign, not once. They were not to be photographed. She wouldn't make any comment on who were the fathers of her children, and no one around the table was ever to make any public comment on her behalf. They were to say and do nothing which would aid any speculation in any way. If anyone breaks any one of these rules, then she would stop immediately, she told them.

"I'm doing this for Stelian and Yulia," said Tania. "They will suffer enough by me not being there for them. They are not going to suffer more by becoming public property too, not now, not ever!" The tone of Tania's voice was as cold and determined as anyone had ever heard her speak.

There was a nod of approval as Tania slowly and deliberately looked into everyone's eyes around the table, getting the confirmation she expected.

"We should do another TV interview," said Evelina to Tania when their eyes touched. "It would be a good opportunity now your new book is out. We could cover all the difficult family matters in a controlled way. Serghei will edit it so that it is just as you want it."

Tania nodded her agreement.

"We will need a campaign slogan," said Serghei. "I know John Kennedy's was 'A Time For Greatness, and Nixon's was Vote as though your Whole World Depends on it,"

"How do you know that? I didn't know that, and I followed both campaigns," protested Henry.

"The best one must be Harry Truemans - I'm wild about Harry, but the one everyone knows is: "Let's Make America Great Again" by who ...?" asked Serghei, looking at Henry expectantly, who, in ignorance, shook his head and shrugged a negative reply.

"They're questions in Trivial Pursuits, the US Edition, which we played when I was in language school," answered Serghei with a huge smile. "Make America Great was Ronald Regan's slogan. He was said to be the great public communicator."

"What do we want to say?" asked Evelina taking charge and, in the process, making it clear she'd had enough of Serghei's showing off. "I want to say we care. Above all, I want us to care. Our orphanages have shamed us around the world. We've looked heartless. We must care."

"And we have to have integrity," contributed Osip." "It is the one thing which can differentiate us from the rest. Integrity and competence. We must have competence too."

The problem with care is everyone cares. I care about what I have for lunch. I care about the brand of toothpaste I use. It doesn't say enough," added Serghei, getting his own back for Evelina's earlier chide.

There was silence as everyone thought of the problem

"Compassion, we should use compassion instead of care," contributed Valeria Ceban, the woman whose former affair with her former professor had been a matter of extensive debate with anyone who would listen to her, which included Tania. Valeria's folly in her personal life belied the fact that she had developed a skill in political analysis which all those sat around the table had grown to admire

There was a murmur of approval.

We're saying nothing about our policies. Shouldn't a slogan say something about those?" asked Tania.

"None of the US ones did," replied Serghei.

"We need something which we can fall back on if we get asked a question on something we don't have a policy on," Tania persisted.

"Such as?" enquired Valeria.

"I don't know. Our relationship with China, or timber logging, or anything which we haven't thought of," answered Tania frustratedly.

"In which case, our policy is based upon common sense. It's the best we can offer," replied Osip.

Evelina played with the words aloud for everyone to hear: "Compassion, Competence and Common Sence." She repeated it a couple of times. "That's what we want. It's what we stand for, isn't it?"

"And integrity. We must have integrity. Integrity is our differentiator," insisted Osip.

"Compassion, Competence Common Sence and Integrity - is that what we stand for?" asked Evelina.

Everyone nodded, which they followed by a modest cheer and a small round of applause.

"A toast," proposed Henry, still seated: "To Compassion, Competence, Common Sence and Integrity in politics," he said with his glass of water raised high.

Everyone raised their glass and repeated his words.

The Freedom Party had its first campaign slogan, and with it, the party was born.

It was late when everyone left, which they did altogether as no one wanted to miss out on any part of the discussion.

"Why didn't you say?" asked Henry as they walked back to their apartment block. "You could have said when we were walking there."

"I wasn't sure I wasn't going to change my mind when I got there. I knew what you would say, and I didn't want the pressure of letting you down if I sensed that not everyone was with me."

Henry nodded his head, fully understanding her concern.

"What made you decide?" he asked.

"Many things. Obviously, what happened to Mitina Denisovna, and lots of what you said, but probably it was when I was with Grandma Brigita on Sunday. She told me that, in December 1917, one of my great grandfathers, too many greats to count, a man called Count Donici-Solokov, stood for election to the Sfatul Tării, our parliament. He didn't get elected. She said it was because he had another family with his Jewish mistress. She said the Count and I were the same. We had the same blood. He was one man with two women, and I was one woman with two men. She said it was history repeating itself. Grandma Brigita then made it clear that, as a direct descendant of the Donici-Solokov family, I had a duty to fight for Moldova. She reminded me she'd fought against the Nazis in the war to give this country its freedom. She told me it was now my turn to fight; my job to make this the best country I can. I think I'm doing this for her, as much as anybody."

Chapter 49

Kishinev November 1995

TANIA CHOSE HER old school, sitting in her old classroom at her old teacher's table for the interview with Evelina. As Serghei set up the camera and the lights, Evelina studied the notes she had made. Tania tried to prepare herself mentally, for they had agreed that this would be no fireside chat like last time. It was to be a hard-hitting interview, proving that Tania could survive under pressure.

Evelina did a small introductory piece to camera, turned to Tania and asked bluntly: "Why have we come to your old school to talk about your latest book, 'A Partnership for Moldova'?"

The question took Tania completely off guard. It was not the first question that they'd agreed on. Evelina had deliberately changed it to put Tania on the back foot while, at the same time, making sure it was an easy one to answer.

"My last book, 'A Manifesto for Moldova', set out the things that were wrong and the things I was against, like corruption. It made suggestions as to how those issues should be dealt with, put right. To some extent, it was an angry book. My new book, which includes some of my past magazine articles, is far more positive. It's more optimistic. It sets out a vision of what our future should look like.

"What does it look like?" asked Evelina.

"It's a fairer society. A society that works in partnership. A society that works for the common good. It eschews a system divided into capital and labour, each fighting the other. It rejects a system where one group is pitted against another in a winner takes all battle. It's a society in which nations work in harmony with other nations, governments work for and with their people, and the people work in partnership with each other."

Tania took a sip of water. Evelina was conscious of the silence, but deliberately said nothing. Instead, she allowed it to build pressure on Tania to speak.

"In a true partnership, there are no winners and losers," she said. "In a true partnership, you want your partners to do as well as you, if not better. In a partnership, there is a generosity of spirit. So, to come back to your very first question, we are filming here because I think our schools are one of the best examples of partnerships working for the common good that we have.

"Would you describe your political philosophy as being founded in the principles of the common good?" asked Evelina.

"It's an easy catchphrase, so I need to ask; what do you mean by the common good?" said Tania trying to deflect the question.

"It was your phrase, so I think you should define it," responded Evelina tartly.

Tania paused to think: "They are the principles which a society has to adopt so that it works for the benefit of all ... for the advantage of everyone ... in peace and security," she said, shaking her head slightly, not completely satisfied with her answer.

"Our state schools are a classic example of an institution both being and working for the common good," she continued. "They epitomise that generosity of spirit which we must instil in our whole nation. For months on end, the teachers here worked unpaid. The bigwigs in government got paid; somehow, it found the money for them, but not for us, the teachers. Despite having bills to pay and families to feed, the teachers here and throughout the land never stopped working. They continued to work unpaid because it was in the best interests of their students. They did it for the common good in a generosity of spirit, which I think we should try and capture throughout the nation, right from the very top to the bottom.

"So, you're saying that a school is a partnership?" said Evelina.

"Yes, most definitely. It's a place that has, at its heart, a generosity of spirit, the very essence of a good partnership. I believe the generosity of spirit should be encouraged to run throughout our whole nation.

Yes, the teachers are in charge. Yes, there are rules, and yes, the children have to obey the rules and do as they're told, but in a school, you see a true partnership at work; a partnership between the institution, the parents and their children."

"Do these partnerships of yours work like co-operatives," asked Evelina.

"No, I'm not talking about democratically controlled enterprises which are managed either for the benefit of the people who work there or who use its services. It seems obvious to me that the state should own and provide things like roads, water, electricity, and telephone networks. You cannot have two roads running side-by-side or two water pipes coming into a person's home, so these can compete. As I hope I've made clear in my new book, I am in favour of a mixed economy where large elements are owned by the individual but where the state owns essential community property like roads or the gas network."

"I am sorry, I don't get this partnership ethos of yours," said Evelina. "It appears as though you are bringing nothing new to the debate."

"It's not my intention to bring anything new. I am just setting out my thinking for people to agree with or not as they choose. Maybe my contribution is just a different emphasis, that's all, but let me try and help you," said Tania. "I do not believe in a society where one person gets one hundred and a hundred other people get one each. I also don't believe in a society where everything is divided down so that a hundred people get two each. What needs to happen is to reduce the one man who has one hundred to say fifty or sixty through taxation and use that money for the benefit of all, to pay for roads and schools and hospitals. That way, the government will create more jobs and more economic growth."

"Does that mean you don't believe in winning? Did you not want your school team to win when it was playing another school?"

"What a strange question; of course, I believe in winning. But I don't believe in winning at all costs. We are at peace. The need to fight a total war has long gone. Our culture should have changed to recognise the new reality, but it hasn't. I don't believe in winning by cheating. I don't believe in winning more than my fair share. I don't believe in winning to the point where it leaves the other person destitute or humiliated. I think that as a nation, we should have far more humanity than that."

"Do you have a philosophy that brings all this together?" asked Evelina. "For example, do you believe in God?"

"I enjoy going to church," said Tania. "I find it gives me peace and imbues me with calm. However, like many people, I find the lack of a logical relationship between today's science and the teaching of God in the scriptures of the Old and New Testaments so confusing that it is not a subject I find easy to express an opinion, let alone debate."

"Would you say your philosophy is more humanistic, then?" asked Evelina.

"Yes, I would say I tend towards that, but I need to make it clear, I don't rule out there being a God. I just don't believe we know all the science we need to know to make that decision, that's all. What I do know is that, on too many occasions, God has not been kind to the human race."

"Does this mean that you are a pragmatist," asked Evelina.

"Yes, I believe so. I think everything should be in moderation. I find extremism, whether it be in religious or political life, to be offensive.

This was the opening Evelina had been looking for.

"Your personal life cannot be said to be moderate, can it?" said Evelina. "You were married?" she asked.

"Yes, I'm now divorced."

"And you aborted your husband's baby before you and he were married."

"Yes, we were both very young," said Tania defensively.

"Is it true that, when you were married, you miscarried your husband's baby?" asked Evelina.

"Yes."

"And now you are a single mother with two young children from two different fathers, neither of whom were your husband. Is that right?"

"Yes," said Tania trying to remain calm while hating the fact that, at some stage soon, her mother would be watching this recording and would be squirming with discomfort.

"How does this fit in with your partnership philosophy? It looks highly hypocritical to me!" said Evelina.

"I remain close to each of my children's fathers. It works for them, it works for my children, and it works for me," said Tania. "In fact, now I think about it, we operate a partnership philosophy because everyone is generous in spirit. It works because we all want it to work for our children's sakes."

"But the father to one of your children is still married with children of his own, isn't that right?" asked Evelina. "Surely, that's in direct contradiction to your philosophy because in creating your partnership with that man, you have effectively broken the partnership he had with his wife?"

"I would never claim to be perfect, far from it," said Tania defensively. "I would only say that his children are now grown up. Do I think my relationship with him is doing harm to someone else? From what I know of the circumstances, I am fairly certain that it is not."

"What are those circumstances?" probed Evelina.

"I am not going to answer that," said Tania firmly. "I think everyone is entitled to a private life, and in particular that includes my children and their respective fathers. We have just discussed issues that I would have preferred not to have discussed. The facts are now in the public domain. I won't answer any further questions or expand on what I have said ever again, not now, not ever!"

"Not all the facts are in the public domain, are they?" protested Evelina, thinking the world would love to know that the father of Tania's child was married to Sophie Elleswell, one of the world's top supermodels. What a coup it would be to break that news, she thought.

"Don't you think we have a right to know who the fathers of your children are?" asked Evelina. "Are they not relevant to your experiences, your thinking, your writing?" she continued.

"Miss Kirillovich," said Tania firmly, "I do not think anyone has the right to know now or at any time in the future. If you have further questions on my family, please ask, but you will get no answer, for I will say no more on the subject, not now, not ever!"

Evelina paused and looked down at her notes. Tania tried to look relaxed although her heart was thumping hard and her mouth was dry. Serghei panned the camera onto her face as she leaned forward and took a sip of water.

"You no longer teach," said Evelina, "so what do you do now?"

"I'm a mother!" said Tania in a voice of offended protest. "I have two young children, and looking after them is my top job." She calmed down and continued. "I write quite extensively and am lucky as that gives me an income. In addition, I own 50% of a vineyard and winery, which I help to manage."

"You own a vineyard?" said Evelina, feigning surprise in her voice.

"Yes, or at least half of one. I found an overseas investor who I borrowed from because no one would lend to me here, at least not on reasonable terms. It was very run down when we bought it. Since then, we've managed to create good, well-paid jobs where there were none before. It is a tough business, but I think we're going to get there.

"Is your investor a Russian oligarch? Are you beholden to them?" asked Evelina sharply.

"I am not going to say who they are, but I can assure you they are not Russian."

"What, ... er favours ... did you have to offer them to get them to invest?" asked Evelina, making it clear from her tone that she expected to know whether sex was part of the inducement.

Tania tilted her head down, frowned and looked at Evelina through the top of her eyes. "The way that question was phrased was deliberately rude and offensive," she said. "For that reason, I will not answer it. However, be assured the investment involved no impropriety on my part. You're an investigative journalist, aren't you Miss Kirillovich? If you thought there was anything untoward, I am sure you would be asking me about it now. The fact that you are not, shows that there is nothing for you to find."

Tania was physically and mentally exhausted at the end of the interview. Evelina and Serghei were impressed with the way she had handled herself. By carefully editing the different camera shots of the same interview, Serghei made Tania appear to be a person who everyone would like.

The Watches of de Gressier

Except, on the night the interview was aired, it divided those that watched it three ways. The men couldn't work out which, between Tania and Evelina, they would prefer to sleep with. They were the Moldovan equivalent of Agnetha and Anni-Frid from ABBA, except neither could sing. It was amongst the Moldovan women that opinion was strongly divided. Some disapproved of Tania strongly, describing her as a harlot, a femme fatale and a shameless man stealer. Others admired her independence. They envied the fact that she had taken control of her life and was managing it in a way that put her and her children first, and her men second.

Whatever the feelings there were over the interview, it was enough to take Tania's second book to second place in the list of Christmas non-fiction book sales. Whether many people read it, who knows.

Chapter 50

Kishinev January to March 1996

IMMEDIATELY AFTER CHRISTMAS, the shadow campaign to get Tania elected as president started in earnest. Serghei organised visits throughout the land, to factories, farms, shops, offices, community halls, anywhere that would take them. It was all arranged on the ostensible reason of a book signing tour.

Everywhere Tania went, she would give a speech, answer questions, and circulate, making a point of shaking everyone's hand. Sometimes there would be no more than a handful of people, on other occasions, there could be sixty or seventy. People were interested to see what the woman from the television looked like in real life.

Meanwhile, as Tania sold and signed books, Serghei would be busy recruiting members to the Freedom Association. Many thought they were joining Tania's fan club. Others were astute enough to realise they were joining a campaigning group or quasi-political party. It was these that Serghei tried to identify as people who might when the time came, lead the campaign for Tania locally.

"I've seen you several times on television," said a man who Tania had selected from the crowd to ask a question. "Many times, you've been asked whether you're interested in being President, yet you've always denied it half-heartedly. You've never actually said yes, although that's what today is all about, isn't it? Why don't you just say you can't because of the age restriction. You have to be over forty to be president of Moldova, and you're certainly not that."

It was the first time that Tania, or any of those in the Freedom Association, had heard of the age restriction. For a moment, it left her completely dumbfounded.

"It is true. I've had many people suggest I should stand for election as president," said Tania. "There are many considerations; not least is the age restriction of which you have spoken. It means I have to be realistic, for if I were to stand as President of Moldova, I would have one handicap which no other candidate would have. I would have to change the law first!"

The journey back to Kishinev was acrimonious, with Serghei and Tania blaming each other for their ignorance when they knew that everyone at the core of their campaign shared some of the responsibility too. So enthusiastic were they for the cause that no one had got around to studying Moldova's election law and the electoral arrangements.

What Serghei and Tania feared most was Henry's reaction. He had invested a lot of money in getting Tania's campaign started, and now it was going to come to an abrupt halt. When Henry heard the news, he was more phlegmatic and reasonable than either Serghei or Tania could reasonably have expected. What they did not know was that Henry's whole career had been built on achieving something and then immediately being punished for his success by something else going wrong. To him, it was no more than one of those moments he had faced many times in the past. He'd learnt that, at times like this, the issues had to be carefully examined, alternatives considered, and a new pathway found. There was only going back as long as it meant going forward again, but in a different way. To some extent, Henry was pleased that the campaign might be over before it was started. He was finding Moldova a very lonely place to be without Tania constantly at his side.

It was a defeated group that met at the offices of the Freedom Association the next evening. These had been lent, rent-free, by a man who ran one of Moldova's new online digital advertising companies. He had no interest in politics whatsoever, just in growing his business. It was what he thought about at every waking moment. He had rented an extra floor expecting to expand into it at some stage soon. If, by lending this spare floor, it meant that some of the Freedom Association's advertising budget came his way, then it would be well worth it. If it meant he'd have a better chance of fulfilling his ambition of sleeping with Evelina, then so much the better.

Sitting in the corner of the room, facing his keyboard and typing furiously, was Fomin Granok. He was not a member of the Freedom Association's management board and held the honour of being one of the most ignored men in the room. Yet, he was probably one of the most important, and not because he was about to explode and change the whole mood of the meeting.

Fomin Granok was as unattractive as a man could possibly be. He was so overweight that his blubber would fall around any poor chair he had chosen to sit on. He only wore tracksuits, washed, cleaned and pressed every day, as these were the only clothes he could buy in his size. He wore his thick hair with a short fringe in the front and then tied into a thick bushy ponytail at the back. He was obsessive about many things, including his hygiene. It meant he had the whitest of teeth allowing his smile to compete favourably with that of any top Hollywood actor.

Fomin Granok was clearly on the autistic spectrum. He was undoubtedly highly intelligent but had great difficulty in creating relationships with other people. It was why he was so good at dealing with computers. He could relate to them. They had a logic he understood, whereas people frightened him. He had been sent by the local IT shop to set up the Freedom Association's computer network and had stayed. In the few weeks that he had been there, he had built an interactive election campaigning database that would do everything that the computer systems of any one of the major political parties anywhere in the world could do

Long before anyone else, Fomin had studied the election rules. He knew that to get Tania on the presidential ballot paper, they needed 18,000 signatures from 18 out of the 35 administration units designated by the Central Electoral Commission, with not less than 600 signatures from each unit. He had also been monitoring the growth in membership, and using his projected trend line, he was certain that, if the growth rate continued, then they would easily meet the required target to get Tania on the ballot paper.

On hearing the defeatist talk around the room and the suggestion that they should give up, Fomin did something he had never done before. "No!" he shouted emphatically from his chair in the corner of the room. "No, no, no!" he yelled in Moldovan, for although his shyness meant he refused to speak English, he understood it perfectly.

Fomin's anger shocked the room. "We've discussed all of this," he said. "We've already agreed the plan. We're going to file Tania's nomination form with the CEC[7], with the required number of signatures, long before the thirty-day deadline mandated by law. They will have to reject it. We will then immediately go to the Constitution Court to get the age restriction lifted on the grounds that it is non-constitutional. The OSCE[8] and its ODIHR[9] have already said that an age requirement of forty is a politically motivated restriction and needs to be removed."

Everyone looked around amazed, for none of them could remember having this conversation. Each assumed it had taken place with others, except surely Tania, Henry, Serghei and Evelina would have known? The fact was that Fomin's conversations were all imaginary. The alleged discussions, held long ago, were only in his head. He had discovered the problem long before them, and having considered it carefully over many days, it was what he thought they should decide to do.

Serghei summed up what he thought Fomin had said, but this time in English so Henry would understand.

"We have a plan?" asked Henry, after Serghei had finished his summing up.

There was a murmur of consent.

"We need to change and become a political party. We should register with the Ministry of Justice straight away," said Osip Pasternak, "and we should set a date of 15th September for having all the nomination

---

[7] Comisia Electorală Centrală a Rubublicii Moldova - Central Election Commission of Moldova

[8] Organization for Security and Co-operation in Europe

[9] Office for Democratic Institutions and Human Rights

signatures into the CEC," he added after flicking through the pages of his diary.

"We should hand a petition into the government at the same time," said Serghei.

"The CEC will have to reject Tania's nomination form," continued Osip, ignoring Serghei's interruption. They might try and delay things so that we have less time to go to court. This means when we file with the CEC, we need to have our court petitions already prepared."

I'm sorry," said Henry, "but I can't afford the cost of a legal battle. I have committed all the money I can."

"I think we're alright for money," said Osip. "We could always do with more, but Tania's book sales, the ones she gets free from the publisher and signs and sells at every event, is giving us a decent income. Also, many members are paying ten or twenty lei a month rather than just once as we've thought at the outset."

"I think a couple of law professors at the university will help us prepare a court petition for free," said Serghei. "They want to end the corruption in the courts. I think they'll be supporters. I'll ask them."

Tania nodded and mouthed her thanks in his direction.

"You'll need to do another television interview," said Evelina looking at Tania.

"Yes, but you can't do it," said Serghei, addressing Evelina.

"Why not?" she asked, affronted.

"You're on this committee; you'd have a conflict. I'll get Timinov to do it."

"What, the news anchor on Channel 1?"

"Yes, he'll give her a hard time because he'll want to keep his job, but he won't be unfair, under-hand," said Serghei.

"Stop," said Henry authoritatively. "The time has come to hire a Head of Media, a Press Secretary. Once you're seen as a political party, you won't be setting the news agenda, you'll be responding to it, and we need to make sure we respond with one voice."

"I think this changes things in another way," said Tania. "I think the Freedom Party needs to have its own Members of Parliament. We need to get them elected in the November elections, ahead of the presidential election. If we can win enough seats, then we'll be able to influence what happens in Parliament, i.e., get the age restriction changed."

"How does that work?" said Henry with a sigh as he realised the Freedom Party was about to become an out-of-control behemoth.

"There are a hundred and one seats in Parliament allocated on a party-list proportional representation basis with the whole country as one constituency," answered Osip.

"Let me make sure I understand this. If we get thirty per cent of the votes, we'll get thirty Deputies in parliament, is that right?" asked Henry.

All those seated around nodded.

"It means we've got to find a hundred and one people who are prepared to stand as deputies and somehow find a way of paying their election expenses," said Henry, making sure he understood.

"Yes," said Tania, "but worse than that, we have to rank them in some way from one to a hundred and one."

"It's unlikely we're going to get more than 50% of the voters," said Serghei adding a sense of realism. "In reality, we need to find fifty-one people, and each of those fifty-one will have to raise the money to help fund the campaign. The good ones won't be expecting a free ride."

"So, your constitution locks you into a permanent coalition government," observed Henry disapprovingly.

"Yes Henry, you know that," said Tania crossly, fed up with his past preaching on this subject. "We've discussed this before, and you've lost the argument. The two-party system in the US, or the UK or France is no better. You've already admitted it. The politics there are just as corrupt as here. You've said it yourself. Look at the gun lobby in the US and how many politicians it buys a year." Tania knew that, for everyone around the table, she had to dispel Henry's criticism. These were the rules they had to fight under and to undermine them was not helpful.

"Perhaps the two party system is even worse than the money corruption, which dominates all politics because it is also dishonest," Tania continued after a short pause. "In countries where two parties dominate, like the US and UK, each of the two main political parties sees the other as so evil that they are prepared to say and do anything, tell as many lies as they need to get elected. You've already an expression for it, haven't you Henry? – 'good cause corruption'. It's an expression you've used time and time again. You're being arrogant when you think your election system is the best. It's not! It's only because they're yours that you think so. Any rational analysis will tell you that's just not true!"

Those in the room listened somewhat shocked as they hadn't heard Tania speak to Henry like that before. Everyone recognised the moment for what it was. Tania was taking control of her own election campaign. From now on, she was undoubtedly in charge.

"Finding fifty-one people wealthy enough to campaign, who can also afford the time to be involved, and haven't paid more than a token bribe is going to be impossible to find, isn't it?" said Henry recovering quickly from her onslaught at the same time as bringing further realism to the task.

"The one thing we have to be absolutely clear on; no one who represents us is ever to have taken or made a bribe," said Evelina. "If we don't keep to that, then I'm leaving," she said aggressively.

"We agree, we agree," said Tania rapidly, "but it has to be a significant payment, a meaningful payment. We've all had to pay someone at some time to get something done."

"We need to form a selection committee," said Osip, bringing his focus on the practicalities to the fore once again.

"Good idea," said Henry, equally as quickly, "and you're its chairman."

Osip looked around the room with a grimace that could have killed. He was seriously upset with the way he'd been delegated the burden of another job. Didn't people realise how hard he was already working?

"Valeria will help you," volunteered Tania immediately she saw Osip's reaction. "Won't you?" she asked, looking directly at Valeria Ceban.

"Yes," she answered willingly. "We'll make a great team."

Osip and Valeria smiled. Another romantic affair, under the pressure of political life, had just been born.

Chapter 51

Kishinev March 1996

THERE WAS AN air of excitement in the offices of the Freedom Association on the morning of Thursday 28th March. A press release had been prepared and issued, embargoed until 6am. Interviews were booked on all the TV and radio channels, and the feature articles for the weekend newspapers had been written. It was the day Tania was announcing the Freedom Association was transforming itself into a political party. It would be petitioning to change the law so that Tania could stand for election as President of Moldova in the December elections.

There was a large deputation who went to the Ministerul Justiţiei to lodge the papers to register the Freedom Party as a political party. There was a celebratory atmosphere as they stood on the steps outside the white modern government building and had their photograph taken before Tania was called away for street interviews with the newspapers.

The only one missing from the photographs was Henry. He was in South Africa seeing Harriet Russell. He might have gone back to Kishinev for the event, but it had been agreed between him and Tania that his being there and photographed with them all, would not be a good idea. It could raise questions as to whether it was this wealthy Frenchman who had financed the Freedom Party.

If life for everyone involved in Tania's campaign had been busy before, it became hectic immediately after they had transformed into a political party. Working eighteen hours a day, seven days a week, became the norm as they attempted to control the beast they had created. No longer were Tania and her colleagues creating the news agenda. They had to respond to it. This meant that every moment of the day, they had to be prepared to express an opinion on every single issue which might crop up in the news cycle.

The biggest burden placed on the Freedom Party was the decision to try and win parliamentary seats in the November election. Dealing with applications, interviewing, and vetting candidates placed a load on those at the centre, which no one could possibly have imagined at the outset.

For Tania, there was one day of the week that was sacrosanct. It was on Sunday when she would take Stelian from the care of Serghei's parents, and Henry if he were around, and go to the Woodman's Dacha. There she would spend the day with her daughter Yulia, who was being looked after by her mother and father, Heidi and Vlad, while she campaigned. Her grandmother Anna and her great-grandmother Brigita would be there too, wanting to know everything that had been going on, every twist, every debate, every problem. It wasn't that Tania needed to be there to have time to think. She had plenty of time to do that as she sat in the car travelling from one end of Moldova to another.

Sunday at the Woodman's Dacha was the one time when her life could go back to being normal. When she could cuddle her children, smell them as they would nestle their faces into her neck, fight them as they did not do as they were told and enjoy the magic that children bring to everyone's lives.

For both Tania and Henry, the days they spent at the Woodman's Dacha were truly magical. Often, when the sun was shining, they would all walk into the woods to the clearing and the Donici-Solokov food den. Tania found there was something calming and spiritually renewing about walking through the trees to that spot.

Chapter 52

Kishinev March 1996

PRESIDENT MIRCEA STANESCU and his son Costin were physically miles apart when they saw the evening news announcing the formation of the Freedom Party.

The President took the news pragmatically. He had the money. He controlled the voting system. He controlled the courts. He controlled the newspapers. The Freedom Party would come and go. He was sure of it. It would shine brightly as a new star for a few months, as all new political parties did, but it would soon fade and die. He was sure of that too.

Costin Stanescu's attitude was completely different. He was livid.

"Why didn't you take that bloody woman, screw her and sell her as I told you," he yelled at Frolov Ilyich immediately he saw him at the Steffaco Hotel.

"She's bloody holier than thou. She's telegenic. She's got fucking charisma. She's gonna take votes from everybody," he protested loudly.

"If she takes votes from everyone equally, then your father should still win, shouldn't he?" said Ilyich, not understanding political maths.

"No!" shouted Costin angrily. "She'll take votes from us, and she'll take votes from everyone else. That way, she gets the most votes and wins."

"Why the fuck didn't you fuck her?" shouted Costin. "If you'd done your job properly, she wouldn't be here now," he screamed, his slang getting in the way of his diction. "For God's sake, find some way to fuck the bitch. She's got to be got out of this," he ordered as he picked up a briefcase containing 10,000 lei in cash. It was the winnings from the hotel's casino over the last couple of weeks.

Chapter 53

Kishinev April 1996

IT WAS NEARLY 3 am and Fomin Granok was about to leave the offices of the Freedom Party to go home before he returned after having just had a few hours' sleep. As usual, he was on his own. Always the last one to leave, he had in his hand the hard disk on which he had religiously backed up all the Freedom Party's computer data. He would take this home and bring back in the morning the hard disk drive he had taken home the night before. In this way, Fomin made sure he had a backup of the Freedom Party's data, which was never more than one day out of date, off the premises.

It was the sound of a massive whoosh of exploding petrol in the stairwell outside his office which caught Fomin's attention. Petrol had been poured down three flights of concrete steps and into the lift shaft. A large amount of fuel had been thrown around at the bottom before a flame was thrown through the letterbox of the closed front door.

Fomin could see the fire through the windows of the door between their offices and the communal stairwell. His main escape route had gone, and the glass in the door was already beginning to crack in the heat.

Urgently Fomin looked around the room to find a way out. There was no obvious escape, for he was four stories up with no exit to the front or back of the building. There was only one way out: through the windows to the side of the building directly opposite the flames. Even if he could get through one of these, it still meant a fall of three metres onto the flat roof of the building next door. The problem for Fomin was that the windows were too narrow for him to climb through. In a panic, Fomin picked up the phone to dial the fire brigade, but the lines were dead. They had either been cut or had melted in the heat.

Taking a chair, Fomin smashed the glass and the window frame as hard as he could so as to create an aperture through which he might be able to squeeze. Fomin frantically chipped off the shards of glass and splinters of wood stuck in the frame as he heard the roar of the fire behind him.

As poisonous smoke began to billow through and under the doors, Fomin knew he could no longer stay. He had no alternative but to try and squeeze his huge body through the jagged aperture he had made.

With his precious hard disk in his hand, Fomin pushed his head through the window until he had no alternative but to lay his massive belly on the bottom of the frame and allow his head to fall. He wriggled on one side and then the other, cutting himself badly as he went until he was stuck upside down suspended by his trousers. Still holding his disk, he threw himself around, unable to go back and unable to fall down. He undid the cord around his waist, which held up his trousers and, leaving his underpants behind, he dropped further until his shoes became trapped in the narrowing at the ankles of his track suit trouser legs. Kicking at one shoe with another, he managed to free one foot, but he was still stuck there, his body grazing badly against the rough wall, blood pouring out of his badly cut belly. With his free foot, he kicked the other shoe off, and with that, he fell hard, head first, onto the bitumen, the protective stones implanting themselves into his skull. Still, he had the hard disk in his hand.

Fomin climbed to his feet, hobbling as the stone chips dug through his socks into his soles. Very conscious of his nakedness from the waist down, Fomin tentatively wandered around the flat roof. He hated heights, and there was no obvious fire escape. On his hands and knees, he looked round and over the edge. There was no way down. He would need to be rescued.

Fomin stood on the roof and screamed and yelled, like a man demented, until a taxi driver, whose attention had first been drawn by the huge fire behind the glass front doors, stopped and wound down his car window to look properly. It was a peculiar sight for high up; there was an obese man, naked from the waist down, bouncing around as he moved from one foot to the next, screaming from a mix of fright and pain.

"Call the fire brigade, get the fire brigade" yelled Fomin. "The building next door's on fire, and I'm trapped. I can't get down."

The taxi driver radioed his control station, who called the fire brigade. It was eleven long minutes before a fire engine arrived and another five minutes before another one came with a ladder long enough to get Fomin off the roof. Eventually, and only after the hard disk was safely secured inside the fireman's jacket sent up to rescue him, was Fomin coaxed off the roof and down the ladder where he was wrapped in a blanket.

As soon as Fomin was down, but only after he had his precious hard disk back in his hand, he was popped into an ambulance where his wounds were quickly checked before the decision was made that he had to go to hospital. No sooner was he admitted as a patient than Fomin discharged himself and went home. He told no one what had happened or where he was.

The first Tania knew of the fire was when she turned up at the offices of the Freedom Party for their regular 7.30 am meeting, only to find a burned-out shell. The press and television cameras were already there streaming live broadcasts.

Osip had earlier established what had happened, so he was able to brief Tania quickly before she was called upon to make a statement to the assembled news reporters.

Tania stepped into the area cordoned off by the police and, making sure she had the fire engines in the background, she started to speak:

"Thanks to the skill and bravery of our firemen, lives have once again been saved. We are eternally grateful to them for their dedication to duty. I say a heartfelt thank you."

Tania paused.

"I am in no doubt that this attack was politically motivated. It shows why the Freedom Party is so important. Burning out your opponent's offices, and putting lives at risk, is not the way to conduct political debate in a civilised society. It is not the way we should be conducting politics in Moldova close to the start of the twenty-first century. We are all better than this. We deserve better than this. All those decent people who abhor such actions, who condemn violence in politics and corruption in public life, need to join us. It requires the majority of good people to stand up against the evil behaviour of the few. Only then will evil be defeated. If you want to join us, to work with us, to make Moldova a place to be proud of, then please go to our website and become a member. Work with us to defeat this kind of evil."

Costin Stanescu had given Tania and the Freedom Party the Public Relations coup of the decade.

Chapter 54

St. Sophia Estate and Kishinev March 1996

"COME QUICK, COME quick boss," shouted one of the women who worked on the St. Sophia Estate. She was five hundred metres away and running towards Henry as fast as she could.

Henry had left his apartment in the centre of Kishinev just after 6 am. He wanted to get to the vineyards early so he could supervise the re-planting of the trees and hedges. They had been wrongly planted before and had just been dug up. He was determined to make sure it was done correctly this time. It meant he had no idea of the fire attack on the offices of the Freedom Party the night before.

As soon as Henry reached one of the newly built cottages, which had been taken over as an office, he was urged to watch the television which had been switched on. There was a picture of Tania being interviewed against the backdrop of fire engines with blue flashing lights.

"What's happening, what's happened?" asked Henry frantically.

"Fire at office," said one of the men who had gathered around the television.

"Accident or deliberate?" asked Henry.

"Prednamerennyy," answered one of the women in Russian who had understood his question.

"Predetermined, predetermined?" asked Henry nodding his head furiously to make sure he had understood.

"Yes," said the man who spoke first. "Prednamerennyy, deliberate."

Henry watched and listened to Tania carefully. He couldn't understand a word of what she was saying.

"Is anyone hurt, anyone hurt?" he asked panic now in his voice. "When did it happen?" Henry's reaction was quite different to Tania's. His very being was falling apart.

"Last night, one man, he was taken to hospital, but he's OK. He's been let out," said the distiller, who had been listening to the news on the radio and had come to the office to tell Henry what had been happening.

Henry dived for the phone where he dialled, first Tania, then Evelina, then Serghei's mobile phones. There was no answer from any of them, so he was forced to leave messages, and with each unanswered phone call, he was transforming into a shaking, gibbering wreck. In his mind's eye, he was reliving the firebombing of his family home in London years before. It was the very moment when his life with Sophie, his ever so precious Sophie, had started to fall apart, and it was happening again, but this time with Tania. He couldn't bear it, not twice.

Those around Henry were shocked to see how quickly he was physically and mentally degenerating. They'd always seen him strong, fit, determined, detached and unemotional, but now he was just the antithesis of the man they thought they knew.

Henry drove back to Kishinev and his apartment like a maniac. He couldn't get there fast enough, and in his frustration, tears poured down his cheeks.

Henry didn't care about parking as he pulled his car to a dramatic stop outside Tania and his apartment block. As he climbed the concrete stairwell, he realised what a fire trap this place was. The steel front doors would act as a fire barrier, but once inside, there would be no way out.

Henry didn't go into his apartment. Instead, he let himself into Tania's, shouted out her name hopefully and then screwed up his face in agony when he realised she was not there. Once again, he worked the phones, constantly calling Tania, Serghei and Evelina, this time using his mobile phone as it worked in the city. He managed to get hold of lots of other people, but no one could tell him where these three were. What he did learn, from a stilted conversation with Serghei's mother, was that Stelian and Yulia were safe with her.

As the minutes dragged into hours, so Henry became more determined that the Freedom Party would stop, and it would stop now. No one should die for a political cause. That quote by Patrick Henry, 'give me liberty or give me freedom', was the biggest load of bollocks ever said, he thought. What was his duty? What was Tania's duty? It was survival, that's what their animal instinct required, and this political crap was just putting all that at risk. It just wasn't worth it.

It was Evelina who contacted Henry first.

"Where is she, where is she?" demanded Henry fiercely.

"She's with Serghei," answered Evelina. "After she'd given her statement to the police and given a couple of one-to-one press interviews, Serghei and she agreed that they should keep to their original schedule. They wanted to prove that nothing was going to get in their way. Almost pretend that nothing had happened."

"Nothing has happened," repeated Henry, incredulity and frustration oozing from every syllable. "How can they say that?"

"Because no one's been badly hurt, and all the electoral data has been saved. The only thing that has happened is some desks and chairs have been burned. Tomorrow, we'll find somewhere else to work from," answered Evelina pragmatically.

"Someone was hurt, who was hurt?" shouted Henry, as he paced like a trapped tiger.

"Fomin," replied Evelina, "but he's fine, a few cuts. Look, stay there. I'll be with you in fifteen minutes."

As soon as Evelina arrived at Tania's apartment, Henry clasped her in a protective hug and then hung on to her as though he were a drowning man hanging onto his rescuer.

In the outpouring of Henry's emotions, Evelina found that her strength and determination evaporated too. She had been frightened by what had happened, and now, in Henry's arms, she could admit that fear. She needed to hold onto him too. Each was getting the human comfort they required from the other.

They had held on to each other tightly like this once before. That was when they were naked in the swimming pool, each teasing, daring the other. Now it was different. They were sharing the nakedness of their raw emotions. Each knew, at that moment, that a bond had been created between them which would never be broken.

"Tania has to give it up. She has to stop it now," said Henry.

"She won't," said Evelina. "She's made it clear already. Serghei and I have talked to her about it, and she won't listen. Instead, it's made her more determined."

"She can't, she can't, you have to stop her," pleaded Henry.

"I can't make her Henry," said Evelina. "You're the only one who could do that, and I don't think you should. She won't like you for it."

Surprised at the rebuttal of his request, Henry slowly let go of Evelina's slim muscular frame and stood back to look at her contemplatively. Evelina smiled and nodded her head slowly with encouragement. He smiled back. They both knew Evelina was right.

Henry went to the bathroom. He washed his hands and face and brushed his hair with Tania's comb. When he reappeared the dependable, unshakable, reliable Henry, which everyone knew, had returned. His emotional breakdown was over, and so was Evelina's. She had taken the opportunity to apply some lipstick and top-up her eye makeup. She too, was ready to take on the world.

"Let's get out of here and get some coffee," said Evelina. "I think it would do us both good to be somewhere else right now."

Sitting at a street table belonging to a restaurant on Strada Vasile Alecsandri, Evelina recounted the scene of poor Fomin, naked from the waist down, being led from the roof onto the fireman's ladder and then to the ground. The image of Fomin's huge bare buttocks descending onto the poor fireman, who was stood at the top of the ladder, brought the first chuckles of laughter to what was a dreadful situation.

"Do you know it's the second time I have been firebombed?" said Henry. "My house in London was firebombed when I was just married, and my kids were very young."

"Yes," said Evelina. "When I was working at Anderson's, they put together a whole file on you from press cuttings as you were a client who'd been categorised as a Person of Influence."

"Influence," scoffed Henry. "Influential at what? I can plot my wife's illness directly back to the moment our home in London was set on fire. Do you know she never went back, not once." His voice reflected his emotional upset.

For the second time, Henry told of Sophie and his story. Evelina listened carefully noticing how differently he told it this time, blaming himself all the way through its re-telling. Instinctively she knew she should say nothing. He needed to talk, and as women have done through the ages, she would listen.

Tania got back to her flat late in the evening with Serghei in tow. Evelina had only stayed to keep Henry company and stop him from becoming melancholic again. Immediately Tania was in her flat, Evelina and Serghei left. They knew these two needed to be alone.

"Tell her, Henry," said Evelina, as she kissed him on the cheek goodnight. "Tell her Sophie's story. I think she will understand better."

Tania had, throughout the day, created a shell of self-preservation around herself. It meant that she was aloof and distant when she walked through the front door of her flat. She was not in the mood for the scolding from Henry, which, from the messages on her mobile phone, she was expecting. Instead, and to avoid the confrontation for which she had no energy, Tania went and showered. Under the hot water, she washed away the hard coating she had wrapped herself in during the day. She would put it on again tomorrow morning.

Tania reappeared in her dressing gown with her hair wrapped in a towel. Henry wanted to complain about the way he had been abandoned, kept in the dark and worrying all day. But now, he saw how vulnerable she looked, he knew he could say nothing. It would not be fair. Instead, he took her in his arms and cuddled her, and they shared the most loving and sensitive of kisses.

"Evelina says you won't give up," said Henry as he and Tania sat around the small kitchen table, sipping at mugs of tea.

"No, I won't," said Tania firmly. "The whole thing was designed to frighten us, warn us off, that's all."

"It's done that alright," said Henry jocularly, trying to bring some normality back to their lives.

"They won't do it again," said Tania, not believing a word of what she was saying.

"I'd like you to stop," said Henry. "Please stop."

"Please don't ask me," replied Tania. "Please don't ask. I'm sure I'll be alright. I promise."

"How can you be so sure?"

"I can't. I just don't believe they will be stupid enough to try the same thing twice. They'll be the usual intimidations, but I'm Moldovan. I live in a country with a secret police force. I have to deal with these things. It's just the way it is."

"And Stelian and Yulia, how do they play into your thinking?" asked Henry gently, believing this was his trump card.

"I'm doing this for them," she answered defiantly, for it was the truth. It was the only reason she was doing it. It was all so hard that she would have given it up long ago, but for the fact that she knew she had to make Moldova better for them, and this was her way of doing it.

"Come, let's go," he said, taking her hand. "Let's go and lie on the bed."

Reluctantly Tania got up from the table to go with him. The last thing she wanted right now was sex, but she had misread the situation. It was the last thing on Henry's mind too.

They lay side by side on her bed, holding hands, their faces turned towards each other, enjoying the silence.

"If I'm not to ask you to stop, then there are some things you are going to have to do for me, for us," said Henry softly.

Tania didn't say anything. Instead, she just smiled weakly.

"You need to move out of here," he said. "If it were firebombed, you would never get out."

"It's not going to happen," said Tania dismissively.

"It's happened once already," retorted Henry. "We could move into our cottage at St Sophia. We've been meaning to do that for a long time."

"It's too far out. I couldn't campaign from there," she answered. Henry knew she was right.

"Well, we're not staying here," said Henry emphatically. "We're going to find somewhere else to rent, at least until after the election."

Tania nodded. It was an easy condition to agree to get her own way.

"There's one other condition," said Henry. "I want you to have a bodyguard. I was with Evelina sitting in a street cafe this afternoon and I realised how vulnerable you are. How easily you could be shot by someone passing by."

Again, Tania smiled. "Only so long as he's damned good looking," she said. "If he's anything less than Kevin Costner, then I'm not having him."

"You saw the film?" asked Henry.

"The Bodyguard, yes twice. He's been my heartthrob since 'No Way Out'," she smiled teasingly.

They squeezed hands affectionately.

"Stelian, Yulia," said Tania. "You'll take care of them if anything happens?" She looked at him earnestly.

"Of course, of course," he replied, squeezing her body into him for reassurance.

That question was the first and only time that Tania gave any sign that she was worried too.

They lay still for some time, enjoying the comfort of having someone by their side until Tania moved abruptly.

"I have to go and see Fomin," she said, suddenly sitting up. "He's been cut and is quite badly hurt. I need to make sure he's alright," she continued. "Did you hear what he did to save our data? I have to thank him, and tomorrow will be one day too late."

Henry looked at his watch. It was 11 pm. "Do you know where he lives," he asked, still languishing on the bed.

"Yes, yes, come on," urged Tania as she wriggled into a pair of tight jeans, pulling Henry from the bed as she did so.

The bodyguard would come, but they never moved out of their two apartments. They could find nowhere safe, and the days were always too packed with other things to do.

Chapter 55

Kishinev March 1996

WHILE TANIA WAS lying alongside Henry, Evelina was phoning Edik. They had only spoken a few times since they had split just over three years ago. As Evelina dialled, she wondered what she ever saw in him.

"You need to tell your mate ..." said Evelina as soon as Edik answered the phone.

'My mate?" interrupted Edik, before asking, "Evelina is that you?"

"Yes, your mate, Costin Stanescu. Tell him to leave Tania Plesca alone!" she said. "We have evidence that he was directly involved in last night's attack on the Freedom Party."

"We?" asked Edik.

"Yes, I'm its General Secretary."

"What, you've gone into politics!" exclaimed Edik, aghast. "Why? When?"

"They asked me."

"Why do you think Costin's involved?" asked Edik, returning to the reason for Evelina's call.

"You know the whip Ilyich uses, the wire flex?"

Edik didn't say anything.

"The guy that helped firebomb the pizzeria; you know, the time when the manager's eye was cut in two with a flex wire whip, well, he's the same person who firebombed the Freedom Party," said Evelina.

"How do you know?" asked Edik.

"It's the same man on both CCTV recordings," she lied.

"What, how do you know that?" continued Edik, surprise in his voice.

Evelina didn't know; she was working on a hunch because the modus operandi was the same. "Believe me, I know, and if anything happens to Tania, or me, then the rest of the world will know too. We've secured the evidence safely, just in case," she lied again.

Edik said nothing. He knew from being with her at the Academy of Foreign Intelligence[10] in Chelebityevo that Evelina was the one person you didn't want as your opponent.

"I'm just phoning to tell you and Costin, do yourselves a big favour. Leave the Freedom Party alone; leave us alone!" she said before rapidly hanging up.

It meant that Edik didn't get to ask the question he had wanted to ask her for many months. Would she like to have dinner with him?

The next day Costin, accompanied by Notary Nesto Ivanov and two bodyguards, met with Frolov Ilyich at the Steffaco Hotel. It was a short conversation. Ilyich had to transfer his shares in the Steffaco Hotel to Costin forthwith. Shortly afterwards, Ilyich and his bodyguard left the Steffaco hotel. No one would have thought anything was wrong. They were never seen again. Their bodies were never found.

---

[10] The KGB training school also known as the SVR Academy.

Chapter 56

Kishinev March – September 1996

THE FIREBOMBING OF the Freedom Party played straight into Tania's hands, although the story was missing from the evening news on all state television and radio channels. It made only a few column inches in a couple of the leading newspapers. President Mircea Stanescu had made sure of it.

But there was a new tool on the market - email. Within two days of the attack, every Freedom Party member, who had access to email, knew what had happened and were asked to share the news. Soon the story was repeated in every local newspaper wherever Tania had spoken and in the numerous news-sheets and pamphlets circulating throughout the country.

At every meeting Tania attended, Serghei made sure she spoke against the backdrop of a large photograph of their firebombed offices. As the news of the treatment of the Freedom Party spread throughout the land, so Tania's invitations to appear on radio and television dried up. Producers didn't dare risk upsetting President Stanescu. Nevertheless, by June, the membership of the Freedom Party had grown to over 37,000 and was continuing to grow daily.

Evelina's conversation with Edik didn't end the intimidation. Its form changed so that it could not be traced back to Stanescu or any other party. Several times Tania's village and town hall meetings were interrupted and shut down by the threatening behaviour of thugs, who distinguished themselves by their uniforms of jeans, t-shirts, black trainers and no socks. Serghei's solution was to book two venues, and as soon as people arrived at the first, if they looked respectable, he would send them on to the second.

Henry's inability to speak either Russian or Moldovan fluently meant he had become almost an outcast from the Freedom Party he was funding. As it grew, the need to share information and ideas quickly, meant English was no longer used. He understood a little of what was going on but only enough to leave him in a state of permanent confusion. In truth, as anyone who has ever worked on a major political campaign will tell, you can't help but wonder what the hell is going on as elections take on a life of their own. Unplanned events create chaos, causing party workers to get buffeted from and to all points of the compass. It was hard to keep to their campaign message 'Kill Corruption because Corruption Kills'.

Tania was busier than ever, so she and Henry saw less and less of each other. Big donors wanted to meet her, and she wanted to meet those who had been shortlisted for approval as parliamentary candidates. This meant that Henry was also seeing less of Yulia, who was now spending the majority of her time with Heidi, Tania's mother. What upset Henry about this was the way Heidi made it clear that she thought Henry's presence, when Tania was not there, was unwarranted and an intrusion.

Henry left Moldova at the end of June and returned to Château de Gressier. He felt overwhelmingly melancholic. It seemed to him that his strange family life with Tania, which had at one stage worked well, was now rapidly unfurling, and he hated it.

What he hated most was his inability to do anything about it. The last time things went wrong with his family life, Henry knew it was substantially his fault. He was working all hours God gave. This time it was different. It was Tania who was operating at both ends of the spectrum, either in a state of hyperactivity or total exhaustion. He wanted to say something, but he didn't feel he could as Tania's mission was on a higher moral plane. It was one in which she had to be both lauded and supported.

A visit to Château de Gressier did nothing to lift Henry's spirits, so he went to see Sophie and sat by her side for a few days. He ended up getting more depressed as, with Sophie being unable to string no more than a few words together, they mainly sat in silence. It meant he thought more and more about Tania and how their relationship was going wrong too.

In August, Henry spent a week with his sons and their girlfriends on a flotilla holiday sailing around the Greek islands. It was a wonderful time as their father-son relationship had long gone, to be replaced by one of equals and friends. Not once did the conversation turn to what Henry was doing in Moldova. There was too much going on in Andrew and Peter's lives for them to worry about their old man.

After Greece, Henry flew to Odessa for a beach holiday with Tania, Stelian, Yulia and Tania's parents. There were so many places Henry and Tania would have preferred to have gone, but when you're a politician seeking election as an 'ordinary woman', then the places you can go are limited.

It was a happy time too, primarily because it involved the simple pleasures of relaxing, building sandcastles, and playing in the swimming pool. Once the children were in bed, and in the quiet of the evening, Tania and Henry rediscovered the deep love they had for each other, a bond made even stronger by the intimacy of their lovemaking. Any fear Henry had that he was losing Tania melted away in the simplicity of their family life and the care and attention they showed each other over those precious six days.

When Henry returned to St. Sophia Estate at the beginning of September, he suddenly realised what it was missing. It lacked a soul. The cottages, the winery and the vineyards had all been beautifully restored, looking as though they belonged on a Hollywood movie set. Everything was working as efficiently as any vineyard, winery or distillery he knew; except, it was without a personality. That sprinkle dust that turns a house magically into a home or gives a vineyard its distinct character was missing.

What added to Henry's upset was that he realised he had repeated the mistake he'd made when he refurbished La Maison Presson in Paris many years before. It was at a time when he was trying to make it perfect so Sophie would come back to him. However, all he had succeeded in achieving then was typical of the blandness of a bedroom in a five-star hotel. He'd done the same again, but this time the newness of the inside of the four cottages gave them a feeling more attuned to a three-star motel. Perhaps, wondered Henry, that was the reason why Tania never came to stay, and whenever he did so, he lived out of a suitcase.

Henry was sure St. Sophia Estate needed a woman's touch. It needed the touch that Sophie had bought to New Found House in London. The touch his grandmother, Juliette, had brought to Château de Gressier. Above all, St. Sophia Estate needed a family living there to bring it alive.

Chapter 57

Kishinev September 1996

PRESIDENT MIRCEA STANESCU was livid. Above all, he was furious with himself for not having acted sooner.

He was one of the very few Moldovan politicians who could afford to commission opinion polls. The first poll taken in the first week of September, at the end of the summer holidays, had shown that his share of the vote had fallen by thirty per cent. The only consolation was that every other party had fallen by a similar amount. The undoubted winner was Tania and her Freedom Party.

The results were staggering in one other respect. It was the electorate aged 40 and under who were attracted to the Freedom Party. Those aged over 60, who remembered the times when their pensions were not paid, sought safety with the status quo.

Tania's greatest electoral strength was shown to be in the universities, where the academics and students were solidly on her side. Those students, who had gone to England for four weeks in 1992 to work on and study the UK's General Election, had become the kernel of the Freedom Party's voluntary workforce. The knowledge they had gained from being involved in that election campaign meant that, by the autumn of 1996, the Party's voluntary wing was well organised and well prepared. Above all, they had an enormous enthusiasm for the new politics that Tania offered.

To Mircea Stanescu's chagrin, his opinion poll told him it would be Ms Plesca, with 'her two bastard children' as he called them, who would be representing Moldova on the international stage. He could not, he would not, see his country embarrassed like that.

It was a phone call from Stanescu to Vanya Cojocari, who was the Head of the SIS, which resulted in a police raid on the Freedom Party's new offices the very next day. Men wearing balaclavas seized computers, papers, everything and anything that was to hand. Everyone who was in their office was arrested which, on this occasion, included Fomin who was making one of his rare visits.

Each person arrested was roughly beaten up, locked in a cell, interviewed, thrown back into a cell and, after this had been repeated three or four times, were released without charge or comment.

Fomin, because he looked and behaved differently to everyone else, was subject to bout after bout of horrendously inexcusable bullying. It showed the innate stupidity and cruelty of man. Never again would Fomin go into the offices of the Freedom Party. However, the treatment of him by unknown men in masks made him one of the Freedom Party's most determined members.

Evelina was one of those arrested. Tania was not. Evelina fared better than most for, as an ex-KGB officer, she had been trained in how to deal with such events. However, she found it much harder than she had expected. It was easy for her to explain why. In training, she knew they would never kill or permanently harm her, but in real life, given the animals she was facing, she felt there was no such certainty. As a result, she found it a genuinely frightening experience.

Chapter 58

Kishinev September 1996

"WE HAVEN'T GOT them," said Vanya Cojocari, the Head of the SIS, when he phoned Stanescu to report on the success of the raid on the offices of the Freedom Party.

"Haven't got what?" asked Stanescu.

"Plesca's nomination papers; we've got the photocopies, so we know who's nominated her. We've also got their membership list, but not the forms themselves."

"Where the hell are they?" asked Stanescu.

It was Evelina who had insisted that it was only photocopies of the nomination forms which were kept at the Freedom Party's offices. After the fire, she had started to put herself in the shoes of their opponents, spending time thinking about what she would do if she were them. As a result, all the original signed petition and nomination forms had, once they'd been logged, been taken to St Sophia Estate, where they were hidden waiting for presentation day.

"We were told by everyone we arrested that the originals had been photocopied and sent back to the local captains who'd got the original signatures, or the captains just sent in photocopies keeping the originals themselves. Apparently, it was the intention to file just photocopies," reported Cojocari.

"Who are these captains? What are they?"

"That's what they call their local party organisers. It's an American expression. In the UK, they're called election agents."

"The Central Election Committee wouldn't accept photocopies, would they?" asked Stanescu.

"No, I wouldn't have thought so," said Cojocari.

"I couldn't give a damn about the petition to Parliament, but she's not, I repeat not to deliver the nomination forms to the CEC, do you understand," said Stanescu

"Why are you so worried about the nomination forms but not the petition?" asked Cojocari

"Parliament doesn't have time to consider the petition before the next election, and a petition presented to one parliament can have no influence on the next because they never received it. For Plesca, it will have all been a big waste of time. However, the CEC will have no alternative but to reject her nomination form. That'll allow her to appeal to the Constitutional Court, and they have a mind of their bloody own. They could well rule the age restriction is unconstitutional and allow her name on the ballot paper. It's why she's got to be stopped before she files them with the CEC."

I am pretty sure we will know when she's going to file," said Cojocari.

"How?"

"She's a politician. She announces the arrival of every fart with a press release," said Cojocari choosing his words carefully to show an appropriate amount of contempt which he felt towards his political masters.

Stanescu chuckled at the expression, not realising it was a dig at him too.

"Seriously, she'll send out a press release to the TV and radio stations telling them what she is going to do and when. We'll pick it up from there," said Cojocari.

"Do it," said Stanescu. "Make sure those nomination papers never get to the CEC. Speak to Costin. He'll know what to do."

Cojocari didn't phone Costin. He thought him an unsophisticated thug, a liability who was best kept well clear of.

Chapter 59

Tiraspol September 1996

EVELINA THOUGHT IT had been a successful morning. She had made a speech at a factory that collected scrap metal and recycled it into cutlery and kitchen utensils. Her speech had been well received, with over half signing the petition and nomination forms she had bought with her. Evelina had gone into Bender, a small city located in the buffer zone established in 1992 at the end of the Transnistrian War. Although Transnistria had de facto administrative control of the city, its people could still vote in the Moldovan president elections.

Evelina had met with the Freedom Party's local captain and volunteers to collect the signed petition and nomination papers they had gathered. It was a happy and positive group of people who had assembled in a room close to the Russian Orthodox Transfiguration Cathedral for her to thank them for everything they were doing and answer their questions.

Evelina was in a contented mood as she left. It was a beautiful day, and the next hour could be taken in relative leisure as she drove back to Kishinev. Just as she was joining the complex road junction near the Monument to Russian Glory, close to the town's 16th Century Ottoman Fortress, Evelina saw Costin's car in front of her. It was turning left on to the R26 towards the Dniester River Bridge and heading towards Tiraspol. Evelina frowned as she puzzled as to why Costin's car was here at all. It made no sense to her. She knew there was a casino in Bender, which was his, but he hadn't come from that direction. He had come from Kishinev, and there was only one reason for Costin to go to Transnistria, she thought. It was to buy a gun! It was a huge assumption, but Evelina knew her instinct was right, so she made an instant change of plan and decided to follow him.

When Costin heard the results of his father's opinion poll, he decided it was time to go shopping. Taking a briefcase of US dollar winnings from two of his ill-gotten casinos, and with his bodyguard sitting in the front passenger seat, Costin was chauffeured to Shevchenko Strada in Tiraspol in Transnistria. Here Costin and his bodyguard were dropped off. They walked for about five minutes through a market, past stalls selling clothes, household supplies, vegetables, meat and fish with all the smells that go with them. It was crowded with buyers looking for bargains and value for money.

Costin's destination was at the back of the market, where it was far less crowded. In this area, there were not the usual scruffy, broken down, old vans that typically surrounded Moldovan or Transnistrian markets. Instead, there were large white vans, each about two or three years old. They had been reversed in so that the rear doors opened close to each individual market stall. A grubby canvas roof and flapping canvas walls provided minimal shelter from the elements.

There, laid out on trestle table after trestle table, each with a dealer standing behind, were exactly what Costin had come to buy - guns. There were displays of every shape, size, age and make of gun, ranging from mini guns, small derringers, pistols, revolvers, rifles to machine guns, but none of those were what Costin was looking for. He had a specific requirement, a bolt action bullpup sniper rifle.

Costin wandered up and down the stalls picking up items, talking, learning, often changing his mind as to what he wanted. Eventually, he chose an American Barrett N90 rifle, firing a standard 0.50 BMG bullet. One of the reasons he chose it was that it was brand new. The gun had only started being manufactured the year before. Costin knew of the inherent dangers which came from the incriminating evidence attaching to a second-hand gun which he was determined to avoid. It was why he was prepared to pay almost twice as much to buy a new rifle.

Costin was also wise enough to know that he shouldn't be seen buying the gun. It should not be traced to him in any way. A nod from his bodyguard drew Costin's attention to the small discretely hidden video cameras focused on the stalls and the customers. Not all gun stallholders had video equipment, but many did. They saw it as some, albeit minimal, protection against the activities of the mafia and a corrupt police force.

Having completed his window shopping, Costin and his bodyguard returned to the car, where Costin moved into the driver's seat. Stuffing their pockets with precisely the right amount of cash, Costin's bodyguard and chauffeur made their way back to the chosen gun dealer, but this time they approached from the back of the market. In the small gap between two white vans, and away from the video cameras, a deal was done. One brand new, boxed, sniper rifle with telescopic sights in its own case and with 50 bullets was acquired for $11,750. It was nearly $2,000 more than the manufacturer's advertised retail price, but it was here, it was now, and needs must. It also explained why it was the arms dealers who were driving the newest vans.

Meanwhile, as Evelina crossed the Dniester River, her petrol warning sign had started to flash rapidly. It had flashed intermittently before, but now it was clear she was running out of petrol, and the need to fill up was urgent. She had watched disappointedly as Costin's car turned left on Shevchenko Strada. He was heading towards the gun market, and with that realisation, her stomach went into her mouth, and her fears took a grip of her whole being.

Evelina didn't follow Costin as she wanted. Instead, she felt she had no alternative but to continue to the R27 and find the nearest petrol station. It was some way out of the city, but she daren't rush. She knew she had to eke out what little fuel she had as it was vital she didn't waste precious minutes with a breakdown

Once her car was full of petrol, Evelina responded to the adrenalin flowing through her body by driving as fast as possible into Tiraspol. She drove up and down Shevchenko Strada several times searching for Costin's car, but it was not there. In a panic, she parked badly in a gap between a row of cars and vans close to the market. Rummaging in her boot, she found an old torn magazine which had a picture of Costin in it. She tore the page out, locked the car and ran into the market.

The arms dealer who had sold Costin a sniper's rifle had long since packed up. He taken his super profit for the day and had gone home to celebrate. The others, not so fortunate, were still there with their goods on display.

"Have you seen this man?" Evelina asked each arms dealer in turn, showing them a picture of Costin as she did so.

They were reluctant to talk. Even tousling her hair, undoing the top button of her blouse and shortening the length of her skirt didn't have the usual desired effect. It was only when she produced her out of date KGB identity card that the men gathered around her. Long ago they had learnt it was best to co-operate with the KGB. After all, over the years, they had proven to be a good customer.

"He wanted to buy a sniper rifle," one of the arms dealers told her, "But he never came back to buy it."

"Except one of our colleagues has made a good sale today, 'cause he's packed up and gone home," said another.

Evelina immediately recognised Costin's modus operandi. He would shop, do the choosing but not buy. He would be clever enough to make sure that there was a break in the chain of evidence.

"Could the dealer who's gone have sold a sniper's rifle today," she asked urgently.

"Could 'ave done," came the non-committal reply. "He 'ad a good yank gun in his stock. I know that 'cause I want to get a couple of 'em to sell too."

"What would have been the price?"

"About two grand over askin'."

"And what's that?"

"Say eleven, twelve grand in total."

With that answer, Evelina made a point of rapidly shaking every man's hand, looking into their faces and smiling sweetly. She then turned and darted into the crowded market and back to her car.

She was now sure of one thing, Costin was in possession of a sniper's rifle. It was what she should do with that information that now worried her the most.

Chapter 60

Tiraspol September 1996

COSTIN FELT A sense of achievement as his car crossed the bridge over the Dniester River at Bender, heading back towards Kishinev. He knew his next challenge would be at the security checkpoint just outside of the town. It was manned by Moldovan soldiers and was a relic from the Transnistrian seven-day war.

They had shown their identity papers on the way out, but on the way back, Costin knew there was a high probability the soldiers would want to search his car. Firstly, they were looking for contraband of the kind Costin was importing, but the main reason was that a large and expensive vehicle meant a bigger bribe. Costin knew he would pay. It wasn't worth the hassle, so he had already prepared and wrapped around his identity papers three twenty-dollar bills, one for each soldier. It was far more money than they would ordinarily get. It would be an excellent payday for them.

When the chauffeur was asked to open the boot, Costin got out of the car and walked to the guardhouse. He didn't introduce himself. Instead, he handed over a further $10 bill and a copy of his father's business card to the corporal who was in charge.

"I think you'll want to see this; perhaps dial the number on that card before your soldiers go any further?" said Costin.

The corporal looked contemptuously at Costin, then at the card. It was when he saw the name of the president of Moldova that he went into panic mode. Rushing outside, the corporal called his colleagues together as he urgently grabbed the three identity cards from one of them. Spotting Costin's name, he swiftly handed all their identity cards to him before he stood to attention and saluted. Costin's birthday present to himself would now get to Kishinev without further hindrance.

A few hundred metres past the checkpoint, there is a large forest. It runs for several kilometres on either side of the road. As they entered the forest, Costin ordered his driver to slow down and then, finding a track on the left-hand side of the road, instructed him to take it. As they drove deep into the forest, the huge car wobbled from side to side as the driver sought to navigate his way around the deep ruts. About seven hundred metres from the road, Costin ordered his driver to stop.

Putting on his thin leather driving gloves to make sure he left no fingerprints, Costin tried out his new toy. He fired shots at a tree, firstly 100 metres away and then 200 metres away. Costin handed over his rifle to his bodyguard and then his chauffeur in turn for them to have a try. Unquestionably his bodyguard had, once again, proven to be the best shot. It meant that he had just qualified for a new job; a new mission he didn't want but knew he couldn't turn down. He also knew, if history were to repeat itself, it would come with the benefit of a large performance bonus.

Chapter 61

Kishinev September 1996

THURSDAY, 19TH SEPTEMBER was a beautiful autumnal day. Tania had dressed Stelian and Yulia in their best clothes. Although they wouldn't be with her as she climbed the steps to the presidential palace, she had decided that today would be something of a family celebration. After all, it is not every day that one gets nominated to be president of one's country.

As soon as Serghei arrived at Tania's apartment, they summoned Henry, and the five of them walked to Biserico Stantul Muscenci Haralambie, the church on Strada Alexandrue cel Bun. It was less than five minutes from where they lived. It was important to Tania that she went to church on this day with Stelian and Yulia and their fathers.

Tania had already decided she was not going to pray for help in her campaign. She already knew that if fate intended her to win, then that is what would happen. Tania wanted to go to church for one reason only; to say a personal and sincere thank you. She thought she and her children had the most fortunate of lives, and she thought it the best place to go for a quiet celebration. There, in front of her God, she wanted to bless them by gently placing her hands on their heads.

After the service, the five of them, led by Tania, walked through Park Katedrainy to where Serghei's and her parents were gathered. It was here that they stopped and took family photographs. Tania always in the middle with Stelian, Serghei and his parents on one side and Yulia with Henry and her parents on the other

Just before 11 o'clock, they all walked Tania to the edge of the park. As they passed the Caterdrala Nasterea Domnului, Henry and

Tania looked at each other; both remembered their eyes meeting all those years ago and, with a wry smile, both of them recognised it as the moment their love affair started.

One hundred metres before the edge of the park, Tania stopped and ordered her family to wait there. She would be back in fifteen or twenty minutes, she told them.

Her family watched as Tania walked off, each of them really proud and happy for her, an emotion only matched by the terrible feelings of apprehension which each of them felt.

Unlike the others, Henry followed on behind her as she headed towards the assembled throng of television crews, journalists and well-wishers gathered on the steps of the Presidential Palace. He was like a dog following its master, allowing her, with each additional step, to get further ahead of him.

The night before, the Freedom Party had issued a press release. It announced that at 11 am, Tania was going to deliver to the Presidential Palace a petition to reduce the eligibility age of presidential candidates to those aged 21 or over. They had deliberately not mentioned that Tania's nomination papers were being delivered to the Central Election Commission by a small team led by Evelina at precisely the same time. They wanted to avoid any interference which might risk their delivery. They certainly didn't want photographs circulating of their nomination forms being rejected on the steps of the CEC, which they feared might happen if they gave prior warning.

A further press release would be made once they knew the nomination papers had been safely lodged.

Chapter 62

Kishinev September 1996

THE STAFF AT the bus station didn't realise that one of its white transit van buses was missing. Most of the drivers were back at base after the morning rush hour with the vehicles parked up. They would only be going out again once the lunchtime timetable started. Therefore, it was incredibly easy to 'borrow' a small bus without permission, which is exactly what had happened.

The bus driver and the sole passenger in the 'borrowed' bus were in a state of panic. In their planning, they had not considered that there might be a large number of people who were now standing on the steps of the Presidential Palace. This meant they would not have a clear view of Tania as she made her speech to the crowd before knocking on the palace door and presenting her petition to a president who, unknown to them, had deliberately decided that he should not be there.

Four times the driver drove the bus around the block, always stopping opposite the spot where Tania would be speaking. Not only were there crowds to deal with, but their planning was so bad they had failed to appreciate that they also had to contend with traffic coming in the opposite direction, which constantly interrupted their line of sight.

On the fifth time of driving around, and as the two men were waiting at the pedestrian crossing opposite the monument to Stefan cel Mare, debating what they should do, the driver suddenly shouted.

"Now, now," he yelled, spotting Tania coming out of Park Katedrainy on to Strada Mitropolit Gavrill Banulescu-Bodoni at the junction with Stefan cel Mare si Sfant Boulevard. "She's there," he pointed, just as his passenger saw her too. "Now's your chance," he continued excitedly, pulling the bus away as the lights changed green only to stop on the other side of the junction directly opposite where Tania was standing.

Tania was on the pavement just outside the park. She had stopped to look back and wave to her family. As she turned around to focus on crossing the road, she noticed the white bus as it had no obvious reason to be stationary in the middle of the junction. Tania frowned slightly as she spotted the printed number on the side of the bus. She turned towards it to look more closely. Immediately she knew it was off route for it was the same number of the bus which she used to catch to go to school every day as a child.

Tania's eyes didn't focus on the driver or his passenger, just the bus number. If she had, she would have seen the passenger look through his telescopic sights, aim his rifle and fire one shot straight into the middle of her chest.

As soon as the driver heard the muffled sound of gunfire, he drove off as calmly and normally as he possibly could. He was determined that nothing was going to draw attention to them as they made their escape.

Five minutes later, the passenger was dropped nonchalantly at an ordinary bus stop with his rifle carried in a non-descript black plastic bag. Fifteen minutes later, the bus was parked just around the corner from the bus station, and once again, the driver calmly walked away. The fact that the bus was left in the wrong place drew nobody's attention, for buses were moved all the time.

At the exact moment the rifle was being fired, Costin Stanescu was in the lobby of the Parliament Building. He had no particular reason to be there, except it provided him with the best possible alibi there could be.

Chapter 63

Kishinev September 1996

HENRY WATCHED AS Tania rocked slightly and then deflated into a heap on the ground as her legs buckled beneath her. So quickly did Henry realise that something was wrong that he had started to run towards her before her head hit the ground. Immediately he was by Tania's side, he rolled her on to her back. As he did so, he saw her blood had flowed into a pool on the ground. He stopped, squatted down, and scooped her into his arms.

Henry didn't notice the general chaos around him as he cradled Tania closely to his chest. He couldn't, he wouldn't let her go. His eyes looked deeply into hers as she looked at him with an expression that changed from quizzical to urgent pleading. She wanted to speak, but no words were possible. Mercifully, she was numb with shock, but the frightened look on her face told Henry that she knew something was desperately wrong.

Henry stroked the hair from her face with his blood-soaked hands as he watched her eyes fade out of focus and her eyelids close. As she fell into unconsciousness, he tried to squeeze his own life into hers, but it would have no effect. Tania's heart had stopped pumping and blood was no longer flowing into her brain. Death would fall milliseconds later. Unquestionably, Henry felt her spirit leave her body exactly at the same time as he felt her fall limp.

"Tania, Tania," he said to her softly, pulling her face closer to his so that she might hear him, but there was no one there. The person she was, had gone.

Every time someone tried to break their bond, Henry shook his head and held Tania even tighter. It was when they saw his tears and the desolate agony on his face that they left him alone, miserably holding on to Tania as though his own life depended on it.

Tania's mother and father hugged each other as they stood close by, looking down on their daughter's dead body, not knowing what to do.

Serghei's focus was on Stelian and Yulia. He wanted to get them away from seeing their mother die. Without a word to anyone, Serghei grabbed the two children in to his arms, and with them bouncing vigorously on his hips, he chased back to Tania's apartment as fast as he could go. His job was to keep them safe, and he knew they would be safe there.

Just as Serghei was opening the door to Tania's apartment, Evelina phoned. "It's in," she said excitedly. "The CEC has taken it."

Serghei couldn't speak. His voice was choked, and tears were pouring down his cheeks. He had been calm and purposeful until the moment he heard Evelina speak, and now he had to tell her the bad news.

"How did you get on?" Evelina asked.

There was no reply, just silence.

"Serghei?" asked Evelina, sensing there was something wrong.

"Tania...," he said, and then he could say no more.

"Where are you?" she asked.

"Tania's," he said, struggling.

"Stay there, I am coming," said Evelina, starting to run, then stopping to take off her high heeled shoes before setting off again, this time in bare feet, ignoring the sharp stones as they dug deeply into the soles of her feet.

"Take care," said Serghei, "for Christ's sake, take care," but she didn't hear him. Evelina was already running.

Serghei composed himself. He needed to be calm for the sake of Stelian and Yulia.

It was only when the ambulance came did Henry allow Tania to be taken from his arms and placed on a stretcher. Very gently, the two paramedics did their tests, and then, with words of regret, they confirmed what everyone there knew. Tania was dead. They covered her body and face with a blanket.

Henry sought to stay with Tania in the ambulance, but he was aggressively pushed aside by Tania's mother and father. This was their daughter, and they were not going to share these last few minutes with a man, who they had always thought, had been an intruder in to their lives.

The police very rapidly cordoned off the area where Tania had fallen. They gathered witnesses inside the cordoned area, which included Serghei's mother and father and Henry. He showed the police his passport. When it became obvious that he couldn't understand, let alone answer their questions, did the policemen lose interest in him. Instead, they focused on Serghei's parents and other passers-by who had seen what had happened.

Henry's mind quickly changed to focus on one thing, finding Yulia. He thought she might be with Serghei but, remembering Evelina's warning of children being kidnapped, he started to panic. Observing the chaos and melee, Henry decided to see if he couldn't sneak away unobtrusively. He started to walk very slowly, going deeper into the park, as though he was going to find somewhere to sit but, once out of the sight of the police, Henry started to run, only stopping when he crashed through the front door of Tania's flat.

"She's dead, she's dead," said Henry to Serghei and Evelina, but the look on their faces told him they already knew.

The three of them stood formally, as sentinels, until the two men looked at each other uneasily. Immediately, they saw the reflection of their grief. At that moment, each unmistakably knew that the other had loved her just as much as they did. The two men threw off a lifetime of inhibition and, unable to speak, they instinctively clutched each other, neither knowing, as they rubbed arms and backs, whether they were giving or receiving comfort.

Henry turned to Evelina who, whilst in shock, had managed to keep her composure. That was until she came to take Henry in to her arms. It was his broken emotions that took her over the edge. The two burst into tears as they cuddled while Stelian and Yulia looked on, frightened and bewildered.

"Costin Stanescu, Costin Stanescu," repeated Evelina time and time again, as Henry held her close.

'How do you know?" he asked.

"I know, believe me, I know," she said with quiet determination before she gathered her composure and broke away from him.

"Go and change Henry. You need to change your jacket and shirt," said Evelina. For the sake of the children, you cannot go around like that."

Chapter 64

Kishinev September 1996

IN HIS APARTMENT, Henry stripped to the waist then, seeing Tania's blood spread across his hands, arms, chest and legs, he stripped completely and climbed into the shower. He watched as Tania's blood washed from his body into a red-brown pool, swirled around the plughole before disappearing into the drain. It was a sight Henry would never forget. He felt as though he was washing away Tania's life. It was a feeling which hurt so much that he collapsed into a heap on the shower tray floor with his back lolling against the cold tiled walls. He wanted to die too, he needed to die. He couldn't go on living. He didn't want to go on living.

It was Evelina, worried about the length of Henry's absence, who shook him out of his state of torpor. If she had not called for him, he might have sat there all day, so deep was his depression.

Once dressed Henry re-joined Serghei and Evelina in Tania's flat. They sat around not knowing what to do. They answered phone call after phone call as the shooting was now being widely reported on national radio and television. They refused to tell anyone where they were.

It was Henry's anger which made Serghei and Evelina turn off their phones. "We're responding to events. We're not making them," he said firmly. "We need to plan. We need to plan for our safety and for the safety of the children, and we can't do that if we're operating on the back foot!"

"What do we do?" asked Serghei.

"We need the Party press officer to issue a press release," he said. "It will buy us time. After that we will make a cup of tea and write a list."

Serghei and Evelina nodded their agreement. Henry dictated as Evelina, using Tania's laptop, translated his words into Moldovan and typed simultaneously, inserting Serghei's suggested amendments as she went. As they spoke Serghei had Stelian in his arms, and Henry had Yulia in his, trying to bring what little comfort they could to two confused, bewildered and very frightened children.

Eventually, the press release was done. It read:

Freedom Party
Press Release
For Immediate Release
Dated: Thursday, 19th September 1996
Timed: 11.42am

Subject: Death of Ms Tania Plesca
  It is with deep regret and sadness that the Freedom Party confirms the death of Ms Tania Plesca earlier today.
  Ms Plesca was shot 100 metres from the Presidential Palace just before 11.00am by a bullet fired from across the road from where she was standing. She died in the arms of a long-standing but unnamed friend and in the presence of her two children and her parents. Also, with Ms Plesca when she died were Serghei Stoica and his parents. Mr Stoica is the Campaign and Membership Director of the Freedom Party and was instrumental in Ms Plesca's campaign to be elected President.
  Just before Ms Plesca was assassinated, nomination forms signed by 26,347 Freedom Party supporters were handed into the Central Election Commission, proposing her as a candidate for president in the forthcoming presidential election.
  Ms Plesca was shot on her way to deliver a petition to the President requesting that the qualification age to be a presidential candidate be reduced from forty to twenty-one with immediate effect.
  Tania was one of the founding members of the Freedom Party, whose creation was inspired by the philosophies and policies set out in her two award-winning political books - 'A Manifesto for Moldova' and 'A Partnership for Moldova'.

Ms Plesca's assassination is proof that our country needs an urgent and dramatic change of direction, as proposed by her writings.

Ms Plesca's death at the age of 31 is a tragedy for us all, but particularly her two young children, her family and close friends. They ask that they be left alone at this difficult time so they may grieve in peace.

Out of deep respect for Ms Plesca, the Freedom Party has suspended all election campaigning for seven days or until the day after Ms Plesca's funeral if that is longer. We trust other political parties will do the same.

The Freedom Party will not be involved in any speculation, nor will it comment on who might have caused or commissioned Ms Plesca's killing. This is a matter solely for the police. We urge anyone with any information about Ms Plesca's murder to contact the police as a matter of priority.

The Freedom Party will issue no further press release regarding Ms Plesca's death, nor will any spokesperson be speaking on its behalf for at least the next 48 hours. We need time to grieve.

With the press release done and faxed to the Freedom Party's Head of Communication, Serghei, Evelina and Henry sat quietly with mugs of tea in their hands as the two children rested in the two men's laps. They were each in their own thoughts, albeit that they were all remarkably similar. It was over. The Freedom Party was finished. Their hopes and dreams for a better Moldova had ended in the pool of Tania's blood spilled on a Kishinev pavement, just as hundreds of others, who had challenged Moldova's mafia, had done in the last seven years.

"We've got tea," said Henry after a long period of silence. "We need to make a list."

"What?" asked Evelina, not certain what Henry was saying.

"It's a family saying," explained Henry dolefully. "It comes from my great-grandfather. He always said that: *in a crisis you make a cup of tea and write a list.* We have the tea. We must write our jobs list."

"Oh," said Evelina, unimpressed. "I've only one thing on my list, and that's to get out of Moldova tonight. It's too dangerous for me to stay. Costin's already got Tania, and he'll come for me next."

"If you're going, then I'm going too," said Henry rapidly. "I don't need to be here. In fact, after all of this, I don't want to be here at all, and I don't want Yulia here."

It was at this moment that Serghei's parents arrived. His mother was still physically shaking.

"Where was Tania's bodyguard?" demanded Serghei's father immediately he saw his son.

"He was guarding the petition papers," Serghei replied defensively. "Even if he had been there, he would never have been able to save her," he continued, trying to give himself comfort from his explanation. "Look how it happened, a shot from somewhere and none of us knows where."

Evelina served tea once more and they shared their stories as the fridge was raided and the children were fed.

With Serghei's parents there to supervise the children, Evelina and Serghei disappeared onto the landing to make the phone calls they were desperate to make, having not dared to call earlier for the fear of upsetting Henry.

Their message was the same to everyone - their script taken from the press release.

When Evelina and Serghei returned to the fold, they found Serghei's parents ready to leave to go home. They wanted to take Stelian with them, and out of Henry's earshot, they enquired about taking Yulia too. Serghei shook his head in reply. He knew it was inconceivable that Henry would allow Yulia out of his sight.

"I'm going home too," confirmed Henry, very shortly after Serghei's parents had left taking Stelian, "and I'm taking Yulia with me."

"What about Tania's grandparents?" asked Serghei. "Shouldn't she stay with them?"

"What about them," said Henry, still feeling sore at the way they had dismissed him from the ambulance. "She's my daughter, and she should come with me."

Serghei looked at Evelina and pulled a face to show he didn't really agree, but she didn't respond.

"You've got Stelian and I've got Yulia. How can you suggest that's unfair? In any case, she can't stay here. This country's too dangerous for her."

Henry looked at his watch. "I, we need to leave now if we're to get a plane to Vienna this afternoon," he said.

"Can I come too," asked Evelina. "Honestly, Henry, I can't stay here." The emotional cracking of her voice gave away the fact that this time, she was truly frightened.

"Of course," he said. "In fact, I'd be pleased if you came too. A man travelling on his own with a young child always looks suspicious."

Henry got up and started to throw a few things that Yulia might need into a bag. A few nighttime nappies, a change of clothes, her pyjamas, just the bare essentials.

"Where's her birth certificate?" asked Henry.

There was no response from Serghei or Evelina.

"Do you know where Yulia's birth certificate might be?" he asked again.

Both Evelina and Serghei shook their heads.

"Have a look in the box above her bed," suggested Serghei after a little while. "It was her grandmother's. She kept most of her precious possessions in there."

Henry took down the box and placed it on the table. Inside were Stelian and Yulia's birth certificates, which the two men shared between them. It was then that Henry saw the ring which he had bought Tania when Yulia was born. Tania wasn't wearing his ring because, immediately he had given it to her, she had sworn to herself that she would never wear it in Serghei's presence in case it upset him. It was a promise she kept even on the day she died.

"I think this should be Yulia's, don't you?" asked Henry, showing Serghei Tania's ring.

Serghei nodded silently.

Henry looked into the box once more. Immediately he saw the cardboard outer sleeve of a jewellery case, he instinctively knew, without opening it, what it was.

In shock, Henry needed to sit down. Very carefully he slid the velvet case out of its cardboard sleeve. He then opened it up to see a pocket watch identical to his mother's. It was gold with a clear white face and large brilliant diamonds marking each hour. Henry took the watch out of its case and looked for the engraving on the back. He found the word he was looking for, Victor!

Without saying anything Henry sunk his head into his hands. How is this? How can this be here? he asked himself.

"You'd better take that too," volunteered Serghei. "Tania was insistent it would go to Yulia. She said it had to go down the first in the female line."

"Why?" asked Henry confused, while stopping himself from telling Serghei that this was his uncle's watch.

"I don't know," said Serghei. "It was just the way it was. I think it was given to Tania's grandmother by Tania's grandfather."

"By Tania's grandfather?" questioned Henry confused.

"Yes, I'm sure that's what she said."

Henry put Victor's watch back in its box, which he slipped back into the cardboard sleeve.

"What's this?" he asked holding up a jam-jar with the name of Donici-Solokov on it.

"I don't know," said Serghei. "Probably another family heirloom. I think you'd better leave that one here."

"Do you have a letter from Tania giving you permission to take Yulia out of the country?" asked Evelina.

"No, of course not, why would I?" replied Henry perplexed.

"You'll need one if we're to take Yulia out with us," Evelina explained. "I'll prepare one," she volunteered, going to Tania's computer once again.

"So Yulia's name is not in your passport?" asked Serghei.

"No," said Henry getting quite perplexed.

"Get me your passport," instructed Serghei, "and I'll fix it."

Henry watched as Serghei wrote the name Yulietta Heidi Plesca Guégan in his passport in black ink before he set about carving what he imagined an official UK stamp would look like into the edge of a rubber eraser.

"Heidi? asked Henry. "Where did the name Heidi come from?"

"It's on Yulia's birth certificate. Didn't you know?"

Henry shook his head.

"Heidi, its Tania's mother's name. Surely you know that?" said Serghei.

"Oh yes," said Henry, remembering. Then it slowly dawned on him. Was Heidi named after Heinrik, just as he had been? Was Heinrik Heidi's father too? Was that how they came to have Victor's watch? Did this mean Heidi was his half-sister?

Taking a pen, Henry sketched some boxes in the form of a family tree on the back of an envelope. He checked once, then twice, and then a third time before he had it confirmed in his own mind. He had been sleeping with his father's granddaughter.

Saying nothing, he looked at Yulia, concerned. She was the most perfect-looking creature, a beautiful child with all the intelligence that a two-year old could muster. He sighed in relief as any harm which might have been caused by incest had luckily passed them by.

Chapter 65

Kishinev September 1996

THE AIRPORT WAS operating on high-security alert, with police officers everywhere. It meant that it took Serghei much longer than usual to drive into the car park as the car was carefully inspected at the barrier.

"Only buy tickets for Vienna," said Evelina as they got out of the car. "We'll buy onward tickets from there," she instructed, her counter-surveillance training coming into effect once again.

"I've already an open return ticket to London via Vienna," protested Henry.

"Then buy tickets to Vienna for Yulia and me," she instructed curtly. "We must try not to leave an onward trail," she added.

Henry purchased the tickets and, with no luggage to go in the hold, he was immediately issued with three boarding cards. At the security gate, Evelina whispered her insistence that their goodbyes should appear formal, so Serghei and Henry shook hands as though they were parting business colleagues whilst Evelina and Serghei hugged.

It was saying goodbye to Yulia which Serghei found incredibly hard. He felt intensely resentful towards Henry. Not only was he taking away from him someone whom he had cared for since she had been born as though she were his daughter, but it was the splitting of siblings which he found unforgivable. Did Henry not realise how empty Stelian and Yulia's lives would be without the other. Of course Henry didn't. How could he contemplate such a notion when he had been brought up as an only child?

The number of people in the airport was light, so Henry, Evelina and Yulia quickly made it through security. It was at passport control that their problems began. The forged letter, ostensibly giving Henry permission to take Yulia out of the country, caused great consternation as it was signed by the woman whose assassination was leading on every news channel. The passport control officer was certain that the decision to allow Ms Tania Plesca's daughter to leave the country was way beyond his pay grade, so he telephoned for advice as the queue started to lengthen.

Very quickly, an officer with an enormous military cap and impressive epaulettes appeared. He gathered Evelina and Henry's passports into his charge as he called them aside to find out what was going on.

"Aah, Mr Guégan, we meet again," said the officer. "I hope it's not attempted skyjacking again?"

On this prompt, Henry recognised the man from his earlier encounter, and remembered both the pain and cost of that experience.

Do you know Tania Plesca? Do you know she's been killed today, murder, assassinated? asked Henry, ignoring the question he had been set.

"Yes, I do. it's why we are on such high alert," confirmed the officer.

Well, she was my partner. This is our daughter," he added, looking down at Yulia who was resting on his hip. "I taking my daughter, our daughter home with me, until everything is quieter here."

"I am so very sorry. I didn't know. It's been very upsetting for the whole nation. She was extremely popular. Everyone's terribly upset," said the officer.

"Thank you. It's been a dreadful day," said Henry as he shook his head slowly.

"Tania Plesca was your wife? asked the officer, making sure he understood.

"Yes," said Henry. "She was my common-law wife," he added to make sure there was no misunderstanding.

"And this is your daughter," the officer continued.

"Yes"

"And this is a letter from Ms Plesca giving you authority to take her daughter with you?"

"Yes," said Henry, "because she's my daughter too."

"Have you used this letter before?"

Henry thought for a moment and decided to lie. "Yes, when we went for a holiday in Odessa," he answered. "It gave me no problem then."

"When was that?" asked the officer.

Henry felt his heart thump for he feared he was going to get caught out because he could not remember the date Evelina had typed on the letter.

"Last month, August," he replied.

"Where are you going to?" asked the officer.

"London.

"How long are you going for? When will you and your daughter be back?"

Henry wanted to answer never, but he knew it was not the best answer. "Two weeks at the most, maybe three," he lied.

"And the police have said you can go?" asked the officer.

"They interviewed me this morning at the scene where Tania was shot," replied Henry, deliberately not answering the question.

It was at this point Evelina stepped forward, deciding it was time for her to take control.

"Please, this gentleman and his daughter are with me," she said as she showed her old KGB identity card with her finger, once again, hiding its expiry date. "If you have any doubts as to whether you should let this man and his daughter leave, you should phone this number," she added as she handed over President Stanescu's business card with his personal telephone number. "He will order you to let us leave," she said confidently, pointing to the name on the card.

The officer returned to his office with Stanescu's business card and Henry and Evelina's passports in his hand. He started to dial the number on the card but decided to put down the phone before it could ring. He remembered taking a hefty exit fee from Henry, which, he now realised, could come back and haunt him, particularly if the President was involved.

The officer rose from his desk and moved to the door of the neighbouring large airport administration room. "Have we had any instructions from the police about suspects we should detain in respect of the Plesca killing?" he shouted. No one took any notice, so he shouted again, even louder.

He was answered with either silence or a shake of the head. Back in his office, the officer worried about what he should do. He knew it should appear to the KGB officer that he had phoned Stanescu, so he sat there contemplatively for ten minutes.

When Evelina saw the officer return on his own, she knew they were through passport control for, if they were not, he would have brought soldiers with him.

"As I said, it's my job to make sure they leave and arrive in Austria safely," said Evelina to the officer cockily, who wisely chose to ignore her remarks

"Once again, can I say how sorry I am about Ms Plesca's death," said the officer directly to Henry, as he handed back both passports duly stamped with exit visas. "It's a tragedy. It really is. I think my country lost hope today."

Henry nodded to the officer as, with Yulia in his arms, he bent down to pick up his briefcase and her bag. He walked into the newly built airport departure lounge. Investment had come to Moldova.

With Evelina sitting next to him and with Yulia on his lap, Henry stared at the grey tiles on the airport floor. His eyes were swelling with tears, and there was a tightness in his throat. His brain felt as though it was about to explode.

He thought about Tania and their past. For the thousandth time that day, he cursed himself for his political ambitions for her. He was so damned stupid!

In all the bewilderment, Yulia started to cry, calling, and then sobbing for her mummy. Her plea: "mummy, mummy" broke his heart.

Henry reached inside the bag he had bought for her things and took out a teddy bear. He had given it to her when she was first born. It was no comfort. He took out her soft blanket on which she went to sleep every night and put it to her face in an attempt to dry her eyes. He offered her a drink, but Yulia was not interested. It was when she saw a toy helicopter, which was being flown around the demarcation lounge by a shop assistant, keen to make a sale, that Yulia left his side and started to chase after it. Yulia's tears and the thoughts of her mother had gone as quickly as her new fascination had arrived.

With Yulia contented, Henry reflected on how Moldova had come into his life. He remembered being told by a fellow passenger on his first trip that it was "downhill all the way from here," and that was true then. But now, Kishinev had a new airport. There were bight clean supermarkets with packed fresh vegetables, where there were none before. The streets, once choked with fumes from old soviet diesel engines, were easier to breathe in, and there were no power shortages. Capitalism appeared to be working for many but not all.

At that moment, Henry wanted to bring back Marx, Lenin, Trotsky and Stalin to show them how capitalism had made life so much better than communism. But then he knew they would point out the self-evident horrors that untamed, unregulated, inhuman capitalism had brought to Moldova. The old were now destitute and living on impoverished state pensions. Those who were young and without family or infirmed were destined to a frighteningly cruel life. And Tania's death was certain proof as to how feral free-market capitalism could be when left in the hands of the corrupt and unscrupulous.

It was at this moment that Henry remembered the hundreds of people whose kidneys had failed, many of whom were now dead because they thought they were buying a soft drink only to learn later that the colouring was a highly toxic leather dye. This single memory was sufficient to confirm Henry's conviction. He was right to take Yulia out of the country.

Their flight was called and, with his daughter in one hand and, with her bag and his briefcase in the other, Henry and Evelina made their way to the boarding desk. Evelina handed over three boarding cards and two passports as Yulia buried her face tightly into her father's neck.

"I'm so sorry about Tania ... Miss Plesca," said the boarding attendant, for it had quickly gone around the airport staff that her husband and daughter were here. "She would have won," she added. "I was going to vote for her. I don't vote, but this time I would have. I would've voted for her."

"So would I," repeated many voices around them.

Henry and Evelina smiled, looked around and mouthed 'thank you' to an embarrassed crowd.

A bus took them from the gate to where the aeroplane was parked. The sun was still warm, and the concrete apron was releasing the heat it had gathered earlier in the day. There was the smell of kerosene in the air.

Evelina helped Yulia off the bus allowing Henry to walk away from the crowds to take his last look at Moldova and the fields around. A few metres away from the aeroplane and the kerosene, he found a strong, powerful and as emotive a smell as he had ever known. It was the smell of dry soil blowing in the wind. It was the same smell he found in the vineyards in France. At that moment, he knew what it was that had attracted him to this country. It was its land. It was in his blood as strong as the soil of Bordeaux coursed through his veins. Irrespective of this, he knew he would never return.

Chapter 66

Vienna Airport September 1996

IMMEDIATELY THE AEROPLANE had taken off, Yulia stood in the window seat looking out. She watched in fascination as the world below went by. Henry sat next to her in the middle seat, holding on to her cardigan in his left hand to stop her from falling onto the floor. Evelina sat in the aisle seat. She and Henry held hands as though they were lovers, but this did not reflect their emotions. Some experiences are so extreme that they can only be shared with those who were there. By holding hands, Henry and Evelina were sharing the awfulness of Tania's assassination. It was a long time before either of them spoke.

"When we get to Vienna will you buy me a ticket to New York, asked Evelina?" I will pay you back," she added instantly.

"Yes, of course," answered Henry. "Why New York; why not London?"

"I promised myself I would do an MBA at Harvard," she replied.

Henry nodded as he remembered her ambition.

"I will get my father to sell my flat, my car and my video camera and all the film equipment. That will pay you back, and with luck, it will get me through the first year. After that, well, I'll have to see."

"I've got quite a lot of US dollars in my briefcase," said Henry. "I won't be going back to Moldova, so I won't need them anymore. I'll let you have them when we get to Vienna."

"Thank you," said Evelina. "I have a credit card so I will be able to survive a few days on that, at least until I can get some money transferred from my bank account back home. I will see if I can get a job with Arthur Andersen. With a bit of luck, their office in Kishinev will be happy to recommend me."

"If you need a reference, I'll be happy to provide one," said Henry.

Evelina nodded appreciatively. "Where are you going?" she asked, "France, England?"

"I've just been thinking about that. I think I'm going to Cape Town," said Henry. "I have a friend there who will help me look after Yulia, at least for a few days." He paused. "It will be too complicated for her to come and live with me, at least for a little while."

Evelina looked at him puzzled but said nothing.

At Vienna airport, and without any luggage, Henry, Yulia and Evelina made their way straight to the Air Austria business lounge in international departures. There they bought Evelina a business class ticket to Chicago as that was the only direct flight with seats available going to the United States that evening. She protested at the cost, but Henry couldn't care less. It was his gift to her. In fact, after Tania's death, he would have paid almost anything to make sure Evelina was safe. It was only then, while standing at the ticket desk that he made up his mind where he was going next. He bought two business class tickets for himself and Yulia to go to Cape Town.

"I don't know how to tell her story," said Evelina once they were settled in chairs in the lounge near to a play box that kept Yulia occupied.

"I don't know either," said Henry, "but one day it will be told. I'm sure of it."

"They won't tell it properly," said Evelina, "not unless you, or Serghei or I do it."

"Why?"

"Because even we would struggle," said Evelina. "How do you explain to people how someone so ordinary suddenly becomes extraordinary? How someone who's just like you and me becomes someone who is incredibly special. It is as though one day Tania was touched by God, and we all followed her knowing she was leading us in the right direction."

"That makes each of us one of her disciples," said Henry.

"And Serghei, and Osip and the other 26,344 who nominated her," added Evelina.

"26,344, was that the final number of nominations she got?" asked Henry. "I thought it was 26,347."

"Yes, it was 26,347 in total, but I took off Serghei, Osip and me from the number I gave you; otherwise, I'd have double-counted."

Henry shook his head as, like countless of times before, Evelina proved she had an incredible brain.

"Can I ask one question?" she asked.

Henry nodded.

"I could never understand how it worked; the three of you, Serghei, you and Tania?"

"I don't know either," said Henry. "Perhaps it's because neither of us is an alpha male."

"No," said Evelina assuredly. "You're one of the most alpha males I know. You, Edik, and Stanescu, you're all very dominant. You have to win."

"I don't have to win every time," said Henry defensively. "If I were an alpha male, we'd have been lovers many times," he continued, before adding, "the first time would have been at your aunt's swimming pool, remember?"

"Just saying that proves you're an alpha male," said Evelina. "But yes, I remember. How can I forget?" She threw out a false laugh as she cast her mind back to that moment when he was holding her tight in the water, open, exposed, and so very vulnerable to him.

"It was your eyes," he said. "They looked frightened. An alpha male would have taken no notice."

"I was frightened," said Evelina with emphasis on the word 'was'. "I remember it. I was surprised at how strong you were. Your age ... well, I didn't expect it."

"Although you said nothing at the time, your eyes said 'no' to me," explained Henry. I've thought about it many times since, but it's never been quite right, has it? Also, I was with Tania, and it wouldn't have been fair to either of you.

"After the initial shock, I'm sure I wasn't frightened of you physically," said Evelina. "I do remember being scared at what I, we might be getting ourselves into. We've had several strange, complex, powerful moments, haven't we?"

"Yes, we've had one or two of those over the years, where it could have gone one way or the other," admitted Henry.

I wouldn't be frightened now."

"Goddammit, now you tell me. When it's too late for us to get a room," teased Henry.

"Perhaps when you come to America to see me," she said as her eyes lit up and a beaming, teasing smile fell across her face.

Immediately her flight was called, the two of them stood up, hugged, and wept as they said their goodbyes.

Henry taking just his briefcase, and with Evelina carrying just her handbag and each holding Yulia's hands, they walked to Evelina's gate. Boarding had already begun. Henry put down his briefcase and picked up and held Yulia in his arms. The three hugged once more. Evelina shed another tear, and then she smiled as she told herself she was being silly. At that moment, Henry saw her transform herself. The former KGB agent made herself stand tall, and with it, she regained her confidence, She put on her actress mode and bounced confidently away, ready to take the United States by storm.

Just before she went out of view, she turned and looked at Henry once more. "I love you," she mouthed. "Come and see me, please," she said, as she yielded the most powerful come to bed eyes that had ever been shone.

Henry smiled back at her nervously, not knowing whether she was teasing him or not, and he gave a faint wave. For the umpteenth time, he admired her figure, and he thought exactly the same thing as when they had first met. If you are going to get honey-trapped, then Evelina Kirillovich was the one person in the world you would want to get trapped by.

Chapter 67

Vienna Airport September 1996

WHILE AT VIENNA airport, Evelina had slipped away from Henry, saying she was going to do some shopping. Using a small amount of the large bundle of US dollars Henry had given her, Evelina bought an international phone card. Taking a slip of paper from her handbag, she dialled the first of two telephone numbers on the list. Getting these two numbers was the last job she did before leaving Kishinev airport.

"Vanya Cojocari," said the head of the SIS on answering his private telephone line.

"This is Evelina Kirillovich," said Evelina. "I think you know who I am."

"I do," said Cojocari, for although the SIS was in the Ministry of Public Order, and the KGB had the year before been turned into the SFB[11] and then transferred to the Ministry of National Security, the two agencies made a point of knowing each other's operatives, including past ones. "How can I help you?" he asked.

"Costin Stanescu killed Tania Plesca," Evelina pronounced boldly.

"That's not possible," said Cojocari. "We know exactly where he was when Ms Plesca was shot."

"It was unquestionably his rifle," said Evelina. "He purchased it in Tiraspol on Monday 16th September. You'll find from the border guards that he went there and back on the same day, and if you ask the arms dealers in the market there, you'll find that an associate of his purchased an American Barrett N90 rifle with telescopic sights when

---

[11] Federal Security Service

he was there. I bet Tania Plesca was killed with a 0.50 BMG bullet. It's the same bullet that the Barrett N90 fires.

"How do you know this?" asked Cojocari.

Evelina did not risk answering the question. Instead, she said: "You'll find the rifle at his house at Strada Nucarilor."

"He doesn't own a house there," said Cojocari confidently.

"He does," said Evelina. "It's a new modern place. I know because I've been there. In one of the basement rooms there is a large safe inside a huge cage, but don't look there," she said as she revolted over her memory of bending over, holding on to the cold bars, as Costin sweated over her. Why did she allow him to use her like that, she thought crossly?

"Look at the stairs; they're fake. They're built on top of an existing staircase. They're the kind used after the famine to hide food in. The rifle will be in a box created between the original stairs and the false stairs on top. But you don't get at it from the top but through a panel at the side. It's well hidden."

"How do you know?" asked Cojocari.

"Men like Costin like to show off," she answered as she put the receiver down. They particularly want to show off when they've failed to perform, she might have added, and she probably would have done if she was talking to a girlfriend, but with Cojocari it was best to give him just the bare minimum.

Cojocari considered his options. Given the quality of the tip-off, he was fairly certain it would be right. If Costin Stanescu had commissioned Tania's killing and it became public, it would be the end of Mircea Stanescu's presidency but also his own reign as head of the SIS. It was inconceivable that any other president would keep him in post.

Cojocari phoned the commandant of the Trupele de Carabinieri[12]

"I've just had a tip-off that Costin Stanescu was responsible for Tania Plesca's death," said Cojocari as soon as he had announced his name.

---

[12] The gendarmerie-type police force of the Ministry of Internal Affairs of Moldova.

"I've had exactly the same tip-off about five minutes ago. Do you know her?" asked the commandant. "Is she a reliable source?" he continued, deliberately giving away the gender of his tippee in the hope that it might generate a response from Cojocari as to who had called him; for Evelina had deliberately not given her name to the Commandant.

The two men shared the gist of the conversation each had had with Evelina.

"We can't arrest him," said Cojocari. "We can't even raid his house."

"Yes," agreed the Commandant. However, if there's any hint, any public hint at all, it will be the end of Stanescu's presidency and the end of our positions. Our jobs depend on him winning in December," said the Commandant in an unusual recognition of the truth.

"I think you'd better leave this to me to deal with," said Cojocari.

"Whatever you do, make sure it's done quickly. If this were to get out, into the hands of the press and well, we'll ..." The commandant didn't finish his sentence. He didn't need to.

Three days later, Costin Stanescu suddenly felt very unwell. His eyes lost focus, and he found it exceedingly difficult to breathe. Such was the strain on his body that, as he fought for breath, Costin Stanescu collapsed on to the floor in front of the reception desk of the Steffaco Hotel. He was to die in hospital a couple of hours later. His autopsy reported a heart attack. No one thought to get a toxicology report. If they had, it would have revealed gelsemium elegans coursing through his veins. The toxin, taken from the rare flower of the same name grown only in Asia, had done exactly as Cojocari intended.

Chapter 68

Vienna to Cape Town September 1996

YULIA AND HENRY slept reasonably well on the flight from Vienna to Johannesburg, where they would change planes to get to Cape Town. In Henry's case, his sleep was induced by total mental exhaustion. He woke up with still two hours of the journey to run and stared at his most precious daughter.

Getting up carefully so as not to disturb Yulia or the other passengers, he lifted down his briefcase from the locker above, sat down again and took out the gold pocket watch that had been in Tania's safekeeping. Had it really been given to Tania's grandmother by his father? he asked himself.

He studied the watch meticulously, and as everyone did, he rubbed his thumb gently over the glass watch face and stroked its solid gold back. He moved it about under his seat lamp, causing the large diamonds at each hour to sparkle. It was identical to his mother's, except it was engraved Victor. Just as he had been told, the 'ia' was missing from the name. Henry felt a sense of relief as he knew how important it was to his mother that her brother's watch came home to her, but now it was too late for her to know.

As Henry was putting the watch back in its velvet box, he noticed the base had become loose, almost forced upwards. He looked closely, and there, hidden under the cream silk covered encasement, was a folded piece of worn and damaged paper. Very gently, Henry opened it up. It tore in places because it had become so delicate with age. He looked at it carefully. He couldn't make out its writing, so he switched on the reading light above his seat to study it better.

The writing was neat but tiny and in pencil. It appeared that some parts had been written in Russian and other parts written in German. He looked hard at the signature at the bottom. He was in no doubt, it was signed, Hauptman Heinrik Klugman, the name of his father. This was the only thing of his he had ever seen. On this realisation, Henry looked up to the cabin roof and exhaled strongly as his heart started to beat rapidly. Henry's emotions were, once again, out of control.

When he had calmed down, he studied the document further. He found printed at the top and in the smallest of writing 26.XI.44 Belgrade. "Was my father in Belgrade in November 1944?" he asked himself out loud, not believing what he was reading. Then Henry remembered hearing the translation of Tania's words from her interview with Evelina: *"my grandmother served as a nurse with the Russian army and travelled with them as far as Belgrade."* Was that when Heinrik and Tania's grandmother met, Henry asked himself. It must have been when his father was a prisoner of war, but it made no sense. How come a German prisoner of war and a Moldovan nurse not only made a baby, but they could write about it, he wondered.

As a result of his marriage to Sophie, Henry's German had become reasonably competent. He, therefore, knew the three words at the start *Mein liebes kind* translated to *My Dear Child*. But Serghei had said that the watch had been given to Tania's grandmother. Why would he address her as a child, and why did his father sign this letter with his rank? he asked himself. Then it dawned on him. This letter wasn't written to Tania's grandmother. It was written to Heidi, Tania's mother. It was a letter from his father to his unborn child.

Where's my letter, where's my letter? thought Henry jealously. With that, he very carefully folded the letter and put it back in precisely the same place as he had found it. It had been there for fifty years, he thought. It could stay there for a few more years until he had time to think about it properly.

Chapter 69

New Found Estate September 1996

CHANGING FLIGHTS AT Johannesburg to fly down to Cape Town made both Henry and Yulia fractious. It meant hiring a car at Cape Town airport, complete with a child seat for a complaining two-year old, was not as painless a task as it usually was. Henry did some essential shopping at a hypermarket, buying everything that his daughter might reasonably need in the short term. He bought nothing for himself, although he was as badly equipped as Yulia.

As he travelled towards New Found Estate, placed between Wellington and Paarl in the Southern Cape, Henry wondered what he was going to say to Harriet. She wasn't expecting him, and he had never mentioned anything about Yulia to her before. He knew it would come as a shock, most probably an unpleasant one.

Harriet watched as a strange car parked on the drive of New Found Estate in front of the house. It was in exactly the same spot where Henry had first parked his motorbike thirty-four years before when he had called in on the off-chance. He was then twenty-two years old. He was to discover, much later, that the people he was meeting would turn out to be his great-uncle, who had been estranged from his family since 1919, and his wife.

Immediately Harriet spotted Henry, she was thrilled, but this response turned immediately to apprehension when she saw him climb from the car. Her instinct told her something was wrong. Rather than run to him, as she normally did, she was rooted to the spot. It was obvious that Henry had changed, and dramatically.

Without acknowledging Harriet, Henry went around to the other side of the car, where he opened the door and picked up his daughter from the child seat.

For the first time, Harriet noticed Henry's hair had turned grey and his skin was pale, but it was his deportment that told the story. Normally he was tall and erect, now he was as bent, curved, and humbled as any human being might be. It was as though he was broken, destroyed.

Everything Henry had planned to say to Harriet, as he travelled from the airport, that witty, clever remark, was instantly forgotten when Harriet asked: "Are you okay?" Followed quickly by, "who is this?" as she saw Yulia for the first time. There was deep concern in her voice.

"I wonder if I could, we could stay here for a few days," said Henry wearily. "It's just we've had a terrible, ghastly time."

"Of course," said Harriet. "Who's this?" she asked again, as she took Yulia into her arms. She could see that Henry was mentally exhausted and was buckling under the weight of the child he was carrying, albeit that she was still light.

"This is Yulia," he said absentmindedly.

"Come on in," said Harriet. "Big Joe's moved in here now. He's here with his wife and children. With his kids growing up, well, it's so much bigger than his bungalow." Her explanation had a tinge of apology about it, which in other times, Henry would have noticed, but not today.

Henry followed Harriet up the steps on to the veranda and into the house, which he knew well. He had visited many times over the years. The last time was for the funeral of Satutu, Harriet's mother and his great-aunt by marriage.

Henry instantly noticed the change in the house. It had all the chaos of a family home rather than the formal, stuffy atmosphere which had matched Satutu's character.

"Have you seen the news, read the papers?" asked Henry anxiously, as he followed Harriet into the house and the kitchen where everyone had always congregated.

"No," said Harriet. "Should I?" she asked.

"You've not seen or heard anything about a presidential candidate for the Moldovan elections being shot?"

"No," said Harriet. "There's been nothing on our news about it."

"Nothing about a Tania Plesca being shot?" asked Henry with surprise in his voice.

Harriet would, at this point, normally have got cross with Henry's persistency but, recognising his delicate state, she held her peace.

"Tania was shot yesterday morning in Kishinev. I was there when it happened," Henry spoke rapidly. "This is her daughter Yulia," he said. "She's my daughter. She was there when it happened too."

"Your daughter?" said Harriet shocked. Henry's words felt like a knife stabbing her hard in the chest. She had tried to become pregnant by him so very many times. At that moment, she could have walloped him in the face, but her anger turned to pity as, once again, she saw his truly terrible demeanour. Henry's mental anguish devoured his whole body.

"You, she ... you saw her mother killed?" asked Harriet in a whisper. She needed to make sure she understood what she was being told.

Henry nodded silently. The expression in his eyes showed the emotional pain it gave him just to confirm that awful truth.

"How old is she?" Harriet asked.

"Yulia, she was born in ..." Henry searched his mind for her date of birth, but it would not come. "She's aged two," he replied.

"And you've said nothing all this time," said Harriet accusingly, the disappointment in her voice plain to hear.

"No."

"Why?"

"I don't know." Henry paused. "It's complicated," he said.

"Does Sophie know? she asked. This time there was bitterness in Harriet's voice.

Henry looked quizzically at Harriet, then after a little while, he replied, "No."

"And Andrew and Peter?"

"No," he answered again.

Harriet looked at Henry disapprovingly as she served him a mug of tea and Yulia some juice as they sat at the kitchen table. It was the same table that Harriet had sat at ever since she was born.

Harriet found some paper and pencils to keep Yulia amused, but it was the pack of family dogs, not wanting to miss out on greeting their new guests, that she chose to play with.

Harriet listened as Henry told Tania's story. His telling was less on their relationship, which is what Harriet wanted to hear, but more on what drove them to get into the murky world of Moldovan politics and her murder.

During the telling, Harriet had many questions, but she had one burning and incredibly sensible one. "How long are you staying?" she asked.

"Can I stay for a few days in the bungalow?" he asked, "if that's alright?"

"Of course it is," she replied, somewhat relieved as she was worried about him. She also knew it would give her time to get the answers she needed.

As soon as tea was finished and the shortened version of the story told, Henry, Yulia and Harriet made their way to Harriet's bungalow, which was no more than 100 meters away on the same estate. It was one of three built by Harriet's father, one each for his three children.

You have no luggage, observed Harriet?" as they unloaded his car together.

"No, we ran for our lives. We left everything behind," said Henry, who was so exhausted that there was no emotion attached to this quite extraordinary statement.

In Harriet's bungalow, Henry was shown to his usual bedroom. "Have a shower," Harriet instructed, "and I'll look after Yulia."

Henry showered, shaved and cleaned his teeth using the complimentary wash bag from the airline. He put on the dressing gown, which was always hanging ready for him in the wardrobe. Without any further thought, he wandered through to Harriet's bedroom and climbed onto her bed. It was where he always slept when he was here. He had no thought that the news of Yulia might make things different so far as Harriet was concerned.

As soon as Henry's head touched Harriet's pillow and her calm scent percolated through his nostrils, he was asleep. He fell into one of the deepest, most re-generative sleeps he had ever had.

Chapter 70

New Found Estate September – October 1996

IT WAS EARLY evening when Henry woke up. During those few seconds before becoming fully conscious, he thought that, for one very brief moment, Tania's murder had just been a bad dream, but the awfulness of the situation was confirmed as he saw his surroundings and remembered how he came to be here.

He was still grey and gaunt, but on climbing from Harriet's bed, his stance returned to normal. He stood tall, erect and looked ready to take on the world, but this would have misread the signs. Undoubtedly, Henry had found his old physical form, but his mental anguish was still compressing his brain. He felt as though it were in a vice that was slowly but surely tightening.

Henry soon found Harriet, who was playing with Yulia on the sitting room floor. His daughter beamed at him with a broad smile. It was the first time in a long time he had seen her happy.

"We went swimming," said Harriet, as she observed Henry closely.

Those few simple words overwhelmed Henry with guilt. He could remember teaching his two sons to swim in the river at Château de Gressier, but not once had he taken Yulia swimming. He'd had a swimming pool built at St. Sophia Estate, but they had never swum in it because it had never become their family home. As a wave of remorse swept over him, the pressure in his brain increased one more notch.

"It's nearly six o'clock. Sunset will be in half an hour. Come on, let's go for a walk around the estate," said Harriet enthusiastically. "Tania's had her tea. She's been changed and will be ready for bed as soon as we are back."

"Yes, I suppose so," replied Henry, showing less than his customary willingness for a tradition established at Château de Gressier by his grandfather Étienne Guégan in March 1919, on his return from the First World War.

By the time Henry was dressed, Yulia had fallen asleep on the settee. The comfort and security she had got from seeing her father had given her the permission she needed to give up on the day.

With a maid from the main house called to babysit, Harriet and Henry set out for their walk. The southern hemisphere was waking up for spring after a long and brutal winter. The grass was enjoying an early period of greenness before it would be burnt, once again, in the summer sun.

Harriet and Henry held hands as they walked around the estate. It was what they had always done ever since Harriet's mother had encouraged her to take Henry to her bed, even though both knew that Henry could not marry her. It was the first of many long, cathartic walks that Henry and Harriet were to take over many days.

From the age of 27, Harriet had tried to get pregnant by Henry, but without success. Harriet knew the odds were against her because she had suffered the medical consequences of being a sexually liberated and liberal young woman. Since coupling with Henry, Harriet had become monogamous, truly faithful to him. It was why she was initially furious when she learnt their relationship had not been exclusive. This anger was fully expressed in the first one hundred metres of their walk. The anger then turned to rages of jealousy when she thought of another woman, any woman, having Henry's child and her not.

Henry felt the full force of this rage which were to crop up frequently over the next few days, but they settled down immediately Harriet came into contact with Yulia, for her maternal instincts would take over. It caused a close bond to be created between them.

"I never told you this, but so many times I tried to have your baby," said Harriet to Henry, as they were on the return leg of their first walk.

"I know."

"How do you know?" she asked, surprised.

"Sometimes, you said, you asked, you'd even demand."

"No, I wouldn't! When?"

"When we were making love."

"I didn't," protested Harriet. "Did I?"

"In any case. It was obvious in so many ways. You would tell me I could come and stay these days, not those. The constant monitoring of your temperature and the strange times we would go to bed. Your insistence that I should wear loose boxer shorts when I was here. The fad diets we would try, and then there were the various versions of the Kama Sutra you would put me through."

"You knew and didn't mind?"

"Far from it. I wanted you to have my baby. I tried hard, but as time went on, well, I knew it was not going to happen. Just think, it's twenty years ago since your father died. We've been together a long time.

"Is that why you got Yulia's mother pregnant... because you knew I was too old to have ...?" She didn't say the word child. It wouldn't come. Instead, there was a horrible, painful sadness in Harriet's voice.

Henry squeezed her into him. "No, of course not. It was an accident. It shouldn't have happened," he lied. "You can tell it was unplanned because, look at me, I'm far too old to do the father thing."

"You didn't choose her over me, did you?" repeated Harriet seeking extra reassurance.

"No, as I said. It was an accident, and I'm sorry, really sorry about you and me, ... we weren't able to ... I did try, I promise but it wasn't to be, that's all."

Henry's assurance seemed to satisfy Harriet because she never spoke of her inability to conceive with him again, but his unfaithfulness was not a subject she was prepared to drop. Time and time again, Harriet would return to the subject of Tania and what she was like for, deep down, she was comparing and contrasting herself to her rival d'amour.

When Henry was alone, he would go through the gamma of emotions, mostly blaming himself, often angry, often depressed, often expressing despair, and despite having both Harriet and Yulia with him, he had a sense of being very, very lonely. No one, he thought, could ever identify with what he was going through.

It was the small things that stopped Henry from being totally absorbed by the physical and mental pain which came from his uncontrolled and uncontrollable cacophony of feelings.

The first was when he focused all his attention on studying several of the books on ciphers and codes that had enthralled his great-uncle. By concentrating exceptionally hard he forced his brain to exclude all the other thoughts which hurt him so much

The other times were when he marvelled at seeing the thousands of little mannerisms Yulia had inherited from her mother. The way she would cock her head to the side when listening. The way she would sit bolt upright, defiantly when she disagreed with him, but above all, it was the way Yulia looked. She had the same understated charisma which came from being assured and self-confident. But what fascinated him most was the fact that, despite being just two years old, Yulia instinctively accepted that, in the absence of her mother, it was her job to look after her father

"I need to go home'" said Henry to Harriet on one of their evening walks after he had been with her for nearly four weeks. "I have so much to do. Would it be alright if Yulia stayed here with you until I get back?" he asked.

"Yes, of course," said Harriet.

"There's something belonging to Yulia which needs to stay here with her. It's an heirloom given originally to her great-grandmother, but now it's Yulia's to have. It's incredibly precious, not because it is, but it's a clue to the whole of her heritage. I could take it to de Gressier, but it would cause immense complications. Would you look after it for her here, please?"

"Of course," Harriet nodded before asking: "Will you tell Andrew and Peter about Yulia?".

Henry hesitated before replying. "Yes, if the moment is right."

It never was. Andrew and Peter were never told they had a sister. As a result, Yulia never got to go to England or France, but Harriet got the daughter she yearned.

It was life repeating itself. Andrew and Peter had been abandoned by Henry to be brought up by his mother. Yulia was being left to be bought up by Harriet. For all three of his children, Henry was not the companion father they yearned him to be.

Chapter 71

London October 1996

ROBERT GLENN WAS fluent in French and English. It was the reason Henry chose him to be his personal lawyer. Like Henry, Robert was privately educated, but there the similarity ended. He was ten years younger and a well established senior partner with one of London's leading law firms. He had a turn of phrase and depth of vocabulary which came from sitting amongst the most erudite of men. In addition, Robert benefited from a grace, charm and intellect which, quite frankly, Henry envied.

When Henry made his appointment to see Robert, he was anxious. Now the time had come for their meeting his anxiety had turned into tummy crunching nerves. They met in a small meeting room. Robert appeared as Henry had never seen him before. His hair was long and tousled, he had no tie on, and his shirt was creased, making him appear a little frazzled, which was precisely the state Robert was in. He had been in all night negotiations and had not slept. Their opening conversation was not as amicable as they usually were.

"I have a problem," said Henry sheepishly.

Robert said nothing. His mind was still in the meeting he had just come from, so he was only half-listening. Long ago, Robert had learnt that too many of his wealthy clients just wanted to talk through their problems, not expecting any answers.

"You know Moldova, the Presidential candidate who was killed there?" said Henry as his opening remarks.

"I know of Moldova, and I know of the woman's death, but I didn't know her," replied Robert stressing the word know. He had learnt, long ago, of the need to be precise in all his dealings.

"I," said Henry before pausing. "I," he said again, stopping as his emotion took over his ability to speak. His eyes filled with tears. "I was responsible for her death. I killed her," he added.

"Henry, stop!" said Robert firmly, as he touched his arm in an act of comfort. "We need to start this meeting again." He got up and left the room allowing Henry time to compose himself.

Robert returned five minutes later. He had shaved and washed his face, cleaned his teeth, put on a clean shirt and with his tie tightened, he was renewed and invigorated. He was now ready for work.

"Tell me again," said Robert as he turned on the small dictaphone which he always carried with him. "You knew Anastasi Plesca?" He had taken the time away to get his secretary to retrieve the old newspapers from the firm's library and to re-read the reports of her murder.

"Yes, although everyone knew her as Tania," replied Henry.

"Tania had a son and a daughter, didn't she? They were incredibly young. It made the whole thing tragic," continued Robert, trying to prove he knew something of her death.

"Yes," said Henry rapidly, "and here's the point, her daughter's mine. She's called Yulia, named after my grandmother."

"Are you sure?" asked Robert in a very straightforward manner.

"Yes," said Henry firmly.

"How do you know?"

"I know," said Henry.

"Have you had a DNA test?" asked Robert.

"No need, she's mine. In any case, if she's not mine, she is now. Even the father of Tania's son accepts Yulia is mine," said Henry emphatically, as though that were proof enough.

"Could he be Yulia's father?" asked Robert.

"He could be, but he's not!"

"Where's your daughter now? Who's looking after her?" asked Robert.

"She's staying with a friend in Cape Town. I took her there the night her mother was killed," said Henry matter-of-factly.

"How did you get her out of the country?" asked Robert as he scribbled thoughts on his notepad.

"We just flew out. Contacts in the President's office helped. They were behind her mother's killing, and the last thing they wanted was a two-year old girl being filmed at her mother's funeral."

"Are you sure you can't be accused of abduction?" asked Robert.

"Of course not; you can't abduct your own daughter, can you?" said Henry, concern coming into his voice for the first time.

"I'm afraid you can. What paperwork did you have which allowed you to take Yulia out of the country? For example, did you have a consent letter from her mother giving you permission?" asked Robert.

"Yes, we created one after Tania had been killed so I could take her out," said Henry innocently. "Evelina was able to copy her signature almost perfectly."

"Are you telling me you forged an authority letter so you could abduct a child," said Robert re-presenting the facts as only a lawyer can.

"It was nothing like that," protested Henry. "Everyone at the airport was so sympathetic, and with the help we got from the President's office, they just let us go."

"Are you named on your daughter's birth certificate?"

"I don't know. I don't think so. It may have been written in Moldovan Cyrillic, so I wouldn't have known. I can't remember, although after the wall came down, Moldova readopted the Latin Alphabet, so it could have been either or in both. What I do know is that when we wrote her name in my passport, we used both the Plesca and Guégan names."

"You wrote Tania's name in your passport?" said Robert sounding like a disapproving headmaster.

"Yes, Serghei did it. He's the father of Tania's son. We needed it in there to get her out," said Henry as though he was making a statement of the obvious

Robert shook his head and sighed his disapproval. "So you might not be named as her father?"

"It's possible, yes, but that doesn't matter. She's mine."

"What if she's not?" asked Robert.

"I don't care if she is someone else's. She's mine now, and I can't let her go," he pleaded. There was desperation in Henry's voice as once again his eyes filled with tears.

"Henry, we need to make you Yulia's legal guardian to avoid any difficulties later," said Robert.

"Okay," said Henry, pleased he was being given constructive advice.

"We will need DNA evidence," said Robert.

"I'm not doing that," said Henry stubbornly.

"Why not?" asked Robert, completely astounded. "Do you doubt her paternity?"

"No, of course not!"

"Then why?"

"If I do a test, it shows I'm doubting it, and I am not doing that. I won't ever let Yulia know, not even once, that I doubted for a millisecond that I was not her father, not once, not ever."

"She need never know."

"These things never remain secret. It will all be in the court papers."

"The family court in the UK operates in secret," responded Robert, as he wondered in which jurisdiction they would have to make the guardianship application.

"In any case, this is all nonsense. No one else wants her but me," said Henry. Serghei wanted her son as he was the father. I wanted Yulia as I'm her father. It was all agreed between us in Tania's flat just after she was killed."

"You sound as though you were two men dividing treasure trove," said Robert, now getting cross with Henry's naivety.

"It wasn't like that," said Henry, affronted at Robert's disparaging remark.

"What about Ms Plesca's mother and father?" asked Robert, deliberately choosing to use her family name. Won't Yulia's grandparents want her? I am sure they will be able to make a custody claim for her."

"Yes, maybe, but they know she's with me. I'll arrange for them to come and see her. Honestly, she's best out of that damn country. She's best with me! Can't you see that?" said Henry, desperation pouring out of every syllable.

"No one is looking for this girl?" asked Robert.

"No," said Henry firmly. He was astonished that Robert was continuing to concern himself with this aspect. "In fact, it's the other way around. There are a lot of people in Moldova who don't want her found."

"Okay, said Robert, recognising it was time to move on. "What's this about you being responsible for Ms Plesca's death?"

Henry told of the evening discussion groups. The essays Tania wrote and his present to her of 'A Manifesto for a Modern Land'. He explained how he encouraged her to seek the presidency and how he helped finance her campaign.

"You didn't actually kill her, did you?" said Robert as a statement of fact.

"No, of course not, but I am responsible. It was me who encouraged her. She was living out my fantasy. Honestly, Robert, if you had been there and seen what goes on, you would have encouraged her too," he added by way of self-justification.

"But you didn't kill her, did you?" insisted Robert.

"No, not directly, but certainly indirectly, so yes, I did!"

"How precisely are you indirectly responsible?" asked Robert getting a little exasperated with Henry's cry of mea culpa.

"Because she stood in the presidential elections. I wanted her to stand. She did it for me. She did it because I asked her to," said Henry, slightly raising his voice in frustration that Robert didn't understand what he was trying to say. "If she hadn't stood, she would not have been killed. It's cause and effect; can you not see that?"

"Henry," said Robert firmly. "You are not responsible for her death. It's the person who fired the gun, anyone who assisted them and those that commissioned the shooting. They're responsible, not you!"

Henry looked at Robert wishing what he said was true, but he knew in his heart that she'd been killed because of his ambition for her.

Robert switched off the dictating machine. The confession he thought he was going to hear was no more than a man overwrought with emotion by the death of a loved one.

"You may choose to bear some kind of moral responsibility; that is up to you, but from what you say, I very seriously doubt whether you should. What I am sure of is that you are not legally or criminally responsible.

There was a moments pause in the conversation as Robert allowed Henry to digest what he had been told.

"Who else have you told that you are responsible?" asked Robert.

"No one, only Harriet in Cape Town. She's a long-standing friend and is looking after Yulia for me."

"I want to change my will," said Henry, revealing the main reason he'd made the appointment to see Robert.

"To include your daughter, Yulia?" asked Robert, his voice revealing his scepticism that Yulia was his daughter at all.

Yes. I own fifty per cent of a vineyard in Moldova. Because I'm not Moldovan, the other 50% was owned by Tania. I think Tania's shares in the vineyard will now go equally to Stelian, that's Tania's son and Yulia. The shares are worthless because the Moldovan company owes me far more money than the vineyard's worth. One day the whole thing will be worth more, but today it's in negative equity."

"You've never said anything about this before," said Robert.

Henry didn't respond. "I want Yulia to buy the 25% which is now owned by Stelian for $50,000," he said.

"You just said the shares were worthless," said Robert.

"They are, but I don't want to have a fight about money with Serghei; that's Stelian's father. Fifty thousand dollars is a lot of money in Moldova. It will look after Stelian for a long time."

"It's a lot of money anywhere," said Robert, shaking his head, for while he understood his instructions, he couldn't understand the rationale.

"I want my shares in the Moldovan vineyard and my loan to be gifted to Yulia when I die. It means she'll own one hundred per cent of it. Just as Andrew will own all of de Gressier and Peter will own all of Rabôut. The thing is, I don't want anyone to know of the gift, and I certainly don't want Andrew or Peter to know about it."

"Why?" asked Robert, perplexed.

"I can't tell them, said Henry.

"They don't know! They don't know they've got a sister?" There was shock in Robert's voice.

"No, I had an opportunity to tell them once. It was when my mother died, but it went away and has never come back."

Robert raised his eyebrows to express puzzlement.

"I can't bear the thought that, by having a daughter with Tania, my boys will think I let their mother down."

"But Sophie's no longer in a position to know, is she?" said Robert.

Henry nodded his head. "But do you know why Sophie's brain is addled?" he asked.

Robert shook his head.

"Because of me. I was so obsessed with work that she felt lonely and abandoned and started taking drugs. That's what destroyed her memory." Henry's voice crackled again with emotion.

"Who told you this nonsense?" asked Robert.

"Sophie's best friend ... and she's right. Don't you see, I let Sophie down then, and I can't let her down again. I can't!"

"But she hasn't got the mental capacity to know; you've just told me that," said Robert.

"If Sophie could've come back to me, none of this would have happened," said Henry in self-recrimination. "Without her, I found someone else to love and who loved me. Honestly, when Tania told me she was pregnant, we were so damn happy. We didn't care what anybody else thought. When she was alive, it didn't involve anyone else. But now she's dead, well, it's got so damn complicated."

"Henry," said Robert firmly. "I'm sure Andrew and Peter will understand."

"No, they won't," said Henry. "Every parent is a mystery to their children. It's just nature."

"What about Yulia. Won't she want to know about her brothers?"

"She'll know. I'll make sure she knows and understands."

"Henry," said Robert sternly. "The longer I do this job, the less I find I understand people and their motives, but this I can assure you. Yes, Yulia will understand. Yes, her curiosity as a child can be contained. When she becomes an adult, she still might have no interest in the question, but believe me when I tell you, when a woman becomes a mother, then there will be no bounds as to how far she will look to find her close relatives. It's what women do."

"As long as it's after Sophie and I have died, then I don't mind," said Henry. "It's just I think that, in a man's lifetime, he should be allowed to keep his own secrets."

"In my experience," said Robert, "there is no such thing as a secret, just delayed truth."

"Well, as long as the truth is delayed until Sophie has died, that is all I seek," replied Henry.

"At the moment, we have Andrew and Peter as Executors of your will, along with me. This means they can no longer be executors. You'll need to find someone else to act alongside me," instructed Robert.

"Yes, okay," said Henry. "I have someone in mind. I'll ask them."

"Will they be able to keep a secret?"

"Yes, he's my former accountant. He's gay and kept that a secret for years."

"So we will re-write your will so that everything you want to go to Yulia is given to your executors who then deal with those assets in accordance with a Letter of Wishes, which you will leave with us," said Robert summarising the situation.

"But then my kids will know something is up!" protested Henry.

"Yes," said Robert, "they're intelligent boys."

"Why don't we just miss out on the Letter of Wishes bit?"

"They would then think that these assets had been gifted to your two executors as a result of something untoward. They wouldn't know we were holding these assets on trust to be dealt with as you proscribed. They will think there is something fishy. Undoubtedly, they will wonder if your will can be challenged and may even apply to the courts to do so. You don't want that."

"Okay," said Henry reluctantly. "If that's what you think is best."

"It is", said Robert firmly.

Henry left Robert's office exhausted but relieved. Very shortly, his affairs would be in order once again.

Chapter 72

Paris and Egypt October 2000 - November 2006

FOUR YEARS AFTER his meeting with Robert Glenn, Henry sat by himself in the library at Château de Gressier and reflected on his life. He remembered the time between selling his businesses and starting the Moldova consultancy project. It had been one long hiatus where, each day, he achieved little and socialised even less. He knew he was repeating that experience, but now in a never-ending form.

He thought of Evelina often and contemplated contacting her. He knew there was something spiritual between them, but was it of that moment. Had the time passed, he wondered. In the end, it was not knowing where she was which made the decision for him, but it was one tainted with regret.

In an effort to stop himself from falling into a deeper quagmire of self-pity and inactivity, Henry decided it was time to transfer the ownership and management of Château de Gressier to Andrew and Château Rabôut to Peter. They had been aged 30 and 27 respectively when they took control. His intention was to free his mind for other things. In the same way as his grandmother, Juliette had transferred de Gressier to him, Henry insisted he was to be paid a pension of an amount which they were to agree with the family accountant as being fair. He didn't need the money, but he liked the idea of continuing the family tradition. Unlike Juliette, he insisted that each of his sons lived on their estates. They couldn't be absent landlords. He would not allow it. The businesses were far too important to him for that.

At the same time, Henry moved out of Château de Gressier and into the small Gîte at Château Rabôut, which had been occupied by Maurice Rabôut until his death. It was from Maurice that Henry's

Grandmother had bought the Rabôut estate in a move which was to nearly bankrupt Henry, and was one of the reasons Sophie started using recreational drugs and become ill. However, the move into the Gîte brought Henry an advantage. His neighbours were Robert and Pascale Rabôut. The two people whose company he enjoyed the most.

Henry's retirement was a good decision for both vineyards because his negative disposition was creating a general gloom. It was adversely affecting the daily running of both estates such that his two general managers no longer wanted him around.

In the surrounds of his small bungalow, Henry tried to write. First, he tried to tell Tania's story. He wanted to do it so that Yulia could read it one day. However hard he tried, Henry found it an impossible task for, as he put ink to paper, he discovered how little he knew about her. To make matters worse, the book started to become focused on him as he reflected, in detail, on the small decisions he had made, subconsciously arguing that, if these had been different, Tania would still be alive today.

Henry also tried to write a comprehensive encyclopaedia of wine, but the reality was that, after he had scoped the book and seen what else was in the market, the task held little attraction for him. He could only think of producing something which was bigger but not better.

Henry should have been a man without a care in the world, except he was burdened with guilt for all that had gone wrong. He might have been wealthy, but he was living his life as though he were a poor little rich man - long in money, short in love and companionship.

His sons were too busy leading their lives, his wife was too sick to be a companion, and his daughter reminded him of Tania, causing the pain of grief to come flooding back every time he saw her. His few friends had long gone in the mist and chaos of life. Several times he thought of suicide, but abandoned the idea knowing it would distress his children. Life had to have a purpose, but he could find none he wanted to pursue.

In an attempt to keep busy, Henry tried travelling, both sea and river cruises, but he found the conversation of the rich tedious. Certainly, he did not want to hear the incessant stories of illnesses that dominated the conversation of those who were retired.

Henry tried ocean sailing and found he was seasick. He tried learning to fly a plane. Like his father, he was a good pilot. He had inherited the same homing navigation gene, but there the similarity ended. Henry found little pleasure in going from somewhere he didn't want to be to somewhere he didn't want to go to.

At first, Henry travelled to New Found Estate to see Yulia every three or four weeks. There he would agree with Harriet that Yulia would stay another little while. It was a strange ad hoc arrangement that worked for all three of them, not least for Yulia, who had the certainty and discipline of a home and all the love that Harriet could bestow. In Harriet's nephews and nieces, Yulia found friends she could happily play with.

When Yulia was about to start school, Harriet and Henry found the need to formalise their arrangements, which they did for one term, and then later for the academic year. As each period lengthened, the time between Henry's visits increased. He would be there for Christmas, Easter, Yulia's birthday and the anniversary of Tania's death, but those were the only times it was certain he would visit. He had no reason not to see his daughter. He just felt disinclined. Just as happened with Andrew and Peter, Henry missed Yulia's growing up.

When Yulia's class at school started studying the Egyptian Pharaohs, Henry was inspired to fulfil one of his dreams. All his life, he had wanted to visit the pyramids, see the night-time sound and light show, and sail up the River Nile in a dhow to Luxor, from where he would travel to the Valley of the Kings.

With Yulia granted permission to be out of school, Henry, Harriet and Yulia made the journey of a lifetime. The trip up the Nile was not in a dhow but a luxury riverboat. For days, it seemed as though time had stopped as they watched the local Egyptians go about their ageless work, and then at night, they would sleep on the deck directly under the stars. On the first night, they listened to the onboard astronomer point out the features of the night sky.

Throughout the trip, Henry was incredibly proud of Yulia. Aged 12, she was a delight to be with as she had just started those special years. She was leaving pigtails and moving to ponytails, leaving play toys and thinking about real boys. What thrilled Henry most was the deep friendship between Yulia and Harriet. It was as close as between any mother and daughter, made more engaging by the fact that they both needed to dance. For Yulia, like Harriet at that age, it was not a choice, it was a craving. It re-awakened Harriet's suppressed desire, allowing her to re-discover the joy of movement which she had found so pleasurable in her youth.

"Look up there," said Henry to Yulia, as their boat drifted slowly along. It was their last night on board. It was a particularly clear moonless night. They were miles from anywhere. "There are over 200 billion galaxies out there, may be far more, and each galaxy has around 100 million stars."

Yulia nodded. "Yes, Papa, the astronomer said so on the first night".

"Do you know stars are born, and stars die just like us"?

Yulia said nothing because it was a concept she found hard to understand.

"One thing is certain; this universe was here long before us and will be here long after us." Henry paused: "as I look up at the sky on nights like this, I realise how unimportant, how insignificant I am. I find it very humbling. Here we are, tiny things on a spinning rock which we call earth and home. The thing is – it's the only one we've got, so we have to look after it."

Yulia didn't respond. She was mesmerised by the night sky too. She was sharing her father's feelings of meekness, perhaps even, insignificance. Is this where God is? she asked herself silently

"When we have electric light all around us, we don't see all the stars. Only the big ones and sometimes not even then. Light pollution crowds them out." Henry continued: "I think problems are like the night sky. When the lights are on, you only see the big stars, the big problems. When the lights are off, all the stars are seen, and like a problem, each star doesn't seem so big when it's put against all the stars in the universe. I find my problems, when put against all the other problems of the world, never seem as big or worrisome after that."

"That's most profound," commented Harriet, who had been listening quietly nearby. "Sometimes I think people have stopped believing in God because we can no longer see the night sky as they did two thousand years ago. When you see the universe like this, you know there must be a God, don't you?"

Everyone stayed silent as they listened to the quiet hum of the engine and studied the sky. It was a powerful moment as Henry and Harriet's comments were ones which Yulia would remember every time she looked up at the night sky

"Do you know my mother, my grandmother and her brother used to share a poem? They would say it on nights when the moon was high, and they wanted to think of the other. It went:

When the moon is high
And its beam shines bright.
Then think of me, for
I will think of you.

I think we should have the same poem, don't you?" asked Henry.

"Tomorrow, I will write it down," replied Yulia, enthusiastically. "Then we can use it too."

Their holiday, which they all agreed was wonderful, ended at Cairo airport. There Harriet and Yulia said their goodbyes to Henry as they were returning to Cape Town. He was staying in Cairo a little while longer. He had never visited any of the Egyptian vineyards before. He thought this would be a good opportunity to find out why the reputation for Egyptian wine was so bad when they had been making it for over four thousand years. Was it really the Muslim conquest of Egypt in the seventh century, with its ban on alcohol, which had killed off an otherwise successful industry, he wondered?

The first day of Henry's visit to a vineyard confirmed everything he had guessed. It was the same problem as in Moldova. The industry had failed to make the necessary investment in its production facilities necessary to improve quality. However, there was a second reason which he hadn't guessed and which he knew would be impossible to solve. The wine producers were all Christian in a society that was overwhelmingly Muslim. They were operating in a country with enormous religious intolerance to their products. As a result, viticulturists and oenologists were constantly persecuted, and no reasonably minded person invests when they feel their very being is threatened.

On the second day of his vineyard tours, Henry got up late. He had spent the previous evening chatting for a long time with Harriet in one of his rare phone calls. He had phoned to make sure Yulia and she had got home without a problem, and unusually, they had stayed on the line chatting. Henry then read until late, un-enthralled by the choice of television.

Henry left his room on the fourteenth floor of the hotel about half an hour before it stopped serving breakfast. He walked to the lobby to take the lift to the top floor and the Executive Lounge, where breakfast was being served to those in his grade of bedroom. Henry pressed the button for the lift and waited. As the door opened, he walked through, expecting the lift to be there, but it wasn't. Without a sound, Henry fell thirteen stories to his death. He landed on top of the lift passenger cage and broke his back, but it was his head hitting the cast-iron hook and pulley on the top of the cage which killed him. The thud was heard in the reception area, but no one took any notice.

No more than a minute later, a young businessman from Germany did exactly the same thing; falling to his death on top of Henry. Still, no one noticed. It was only when a mother and father from the United States saw their five-year-old son fall to his death, in the same way, that the alarm was raised.

In a city that holds the record for the worst number of car fatalities in the world, and every statement of intent is predicated with the word *Inshallah*, God willing, the death of three foreigners was a nuisance. Only one aspect was of interest to the authorities. It was keeping the news out of the papers so as not to damage Egypt's tourist trade.

It was the American Embassy which eventually discovered the cause of death. New software had, that morning, been installed on the lift to make it operate more efficiently, except there was a coding error. An earlier version of the software had made it impossible for the door to open if the lift was not there, but a programming error in the new version meant that, whilst the code was still in the program, it was not read and thus did not operate. Even with this software error, it should still have been mechanically impossible to open the doors when the lift was not there. However, a subsequent investigation showed that when the lifts were first installed, not one of the safety leavers and catches had been fitted properly. They would never have worked.

The fact that all three deaths were of 'non-believers', and most Muslim's had heard of Allah's teaching that non-believers deserve to die, meant no one was ever held responsible. After all, it was Allah's will that they died. But this was just part of the story; the country was also an administrative shambles, as Andrew and Peter discovered when they tried to extradite Henry's body to France for burial. There was a protocol that required an Englishman's body, with an English passport, be repatriated to England as that was what they had always done. To the Egyptian mind, that was the logical thing to do. Except, Andrew and Peter wanted Henry's body to go to France, and that was one process too far.

Chapter 73

Château de Gressier November 2006

AFTER THE INITIAL shock of learning of their father's death, both Andrew and Peter adopted the appropriate amount of reserve and phlegm as befitted former students of an English public school. Immediately they met at Henry's gîte at Château Rabôut, and with great fortitude, they had several cups of tea, and as the family tradition required, they made a list of the things to do.

The two boys reacted differently to their father's death. Andrew showed little emotion for he felt that they had never been that close. Peter found it harder. All his life he had strived to please his father, feeling he had never received the approval he yearned. He regretted that they could never now be the best of friends, which is what he so wanted to happen.

Henry was buried in Latoire Village churchyard, next to his mother, Victoria, in the line reserved for the Guégan family.

Andrew and Peter debated about taking Sophie out of her sanatorium to attend her husband's funeral, but decided that, not only would it be pointless, but it would cause their mother too much stress. Although they visited to tell her that Henry had died, she had forgotten the news as soon as she had heard it.

The funeral service was a dull and ordinary affair. No one put any thought into making it personal, so it didn't reflect Henry's life or the person he was. No one prepared a eulogy. The priest said a few words about Henry being a pillar of their community, but it was not said from the heart. His little speech could have been given by almost anyone there.

Apart from those who worked, or had worked, on the estates at Château de Gressier and Château Rabôut, and some of the villagers, there were very few attendees. Vincent Ainsworth came, as did Robert Glenn, both doing their duty as the Executors of Henry's Estate. His former Chauffeur, John Chabani, came with his long-time partner Imra Blanche who had been one of Sophie's former supermodel friends.

Of all the people there, it was Robert and Pascale Rabôut who Henry had admired most and thought of as true friends. When he and Robert were together, they had a kinship which only those born into one of the great French wine families could understand.

Harriet and Yulia didn't come to Henry's funeral. No one knew to tell them that Henry was dead.

The reception at Château de Gressier was a dull affair where strangers found it hard to find things to talk about, except the age at which Henry had died. He was sixty-four years old.

Chapter 74

Bordeaux September 2009

"WHAT DO YOU know about A Manifesto for Moldova?" asked Peter Guégan, as soon as his brother Andrew came on the phone. There was no hello or other opening remarks.

"What?" asked Andrew.

"A Manifesto for Moldova, what do you know about it?" repeated Peter.

"Nothing, why?

"Because our father edited it."

"Don't be ridiculous. He didn't have the temperament needed to edit anything, let alone a book."

"Unless there's another Henry Guégan, and there isn't, - I've checked Google, then he did, because his name is on the cover," said Peter assuredly.

"I know he spent a long time there," said Andrew, "but that was ages ago."

"Yes, when Grandma died, I remember, because he flew there the night she was buried. Do you know, the publication date is the same year she died?" said Peter, giving what he thought was an important clue. "Do you know who wrote it ?" he asked.

"No, of course not. I've never heard of it until now!" replied Andrew sharply.

"Anastasi Alekseevna Plesca, otherwise known as Tania Plesca," said Peter proudly, answering his own question.

"Never heard of her either," said Andrew.

"Neither had I, except I've now discovered she's quite famous. She was a candidate in the Moldovan presidential election, but she was shot and killed outside their Presidential Palace on the way to hand in her nomination papers. Apparently, it was the success of A Manifesto for Moldova which persuaded her to put her name forward for nomination, and the contents of the book provided the basis for her election campaign. There's a whole Wikipedia page about her."

"Papa never said anything about this, did he?" said Andrew puzzled.

"Do you know she died leaving two young children?" said Peter.

"No. As I said, I've never heard of her before."

"Andrew," said Peter earnestly. "Would you do me a favour and have a look in the Cellars library and see if we have a copy of this book in there?"

That night, next to the de Gressier diaries written by the chatelaines of the Château, Andrew found a leather-bound version of 'A Manifesto for a Modern Land'. It was the English version of the book Peter was looking for. It was physically signed both by Tania and his father, each dedicating the book to her two children. There was now no doubting that they knew each other and that his father was the editor. Another book accompanied it, but in a foreign language, also signed by Tania and Henry. His father had written on a label, stuck across the front, a translation of the book title. It was called 'A Partnership for Moldova." Why was one book in English and another in a foreign language, he wondered.

As Andrew studied the pages of 'A Manifesto for a Modern Land', he could hear his father speak the words which had been written. Some of the words, the turn of phrase, were his, not hers. He was sure of it. Seized by a need to know more, Andrew searched the internet, reading everything there was on Tania Plesca. Time after time, he found coincidences between his father, Tania's book, and Yulia's birth.

Suddenly, and for no good reason, it dawned on Andrew that this might have something to do with the Letter of Wishes attached to his father's will. There was a mystery there that had never been resolved.

First thing the following day, Andrew phoned Robert Glenn, who had acted as an executor of their father's will and was responsible for winding up his estate.

After the usual salutations, Andrew asked: "What do you know about Tania Plesca and her children?" He was deliberately blunt.

There was a long pause as Robert thought.

"She was a woman your father knew who lived in Moldova. She was going to be a candidate in their presidential election, but she was shot," he answered.

"Did you know our father had edited her book 'A Manifesto for Moldova'?" asked Andrew.

"No," said Robert, thinking he was speaking truthfully.

"Is all this tied up with my father's Letter of Wishes? I've since learned that this is a common mechanism where a man, when he dies, can leave money to a secret family. Did my father have a secret family?" asked Andrew in a no-nonsense way.

There was a long silence on the phone. Instinctively, Andrew knew he had his answer.

"You know I cannot comment on the Letter of Wishes," said Robert sharply.

"It is just that a Google search shows that Tania Plesca left two young children when she died, so I have to ask: Do I have a brother and sister I don't know about?"

"I am sorry, Andrew," said Robert. There was clear reluctance in his voice. "It's not something I'm allowed to discuss."

Robert's tone said everything Andrew needed to know. Somewhere he had a brother or sister or both that he knew nothing about.

Chapter 75

Vienna International Airport March 2010

IT WAS A hefty fee paid to an international private detective agency which resulted in Serghei Stoica being found and Andrew and Peter meeting with him at the Vienna International Airport hotel.

Andrew and Peter already knew, from the detective's report, that Serghei was the father of Tania's eldest child, a son called Stelian. They'd also had it confirmed that Henry was the father of Tania's daughter, Yulia. It was to talk about the much wider story that the three men met in the coffee lounge, not least because Serghei desperately wanted to know where Yulia was. Her grandparents had lost touch with her on the day their daughter was killed and were worried sick about their granddaughter's safety.

"I haven't seen or heard of her since she flew off with Henry and Evelina that evening," said Serghei referring to Yulia's departure. "On the afternoon Tania was shot, I drove them from her flat to the airport. They were in such a hurry. They didn't take anything with them, clothes, nothing. Your father didn't even pack a suitcase. He left everything behind. The only thing they took was his briefcase, Yulia's birth certificate, the diamond ring your father gave Tania when Yulia was born, and oh, yes, I gave him Tania's gold pocket watch, which she always said Yulia was to have. You have to understand. They were running for their lives."

"A gold pocket watch?" repeated Andrew and Peter together.

"Yes, ever since Yulia was born, Tania was insistent that it went to her. It had to go down the female line of her family. It would identify some mystery father a long time ago. I was told of the relationship. It was complex, and didn't really interest me," said Serghei.

"Did you see the watch?" asked Andrew.

"It didn't have any engravings on it, did it?" ask Peter, following on quickly.

"Yes, I'm sure it had a crest and name engraved on the back, but its most notable feature were the diamonds to mark each and every hour. They were serious jewels," said Serghei.

The two brothers looked at each other and shook their heads with their mouths open but said nothing.

"Do you know where it is now?" asked Andrew anxiously.

"I don't. It will be with either your father or Yulia, but I made it clear to Henry at the airport that it was Yulia's, so I guess it's with her, wherever she is," said Serghei.

"And you don't know where she is?"

"No, as I've said, I really need to find her. I've been looking for her for a long time. I'm looking after an apartment in Kishinev which belongs to her, and of course, there's the St. Sophia vineyard which she inherited from your father."

"St. Sophia?" said Peter, recognising the name and interrupting abruptly.

"Your father bought an old run-down vineyard in Orhei in Moldova. He spent a fortune doing it up. It was known originally as the Faterini vineyard, after the village it was next to, but your father changed its name to St. Sophia Estate."

"What, after our mother?" said Peter, looking straight at Andrew.

"I don't know about that," said Serghei defensively. "What I do know is that the vineyard was owned by Tania and your father equally, and when Tania died, her shares went to Yulia and my son. Henry later bought my son's share so Yulia would own it one hundred per cent after he was dead."

"What's the vineyard like?" asked Andrew.

Very good, very successful, its wines are excellent, but its best-selling products are its brandy and apricots and peach liqueurs. They win prizes."

"Really, do you honestly not know where Yulia is?" asked Andrew. "It's important we find her."

"Honestly, I don't," said Serghei. "I've come to ask you the very same question. I've not seen or heard of her since Evelina carried her through the security gates at the airport on that dreadful day. Your father was so distraught, well we all were. It was awful." Sergei shook his head in pain, as he remembered that moment.

"And that's it," said Peter, not liking the finality of it all.

Serghei shrugged his shoulders. "There was talk of Tania's mother and father, and yes, I think her grandmother too, flying down to South Africa to see Yulia, but I think that was just talk."

"Are they still alive?

"Oh yes, that's why I've come today. They're desperate to know where Yulia is," said Serghei.

"We need to talk to Robert Glenn," said Andrew, as he dialled the solicitor's office on his mobile phone.

"Robert, its Andrew Guégan," said Andrew abruptly once they were connected. "We know we have a half-sister born in Moldova. We also know her name's Yulia, and she owns the St. Sophia vineyard and winery in Moldova. That's what the Letter of Wishes did, didn't it?"

There was a long pause while Robert thought.

"I think, given the circumstances, it is reasonable for me to confirm what you've said is correct," he replied formally.

"He's confirmed it," whispered Andrew to Peter.

"Do you know where she is?" Andrew asked aggressively.

"No, I have no contact details for her at all. The only person I have contact with is based in Moldova, but I can't remember his name."

"Serghei Stoica," prompted Andrew.

"Yes, that's it.."

"Peter and I are with him now. He says he looks after the St. Sophia vineyard and wineries on behalf of Yulia's trust. He doesn't know where she is. He says you must know. He's told us that all her shares in the vineyard in Moldova are held in trust for her until she reaches the age of twenty-one. She's now sixteen and probably doesn't even know she owns it." said Andrew getting quite agitated

"I promise you. I don't know," said Robert, "and the fact that I don't is most unsatisfactory. It's getting almost impossible for me to act on her affairs until I've had confirmation that she's still alive," he added.

"There is a suggestion that our father might have taken her down to South Africa to live. Do you know anything about that? asked Andrew.

"No, I don't but if you find her. I'd be grateful if you would let me know where she is or, at least, ask her to contact me.

"Half an hour after they finished their call, Robert phoned Andrew back.

"I've just been through my files," he said. "Firstly, I told you I knew nothing about 'A Manifesto for Moldova. I did. It's written in my notes of my meeting with your father. I forgot I knew. My apologies. I have another note which says that your father took Yulia to South Africa the day Tania was shot. My notes say that I advised him that he could be guilty of child abduction and he should apply to the courts to get himself appointed as Yulia's guardian. To the best of my knowledge, he didn't follow my advice. South Africa is the only clue I have as to her likely whereabouts."

"Okay, thank you," said Andrew, rapidly cancelling the call.

"Why would he have taken her to South Africa?" asked Andrew with a puzzled look on his face. "That's where Robert has just said they went from Moldova."

"He had a great-uncle in South Africa, remember. Papa talked about him when we were sitting around at Grandma's house just after she died," said Peter.

"He used to do a lot of business down there, didn't he?" said Andrew.

"You said Yulia and my father left with a woman. What was her name?" asked Peter looking at Serghei.

"Evelina Kirillovich," he replied.

"Could Yulia be with her?" Peter continued.

"Evelina could have stayed with your father, but she wouldn't have taken Yulia on her own. It would not have been her thing. Too beautiful, too ambitious, too scared," continued Serghei.

"Too scared, why too scared?"

"Evelina was ex KGB. She was very clever and beautiful, and I mean beautiful, dangerously beautiful. Your father could handle her.

He was older, also rich which is what she liked. He could also be very er...." Serghei searched in his head for the right word.

"Difficult, stubborn, determined, cantankerous, irascible, irritable," offered Andrew and Peter in turn, as the adjectives tripped off their tongues to describe their father.

"Let's just say they respected each other. There would be very few men like your father who would have been able to keep Evelina happy. Certainly not me ... although we made some great television programmes together," added Serghei, with a big smile across his face. "We did a couple of really nice interviews with Tania. I'd let you have a copy, but it's all in Moldovan."

"Why was she frightened?" asked Andrew.

"She thought she'd be killed next," answered Serghei. "Costin Stanescu was a former boyfriend of hers. He was the son of the President and ran the biggest mafia gang in Kishinev. Everyone in Moldova knew it was Costin Stanescu who had Tania shot. I think she was probably the one person who could prove it was him, and he knew it."

Andrew and Peter looked at each other amazed.

"I'll tell you, I did some investigatory work for a film with Evelina once, and what she could find out was truly startling," continued Serghei admiringly. "She's now in the United States, somewhere. I don't know where. All I know was her father sold everything of hers and sent her money there.

"If we found her, would she be able to tell us anything?"

"I don't know, possibly. She and your father might have kept in touch. There was a bond between them, always was."

"Did my father ever contact you after he left Moldova?" asked Andrew.

"Yes, we met in Bucharest several times in the first couple of years after Tania was shot. He put me in charge of running St. Sophia Estate in his absence. There was a lot of administration, lots of papers to sign for banks and the government. I brought him the clothes and personal things he left behind in his flat, but that was it. His biggest interest was in knowing if Tania's murderer had been caught, but no one was ever arrested."

"You don't happen to know how Tania's family came to get hold of the gold watch, do you?" asked Peter.

"Yes, in part. Your father asked me to find out. In fact, I'm sorry I should've said. It was the very first thing he asked me to do when we met for the first time in Bucharest." Serghei paused as he tried to recall what he had been told. "It was a gift from a German pilot during the war. I think there was something about him being Tania's grandfather. Honestly, I don't remember. It was all far too complex. What I do remember was how interested your father was when he discovered how the watch had ended up with the Solokov's."

Andrew and Peter's eyes widened, and their mouths dropped open. They couldn't say anything. Instead, they looked at each other in amazement. A German pilot, it was impossible to believe that this was a co-incidence.

The Solokov's? asked Peter.

"Tania's mother was a Solokov. Their family history is as old as Moldova's."

The conversation drifted on until it was time for the three men to catch their planes.

"You might like this," said Serghei, handing over a photograph. It was taken in the park just minutes before Tania was shot. There's your father and Yulia, and of course Tania," he said, pointing out the faces.

"Who are the others?" asked Peter.

Serghei ran through the names.

"It's yours to keep," said Serghei when he was offered back the photograph. "It's a small thing, and very old, but it might help you find her."

As Andrew and Peter flew back to Paris, each silently considered and analysed what they had learnt, just as their father used to do. Why had he kept it all so quiet? they wondered.

A couple of weeks later, Andrew phoned Peter to tell him that he had spoken to Pierre Hilaire. "I asked him about St. Sophia Estate. Did you know he went there with Thomas Cannen?"

"That's strange," replied Peter "I've just been speaking to Thomas about it too."

Hilaire and Cannen had retired only a few years before as the general managers of the Château de Gressier and Château Rabôut Estates, respectively.

"Pierre said St. Sophia Estate was a complete mess when they went the first time and thought Papa mad. They told him that. When they went back, after the first harvest and before the second, they thought he had a good chance of making a success of it," said Andrew.

"Thomas said roughly the same thing. He also said that they met Tania the first time they went out there but not the second. Father told them she'd just had a baby but said nothing about it being his. When I said it was Papa's daughter, he thought that explained why he was investing so much in St. Sophia. He suggested that Papa wanted to make sure she inherited a vineyard, like us."

Andrew grunted his acknowledgement.

"You know, the answer to this riddle lies in South Africa somewhere, and that somewhere is hidden in the de Gressier files."

"Yes," said Andrew reluctantly and with a heavy sigh.

"Okay, so phone me when you want me to go down there with you," said Peter just before he hung up.

Chapter 76

New Found Estate July 2010

HARRIET RUSSELL AND her brother Joseph, always known as Big Joe, were in the office at the New Found Estate when the phone rang. Albeit they shared a room, their working styles were so different that, for the purposes of harmony, their desks were as far apart as they could possibly be.

The call was first put through to Big Joe. "Sunetta," he called out, using Harriet's nickname as soon as he heard who was calling. "Mr Andrew Guégan's on the phone. He's asking about Yulia."

"Henry's son?" she asked.

"I guess so."

Harriet's heart started to pump as she picked up the phone. It was not a conversation she wanted to have, ever!

"Hello, Harriet speaking."

"I'm Andrew Guégan. I am Henry Guégan son. I believe we are related but I don't understand how," he said.

"Yes," said Harriet coldly. "We're related, but it's a long way back and complex."

"I believe you knew my father," said Henry cautiously.

"Yes, my mother, my father and me, we knew him very well. It was why I was so upset not to have been invited to his funeral or to have been told of his death by a member of his family." There was bitterness in Harriet's voice at the way she had been ignored.

"Oh, I am sorry," said Andrew. "I didn't know."

"I think there are a lot of things about your father's life which you don't know," said Harriet, allowing her intended irony to be carried along the telephone line.

"As I'm just discovering," said Andrew.

"And you might well have discovered much earlier if you'd invited me to his funeral," said Harriet, labouring the point, as the pain she felt then returned.

"Yes, I'm really sorry about that," he repeated, before pausing and saying: "The reason I'm phoning is that I have very recently found out I have a half-sister."

"Yes, you do," confirmed Harriet.

"Her name's Yulietta, Yulia for short. We think she was named after Juliette, our great-grandmother."

"Yes, she was," said Harriet, who then asked: "Do you know how she learnt of her father's death."

"No."

"She got a stereotype letter from your office in response to the Christmas card she'd handmade and sent him. Do you know what it said?"

"Sorry, no."

"I do. I can repeat it for you. It read: Thank you for your correspondence. I regret to inform you that Henry Guégan has died. All future correspondence should be addressed to ... you. Could you imagine receiving such a letter when you're just twelve years old? A reply to a Christmas card, for God sake!"

Andrew was dumbfounded. "No, I can't. I'm sorry. I'm really very sorry," he said apologetically.

"Do you know where Yulia is?" he asked.

"Yes."

"Where is she?" he pressed.

"She'll need to give me permission before I give you that information."

Andrew was shocked into silence. He wasn't expecting that response.

"Would you ask her, please?"

"Yes, I'll do that, but I'm not promising she'll phone you back." There was a long pause. "Our lives have long settled down. I am not sure either of us wants your father's family dragging up the past. Too damn often, the Guégan name has appeared and interrupted my family's history, or should I say Daunier, or Dovingdon, or perhaps Bellanger? I don't suppose you know all the aliases your family have used over the years to deceive."

"It's been that bad?" asked Andrew, recognising some of those names in his family's history.

"In part, yes," said Harriet firmly.

"I am sorry," said Andrew. "Really, I didn't know. Can I ask you one more question?"

"Yes," said Harriet, "but I'm not going to promise to answer it."

"Do you know if Yulia's got a gold pocket watch with the name Victor engraved on the back?" he asked, almost too frightened to do so.

"Mr Guégan," said Harriet. "Yulia left Moldova immediately after her mother had been killed, in no small part thanks to your father with, yes, a gold pocket watch as you describe, the diamond ring your father gave her mother, and a leather-bound book called A Manifesto for a Modern Land, the clothes she stood up in, and her life. Not a lot for a two-year-old, I'd say."

"You just said Yulia's mother was killed thanks to my father. Why did you say that?" asked Andrew.

"Because that's exactly what he told me .... and he told Yulia the same thing, and we have no reason to disbelieve him."

"I am really very sorry," said Andrew. His heart was thumping, and his mind was racing as fast as Harriet's. "I had no idea. I really didn't. I'm so sorry," he continued.

"I think I have said enough," said Harriet. "I might regret it if I say more. I think we should say goodbye."

"One thing; there are other people who would like to know she is safe. Her grandmother and grandfather and her half-brother, they would love to hear from her, to know she's safe."

"She's safe."

"I'm sure they'd like to know by talking to her. Also, my father's lawyer is holding a vineyard in Moldova in trust for Yulia, and she needs to know about it."

"Fax me their details, and I'll make sure Yulia gets it," said Harriet, before rapidly hanging up.

Without saying anything to Big Joe, Harriet walked purposely out of the office up to the tree at the highest point on New Found Estate where her mother, father and youngest brother were buried. With her back resting against the tree, she looked down at their graves. She then looked over the fields, towards the storage barn where she and Henry had made love for the first time. Except damn him, he never remembered her when they met years later.

Harriet thought of the other times she and Henry were together. They were always happy times, Harriet acknowledged. Somehow, whatever the pressure, Henry always made them so. Why wasn't he here now with her, she demanded. She loved him. She knew she did, and yet she hated him for dying, for leaving her. The fact was that, even after all this time, Harriet was grieving for Henry Guégan. Any time his name came up, she would well up in anger and start to grieve all over again.

As Harriet ambled back to her office, she worked out what she was going to do. She would tell Yulia about the phone call from her brother and try to persuade her not to call him back. She would tell her that the Guégan family were trouble.

She would tell about Henry's grandfather, Étienne and the double life he had with a mistress, which led to him being killed.

She would tell about the double life led by her father, using the name Penrose Dovingdon before the war and the name David Daunier after it.

She would tell how Henry was once called Hank Bellanger before he changed it to Henry Guégan. It meant that it was only after her father's death that she learnt that her father was Henry's great uncle.

She would remind Yulia of her father's treble life with his two families, who knew nothing of each other, while he carried on a love affair with her.

She would drive home the fact that duplicity was in the Guégan family genes, and under no circumstances were they to be trusted.

Except, when she came to speak to Yulia, Harriet chose her words carefully. Even though she remained furiously angry with him for dying, in her heart, she loved him; that love came through in the kindness which Harriet showed when she broke the news to Yulia that one of her brothers had been in touch.

As soon as Andrew had put down the phone on Harriet, he telephoned Serghei Stoica. He told him of his conversation with Harriet, that Yulia was safe. He gave him Harriet's telephone number to call.

"There's something I need you to do for me," Andrew asked Serghei. "If you would be so kind, I would like you to talk to Yulia's grandparents and find out exactly how the gold watch, which Yulia has, came into their family's possession. You told us once, but we need to check. We need to be certain. Its Yulia's. We want Yulia to keep it," he stressed. "It's just, my grandfather was a German pilot, and my grandmother lent him that gold watch. He was supposed to bring it back to her when the war ended, but he never did. The watch she lent was one of a pair. Yulia has the one engraved Victor, and we have the other in Bordeaux engraved Victoria. Victor and Victoria were twin brother and sister. It might be that Yulia and I aren't just half-brother and sister. We could be related in another way too."

Chapter 77

New Found Estate July 2010 to July 2014

FOR FOUR YEARS, Andrew, Peter and Yulia knew of each other but did nothing about meeting. Yulia contacted her father's lawyer, had an emotional meeting with Serghei and Stelian in Vienna, and reconnected with her maternal grandparents by holidaying with them for a week each year in Cyprus. She refused to go to Moldova.

It was on their first holiday that Yulia's maternal grandparents gave her an heirloom which they had been keeping safe for her.

"It has no value, but it should be the most precious item you will ever own," said her grandfather confidently, as he placed an old glass jam-jar with a metal top in front of her.

"The jam-jar was made in the Donici-Solokov factory," said her grandmother. "You're a Donici-Solokov. Look, and you will see your family name moulded onto the side of the glass and the year 1903. This factory was owned by your family, our family. Look at the bottom," she instructed. "Those three rouble coins are from the Russian Empire. Now, look at the smooth rounded stones."

Yulia did as she was told.

"Those stones were collected from the gravel works our family once owned," her grandmother continued. "The sticks around the edge, they were collected from our forests, but it's the soil I want you to have. The soil is from Moldova. It is valueless like this, but so important. It's essential for the very existence of human life. We must, you must, never take it for granted. Empires are lost because their citizens didn't look after their soil." There were now tears in her eyes.

"Wherever you go now, you can take a part of Moldova with you," said her grandfather proudly. "It is the land of your birth, and we never want you to forget that." He started to choke-up and began weeping too.

The passion with which her grandparents spoke of Moldova and the love they had for their country, despite all the pain it had given them, genuinely touched Yulia's heart. Maybe it was time to go home, she wondered.

The state of flux in the relationship between the two brothers and their sister was changed when Harriet and Yulia received letters jointly signed by Andrew and Peter. They were invited to the opening night of a musical on Broadway about Yulia's mother, which they had written. The letter also told how they were not just brothers and sister, but how they had discovered that Andrew and Peter's paternal grandfather was also Yulia's maternal great-grandfather.

Andrew and Peter offered to pay for the cost of the trip, plane ticket, hotel, everything. They just wanted Yulia there on that opening night and to bring with her the gold watch her mother had the bequeathed.

Yulia knew she had to be there to represent her mother.

"Are you going to come too?" she asked Harriet.

Harriet thought long and hard. It was all too painful. "No, I'll just cry," she said, as her thoughts moved on to something else. She was already planning. She was going to make sure that her adopted daughter was unquestionably the prettiest, the most attractive woman in the theatre that night.

Chapter 78

New York, USA September 2014

AS ANDREW GUÉGAN looked up from his newspaper, he saw Yulia Plesca was already at the hotel reception desk. Somehow, she had arrived without him seeing.

Although Andrew couldn't see her face, his instinct told him it was her. He knew she was beautiful from the photographs he had seen of her on the web, but as her locks of auburn hair flowed down her long, tailored coat, it was obvious, even from behind, that she radiated an elegance which was not apparent from the photographs of her on a computer screen.

Andrew felt nervously excited about their meeting. If he were honest with himself, he would admit to feeling genuinely fearful. He quickly put down his newspaper, which he hadn't had the concentration to read properly, got up from the settee he'd been sitting on and walked slowly to her side, checking it was her all the way.

"Yulia Plesca?" he asked cautiously, clumsily offering her his hand as he spoke. As she turned towards him, her eyes brightened, and her mouth broke into a smile.

"Peter?" she said, taking his hand and leaning forward to kiss him lightly on his cheek.

"Andrew," he replied, shaking his head ever so gently. "Andy," he added, almost as an afterthought.

Yulia repeated his name, and then as he smiled his acknowledgement, she found she could no longer control her emotions. In an explosion of joy and relief, she flung her arms around his neck and burst into a flood of tears. Andrew was slow to respond. His arms remained open at first, not really knowing what to do. Slowly he wrapped them around her coat, and only then did he take her in his arms. As he held her, he became overwhelmed by her convulsing sobs and, losing control of his emotions, his tears started to fall down his cheeks and into her hair.

Although they were complete strangers, they clung to each other, rocking from side to side, each knowing the other was filling a mysterious gap in their life. They parted for a brief second, asked if the other was all right, and then, when each smiled in acknowledgement, they impulsively grabbed each other and wept once again.

"I'm sorry," said Andrew to the hotel receptionist, finding it difficult to talk as he was still overcome. He was awash with a strange intensity of mixed feelings. They moved away from the desk and back to the settee where he had been sitting. They sat facing each other, holding hands, not knowing what to say, their tears flowing for everyone to see.

"Hello sister," said Andrew after a pause.

"Hello brother," said Yulia. "It's a pleasure to meet you." They both smiled and said little else as they just looked at each other, sharing a pack of tissues as they dried their eyes.

After a while, they returned, composed, to the reception desk. Andrew felt not just a need to explain but to tell someone his news, even if it was to a complete stranger.

"This is my sister," he said proudly, then paused, for even this tiny phrase carried too much emotion for him to speak. "We've never met before ... until now."

"Congratulations," said the receptionist, a little uneasily, not knowing what else to say.

Neither spoke as Yulia checked in.

"Room 707?" said the receptionist eventually, handing back Yulia's passport and credit card before writing the number on the key sleeve. "Room 707," the receptionist said again, this time speaking to the porter as she handed him the two electronic room keys.

At the elevator, Andrew pressed the call button, and the door opened immediately. Yulia went in first and moved to the back wall. Andrew went next, only to be followed by the bellboy with his trolley and Yulia's luggage, invading what might have been their private space. As the three of them rose to the seventh floor, they said nothing. Andrew observed Yulia as she nervously studied herself in the large mirror, lifting and scrunching her hair as they travelled.

Room 707 of the Ritz Carlton Hotel overlooks Battery Park and the seas of the Upper New York Bay. In the corner of the room, by the window, was a white telescope on a stand so you could look towards the Statue of Liberty and watch the ferries sailing backwards and forwards.

Her bags delivered, Andrew stopped the bellboy doing a facilities' guide to the room by paying him off with a tip. Yulia stripped off her coat and threw it across an armchair. She unzipped her boots, kicked them off and then, with a flick, bounced to fall on her back diagonally across the bed, letting out a deep sigh as she went. Yulia's exuberance contrasted sharply with Andrew's highly reserved behaviour.

"Good journey?" he asked as he moved to look out of the window.

"Yes, it was," she said, looking at the ceiling, her mind empty, "except the cab journey from JFK was tedious."

"It always is," replied Andrew.

Suddenly, Yulia became conscious that the dried salt from her tears was irritating the skin on her face. Getting up quickly, she electrified the room with her untapped energy as she attacked her suitcase and started the process of unpacking.

"Have you been to New York before?" asked Andrew, feeling he needed to say something.

"Yes, third time," Yulia replied casually, as she waved her washbag and clean underwear in the air in a show of success at their find. "I danced a couple of tours here a few years ago."

Without thought, Yulia started to undress in front of him, throwing her clothes carelessly on the bed. Any inhibitions or requirements for modesty had been lost a long time ago in the changing and dressing rooms of dance schools, theatres, and fashion shows, where she found most of her work. In seconds she had stripped to her bra and panties.

In ordinary circumstances, seeing a woman he did not know in a state of semi-undress close to him would have made Andrew feel uncomfortable. But this time, with Yulia in front of him semi-naked, he went into apoplexy, for she was just twenty, and there was a generation of difference between their ages. It meant Andrew did not know where he should look, but study her he did.

Yulia was much taller than he expected with the slim, muscular, perfect shaped body of a dancer. Even with jet lag, it was obvious she was nervous, overcharged with energy.

Within seconds Yulia had disappeared into the bathroom, only this time to reappear without a bra, but with an arm across her breasts. Her eyes were focused on her suitcase into which she dug furiously, first with one hand and then with both, unconsciously revealing herself to her brother. Grabbing items of clothing to her breasts, she disappeared as quickly as she came. Her concentration on her task had been so complete it was as though Andrew wasn't there. If their father had been watching her, he would have remarked how like her mother Tania was being.

Andrew paced the room, his discomfort continuing. He took off his raincoat, turned on the television and flicked from channel to channel until he came to CNN, which he settled down to watch. His mindless viewing was only disturbed by the sound of the shower in the bathroom.

Yulia reappeared wearing a white fluffy hotel dressing gown and vigorously rubbing her hair.

"That was quick," he said, "impossibly quick! No woman's ever been that quick in the bathroom before."

Yulia smiled as she moved around the bed and walked purposely towards him, holding out her hands. Andrew stood up, moved just a couple of steps closer to her and opened his arms. They took each other in another gentle embrace. As they cuddled, they rocked, very gently from side to side. He could smell the dampness of her hair and felt the softness of her skin. They both thought of the events which had bought them together. Each felt the nervous excitement, which had dominated their earlier feelings, drain from their bodies. With it, a new-found calm settled between them.

After some while, they separated. Andrew saw new tears in Yulia's eyes, but as he looked at her, she smiled again. He realised the tears were of joy, of finding a family she knew she had but could never acknowledge until then. The feeling of abandonment, which Yulia had carried for over 18 years, could start to leave her.

Andrew wanted to ask her about their father. How well did she know him? How often were they together? But he could not find a way to start. However, he had to know the answer to one question. Did she have the gold pocket watch whose story lay at the heart of his musical which was to be performed for the first time that evening on Broadway?

"Did you bring it with you?" Andrew asked nervously.

"Yes, it's here," she answered, knowing exactly what he was referring to. "It's in my case." She then paused. "Where's yours?" she asked.

"Peter's got ours. It's already at the theatre. Can I see it?" he asked.

"When I can see yours?" Yulia replied, somewhat sternly, and then added more gently, "It's only fair." She had thought about this moment; had prepared for it. If they saw hers before she saw theirs, then they might simply abandon her without acknowledgement or explanation. She had come too far and waited too long for that. She had too many unanswered questions.

Yulia paused, reflected for a moment, and moved to her enormous, business-like handbag.

"I thought you might like to see this," she said, taking out a heavy clear plastic sleeve. "I forgot to tell you about it before. I don't know why. Our father found it hidden in the watch case."

Andrew looked through the plastic at the rough yellow-brown paper torn from a lined exercise book. It was covered in tiny grey pencil writing which had smudged across the page. It was torn and frayed at its crease marks.

"What is it?" he asked. "I can make out the first words, 'mein liebes kind', 'my dear child', but the rest; it doesn't make sense."

"Look at the name on the bottom," instructed Yulia.

Andrew read the words, before saying out loud, "Hauptman Heinrik Klugman. It's not, is it? My grandfather?

"Yes, and my great-grandfather. Look at the date," said Yulia encouragingly.

"26th November 1944, Belgrade." Andrew looked at Yulia quizzically.

"I think it's a letter written to my grandmother by Heinrik before she was born," said Yulia.

"Where did you get this?" asked Andrew.

"It was hidden in the watchcase. Father found it years ago. If you look, it's written in a mixture of Russian and German, some words taken from one language, others from another."

Andrew looked at the letter again carefully. "You think our father knew about this?"

"The letter? Yes. Certainly, he knew of the watch because he was the one who told me of its history."

"You know this proves our story's true, don't you!" exclaimed Andrew excitedly.

Yulia said nothing. She just opened her eyes a little wider and jerked her head quickly in response.

"Do you speak Russian?" asked Andrew after a little while.

"Yes, not brilliantly, but yes, why?"

"How did you learn?"

"I don't know. I had some lessons, but it was something I found easy."

"I don't understand why Papa took you to South Africa and didn't bring you to us in France. Was it always Harriet who brought you up?" he asked. "We were told you and Papa left Moldova with a woman called Evelina Kirillovich. Do you know her?"

"No, for as long as I can remember Harriet's looked after me. I've never heard of her, or heard anyone else mentioned," said Yulia shaking her head. "But I don't understand it either. It's a mystery to me as to why I went to stay with Harriet too. All I know was that she was one of Papa's mistresses for many years until he died. She loved him. She passionately loved him; I know that."

"One of?"

"Oh yes, when I spoke to my great grandmother Anna about Papa, she was certain that our father had been in love with only two women. Tania and your mother, but I don't think that was true as he loved Harriet too. I'm sure of it. She certainly loved him. I think it is why she was happy to look after me – just for him."

"Is Yulia your full name?" asked Andrew.

"No, why?" Yulia paused. "It's an abbreviation of Yulietta," she answered. I'm told I'm named after our grandmother, but I don't know if it is true. Is it?

"Probably after our great-grandmother Juliette. By all accounts, she was quite formidable."

"Like our father," said Yulia.

"True, how very true," said Andrew and they smiled at each other with another knowing smile.

Chapter 79

New York, USA September 2014

IT WAS LATE afternoon, and it was Peter Guégan's turn to wait impatiently for Yulia. As he paced around the reception of her hotel in his tuxedo, he was strangely out of sorts with everyone around him.

Peter should have been thinking about the woman he was about to meet. His elder brother, Andrew, had told him of his emotional meeting with Yulia earlier in the day but, with his senses already coiled as tightly as possible, he had no ability to let any other emotion in or out. His thoughts were focused on one thing, and it was causing his stomach to churn with fear. His career was about to be made, or broken, by a musical he had been working on for the last two years. It was opening on Broadway in just over two hours' time.

For as long as he could remember, Peter Guégan had written songs. He did not know how it happened. Somehow, lyrics and music would coalesce in his brain, and a song would appear. After this, the hard work would start as the song was honed into a story with a beginning, middle and an end.

It was at University, when Peter attended the Edinburgh Fringe Festival, that his song-writing career began. He had been asked by a group of friends, who had written and were performing in their own comedy sketch show, to sing a few of his songs during scenery changes. There he was spotted by the agent of a New York music publisher, who wanted to offer two of the songs Peter had sung to his clients. Peter took exactly twenty-four hours to turn what he thought were scrappy songs on scrappy pieces of paper into sheet music with '©Peter Guégan' at the bottom. Since then, seven of his songs had been purchased, recorded and released to appear in the top ten pop charts somewhere around the world. In addition to his composing, Peter's ability to create repeating melodies took him into the world of the super-groups. From the recording studio he had built at Château Rabôut, he helped them arrange and orchestrate their work. If these super-groups' songs were included in his repertoire, then Peter could be considered as one of the most successful composers of his day.

Thanks to his father, Peter refused to sell any of his songs outright, always getting an upfront fee, a royalty, and a writing credit. This gave him an income that exceeded many of the famous names who were indelibly linked to his songs. While there was a sense of pride when he heard one of his tunes on the television or radio, this was immediately counteracted by the disappointment he felt by his lack of recognition. Every time he wanted to shout out, "I wrote that," but rarely did.

It was when Peter saw Les Miserables on the London stage at the age of thirteen he knew what he wanted to do with his life - write musicals. It was an ambition that was to last until he was eighteen and saw Miss Saigon on Broadway and heard the song 'Bui Doi' (the Dust of Life). It was sung to the click-click of an old amateur cine film, showing the faces of the mixed-race children the American GI fathers had left behind in Vietnam when the United States pulled out after losing the war. The sense of communal guilt was so powerful that it raised the hairs on the back of the necks of everyone in the theatre. Peter decided he could never write a show as good as that, and if he could not, what was the point. He was like his father in that respect, the best or not at all.

As a result, Peter continued to write his 'little ditties', as he called them, but it didn't bring him the career satisfaction he craved. Time after time, he had researched a subject for a musical, but the passion he felt at the outset waned, as he found the storytelling either too difficult or insufficiently exciting to be honed into one hundred minutes of theatre. The story he wanted to tell had to have a meaning, a message and that was proving too hard to find.

Chapter 80

New York, USA September 2014

ISAAC TINNERMAN, KNOWN as Zac, was short, overweight, unfit, and balding. He was a third-tier New York impresario who had never found the big hit he yearned.

On his arrival from Israel, Isaac had set up shop as a talent agent but, he could never find enough work for the actors on his books to earn the income they desired in an overcrowded market. Isaac's solution was to produce his own shows in the smaller theatres off-Broadway. The key to his moderate success was to do short runs of only a few weeks as, within New York's finest, there was a cadre of theatre aficionados who would come to the opening of an envelope as long as it had the word 'theatre' on it. Some of Isaac's productions were rightly panned, for they were truly dreadful, while others were delightful but without the popularism needed for mainstream theatre. Nevertheless, good or bad, the theatre buffs kept buying his tickets.

Isaac made it his business to know everyone he possibly could, not because he was interested in them as a person, but because of what that person might be able to do for him. He was as proud of his rolodex of contacts as any New York stockbroker. In this quest for contacts, Isaac made a point of getting to know both Andrew and Peter. As far as Isaac was concerned, these two were 'old wealth'. This made them potential angel investors for one of his shows. If he kept trying for long enough, then one day, he would find something they would invest in. It was his way; persistence, a small amount of money at first, then bigger and bigger amounts. He rarely returned the accumulated investment to his investors, always rolling it on into the next show. Isaac was as close to operating a theatrical Ponzi scheme as was possible without breaking the law.

In an attempt to shut Isaac up, during one of his incessant investment pitch telephone calls, Andrew and Peter independently told Isaac about their idea for the de Gressier Musical. Andrew told of their family story and how it might be staged. Peter spoke of the music and how the story related to songs he had already written. Although they had spoken in general terms about a musical based upon Tania Plesca, neither knew, for they had not spoken to their brother about the idea, was that each had conceived and shared with Isaac exactly the same idea for the show's climactic ending.

Taking their story, as told to him by Andrew and Peter, Isaac produced the first outline of the de Gressier musical. The scenes, the story and the music were all summarised on four sheets of paper. There was not an original thought in Isaac's writing. It had all been taken from the two brothers. It was enough to get them in a room together to write the first draft of the script, identifying the theme of each song to be performed and ideas for the staging. Neither had done anything like this before, but they had seen enough musicals to know the effect they wanted to create.

As they worked, Andrew and Peter fought like cat and dog, as only brothers can. Each tried to get their way - never conceding outright but gently acquiescing at some later stage by silently allowing the other brother's idea to remain in the draft script.

Andrew worked on the practicalities of the storytelling, staging and script while Peter worked on the look, the feel and the emotion of what they were telling, for they were of quite different temperaments. It was this difference which, when each listened to the other, made them a powerful duo.

At the end of preparing the first fully worked script and score, Andrew and Peter presented it to Isaac with two conditions. Firstly, it had to be performed in one of the major theatres of Broadway, not one of his back-street jobs. Secondly, they weren't going to put any money into the show. They could have easily financed a large part of it between them, but this was not the point. Before it was performed, it had to pass the test that other people thought it good enough to invest in. They did.

It meant that the curtain on the first performance of the de Gressier Musical was to rise on Broadway that night.

Chapter 81

New York, USA September 2014

YULIA PLESCA HAD never been to a red-carpet theatre opening before. She knew tonight was going to make or break her career. She was determined to make an entrance and be noticed at the premiere of 'her mother's musical,' as she thought of it.

Precisely on time, Yulia swept from the lift to where Peter was standing. The bustle in the room noticeably slowed as everyone stopped to look at her. Their eyes were immediately attracted to the deep vermillion red ballgown she was wearing with its wide flowing skirt and tight plunging bodice, then they looked at the woman with her auburn hair falling in waves over her shoulders, and finally to Yulia's face where her make-up had been immaculately applied. She radiated beauty.

Yulia wore no jewellery on her ears or neck, which made her look more youthful. She wore two rings over her gloved hand, each given by her father to the two mothers in her life. It was the first time that they had come together on the same hand. It was a moment Yulia found incredibly poignant, causing her to blink rapidly as she fought back her tears.

As she left the elevator, Yulia thought she looked the best she possibly could, and with it her confidence had been given the biggest of boosts. She might not be the star of the show, but it was her birth mother, Anastaisi Plesca's story which was being told on stage that evening, and she wasn't going to let her down.

"You must be Peter," said Yulia as she stepped up to meet the man in the tuxedo.

"Yes," said Peter, as he smiled back cautiously, now nervous about this meeting too. His earlier worries about his show were briefly removed by the vision of beauty now in front of him.

"Hello brother," said Yulia as she extended her hand formally and leant forward to give him an air kiss on the cheek. Her emotions were steeled for the performance she was about to give.

They shook hands in a manner which Peter found disconcerting. It was nothing like her emotional first meeting with Andrew which had been described to him earlier.

Peter didn't realise, but Yulia was now in character. Dressed in her costume, she was focused on playing the role she had crafted for herself. Her intention was to be the photograph on the front page of every newspaper tomorrow morning, and nothing was going to stop that from happening! The memory of her birth mother deserved nothing less.

"Do you have it?" Peter asked.

Yulia raised her hand in response. All Peter saw was Yulia's long red glove, which matched exactly the colour of her dress; then he saw a small scruffy cardboard box. His heart sank, and then his mouth fell open, for it appeared nothing like the case of their watch. Oh God, he thought, praying that they hadn't got the whole story terribly wrong.

Outside the hotel, Peter patiently helped Yulia fold her ballgown into the back seat of the waiting limousine and shut the door. Peter climbed in through the front door and slid up the leather seat that ran the length of the car so they could sit side-by-side. Throughout the short journey, they asked and answered the usual questions that strangers ask one of the other when they first meet. Peter's instincts were putting him on edge. There was something too formal about the way his sister was reacting to their meeting, and it was making him decidedly uncomfortable.

A small pre-show party was underway when Peter and Yulia arrived at the offices of Isaac Tinnerman. Isaac had the label of co-producer of the de Gressier Musical, but in truth, he was the sole producer. It was he who had encouraged Andrew and Peter, brought in the money, found the stage and musical directors, rented the theatre and had hired the cast and orchestra. All the others in the room with the title of co-producer hadn't done an item of work. They were just the largest angel investors in the show and were now supping Isaac's champagne as part of their reward.

Yulia's arrival at the party had precisely the effect she had hoped. The room noticeably went silent as everyone spotted this unknown but powerfully attractive young woman. Andrew stepped forward and enthusiastically took Yulia off Peter's raised hand, but as they touched, he noticed the difference in her demeanour. Something had changed. He too didn't realise that Yulia's performance had started: cometh the costume cometh the actor!

Andrew had just started the introductions when Yulia suddenly froze. In the centre of the old polished mahogany table, there was a sculpture that she had seen many, many times before. The sculpture was a solid silver casting of two hands shaking. On each wrist, there was moulded into the piece a gold wristwatch. On one watch, the diamonds made the sign of the cross and on the other, the Star of David. Across each watchstrap were engraved the words: *"A true partnership - where each is more generous to the other for then there's more than one hundred per cent to share."* Yulia had always coveted its very existence.

"Where did you get that?" demanded Yulia loudly, pointing to the sculpture. Her sense of shock was apparent to everyone in the room.

"It's mine," said Isaac taken aback by the aggressive nature of Yulia's question. "Why?"

"How did you get it?" she demanded, almost screaming in anger. The room fell silent in response to the tension Yulia was creating.

"It was given to me by my father when I emigrated," replied Isaac, affronted at Yulia's behaviour. "There are only two in the world. One's here and the other's ... I don't know where." As Isaac spoke, he became more perplexed as Yulia's distress was as palpable as was his mystery at her behaviour.

"The other one ..." Yulia paused, for she was now crying. The composure she had been so determined to keep was lost as she physically shook. She started to speak again: "The other one .... the other one's my grandfather's," she sobbed. "I can take you to it straight away. I know exactly where it is!" Her voice was defiant.

"Is your grandfather David Daunier?" asked Isaac patiently. He slowly but deliberately turned the sculpture around so that the inscription of David's name faced her.

"Yes," she cried, wholly overwhelmed, "but he died before I was born."

There was a pause as the news was absorbed.

"Christ," yelled Isaac. "If Daunier's your grandfather, how come you three are brothers and half-sister?" he yelled.

All eyes in the room darted quickly between the object on the table and Isaac and Yulia's faces. They had quickly worked out what this meant for the show. The musical's story was based on Andrew and Peter's paternal grandfather being a German pilot called Klugman and their paternal grandmother a French woman named Guégan. There was no one called Daunier involved! They had all jumped to the same conclusion – the script had no basis in truth. It was a fraud!

Andrew and Peter said nothing. They had failed to see the problem. Wasn't it normal for siblings to share grandparents? they each wondered, oblivious to the point Isaac was making.

"Hang on a moment," shouted Isaac, not reacting well to their silence. "Haven't you guys proved you're brother and sister? Haven't you had a DNA test or som'in?"

"No," said Andrew. "Why would we? We only met today."

"Because I've invested fuckin' five million bucks on the fact that you are ... and now you're telling me you fucking don't know!" he yelled.

The rest of the room moved slowly away from the table, taking a few small paces backwards to get closer to the wall.

"What makes this fuckin' worse is that the fuckin' watch, which is supposed to have gone to fuckin' Eastern Europe, courtesy of some fucking Nazi, has been sitting all the fuckin' time in South Africa courtesy of her bloody grandfather," screamed Isaac. "There's no soddin' truth to the whole bloody story at all, is there?" His was a genuinely prima donna performance.

"Where are the fuckin' watches? Give me the fuckin' watches!" demanded Isaac, now certain he was about to suffer a huge public humiliation.

357

No one moved or said anything, for they knew to do so would just incur Isaac's wrath.

"For Christ's sakes, some'n get this girl a drink ... and a load of tissues," instructed Isaac in that tone that is uniquely reserved for New York's alpha males. He threw his arms in the direction of Yulia, who had retreated to sit on a dining room style chair placed in the corner of the room. She was still shaking from Isaac's onslaught. The grasp on her package was so tight that it would have taken the best of New York's firemen to have prised it off her.

Seeing Yulia's distress, Andrew and Peter ignored Isaac, and together they squatted at her knee, held her hands, and told her that everything would be all right.

"Peter, isn't Daunier some kind of uncle of ours?" asked Andrew, trying to make sense of it all. Isn't he referred to in the de Gressier diaries somewhere?"

"I don't know. Perhaps, yes, I think so. Does it matter?"

"I need to go," said Yulia. "I can't be here. I need to go back to the hotel, please?" she begged.

Words of comfort streamed from Andrew's and Peter's lips as a glass of champagne was thrust into Yulia's hand. A packet of tissues was dismissively thrown onto her dress from another guest who was certain she was looking at the cause for the loss of her investment.

Yulia downed the champagne in one go, forcibly ignoring the bubbles, and passed the glass away. Still grasping her package with one hand, she wiped her eyes with a tissue in the other.

"I say he's my grandfather, but he's not my real grandfather," said Yulia, stressing the word real. "He's really Harriet's father. When she, sort of, adopted me, well, I sort of adopted the rest of her family too."

The two brothers looked at each other. "So, he's not related to us?" asked Peter shaking his head in confusion.

"He is, you know he is. He's our father's great uncle," Yulia answered firmly.

"Oh fuck," said Andrew in one of the very few times he swore. "I don't get this. I really don't get it at all."

"There's something worse, even weirder. You see that jar," said Yulia, pointing towards a non-descript glass jam-jar on a window sill.

The two brothers looked.

"It says Donici-Solokov on it, doesn't it?" said Yulia.

Andrew reached across and picked up the jar, which he examined before handing it to Peter.

Those closely around them were carefully watching the two brothers and their sister in conversation. They were looking for some clue as to what was happening. The others had returned to the task of partying.

"And?" said Peter looking at Yulia in the eye, not grasping its importance.

"It comes from Moldova. My brother and I have one just the same."

Peter and Andrew looked at each other, neither grasping its importance.

"They're family heirlooms," said Yulia.

Peter rose from his squat position and went to talk to Isaac, who had calmed down. He'd realised that the tickets had been sold and the night needed to be a success. If he panicked, his investors would panic too and so, to calm his and their nerves, he was back pouring champagne telling everyone that they had a great show, and everything was going to be alright.

"What's this?" asked Peter, waiving the jam jar close to Isaac's chest.

"Oh that, it's a family heirloom. Why?"

"Yulia says she has one."

"Nah, not possible" whined Isaac dismissively. "There were only very few made."

"In Moldova?" asked Peter.

"Yeh, yeh," replied Isaac." It's where my family comes from."

"It's where Yulia comes from."

"Yeh, yeh," said Isaac snidely, as he turned to refill another glass with champagne. "It's why I liked the story; it sorta connected with me. Is the girl all right?" he asked. Have you seen the watch? Is it a pair?"

Peter didn't reply. Instead, taking the jar, he placed it back on the shelf and returned to Yulia's side.

"He says it's an heirloom too."

"That doesn't make sense," said Yulia as she shook her head slowly.

"It might do when you know his family comes from Moldova too."

"Really?"

"Can I see your watch?" asked Peter changing the subject. He was conscious of Isaac's question.

"No," said Yulia defiantly.

"I think it's best if we see it now," said Andrew in support of his brother. "It means we can be prepared," he added.

Yulia said nothing. She just shook her head firmly and tightened her grip on the box.

"We know we have the same father. There is no doubt about that, but now there's doubt about the journey of your watch, and that's what this whole musical is about."

"It isn't," said Yulia defiantly. "It's about my mother."

"Yes," acknowledged Peter, "and the watches."

"Let's just check, and we can be sure. What's the harm?"

"No," said Yulia determinedly. She didn't know what the harm might be, but she wasn't going to risk it. "You promised me that the watches would be opened together on stage at the very end. Either that happens, or I'm not going."

Andrew and Peter pleaded, but Yulia had said her last word on the subject. It was the reason she had come all the way from South Africa. To her, the watches were just objects, nice objects but objects all the same. But to reveal the letter hidden deep inside the watch case - that would be a sensation.

She had to read it on stage tonight. She just had to!

Chapter 82

Broadway, New York September 2014

YULIA TOOK HER seat in the theatre between her two half-brothers, her extensive dress floating around her. She had appeared on stage many times and knew the anxiety of first night nerves; but the fear she felt was worse than anything she'd experienced before. She sat rigid in her seat as surges of terror swept throughout her body. As the theatre lights dimmed, Yulia exhaled heavily and closed her eyes in silent prayer.

The first song was sung by an actor playing Col. Stoddart Dovingdon, Victor and Victoria's grandfather. The scene was of a lonely man on a bare stage sitting at a writing desk. The stage was as desolate as expressed by the actor in his singing voice. The lyrics were based on the letter written by Col. Stoddart Dovingdon to his daughter Juliette in February 1925. It had been kept safe in the diaries at Château de Gressier. It told of the Colonel's grief at the estrangement from his daughter and how, through these gifts of gold engraved watches to her twin children, he yearned that Juliette would forgive him and come home.

The stage curtain fell as the song ended. There was no movement in the audience - just the faintest of applause. Andrew and Peter's hearts stopped beating as fear of failure gripped their very being.

The curtain rose quickly with the actor playing Heinrik Klugman standing centre stage in a German pilot's uniform, with a backdrop of a city burning in red and orange flames from the bombs which he had just dropped. The Actor had such self-confidence that he controlled the stage by merely standing upon it.

Yulia took a deep intake of breath, for she thought the actor who played Heinrik was perhaps the most handsome man she had ever seen. He was tall, chiselled, with nordic good looks. Yulia did not know, but the actor was as close a lookalike to his real-life character as there could possibly have been. As part of his research, Isaac Tinnerman had discovered a photograph of Heinrik taken at the Wolf's Lair, Hitler's Field Headquarters, when he was awarded the Iron Cross. It was in his Luftwaffe file and had survived the fire deliberately started when the German army began their retreat.

The actor took a deep breath and, in a tenor voice, started to sing:

> *I've seen hope in the eyes of children*
> *And love in the tears of man.*
> *Now I Iook on the red horizon*
> *And I see what I have done.*
> *I've been the man to fight the battle*
> *I've been the one to win the war.*
> *And for it all I've left you lonely*
> *As lonely as before.*
> *Have I not been your hero?*
> *When it was all I wanted to be.*
> *I realised I've been going solo*
> *If only for you, I'll find the hero in me".[13]*

The song was already well known by the audience as it had been released to accompany a video promoting the musical and, because it was a Peter Guégan composition, it had automatically received the radio and television air time needed to take it into the international hit parade.

Yulia may have been the only person who hadn't heard the song before, but it didn't matter. It immediately captivated her. She was certain that the pilot was singing just to her. It was precisely what he was doing because, studying the audience from the wings before the

---

[13] Lyrics and music by James Bunker

curtain rose, he had become enchanted with the girl in the vermillion dress. He had no idea who she was.

Again, the audience clapped politely, causing Andrew and Peter's anxiety to rise even higher, for they could sense that they had not won them over. In their silence, the audience was challenging those on stage: come on - entertain me!

It was the third song that captured the soul of the theatre and took each member of the audience deeply into the story being told on stage. With Victoria standing on the left of the stage, Heinrik in the middle, and against a backdrop of a French vineyard, the two actors sang of their love for each other. They shared the pain they both felt at being parted as Heinrik had been ordered back to Berlin. Victoria tells of her brother's death from drowning at a young age. How lonely this made her feel, and how she was giving Heinrik her brother's watch to remember her by. It was given on the promise that one day he would return, and it would come back to her.

Without any change in the music or its tempo, Heinrik turns from Victoria, and with Victor's watch in his hands, he looks in the other direction as coming on to the stage is Anna Solokov, Tania's grandmother, Yulia's great grandmother.

Victoria fades off stage as the backdrop is transformed from a French vineyard to be lit as a Moldovan wheat field. On stage, Heinrik transforms from being in the smart uniform of a German soldier into the well-worn and world-weary clothes of an escapee.

It is now Heinrik and Anna who sing of the love they have for each other. They share the pain they both feel at being parted as they know Heinrik will shortly be arrested as a prisoner of war and sent to a gulag. It is now Heinrik's turn to pass the gold watch to Anna, asking her to keep it safe because it belongs to a friend. He promises to return as soon as he can so they can be together once again.

The music becomes very soft and balletic as Heinrik recedes deep into the darkness at the back of the stage. Anna remains on the right-hand side with the background of a Moldovan wheat, while Victoria reappears on the left side to the backdrop of a French vineyard.

Victoria and Anna, each standing in ignorance of the other, start to sing a duet with very little accompaniment. Their lyrics were almost identical.

In the purest of voices, the two women expressed their love for Heinrik, tell him that his son or daughter has been born, and each prayed earnestly for their re-union. The only variation in the words was that Victoria sung of the birth of Henry, and the fact that Heinrik had something of hers, whilst Anna told of the birth of Heidi and that she had something of Heinrik's; both were referring to the gold pocket watch engraved with the name Victor.

So powerful were the music and the words of love that, at the end of the song, the audience was spellbound into a strange silence. In response, Andrew and Peter's fright mechanism took them to another level of fear. They both wanted to run. It seemed to them that the silence was the audience signifying contempt and disapproval of their work, but then, very slowly at first, the applause grew and grew until the two brothers started to smile. For the very first time since the curtain had gone up, the butterflies in their stomachs started to abate.

Yulia beamed with delight for, throughout the duet, Heinrik had been standing in the shadows listening to the two women sing, but she was certain that he had been staring at her. Theirs was a magnetic attraction, and she loved him for it.

The first act ended with Heinrik coming forward from the shadows to sit in a park all alone. He is homeless. All his worldly possessions are gathered around him in plastic bags. The lights are dimming as the evening passes into the night. Heinrik starts to sing:

> *Here I lay stranded*
> *The candle burning bright.*
> *Flickering shadows*
> *Dancing in the night.*
> *Do you not know my name?*
> *What are the rules to your game?*
> *Twisting colours in my whirlpool of darkness*
> *Lost inside my head in crazy dreams.*

You cross the streets,
Turn your back,
And you walk on by.
Pretend to not notice,
Don't you see my cry?
When I reach out for your hand.
I only ask you understand.
I close my eyes and I pray for protection.
I pray to God, may I rest in peace.

The streets are bare,
They are my home.
The address I use, it is not known.
All my friends have flown
I lay here all alone.

Through the wind and through the rain
I hide my face
And hide in shame.
No one knows the pain,
Of a man who bears no name.

I wear my life on my back,
My heart upon my sleeve.
It takes no imagining,
It's not hard to believe.
And every day I see your face.
No signs of love,
Just disgrace.
I've been abandoned in a world unrelenting
I reach out,
But you walk on by.

You walk on by.[14]

---

[14] Lyrics and music by James Bunker

Yulia studied Heinrik intensely, for the actor physically changed in front of her as he sang. It wasn't just that his clothes had changed to become dirty and worn, but his whole demeanour transposed before her eyes to one of a broken man. Except he couldn't hide one thing, the brightness in his eyes. They shone with every note in Yulia's direction. She knew he was singing directly to her as he took his last breath and died.

There was complete silence in the theatre for a long time after Heinrik had stopped singing. The moment was too powerful for an instant reaction. Yulia didn't move a muscle as the tears from her eyes flowed down her cheeks. Did her grandfather end up homeless and die just like that, she wondered? It was only when the audience started to clap, slowly at first, that Yulia moved to wipe her face with her gloved hand, spreading streaks of mascara across her face.

Peter offered Yulia the handkerchief from his top pocket, while Andrew tried to encourage her to go backstage, but she was too upset to talk. Above all, she didn't want anyone to see her like that. After all, she was there representing her mother, and she was not going to let her down.

Chapter 83

Broadway, New York September 2014

THE SECOND ACT was set in Moldova and told Tania and Henry's story. The music started on an upbeat note as the lyrics told of a country throwing off the yoke of communism.

The love story between Henry and Tania was beautifully crafted with sensitivity in the words of love which resonated with Yulia. But it was the physicality of the actors to the persons they were playing and the way they had captured many of their mannerisms, which made Yulia feel strangely light-headed. It made it seem as though her parents were still alive.

Although everyone knew it would be coming, when the sharp crack of a rifle shot resounded loudly around the theatre, the audience was shocked into such a fright that the hairs on their bodies stood on end. Adrenaline poured through everyone's veins as Tania's body, hit by the assassin's bullet, collapsed to the ground.

Almost in unison, the audience turned to stare at Yulia. She had stopped breathing. She was numb, rigid and nauseous all at the same time. She couldn't believe she had just witnessed the killing of her mother on stage.

The audience turned back to look at the stage where, with Tania in Henry's arms and clasped to his breast, they started to sing:

Tania: Heaven calls my name,
I'm so afraid,
I'm so frightened.
Each breath my last,
My life has passed,
Fading away.

Henry: Do not be afraid.
I'm by your side,
And will not leave you.
What I would give,
For you to live,
Until I die.

Henry: Now is not the time.
Tania: It's not the place.
Henry: Don't close your eyes.
Together: Please heaven,
Leave my love

Tania: Heaven calls my name,
One last embrace,
One last goodbye.
Touching your lips,
Feeling your kiss,
It makes me cry.

Henry: Wipe away those tears,
I will see you tomorrow.
In time we'll be,
Eternally, above the stars.

Henry: Now is not the time
Tania: It's not the place.
Henry: Don't close your eyes.
Together: Please Heaven,
Leave my love.

Tania: Heaven calls my name.
Henry: Without you I cannot cope
Tania   I'm so afraid, so frightened.
Henry: What will happen when you're gone?

Tania	Each breath my last
Henry	Where will I go?
Tania:	My life has passed,
Henry:	And what will I do?
Tania:	Fading away.
Henry:	Do not die,
	Do not die.
Tania:	Oh my love.
	Wipe away your tears
Henry:	Oh sleep softly and in peace.
Tania:	I'll see you tomorrow.
Together:	Our hearts will meet again,
	Eternally above the stars.
Henry:	Now is not the time.
	It's not the place.
	Don't close your eyes.
	Please heaven,
	Leave my love.[15]

When the curtain fell, there was not a dry eye in the house, least of all for Yulia, who just before the curtain touched the ground, had rushed from her seat in sobs of tears. She didn't know where she was going. She just knew she had to get out of there. To watch her mother's violent death portrayed in front of two thousand others was too much. It bought back the pain of years and years of loss. Yulia was crippled in the agony of it all.

Andrew and Peter had sat through the scene fifty, perhaps a hundred times in rehearsal. They had become inured to its effect, except tonight when they shared it with others. Not for a moment had Yulia's feelings or reaction crossed their minds. They were focused on one thing: making a great moment of theatre.

---

[15] Lyrics and music by James Bunker

It was the Theatre Manager who took charge of Yulia's rescue. He was an old hand in crisis management and had predicted what was going to happen. It was part of his job to prepare for the unusual, for the known unknowns, for moments just like this. His only uncertainty was the door Yulia would rush through, so he had usherettes at every exit. With kind but firm manhandling, it took seconds to have Yulia sitting by herself in an unoccupied dressing room behind the stage. There Yulia sat mute and motionless, looking at her face in the mirror, panic-stricken, not knowing what to do. Clasped tightly in her gloved hand was her mother's gold watch.

Yulia's trance was broken by the Theatre Manager bringing her a cup of tea. "I thought you might like this," he said in a soft Geordie accent.

She nodded and smiled weakly.

"I'll tell you, the bigger the star, the more frightened they get," he said as he very quietly busied himself around the room. He didn't think she should be left alone, and he certainly didn't want Andrew and Peter interrupting what he thought should be her private moment.

"I looked after Sinatra a few times. He would get a bad attack … well best not said," he continued calmly. "What happens in the dressing room stays in the dressing room. That's the rule."

Yulia reached across the dressing table for a wet wipe so she could remove the grey streaks of mascara from her face and started to attend to her make-up. There was little time.

"Don't do that love," said the Theatre Manager in a kind and fatherly manner. "Are you sure you want to?"

Yulia looked at him. In her silence, and from the way she held her head, it was obvious she expected an explanation.

"Da'ya remember Jackie Kennedy when President Kennedy got shot?"

Yulia nodded. "I wasn't born then …," she added with a tone that sounded mildly sarcastic. She knew of the shooting but had no idea what the Theatre Manager was referring to.

"After the President was shot, Mrs Kennedy had an opportunity to change her clothes before President Johnson was sworn in. But she didn't. She wanted the world to see her husband's blood on her suit. She wanted them to know what had been done to him."

Yulia remembered the black and white photograph the Theatre Manager was referring to as Kennedy's death was deep in the psyche of every South African. It was the death of the world's leading anti-apartheid campaigner, and for many, it was the death of hope.

Suddenly, in her mind's eye, came the picture of Jackie Kennedy standing stock-still in a long black widow's veil as John F. Kennedy Junior saluted his father for the final time.

"Did you know the day of President Kennedy's funeral was JFK Junior's birthday?" said the Theatre Manager. "He was just three that day. It broke everyone's heart."

Yulia was shocked, for it was as though the Theatre Manager had been reading her mind. She nodded her head in sympathy.

"You were two, weren't you, when your mother was killed?" he continued, asking a question he already knew the answer to.

Yulia nodded.

"You've both had a lot to live up to, haven't you?"

"You think I should go on like this?" asked Yulia.

The Theatre Manager said nothing. Instead he nodded firmly, just once, as the floor manager sent out a panicked tannoy message saying the final act was about to begin. "Just touch up the eye shadow, mascara and lipstick and leave everything else," he said after further thought. "You'll be a sensation!"

Andrew, Peter and Yulia were not in their seats when the curtain rose. Once again, the scenery was split in two. On the left-hand side of the stage the scene was of the de Gressier vineyards where the actors playing Andrew and Peter were standing. On the right-hand side of the stage the scenery was of a vineyard in South Africa with Table Top Mountain in the background and a child actor in front playing Yulia's role. In the middle was the actor playing Henry. He sings to them separately. First, he hands Victoria's watch to the actors playing Peter and Andrew and then, moving carefully to the right-hand side of the stage, he hands Victor's watch to the young actress playing Yulia. He tells them both that their watch is one of an almost identical pair. One had initially been given to his mother, and the other to his uncle.

He tells them each that if they find the other watch, then their family will be reunited.

The music slowly changed from a ballad into a powerful march, expressing optimism for the future. It meant that the audience hardly noticed Henry drifting out of the scene and into oblivion. At the same time, a young Yulia is replaced by an actress of Yulia's current age.

On every other night, the show would end with actors representing Andrew, Peter and Yulia meeting on stage, showing and sharing their watches and then singing in unison of their family going forward together; but not tonight, the opening night.

As the music ended, from the Western European side of the stage came the real Andrew and Peter, not the actors playing them. Simultaneously, from the right-hand side of the stage, and with the scenery of the winelands of South Africa in the background, should have come the real Yulia, except she was not there. From the anxious shuffles on stage, the audience could tell something had gone wrong.

"Are you sure you want to do this?" asked the Stage Manager gently when Yulia's curtain call came through the tannoy in her dressing room. "You don't have to, you know."

"I do," said Yulia defiantly. "I have to for my mother. I have to do it for me!" The steeled actress, who had first appeared in her costume on the ground floor of the Ritz-Carlton hotel only a few hours before, was back in character. She was ready. She was determined. She was going to give the performance of her lifetime.

Chapter 84

Broadway, New York September 2014

THERE WAS PALPABLE relief on Andrew and Peter's faces when they saw Yulia appear in the wings, pausing to shake down her dress. Then, with her package in her hand, she strode onto the stage. Everyone stopped looking at the two men. All eyes were on the beautiful, radiant woman in her vermillion dress with its colour intensified under the spotlights. There was not a man or woman who didn't want to love her. The applause was deafening.

Andrew held up his hand to speak. "Today," he said and then stopped as the audience quietened down. He started again. "As you probably know now, this is my family's story. Today, I met my sister ... our sister ... Yulia for the very first time." Andrew paused. He tried to say more, but the words wouldn't come out. His mouth was dry. His jaw was clamped tight as he tried to stop himself from crying.

Peter came forward to help his brother out, but he could say nothing either, his distress made worse by his brother's obvious tears. He, too, was overcome by the moment.

Yulia moved between her two much older brothers and held their hands. The audience was crushed into silence, embarrassed for the two men, but as Yulia pulled her brothers into her, the audience clapped and cheered and stamped their feet in approval, creating a noise the theatre had never experienced in its history.

Yulia took the microphone from Peter and stepped forward. The mascara from her tears was still streaked across her face. Nevertheless, she smiled a warm, beaming, welcoming smile. It radiated joy that was immediately felt by everyone.

As Yulia put the microphone to her lips, the audience fell quiet. She thought she knew what she was going to say, but no more. She would just speak as the words found themselves:

"This fantastic story, so brilliantly told tonight, is of our two families," she said. "A family united by a pair of watches, but most importantly united twice by love. Now, as a result of me meeting my brothers for the very first time today, we can say we are reunited in love for the third time."

There was an immediate and obvious gasp of breath as the audience realised that Andrew and Peter had met Yulia for the first time that day but then, in their approval, they rapidly applauded her words.

The sound of the audience's intake of breath startled Yulia, but it meant that, during the applause, she remembered the opening words to her planned script.

"Tonight, we are going to re-unite the de Gressier watches for the first time since they were parted in 1941," she said. "Before we do that, I thought you might like me to read a letter. It was written by Heinrik, Andrew and Peter's grandfather and my great grandfather, to Heidi, my grandmother, before she was born."

Yulia looked up at her audience. She had them captivated, eating out of the palm of her hand. Immediately the sickening feeling she had in her stomach eased, and she started to relax.

"The letter is dated 26th November 1944 and was written in Belgrade," said Yulia. "Heinrik had just been taken as a prisoner of war. He knew he was never going to see his child born or grow up, so he wrote them a letter."

Peter looked toward Andrew anxiously. Andrew had some idea of what Yulia was going to read, so he raised his eyebrows and nodded encouragingly to his brother.

"It was found by my father, ... our father," said Yulia looking in turn at her brothers. It was in the bottom of Victor's watch case. It is written in pencil on very poor-quality paper, and although it is over 70 years old, it belongs to tonight."

Yulia opened the box containing Victor's watch, took out the letter and started to read. Except she wasn't reading. The letter she held in her hand was written in a mix of German and Russian, some words taken from one language, others from another. Yulia had learned the translation by heart. She looked at the grey-brown ragged paper, looked up at the audience and, just like an actress, she started to recite her lines:

"*My Darling Child,*

When your mother told me I was to be a father, I hit the heavens with joy and excitement, but those feelings were instantly crushed by an overwhelming sense of fear. I felt so scared, so frightened for her, for you and for me.

It is hard to describe the depths of despair I am feeling as I write because I know I cannot look after you. It is a feeling that is so low, so painful, that any bubble of hope I might have had is burst; abandoned to the dirt, never to rise again.

Any flames of hope I had for our future have been extinguished by the tears which fall on this piece of paper.

My fears were made much worse by the terror I saw in your mother's eyes when she told me of your coming. And yet, in her face I saw a determination, a spirit, a sense of both right and fight. I knew she would keep you safe. It made me love her even more."

Yulia paused to pretend to read the letter and then looked up again at her audience. Each was straining to sear into their memory the words she was reading.

"*I want you to know I have done nothing wrong. I did my duty in a war which has consumed the whole world. I am on the losing side, and for that, I am a prisoner whose fate is at the mercy of others. Why a baby is deprived of its father and punished too is, my dear child, a matter we will have to leave God to answer, for it makes no sense to me.*

I cannot bear to think of not being there to hold you, to help you, to protect you, to teach you. The normal things a father does for his child, I will not be able to do for you, and so I grieve for the pain you and your mother will suffer through each of your growing days.

Saying how sorry I am is not and will never be enough. Just know that you were conceived and born out of love.

Yulia stopped and looked up at the audience. She paused to make it evident that she was about to say something that was not in the letter.

"I was born out of love too," said Yulia to the audience, which was transfixed. Not a muscle twitched, nor an eyelid blinked. "The one thing my father told me was how much he loved my mother." Still there was no audience reaction. It was embarrassed into silence.

Yulia returned to recite from the letter:

I close with a prayer and, if I may, a request. My prayer is for your liberty, as freedom is the most precious gift; freedom from oppression, freedom from fear, freedom from anxiety, freedom to think and speak as you wish. Something my countrymen, and yours, have been denied for too long.

My request, my most cherished child, is that you be of good cheer, whatever the hardship. I can promise you that no battle, no problem, no worry is half as bad if it is tackled positively, bravely and with a joyous heart."

Yulia paused, looked up to her audience, and recited the last few words:

"I promise. I will love you always.

Papa"

Yulia didn't read out the last three words, which had been written in brackets - (Hauptman Heinrik Klugman).

There was complete silence in the audience. You could have heard a pin drop. Once again, the hairs on the back of everyone's necks were standing on end. Each wanted Yulia to read the letter to them again, just so they could make sure they had heard it correctly.

"I was with my birth mother for just two short years," Yulia continued after a long pause. "I don't remember any of that time as I was too young. I was later to learn that she was permanently of joy and good cheer. Each problem she tackled with the same positivity, bravery and with a good heart, but of course, these attributes made her a formidable woman and ultimately this was the reason she was killed."

It was now Yulia's turn to get emotional. She lowered the microphone to her side and dipped her head onto her chest in a poignant moment of silent prayer. Everyone in the audience took that moment to pray with her.

With renewed strength, Yulia looked up and returned the microphone to her lips. "It is the same positivity, bravery, good cheer and good heart which Andrew and Peter have shown in the creation of this musical about our family and its tribute to my mother. I am immensely proud of them and incredibly grateful. Andrew, Peter, thank you. Thank you very much."

Yulia stood back, allowing the audience to clap Andrew and Peter with unrestrained approval for the show they had just seen. After an eternity, Yulia raised her hand for silence, and the audience obeyed. She had the same public presence, the same strength of character as her mother.

"The question is whether the story of this musical is true," Yulia continued, "Whether our combined history is truly joined; only by comparing ... only by putting these two watches side by side ... will we know."

Yulia raised her red gloved hand and the watch case she was holding high into the air.

Peter opened Victoria's watch case as Yulia opened Victor's. They both took the watches out. All three, ignored the audience, as they huddled together as though they were in a scrum. They hurriedly compared the front and then the back of their watches. They did it once, twice and then a third time just to be sure. The audience was on tenterhooks. There was such tension it could have cut the atmosphere as everyone in the audience had invested so much emotion in the story of the musical they had just seen.

"It's true," shouted the three of them in unison as they broke apart to address the audience. "They're the same!" they shouted.

Nothing more could be said. The musical director, sensing the moment and with impeccable timing, opened up the orchestra with the very last song of the show, still to be sung. The actors who played

Andrew, Peter and the older Yulia came forward to the front of the stage. They sung with such force that the words and tune were carried in everyone's head long after they had left the theatre. The audience knew that they had just witnessed an opening night sensation. The lives of Heinrik Klugman and Tania Plesca were never going to be forgotten.

Chapter 85

Hudson River New York September 2014

THE SUN HADN'T quite started to rise as Andrew, Peter and Yulia left the theatre. From the reviews in the morning newspapers, they knew they had a Broadway hit on their hands; some predicted it would be the biggest hit for years.

The bringing together of the two watches on stage was described as an awe-inspiring moment of theatre, but it was Yulia's reading of the letter to Heidi, her grandmother, which made it a memory all those present would never forget. It was not in the original script, but it had created a cataclysmic moment of theatre that it would be included the next night and every night the show ran. The young woman in a Vermillion dress reading a love letter to an unborn child made it the show everyone had to see.

Yulia insisted that there was one more thing they had to do before they went to bed. Their father had told her it was one of his strongest memories and she wanted to experience it for the first time with her brothers there.

The traffic was quiet at that time of the morning, making it a quick drive off Manhattan Island, through the Lincoln tunnel, where their taxi turned south onto Sinatra Drive. There, as they looked left, they saw it too; the sun rising through the skyscrapers of the most powerful city on earth. It was the same view their father had seen from the QEII liner when he arrived in New York for the first time. An early morning sail past the Statue of Liberty and up the river and looking east as the sun rose was something Henry thought had to be included in everyone's bucket list.

They stopped at Pier A park and moved to the edge of the Hudson River. They found a park bench and sat closely, as brothers and sisters can do. Yulia was in the centre with Andrew and Peter on either side of her. On her lap she held the two gold watches, which she gently rubbed with her thumbs.

"I wonder what they would tell us if they could speak" she asked, lifting the two watches to their eye height. "Do you think that this is the moment when we can leave the sins of our father behind?"

"And our grandfathers," added Peter, poignantly.

"Perhaps it's the sins of our parents which makes us the people we are?" said Andrew.

"Maybe we can't leave them behind. Even if we wanted to," responded Peter.

"Do we want to?" asked Yulia. "After all, they helped make us who we are, and hells bells, didn't we make history last night!

Postscript

New York. USA September 2014

SITTING IN THE audience on the opening night of Andrew and Peter's musical was Evelina Waterman, née Kirillovich. She was seated with her husband, with whom she was happily married. They'd met at Harvard while she was completing the MBA course she had promised herself. Together, they'd had two children and built a successful chain of 24/7 one-stop-shops on the Eastern seaboard of the United States.

As the curtain fell for the last time on the opening show, Evelina was inconsolable. She had not said a word to anyone about her involvement in Henry and Tania's life. It was a chapter she had closed, expecting it never to be re-opened. It was when Evelina heard that a musical had been made involving Tania's life, she knew she had to see it on its opening night. She didn't know what to expect. What she didn't expect was the raw emotions projected from the stage. She certainly didn't expect to see Yulia shot, although later was to wonder why.

"I was there that day," Evelina sobbed disconsolately into her husband's arms. "This is my story too. I knew her. I knew Tania. I knew Henry. We were friends," she whimpered." I carried Yulia onto the aeroplane, away from it all ...." Evelina stopped talking. She was too upset to say more.

"You never said," commented her husband as he wrapped his arms around Evelina to comfort her.

"Because it was so bad. We were all frightened. I was petrified. It was fun at first. We were so enthusiastic, so naive, and then everything went terribly wrong." She shook her head as she thought of those times. "I had to put it away and now it's come back," said Evelina, her voice trembling.

It was a ninety-minute car journey from the theatre to Huntingdon, on Long Island, where Evelina and her husband lived. For the whole of the journey, Evelina told her story as her husband listened with little interruption. She spoke with the clarity of a former senior KGB agent, another fact which Evelina revealed to her husband for the first time. It was a disclosure that was not well received, for he understood how profound the implications would be for their family if this secret were ever exposed.

"Did you sleep with him?" asked Evelina's husband as they were nearing the end of the journey, and Evelina had exhausted her story. Former relationships were a subject which neither spoke about, but she had spoken of Henry with such affection that he could not help but wonder. She had never talked about any man like that before then.

"No," she replied shocked. "Why would you ask that?"

"Because of the way you've spoken of him. It was more than a friendship, wasn't it?"

"We could have been lovers but never were," she said. She hid the tint of regret from her voice. "I don't know why not. Perhaps it was because he was in love with Tania. But yes, ... there was something special between us."

Her husband said nothing, but a rare surge of jealousy swept through him.

"It wasn't an amorous or sexual love," she said, sensing a change in her husband. "I imagine it is like the love soldiers have when they've been in battle together. It is only shared between those that have been there. It's a deep, caring, protective love, but obviously, it was not as deep as I thought, as after we parted at Vienna airport, he never contacted me again."

That night Evelina didn't sleep. How could she; the nerves in her body were so fraught that her skin was tingling. She knew she had to do something to tell Yulia what she knew about her mother and father.

Evelina went back to the theatre the next night. She was compelled to see the show again. She purchased a ticket from a tout at huge expense. She had brought with her a letter for Isaac Tinnerman to give to Yulia.

Huntingdon, Long Island
September 2014

Dear Yulia
I was in the audience for the premiere of the de Gressier musical. What a wonderful show. How beautiful you looked, and you spoke so well.

It was a very poignant night for me as I knew your mother and father well. I was involved in the events leading up to that dreadful day when your mother was killed. It was me who, with your father by my side, carried you from Moldova soil and into your new life. I do hope it has been a happy one.

Your father and I parted at Vienna airport, and I never saw or heard of him again. I would have liked to have kept in touch, but I was so scared, and time moved on. I didn't know he had died until I read the publicity material for the show. I am so sorry. He was a lovely man, and I was so very fond of him.

I am sure your father will have told you that your mother was an incredibly special person. We are all unique, but your mother had qualities that set her apart and above us all.

I wonder whether he was able to tell you the full story of those last few years of her life when she set out to achieve so much? I suspect he will have said little about those times. He would have found it too difficult as he wrongly blamed himself for what happened.

If you would like to learn more about how wonderful and courageous your mother was, then it would be a pleasure to meet and tell you more.

Hopefully, yours.
Evelina

Thank you for reading The Watches of de Gressier. I do hope you enjoyed it. It is the last book in the de Gressier series.

If you enjoyed this book, it would be helpful if you would post a positive review on Amazon at www.amazon.com

I have a book in development called The Iron River. It covers the lives of the Donici-Solokov family from 1878 until the late 20th century. I have to do more research into the politics and living in Russia, Romania and Moldova before I will be comfortable in publishing it. Whether it gets finished will, in large part, depend on the literary and commercial success of the four books in the de Gressier series, for there is little point in being an unread author.

Facebook Page: @DeGressier
Twitter: @deGressier
Website: www.degressier.com

About the Author

Charles Bunker was an international corporate financier and entrepreneurial businessman before retiring to become an essayist, pamphlet writer and author. He uses his experiences in business and politics, his interest in history and international affairs, and his observation of people as the bedrock of his writing. Widely travelled, Charles is the proprietor of the famous Orchard Tea Rooms in Grantchester renowned for its connection with Rupert Brooke, Virginia Woolf, E.M Forster and many other literary, philosophical and scientific talents over the last 120 years.

Printed in Great Britain
by Amazon